SUMMARY

"I didn't come here for you to be nice to me."

Third year medical student Les Wilder has done the unforgivable. When she flees to the door of childhood crush and arson investigator Jefferson "Brick" McGuire, she doesn't come for comfort. With what she's done, she doesn't deserve to let love save her.

Brick feels differently. He's enough of a Master to know his shattered submissive needs more than pleasure or punishment. Though he will give her both, love is the only thing that will heal the wound that threatens her soul.

IGNITION SEQUENCE

A Nature of Desire Series Novel

JOEY W. HILL

Ignition Sequence

A Nature of Desire series novel #12

Copyright © 2023 Joey W. Hill

ALL RIGHTS RESERVED

Cover design by Scott Hill

SWP Digital & Print Edition publication June 30, 2023

The following material contains graphic sexual content meant for mature readers. Reader discretion is advised.

Digital ISBN: 978-1-951544-25-6

Print ISBN: 978-1-951544-26-3

ACKNOWLEDGMENTS

Where do I start? Some books require a little more "expert" guidance than others, and this one surely did.

A big thank you to Laura, Bob, Crimson and Elizabeth for the guidance on fireplay. A special thank you to Elizabeth for letting me use her beautiful language to describe how it feels to have flame applied to flesh for mutual pleasure.

Many thanks to Marcella for her hospital medical liability knowledge, a tricky path to walk. Thank you, Kimberly, for the tweaks on Catholicism, a religion with beautiful rituals.

Without Nancy, I'd have woefully messed up proper EMT practices, and Nick, Vicki and John gave me further vital first responder knowledge on firefighting procedures.

So many things I see and hear, the conversations and experiences I have, inspire scenes, characters and storylines for my books—sometimes even years later. So I want to offer a thank you to the Universe for the interesting young man (and history buff) who helped us move back in 2018. His conversation with my husband about their mutual interest in Civil War reenactment inspired Rufus's character, plus pulled me more deeply into what kind of man Brick is.

I always thank my readers, but in this case, I specifically thank you for your help coming up with a name for the Wilders' hometown. You came through for me with terrific suggestions. Sheila W was the one who hit the nail on the head, so on this, the *fourth* book where the town played an important role, it finally has an official name: Fairhope, North Carolina.

I hope you all love Brick and Les's story!

PROLOGUE

"*I* am strong. I can handle anything, as long as I take it a step at a time, stay calm, and think it through."

Said no one when they were drowning and sinking fast into darkness. The mantra she'd applied to the last few years of her life meant nothing.

The rain hammered down on her in the hospital's serenity garden. Les was cold and wet, but it was the inescapable anguish that permeated her bones. Broken heart syndrome, an agony so powerful it strained the heart muscles, suddenly made a lot more sense to her.

"I am strong... I can handle anything..." Seized by sobs, her voice failed. Les wanted to shut her eyes, but she couldn't. Closing them meant seeing the truth of how spectacularly she'd failed. All the tears, all the ways to be the best, to try to make it better...she couldn't do it. She couldn't meet the challenge. She'd been running a race she'd lost before she started, and worst of all, she'd always known it.

No. What was worst of all was who had paid the price for her delusion that she was smart enough, strong enough.

When she slid down the rough surface of the brick wall behind her, it had snagged her scrubs, making them ride up in back. More cold water dripped down the prominent bumps of her spine. She tightened her arms around herself because the chattering of her teeth and pointless sobs were making her jaw and neck hurt. The rainfall increased. Her tears meant shit to the deluge.

1

She turned to hunker against the wall, her shoulder pressed to the unyielding surface. This wasn't sensible. It was irresponsible. She wasn't a child. She needed to get up and go into the building. Get her stuff out of her locker and calmly ask if anything was required before she went home. As she'd been told to do.

But she couldn't do it. Her conscience slapped her, called her a coward. She'd never thought of herself as a coward.

Get up. *Get up*. Goddamn you, get the fuck *up*.

She made a fist and hit the brick. She hammered it until the drops on her knuckles were tinged red and the physical reaction to pain made her draw her hand back against herself. Her head fell to her chest. Her overwrought heart thudded painfully. Trying to find some meaning, some path, she reached out again.

This time when her fingers slid over the rough mortar to the slick red brick, she followed it like a blind person reading Braille, looking for the answer to a question. Two answers came. One for comfort, one for punishment.

Though she didn't deserve comfort and she didn't know why she thought punishment was something she could seek from him, both answers were the same.

Brick. Not the apathetic force that shed her blows like the rain rolling down it, but a person. Brick.

She'd last seen him four weeks ago, when he'd shown up out of nowhere. Every stolen spare thought she'd had since then had been coated with an incendiary residue of cravings.

Ironic for a man who'd been a firefighter and was now an arson cop.

She had to go to him. It was the only thought capable of making her push against the weight of the world and struggle to her feet.

She didn't need to go to her locker. She carried her wallet, keys and phone in her scrub pockets. As she cut across the courtyard and took the least populated route to the staff lot, she held him in her mind, a target for a desperate arrow.

She took shelter in the memories of that visit four weeks ago. She needed to be steady enough to drive, but more than that, she preferred the baffling emotions and needs he'd roused in her that day to facing the truth.

With one decision, everything she'd believed about herself had been proven a lie.

Confusion was a better driving companion than despair.

CHAPTER ONE

Four Weeks Earlier

"*P*lease tell me we have a new neighbor who's single," Beulah said. "One horny enough not to care about dating and feelings, shit we don't have time for. I can't even see most of him, and I'd fuck him for his biceps alone."

Les rolled her eyes, but like her other three study partners, she turned to see who her roommate had spied. The shiny black truck cruising through their condo parking lot had a red and gold firefighter's plate on the front. Because of the waning light of early evening, she couldn't make out the lettering on the Maltese cross, which might have told her the town and station number. However, as the truck rolled closer, giving them a better view of the driver, she blinked, sure she wasn't seeing who she was seeing.

Denial. In her third year of medical school, when her studies and clinical rotations consumed every ounce of free time, Les denied any need that didn't support that effort. However, denying that Jefferson "Brick" McGuire was parking his truck in front of her condo was impossible. Because instead of being miles away in Richmond, Virginia, here he was, her first serious girlhood crush and her brother Rory's best friend.

Relationships were a time suck. Worse than social media. Even casual sex fell under that axe, at least for Les. Since her broken undergraduate engagement, which was fortunately well in her rearview

5

mirror, she'd had a couple times where her body's needs had over-ridden her good sense. She'd then faced the awkwardness of making sure it wouldn't happen again with that person, without leaving bad feelings. Her mother had raised her right, after all. Never make last night's mistake feel bad.

She was absolutely certain her mother had *never* intended that to apply to a one-night hookup. But hey, rules of courtesy had a universal application.

The closest she got to "sex done right" was with her *very* private fantasies and her vibrator. And the main star of those fantasies was pulling his truck into a parking space.

There was no way he was here to bring those imaginings to life. She resented her subconscious for ignoring that logic. Resented him for getting it stirred up.

A scowl wasn't how a good Southern girl greeted a family friend who showed up out of the blue, but the female reaction to Brick, currently surrounding her like the scent of blooming gardenias, added to the downward pull on her lips.

"He's a fireman," Sue purred, obviously having noted the truck's front plate. "Growl and prowl, ladies."

A pussy magnet. That was what Rory called the original firefighter plate Brick had put on his first vehicle, a battered farm truck his grandfather let him use in high school. Brick had been the youngest firefighter accepted by their small-town volunteer department, prob-ably because of his size.

His commitment was more than a teenager's passing fancy. After high school, he'd gone after a degree in fire science and certifications in fire and crime investigation. During that time, he also joined the Richmond Fire Department. His family had moved back to Rich-mond by then. Through her mother and Rory's updates, Les had heard when Brick moved into arson investigation in Major Crimes.

Basically a firefighter and a cop. A fire cop. What girl could resist that?

Brick had seen her. A smile crossed his face. Home was in that smile, a shared history. The resentment vanished, replaced by some-thing just as appalling. Tears stung her eyes at the gift of it, coming in the middle of a grueling year.

Med school orientations cheerfully suggested if a student organized and prioritized correctly, she could have a social life. Some did manage it, but not her. Beulah said it was because Les was too anal, too wound up, too worried about getting things wrong. "Girlfriend, stick some Zen up your narrow ass to loosen it up."

Beulah Joyner had been her roommate since the start of med school. The compatibility of their differences made them stick together ever since. Including when, like most second year grad school students, they'd had to seek off-campus housing.

Squelching her weird emotional reaction to his smile, Les watched Brick's large hands slide off the wheel. As he unsnapped the seat belt and exited the truck, the girls got a top-to-toe view of him. They weren't shy about taking it all in, viewing him like the Second Coming.

Really wrong thought, since Brick looked capable of giving a woman multiple orgasms. She winced as she imagined her devout Catholic mother's reaction to that.

Brick wasn't pretty. She wasn't sure if he'd even be called handsome. He had the face of a man who routinely pitted himself against the forces of nature. Pre-dawn frosty mornings working his grandfather's farm, subsistence hunting with his dad. Being a battering ram at the high school football games and practices. Running into a burning building.

Cold, wind, rain, heat. Those elements had carved his features, made him ruddy and rugged. He had a square cut jaw and dark brows that slanted toward his nose, giving him a formidable look. But his smile, which easily reached his eyes, drew attention to irises the color of fog in a forest, a smoky gray that could get hints of green or brown when sunlight burned off the fog.

His firm, thin top lip accentuated a tempting and full bottom one. The mouth was an invitation, the brow and hard planes of his face a warning. The combination had become more impactful as he grew older. More irresistible to her woman's body and heart.

What usually attracted female attention was his massive build. Broad shoulders, solid trunk, and a compact ass. All of it developed by the same factors. Working a farm, pushing back a defensive line on the field, or handling the pressure of a charged hose and the weight of the turnout gear that protected him from a roaring wall of fire.

A woman saw a man who could plant himself in front of anything, to keep what he protected safe. Even more important, he *wanted* that job. It was the job he'd been born to do. The message was broadcast not just through his physique, but through his expression, those eyes.

If you think you can get past me to hurt someone I care about, you won't.

He was smart, too. While other girls had focused on his sports exploits, she knew he'd tutored Rory and their friends in science and math. Even English lit.

Especially English lit. She pushed that distracting memory away and focused on the here and now. Since it was March, some days here in Durham, North Carolina still carried a chill. Brick wore a lightweight flannel shirt with gray and camel stripes, buttoned up halfway over a ribbed white tank. The shirts were tucked into tan jeans held with a brown belt, the jeans pulled down over scuffed boots. Not too tight or loose, the clothes worked with the flex and ripple of muscles.

Determinedly shouldering her laptop bag, Les moved away from her study partners and toward him. She tossed a distinct *stay* glance their way. Because it shocked them, they actually did it, thank God.

She crossed the strip of grass between the walkways to reach him. He'd seen her intent to come to him, so had stopped by the truck, one foot braced on the curb. She remained on the grass, but even in her elevated spot, he was taller than her.

His thick, slightly curly dark hair was damp, as if he'd recently showered. At Rory's wedding a few months ago, he'd had a close-clipped dark beard, though today he was clean shaven. As she came closer, she detected the more noticeable aftershave and soap smell that confirmed the recent shower. It suggested he hadn't driven from Richmond. He was staying somewhere in town.

She pushed down another surge of annoyance, that he would come to her unannounced like this. It only pointed out the obvious. She was his best friend's "little sister," not a girl he was worried about offending. He was probably here for some kind of fire conference. Hadn't he said something about that at the wedding?

They'd been best man and maid of honor when Rory married Daralyn. Though Daralyn had lived with their family long enough Les thought of her as her sister, she was delighted to be able to officially call her a sister-in-law.

"I have some training down your way in a few weeks," Brick had said at the reception. "I'll come take you out for a pizza."

A flutter low in her belly, a momentary thrill at the possibilities, was extinguished when Rory teased him. "If you don't get distracted, chasing all those campus co-eds."

Yet Brick's gaze hadn't wavered from hers, and he hadn't responded to Rory's joke.

She remembered walking down the aisle, her hand curved over his arm. She'd been able to feel the strength of it through the wool of his suit. Brick had done something the other groomsmen hadn't. He'd covered her hand with his own as they walked together. His hands were nicked with small scars, the nails kept excruciatingly blunt, his firm grip warm and smooth.

Time to put those thoughts on the over-weighted train back to Fantasy Island. "Did my mother send you to check up on me?" she asked lightly.

"No, ma'am." The warmth in Brick's voice, the gravelly deepness, held her as surely as she imagined his arms would never do. "I decided you needed checking on all for myself. I'm taking you to dinner."

She took the glint in his eye as a five-alarm warning to her sanity. He interpreted her expression a different way, because his brow cocked, and his drawl deepened.

"You know you're safe in the company of a good old Southern boy."

"Actually, the fact you *are* a good old Southern boy is what makes me wary of your intentions. Sir."

She'd meant it as an answer to his teasing use of *ma'am*, but his gaze flickered, his smile getting a more serious look. A blush rose to her cheeks. She shouldn't try jokes. She wasn't good at them. Her timing was always awkward.

She was startled by a healthy nudge from behind. Beulah pulled Les's laptop bag off her shoulder. "I'll just put this in your room for you," she said.

"We were supposed to study—"

"Bye now. You kids stay out late. Don't come home until the police put you in the squad car."

Les sent her a searing look, but Beulah just winked and back pedaled to corral the other women. They sauntered away with a few more lingering looks in Brick's direction and big smiles at Les, promising her an interrogation later.

Probably when she most needed to digest the latest lecture notes.

During the first year, Beulah had told Les, "Right now, it's all about book stuff. This is the time to make friends, the ones who'll be with you in the foxhole when we get to the clinical stuff."

She did make a small group of friends, primarily thanks to Beulah, though when she was talked into going to a house party or out for drinks at one of the popular hangouts, Les mainly went to make sure Beulah and the others who partied too hard got safely home.

In their study group, Les had been dubbed "Search Engine," because she committed the most complicated material to memory. She didn't see it as aptitude. It was balls-to-the-wall hours of striving to internalize all the information poured into them during medical school.

Long and short, if she wasn't in the lab with their assigned cadaver, learning details about anatomy she'd never imagined existed, she was online watching the latest class lecture or in class attending one. Or in her room, going over the coursework and working on her residency application.

On the days she worked at the hospital, her schedule was twelve or thirteen hours there, with nighttime left over for study, and anything else wherever she could fit it in. Like making up a week's worth of reasonably healthy lunches and dinners at one go. She and Beulah portioned them out in Tupperware containers so they could grab them from the fridge each day on their way to the hospital or school.

As Brick gestured Les toward the passenger side of the truck, stepping ahead of her to open the door, those thoughts crowded in and made her feet drag.

"I look like hell," she told him. "I haven't taken a real shower in two days. I did two enemas at the hospital and had a ten-year-old throw up on me. I went through my spare scrubs. This was the only set left in the community bin that didn't fall off of me, and it's two sizes too large."

She didn't think about her appearance as a priority, beyond being presentable for rounds and patient interaction, and brushing her teeth so coffee breath didn't make those patients pass out.

Death breath Code Blue on seventh floor, stat.

"Means I might be able to see down the front of it," Brick said, unperturbed. He produced a pack of cinnamon gum from his shirt pocket. "Want a stick?"

She couldn't suppress the smile, and took the gum. "Do you medical types go commando under the scrubs?" he asked.

That light in his eyes was still there. She sighed to cover her uncertainty over it. "I guess you're here for the fire training you mentioned? No way you drove two hours just to take me to dinner."

"I told you I'd come to see you."

"Yeah, right. Rory mentioned college co-eds, and I was a convenient excuse." She managed a casual chuckle. "If you want, we can have that pizza you suggested delivered, and hang out with my study partners. You'll like them."

"Les." Brick shifted closer, gazing down into her face. His fingers flexed on the door frame. "Get in the truck. Or I'll slap your ass and find out if you're wearing anything under those baggy pants."

Holy crap. He'd teased her before, with Rory. But not like this. The surge of sexual response was alarming. Despite her long-standing desire *not* to be seen as his best friend's little sister, she panicked, grabbing for the surer ground of responding exactly how she would in that role.

"I wasn't the least bit afraid to kick Rory in the balls when we were wrestling as kids."

Brick's gaze kindled. "I'd be willing to take my chances in a wrestling match with you. I'm better at it than he is."

The weird sexual tension she had to be misconstruing became even more confusing. This was dinner with a family friend, she told herself. That was all. "I can't be gone long. I have a lot of studying to do."

Another shift closer, and he slid his knuckles along her face. "Count of three," he said. "One, two..."

He wouldn't. He would. She knew he would, and the reasons why, and how she was responding to it, were a lot more complicated than a flirtatious exchange. Suddenly that light in his eyes wasn't mischief. Not even flirtation. It had the intent of a solid flame, seeking fuel to build it up higher.

The abrupt lack of subtlety startled her. She wanted to be affronted, to tell him to go to hell. Or get into that wrestling match and see how different his technique was from Rory's. Hell, he smelled good. She liked his aftershave.

There was only one way to respond that made any sense. Lifting her chin to reclaim her dignity, she turned to get into the truck.

He shifted behind her as she stepped onto the running board. She intended to rest a hand on his ready arm, but her palm landed on his chest instead. She stopped, one foot still on the pavement, and looked up at him.

Some of those co-eds were passing on the sidewalk, chattering. Girls with shiny hair and bright eyes, and majors that didn't suck up every second of their lives. Les curled her fingers over the placket of the flannel, against a smooth button. Another denial—that she did it to send an ownership message to their ogling faces.

The man really was a wall. Most would assume he'd acquired his nickname on the football team, but he'd been called Brick by his family even before then. He'd lived up to the name, getting broader and more solid after he left behind high school and college to embrace full manhood.

He put a hand over hers, holding it between his palm and the thump of his heart. Doctor's habit, tracking the beat. It was healthy, no skip. "What is this, Brick?" she asked.

"I'll tell you in a minute. How hungry are you?"

She didn't think about hunger. She ate when needed. But a meal eaten in a restaurant, without her tablet open to a medical textbook, a stylus in her free hand to mark paragraphs, held appeal. "I can eat. Just, seriously, it better not be anywhere fancy, or they'll throw me out."

"This is my very favorite look for a woman." His gaze skimmed over her. "Working hard on what matters to her, and it shows. She's not worried if her hair's a little messy and she's wearing mismatched socks."

Her attention flew to her feet. She shot him a glare as he chuckled. "Made you look," he said.

She shoved at him, and suddenly they were on an easier footing, even if it seemed he'd followed her lead and was teasing her the way he would have when she was younger.

"If you feel more comfortable getting cleaned up and changed, I can wait. But I'm telling you, you look and smell"—he leaned in, exaggerating a deep inhale of her hair that made her chuckle, even as it was distracting as hell—"fine, to me."

"No, I'm good." Though she'd dearly love to put on something that would make her look like a date, every minute with him would be borrowed time. She'd be up studying past midnight to make it up.

A reminder it was best to stay in scrubs, and in this mode. Just a casual visit, something she'd tell her mom about on the next phone call. *Brick stopped by.* Elaine would tell Brick's mother, because they'd stayed in contact. They'd talk about what a good boy he was, checking on Elaine's daughter.

Brick handed her up into the truck and closed the door. She watched him circle around the front. The man had a blatant sexuality, as if he was built to command a woman into his bed and then give her so much pleasure, she couldn't find the strength to leave it.

Hell. On a normal day, sexual desire accommodated her by staying dormant, not trying to boil over to upset the pot lid clamped over her life. But her own word choice, *command*, bumped things up several notches.

During her senior undergraduate year, some of her classmates at a nearby lunch table had giggled over a popular book with bondage in it. Beulah teased Les about being a small-town Catholic girl, not as comfortable with bawdy humor. Some of that was true. But she was also afraid if she indulged in it, she'd let the truth slip.

What those classmates viewed with light-hearted curiosity took her into dark and mysterious places, filled with a yearning a giggle couldn't mask. They'd left the book on the table, to shock the next person. Resisting the urge to tuck it into her backpack had been like resisting her mother's peach cobbler, fresh out of the oven.

Brick, with his authoritative presence and the threat to spank her, had the juices bubbling around the melt-in-your-mouth flaky crust. She needed to find a way to turn down the heat. If she didn't have time for casual sex, she definitely didn't have time to delve into that kind of dessert.

Brick got into the truck. With his size, she'd have expected him to rock the metal body with the settling of his weight in the seat, but his grace was always surprising.

It had added to his skill as a football player, and as a firefighter. She'd watched him scale up a ladder to sound a roof at a residence fire, making sure it was stable for him and the other firefighters to use their hooks to tear open a hole and vent the flames.

During her middle school years, when he'd joined the fire department, she learned a lot about firefighting.

In their small community, people gathered to help in a crisis, as well as to see what was going on. So no one had questioned one young girl sitting on her bike watching, though her eyes remained glued to the figure with the number 285 on his helmet and jacket. Her heart had pounded, the creases of her hands damp, as she prayed to keep him safe.

When Brick leaned toward her now, she wouldn't have been surprised if he tried to put her seatbelt on her like she was still that twelve-year-old girl. Instead, he crooked an arm around her neck, another circling her waist. In one smooth motion, he brought her across the seat to him, the console against her hip as he put his mouth on hers.

That *did* surprise her.

A few weeks ago, there'd been a cold snap here, temperatures dropping down to the twenties. When she stepped into the warmth of the condo, the contrast was so welcome and extreme, she had gone still, absorbing the sensations. This was like that. Her eyes closed at the strength of his grip, the first rasp of his jaw against her tender flesh. The dual soft and firm texture of his lips, experienced through full, exploratory touch.

Hard and deep he kissed her, hand moving from her neck so he could cup her head, fingers tangling in the messy bun of her hair. She'd stuck two ballpoint pens into the twisty part, an extra if she needed it. She was distantly aware of the clatter as he plucked them free and dropped them into the cupholder. He pulled her hair down, the locks tumbling against her throat. His fingers followed, thumb along her jaw, her cheek.

When he drew back, he pressed his lips together, taking in her taste. She stared up at him.

He'd kissed her thoroughly, in a way she'd never experienced. Not even from Bart, her undergrad fiancé, who'd taught her that first sex wasn't really love.

But firsts mattered, and this was her and Brick's first kiss. A really fucking fabulous, ground-quaking, first kiss.

"You have my gum," she managed.

He smiled. "A beginning."

"What?" She blinked.

"Outside, by the truck, you asked what this is. That's my answer to your question. That, and the kiss. Do you want the gum back?"

CHAPTER TWO

She shook her head, still dazed. Then he brought her down to earth. Hard. "I've held scarecrows with more weight to them. I'm taking you to Brenda's. You heard of it?"

She had to be cool, calm. Was he cool and calm? She couldn't tell, but if he was, she had to be too. "No, I haven't. You do know how to sweep a girl off her feet with the compliments."

"You're beautiful. But you're too thin."

She intended to move back toward the passenger seat, but he still held her, his arm around her waist, fingers wrapped over her hip bone. He was a big man with long arms, and he filled up the truck, seeming to surround her. "You can stay right where you are. I don't need the space."

"Maybe I do."

"Maybe, but here you're in a better position to look in the back and see the box your mom sent."

Joy flooded her. He eased his hold as she twisted around and saw the medium-sized box. He helped her bring it up front and onto her lap as she settled back in her seat. She hugged the box to her, even knowing she was acting like a kid at Christmas. "You took a round-about way to get here from Richmond."

"About every couple months, I check on my grandfather's place. Verify the people renting it are taking good care of it. Saves my dad having to make that trip during the school year when he's up to his eyeballs in grading papers and doing lesson plans."

The box would be one of her mother's occasional care packages, including baked goods and little household items, like a hand towel with a crocheted top offered at the recent church bazaar, or a goat-milk moisturizer, obtained at the farmer's market.

On top would be a thick letter full of local news. It would refresh the pictures in Les's head of neighbors, places in town, and daily life there.

She tried to call her mother once a week, usually on Tuesdays. Daralyn and Rory ate dinner with Elaine on that night. Sometimes Thomas, her older brother, was there, too, with his husband Marcus. They'd bought and renovated the Hill farmhouse near her mother's a few years back, and traveled frequently between there and Marcus's penthouse in New York City. Marcus was an art dealer and gallery owner. He represented Thomas's work, which was currently in demand worldwide, a thought that always made Les deeply grateful to all the forces—especially Marcus—that had made that happen.

Rory would put the phone on speaker as the meal was prepared. Les would mostly listen, imagining she was in the kitchen with her mother and Daralyn, helping with the cooking or setting the table. Then sitting around the big table laden with food, hearing the back and forth, the laughter, the snippets of things that probably didn't seem like much to them. To a homesick and stressed-out medical student, they were gold.

"I tell her she doesn't have to do this. I'm only a couple hours away." Even though sometimes it felt like she was on the moon.

Brick rested his hand on her shoulder. As he stroked her with his thumb, it moved under the neckline of her scrubs, resting against her bra strap.

"She likes doing it," he said. "I had to exert considerable will power not to tear it open, knowing she probably had zucchini bread in there, or Daralyn's cookies. I should demand a percentage for my fortitude."

She sniffed. "Weren't you just paid for that?"

He chuckled at her tartness, a good cover for the slight quivering of her fingers as he kept playing with the tingling skin under her bra strap.

Removing her mother's box had revealed another package in the back. It was small and rectangular, wrapped in red paper and tied with silver ribbon. "What's that?"

"That's from me, but you can't open it until your birthday. My schedule's not going to let me get back down here then, so I wanted to make sure you had it."

She stared at him. Her father had died two days before her birthday, so for the past several years, that event had eclipsed her own. She didn't resent that. She much preferred to honor her father's memory. But Brick bringing her a gift, remembering it, confirmed the truth.

His visit wasn't an afterthought. He'd come here for her.

"So tell me about this diner." If she didn't move away from thoughts of home or Brick's distracting effect on her, she was going to get teary or try to jump him. "How'd you learn about it?"

"The guys teaching the class. Put your seatbelt on." As he spoke, Brick backed the truck out of the spot. She missed his touch, but set the box in the floorboards at her feet before complying. "Good comfort food stuff, meat, three sides and a dessert for a college student price. Though tonight's my treat. FYI, she's open 24/7 in a safe part of town, so if things get too rowdy here when you're trying to study, it'll be a good spot. There's a bus stop right near it."

It was a fifteen-minute drive, which suggested one reason it wasn't as well known to her fellow classmates. They had plenty of quick eateries clustered around campus and the hospital, like camp followers around a busy army. However, as they entered the diner, the smell of coffee and fried food were familiar scents from any diner back home, and the cozy feel of the place told her it could easily become a new favorite for her.

The décor was an homage to first responders. Framed photos showed firefighters and police on the job, from the 1950s to present day. There were also formal uniform shots of service men and women with serious eyes and young faces. Les suspected the photos had been brought in by patrons. Flags and badges from various precincts, firehouses, and branches of military service filled the rest of the available wall space.

Two police officers were finishing up a meal in a booth while talking to a firefighter sitting on a high stool at the counter. His firehouse logo was printed on his dark T-shirt, stretched over his shoulders and back.

A landscaping crew picked up takeout, while a group of senior citizens shared coffee and pie in a rear booth. Brenda was a pencil-thin older woman in jeans and a blue short-sleeved shirt. Her name was embroidered on the pocket. One of the biggest portraits, a man in a police dress uniform, was mounted behind the cash register. Her husband, who'd died about a decade ago, according to the gold plate on the frame. A wedding shot of the two was tucked into the corner.

Brenda had smiles for her customers, and banter for the fireman and police, while she kept tabs on the three waitresses hustling under her direction. They wore jeans with pink, purple or blue T-shirts bearing the restaurant's logo.

Brick accepted a couple menus from her and guided Les to a booth. He exchanged a nod with the firefighter and cops.

"Specials are up on the board." He pointed at it. "Get something for here and something to go, so I'll know you have enough to eat tomorrow, between enemas and nauseous ten-year-olds."

She glanced at her menu. "You've had food here? Because Brenda looks nice, but people have different ideas about what good Southern food tastes like."

He shot her a grin. "Yes, I've eaten here."

"All right then. Country fried steak, mashed potatoes and gravy, green beans and corn bread. One for here, one to go." She could easily divide into a couple meals what she'd have left over from the one for here. She'd share the to-go one with Beulah.

"Good choice. Drink?"

"Iced tea, if fresh brewed and certain to send me into a sugar coma."

"They don't know any other kind. Dessert?"

"I'll decide if I have a place to put it when I'm done with the rest."

"You can take it to go."

"Not if it's chocolate pie. Gotta eat that before it melts."

"How about we start with it while we wait for the rest? I'll share it with you."

"You're going to spoil me."

"That's the idea."

As she met his gray eyes, she decided this night was going to be one of those one-off memories. Something she could hold onto and cherish, let it keep her warm for a lot of nights. Which, come to think of it, might be a better deal than the ups and downs of a relationship.

Their waitress's nametag identified her as Sonja. Her accent suggested she was Russian or Ukrainian. "What will you have?"

"We'd like a piece of chocolate pie to start off," he told her. Then he placed the rest of the order, including their drinks and Les's to-go selection.

She'd never had a man order for her before. It wasn't a bad feeling, not the way Brick did it. She was aware of his legs below the table, spread around her own feet, aligned and planted on the base in the center. Like in the truck, his presence surrounded her.

"So at the wedding, I didn't get a chance to ask. What made you decide to leave the deputy fire chief role and go all the way into arson investigation? I thought you loved being a firefighter."

"I did, and still do. I occasionally get the chance to pitch in as a pipe man or for search and rescue, when I'm training stations what to notice to help us with our investigations. The investigative process for arson cases is interesting, and forensic science is always evolving, just like with medicine. That alone can keep me busy, but I also do fire code reviews, talking to community groups about fire safety, that kind of thing."

He looked toward the fireman at the bar. "People think setting fire to an empty building for insurance money is a victimless crime, but the financial losses have far greater impacts than they realize. More importantly, every fire can get out of control. Each of them has the potential to endanger the firefighters who have to put it out. Their families sure as hell care about that."

He met her gaze. "So not only can I help firefighters do their job better with what we learn when we investigate a fire, I can catch the assholes who think they can get away with setting them. I like that."

The waitress brought the pie, setting it down with two forks. Brick nudged one toward her. After one bite, she nodded decisively and waved her fork at him. "If I finish this and the tea, I'm definitely dropping into a diabetic coma. Before I pass out, give me an example of the science, how it's evolving."

He grinned. "You're as big a science nerd as I am."

"I don't think anyone is as *big* a science nerd as you are. Physically."

"Smartass." He poked his fork at her hand. "Okay. So there's this phenomenon you see in the aftermath of fires, called spalling. It looks like a shallow gully or chunks chipped out of the concrete. There's also what's known as glazed glass, like that spidery cracked look you see in glassware. For a lot of years, arson investigators took those two things as pretty sure evidence of arson. The concentrated heat level that produces it suggested an ignitable liquid started the fire."

She had a smudge of chocolate on the corner of her mouth, but before she could reach for a napkin, he wiped it away with his thumb. Then he licked the chocolate off of it.

When he continued talking as if doing that was the most normal thing in the world, she thought about hitting him. Or fanning herself with the laminated menu. The heat of his touch lingered next to her mouth.

"In the aftermath of the California wildfires one year, they noted the same phenomenon, the spalling and glazing. They knew for certain no arson was involved. So on one hand, that made our job even harder, because proving arson is tough already. A lot of our evidence gets burned away. On the plus side, we're not sending someone to jail who's innocent."

"Hunh." Chocolate melted on her tongue as he spoke. She watched him take small bites of the dessert. Smaller than hers. He was letting her have more of it. It was the little things a man did that could capture a woman's heart.

"You also have to watch the chemical makeup of accelerants," he continued. She suppressed a smile. Definitely the biggest nerd. "Like diesel fuel and lemon furniture polish. They have very similar elements. If your mom's house caught on fire, I wouldn't want to send her to jail because she uses Pledge to clean the furniture."

Les scraped the remaining crust off the plate. It was really good pie. "Medicine has pitfalls like that, too. Sheila, a girl in my study group, is doing her ER rotation. A mother brought in a baby with a cold who 'just didn't seem okay.' Sheila didn't see anything, and thought the mother was being overly protective. She was going to discharge her, but the resident looked at the baby and asked the mom if she'd given her any home remedies."

She'd intended to offer a similar story of academic interest, but as she paused, the subconscious anxiety that liked to coil up in her stomach like a rusty piece of barbed wire tightened. Her own ER rotation was soon.

Aware that Brick's gaze had sharpened on her, she pushed past that, continuing in an even tone. "The mother was giving the baby honey. When they're under a year old, babies don't have the gut bacteria that can prevent harmful bacteria from infecting them. She had botulism."

"Shit."

She nodded. "The baby was already experiencing respiratory symptoms and lethargy, which fit with a cold. But because of the mother's intuition that something was off, and that key question, they gave her the right treatment."

He frowned. "It seems like there's a fine line. You can't overlook anything, but you also can't second-guess yourself into inertia."

"Yeah." But she was really dreading that ER rotation.

Their food arrived. That anxiety had draped itself over the pie in her stomach, warning her not to put anything on top of it. It was the real reason she'd lost weight, but no way was she passing up something this close to her mother's cooking. She just had to take it slow. "Oh my God. It smells amazing."

Brick's gaze rested on her face, her parted lips. "Wait until you actually put it in your mouth."

Christ on a waffle. Yes, he had an effect on her, but it seemed absurdly juvenile to put a sexual spin on an innocuous food comment. It was his own fault, though. When he'd licked that chocolate, the vision of taking his hand, putting her mouth on the side of his thumb to suck the chocolate off, had been impossible to block.

She wasn't nearly as experienced as the version of herself she was when she fantasized about him. If she tried to do something like that, she would look ridiculous. Especially in Brenda's diner. But as Les kept her eyes pinned on the food, she was terrified he'd see what she was thinking about.

Being on her knees, her mouth sliding along his thigh, over to a very thick, erect cock, tasting the salt of it like the salt in this country steak.

Her friends didn't fantasize about giving their boyfriends oral sex.

They didn't get a visceral thrill, a little shiver and tightening of the thighs, at the idea of serving a dominant male, working his cock in her mouth as he pushed her down on it with strong hands. His demanding, dirty orders falling upon her bare shoulders like a heated release against her bare back, his hand clamped on her nape.

She swallowed the first small bite with a gulp of tea. "I'm going to have to avoid this place," she said. "Or I'll gain a hundred pounds."

"You've got a ways to go on that." He was watching her eat with those thoughtful, penetrating eyes. She hoped he'd attribute her flushed cheeks to the restaurant temperature. "Third year's pretty demanding, isn't it?"

"Yeah, I guess so. But a lot of things start coming together and making sense." Even as they overwhelmed. "When do you go back?" she asked.

"It's a two-day class. Tomorrow they're covering wildfires, helicoptering us up into the mountains for some practice burns. Then I'm due back in Richmond for work." He'd ordered the meatloaf, and gazed at it appreciatively. "A ketchup topping, just the way it's supposed to be made. None of that brown gravy shit."

"Amen." She took another bite of the steak. "It was nice of you to come by, with all that going on."

He set down the fork, crossing his arms on the table behind his plate. The stare he leveled at her had her fighting not to squirm. Her cheeks warmed again. The reason for the blush should have been different, but the sexual hum beneath was hard to ignore.

The temptation to blurt "What?" or otherwise cover what she'd just done was there, but something about that look pointed her toward the only appropriate response.

"I'm sorry," she said.

After a protracted pause, he nodded. "I'm patient. But don't do that again."

The implied threat made those tingles run through her thighs and down to her feet. "I'm off balance here, Brick. It makes me nervous."

"That's okay. I get that. But that's how I want you to communicate about it. No evasion, or doublespeak bullshit. All right?"

He picked up his fork and began to eat, even as he shifted back into the flow of the conversation. "So your ER rotation is worrying you."

23

"Is it that obvious?"

"You're a systematic thinker. You like to have time to gather and analyze data. The ER requires pretty quick decisions. You won't be comfortable with that at first. It'll probably scare the shit out of you. But the more you do it, the more experience you accumulate, the better you'll get at it. Like anything."

Maybe. She could provide book-related answers at the drop of a hat. Yet learning how to respond to attendings, residents and patients, when the answers had to be deduced, by connecting all the dots, was different. She did it, and Beulah said she did it well, but a small tornado had become a frequent weather condition in her lower belly, while the muscles in her neck and between her shoulders remained permanently knotted.

She would get through it. Plenty of med students did. She wasn't unique. Unless her uniqueness was that she couldn't get through it, that the pace was too much.

Nope. It wasn't. Denial. The key to success. She reached for her personal mantra. *I'm strong and smart. I can handle anything, as long as I stay calm and take it one step at a time.* She wouldn't miss something as simple and potentially fatal as honey given to an infant.

"Were you scared, the first time you went into a fire?" she asked.

"Not so much when I was a pipe man. That's an adrenaline rush, and the focus is on your training, everything you learn about technique, strategy, and how fire works, to knock it down or keep it contained. You're wearing gear, and you have faith in it to do its job while you're doing yours."

"But things can go wrong."

"A lot of things can go wrong. That's why you train and train and train. City councils think firemen mostly sit around and play with their shiny toys, while asking the town for more of them. But when the fire starts, you have to be as ready as you can be for what it throws at you. Even as you know there will always be variables you can't predict."

"Yeah."

He touched her hand. "Those variables are what play holy hell with a control freak's compass. It was search and rescue where I had to teach myself to manage fear. The fear of not having enough time to find someone and get them out. Then came the first time it happened."

He paused. "Backing out when the IC, the incident commander, tells you it's a lost cause, knowing someone's still in there, even if there's no chance they've survived...it's tough. Or getting someone out, only to have them die when the EMTs or docs are working over them, because they inhaled too much smoke, or were burned too badly."

"Oh, God. I'm sorry, Brick." She stopped eating and covered his hand with her own. "Was that part of why you decided to do arson?"

His gaze touched on the contact between them before it lifted back to hers. "No. I still miss doing the S and R. The more I did it, the more I learned to manage my reaction to that possibility, even as I fought like hell, just like the others in my firehouse, to make it the exception rather than the rule." He tapped her hand. "But something else I found out. Seconds are a lot longer than you realize. The more experience you get, the more you can do with them."

Her brow creased. "I'm not following."

"New guys often dash around. The more experienced ones take the time to check the perimeter, evaluate the scene. Flake out the line and hook the hydrant up right, rather than fumbling it from being too much in a rush. In the ER, I expect it's the same. Those extra moments to think it through can save lives."

He smiled. "You're a thinker. That's why I know you're going to be fine. You just have to let yourself accumulate the experience to get there. That's the terrifying part. Because we know how much we don't yet know, and lives can depend on our knowledge."

"Yeah." She dropped her gaze to her food again, toying with it.

"Tell me about your current rotation. It's Behavioral Medicine, isn't it? Psych? Do they have a diagnosis that explains Rory?"

She smiled. "I haven't found 'asshole' in the DSM yet, but I'm sure they've given it some convoluted Latin name."

He chuckled. She wondered if he'd intended for the humor to pull her away from her worries. Whether he did or not, as he asked her more questions about her rotation and studies, the two of them fell into a comfortable back and forth, leaning toward one another as he finished his meal and she had the rest of hers boxed up.

The persistent sexual undercurrent gave their conversation a nice edge. It rose and fell, through eye contact and the brush of his legs against hers under the table. And yet…

A crush was about imagining kisses and moments where the other person gave titillating hints about their feelings. Connecting with him in a real way, about things that mattered to them both? He'd said he liked the look of a woman engaged in what mattered to her, and here they were, talking like adults interested in one another beyond sex. Interested in finding out more. Everything, in fact.

Alarm bells went off. If it was just sexual attraction, she could put that away once he dropped her off and left. Like she'd done with every man she'd met since entering medical school. She couldn't make it about more than that now.

She was giving herself whiplash. Wishing he was going to be here longer, even knowing it was better that he was headed home. Wishing they could stay in closer touch, when she had no time for that kind of maintenance.

Shut the fuck up, Les. Sheesh. Maybe with a little time and space, she'd put this in better perspective. After she used her vibrator twenty times.

When Brick paid for the meal, he left a generous tip. He drew her over to the firefighter and cops and shook their hands, mentioning the training that had brought him here. He didn't linger on that, though, before introducing her.

"Les is a med student working at the hospital. She'll be starting her ER rotation soon, handling what you guys send her way."

Sheila had talked about this, yet Les was surprised to feel it herself, a subtle but detectable shift in their attitude toward her. An acknowledgement of the common bond between first responders and hospital staff. She was one of them, or trying to be.

"Her accent's stronger than yours, Brick," the firefighter noted. "A lot prettier, too. She sounds like honey and sweet cream, whereas you just sound like a braying mule."

"Yeah, yeah. You Tarheels are the ones with the accents. We Virginians talk the way you're *supposed* to talk."

The firefighter grinned. Les excused herself to use the restroom. On the way there, she heard them re-engage with Brick on the course work that had brought him here. Easy networking.

"Ready to go?" Brick asked when she returned. At her nod, the firefighter lifted a hand in farewell.

"See you around, doc-to-be."

The cops gave her a warm nod. She felt like she'd been marked and noted, in a good way. Brick had probably told them he'd appreciate them keeping a friendly eye on her, if she came into the diner when they were there.

She'd grown up in a small community where people looked out for each other, so it didn't offend her to feel it in this setting. But the way Brick acted toward her gave it a different quality. Not necessarily bad, but unsettling.

He handed her up in the truck. He was going to take her back to the condo, and what then? She thought about inviting him in for coffee. Which clearly could lead to something else.

Or maybe not. Her study group would be spread out at the kitchen table. He'd be pulled into an inquisition slash flirting session. As pretty as some of them were, it might encourage him in the direction Rory had teased him about.

He'd already warned her not to go down the emotional deflection road with him, but it was hard not to do it with herself. The thought of him flirting with them felt like hitting herself in the face with a bag of oranges. She wondered if he was going to kiss her again. Or if she was brave enough to try and kiss him.

He held her hand throughout the ride, rubbing her palm with his thumb. With any other man, maybe that would seem a casual gesture, but it telegraphed exactly what he intended. Being touched by him, after imagining it for so long, gave her shivers she didn't want to stop.

When they pulled into the parking lot, she collected her mother's box and his gift, holding both against her. Belatedly, she realized it sent the message she didn't want to be kissed again. Or have him come in. Which she did.

Though she shouldn't. *Hell.* She wondered if she could get away with bolting from the truck with a hastily tossed, "I had a great time, thanks, enjoy your training."

She was panicking. The stew in her head was about to overflow the pot and burn. But she couldn't afford to do this. She had no time for this. She needed to set boundaries, be responsible.

Before she could say anything, Brick shut off the truck and turned to look at her. "We need to get something straight between us. *I* need to set something straight."

"Okay," she ventured.

"Put down the box."

Her fingers couldn't move, her heart pounding faster.

"Are you going to make me repeat myself, Celeste Joy?"

Her full name, the one no one used. Except her mother, if Les was about to be in trouble. What would it be like to be in trouble with Brick?

Moistening her lips, she put the box and his gift on the floor by her feet.

"Come here," he said.

This time there was no pulling her to him. He was requiring her to use her own steam to close the gap. When she did, he didn't touch her right away. He just looked down at her face.

He was right. Seconds could take a lot longer than they seemed.

She felt as if she was supposed to stay still, motionless on the outside, while her insides turned to flame. Heat moved to all corners, reaching her cheeks, making her lips tighten.

"Yeah," he murmured. "So you're busy. You're overwhelmed. No time for a relationship. It's in your eyes, your voice, and whatever's churning inside you. Tell me."

His tone stilled the other voices, that clack and blather, all the insecure stuff. It held her on the one point, what the question and answer was.

"I'm keeping my head above water, Brick, but barely. This year, and probably for the next several years, that's all I have the energy to do. I have to see this through before I focus on anything else just as important. I have to succeed."

She'd almost derailed herself with Bart, and she'd promised herself that wouldn't happen again. She glanced down. Their hands were clasped on the console. She didn't know if she'd reached for him or him for her, but the linking helped, the pressure of his fingers adding to the words he spoke to her next.

"Okay. But if and when you have the energy, do you want what I'm offering? No strings attached to the question."

She opened her mouth and said words she hadn't expected herself to say, either from fear of scaring him off, or making herself too vulnerable. With Brick, none of it seemed like an issue. At least in this moment.

"Yes." She swallowed as his eyes flickered. What was there was as intimate a response as his hands upon her, making her repeat the word. "Yes. I've thought about you for a long time, Brick. Long enough I'd decided the reality couldn't possibly be better than what I imagined."

Which she'd used as a way to accept that was the beginning and end of it. A special girlhood memory to cherish in the years to come, a part of her past.

Her heart was emphatically rejecting that idea.

"Hmm." He leaned in, making her lips part, and he brushed his mouth over them. She stayed still, to better absorb the sensation, and because she couldn't move under that penetrating gaze. "I look forward to expanding your reality, doc."

He straightened, the gray eyes focused on her. "So here's the deal. You do what you need to do. But once you get done, once the wheel turns to the right spot, I'm coming for you. Got it?"

Based on one dinner. One visit. Yes, there was a strong connection, probably mostly hormone-driven on his part, maybe hers, too. Nothing about her warranted such a sweeping declaration.

"You're messing with me. Don't do that. And I'm not called a doctor until I graduate." She tried to pull away.

He wouldn't let her. Sparks were in his eyes. "When you were in the bathroom, I told those guys you were my girl. And they should watch out for you while keeping their hands and dicks to themselves, because every one of them saw how beautiful and desirable a woman you are."

He curled a hand in the collar of her scrubs. "When I kiss you, Les, you can tell what I want, can't you? You've been in my head a long time, too. Maybe I haven't made that clear enough."

He kissed her again. She pushed against him, but he absorbed her resistance in his strength, his persuasion, his overwhelming presence. He coaxed her lips apart, stroked her tongue with his, played it over her teeth. When he moved his hands to her waist and back to bring her closer, everything came alive, energy surging through her body.

Okay, maybe sex would be okay. Maybe Beulah and the others would be gone, and they'd have the place to themselves.

"Goddamn," he murmured. It broke the kiss, but told her he felt the power of the energy pulsing between them, too.

His gaze locked with hers again. "You may be Rory's sister, but you are not *my* fucking sister. That's sure as hell not how I see you. I haven't, not for years. We're done revisiting that shit."

He kept that penetrating look upon her, confirming the message had at least taken root, enough to keep her from trying to deny it. "And yeah, I'd be happy to have you twelve different ways, but we're not doing that, either. Because once I'm inside you like that, we're going to be together. I meant what I said. When the time is right, I'll be back on your doorstep. I'll give you the space to finish medical school, figure out who and what you want. But if you're on your own when that's done, I'm coming for you."

"So I get no say in this." Having her desires for a quick sex fix thwarted generated the annoyance she needed to push back. Even if the words came out a little unsteady.

He eyed her. "You have as much say as you want, but you'll have to convince me if what you want isn't me."

"You do realize this is the 21st century? Men don't come and carry off women?"

"I know what I want, and that's you. Tell the truth. When I said I'm coming for you, what happened?"

It had made her toes curl and her breath shorten. No way in hell was Les admitting that. "Firefighters often have brain damage due to testosterone overload. You might need an MRI."

"See, you are a doctor. Making diagnoses and everything."

Ignoring his way-too-sexy grin, she exited the truck, taking her box. And his gift. She slammed the door with an appropriate decisiveness and stalked up the walkway.

"Hey, doc?"

Since he was already out of the truck and coming up behind her, her choice was to face him or do an undignified sprint to her door. She turned and planted her feet, but he disarmed her when he showed her the pen. One of the two he'd pulled from her hair before dinner.

"Didn't want you to forget this. I'll just keep the other. Never know when I might need an extra pen." He threaded it back into the twist she'd redone at the restaurant. His fingers trailed over her collar bone, offering another intimate stroke of her bra strap beneath the neckline of her scrubs.

"Thank you for dinner," she said with dignity. Then she pivoted and marched for the door.

She heard his chuckle, which would help later if she thought she'd been unforgivably rude. She already knew she'd regret not looking back. However, if she took the risk, she knew those intent eyes wouldn't be laughing.

And that look alone might pull her right back into his truck.

CHAPTER THREE

He may not be the guy some girls think of as dreamy... The Gershwin tune with its wistful poignancy came to her, but Les shut it down. She couldn't afford to think about wanting or needing some guy to watch over her. She was too damn busy for that nonsense. She had patients who needed her to watch over them.

She'd been assigned eight in her current Behavioral Medicine rotation. Tonight she'd download and review the current status on their charts. She'd be up at 4:30am to run on the treadmill and do strength training while listening to a downloaded lecture. By six, she'd be at the hospital for pre-rounds. At seven, she'd present to the attending or resident in her care team. The rest of her twelve-hour day would be divided between clinical work and grabbing as much study time as she could for the exam she'd be taking when the rotation was complete.

The pace was relentless, but ironically it also helped her manage her stress. Study, experience, learning from her attendings, residents and fellow students, formed the walls of the tunnel she was chugging down. At the end of the tunnel, she'd have the knowledge to mitigate the fear of screwing up.

Brick hadn't taken her refusal to start a relationship as a dodge. He'd taken her at her word, which yes, could reflect an arrogant confidence—not unjustified—in his impact on her, but his unsettling respect for her honesty made an impression.

It also weighed on her. Once she'd flounced into the condo, her sass and backbone had left, just like he had in his truck. She hadn't faced the main reason she couldn't afford to get involved with him right now.

She couldn't handle losing him. The meaningful stuff she left untended while accomplishing her goals wouldn't be there at the finish. Those essentials would rightly be snapped up by others for the gift they were.

But just for a moment, she let herself believe he'd be waiting at the finish line. Leaning against his truck, massive arms crossed, that body that looked so good...all hers. A crazy, incredible thought. He thought *she* was beautiful? He took her breath away.

His shrewd regard made her feel like he knew everything this was costing her, better than she knew it herself. Did he know her deepest fear, that when she crossed the finish line, all the things the denial had kept glued together would give way, and she'd fall to pieces?

During the wedding, when the vows were exchanged, she'd made the mistake of glancing toward him. He'd shifted his gaze in her direction. The startling revelation of his kiss tonight had unearthed that buried memory. In that key moment, she'd known he no longer saw her as a child.

She'd been afraid of that look, afraid she'd do something stupid. Fortunately, her maid-of-honor duties kept her busy, or rather, she made sure they did. Next morning, she headed back up the road early. She could only afford to be there a few days, which was why her mother had helped Daralyn with a lot of things the maid-of-honor did.

More memories she wouldn't be able to share with her family, to strengthen her bonds with them. How many would she lose before this was done?

She was miring herself down in tiresome things she'd thought through a million times before. *Put some Zen up your ass, sister.* She half-smiled as she thought of Beulah. Then she thought of Brick. Her body was throbbing, but she couldn't handle getting her vibrator. The idea of the impersonal buzzing, the initial chill feeling of its touch, repelled her.

Her hands were often cold. Dr. Morris, one of the Ob/Gyn residents, joked that it was a doctor thing. *When you graduate, the perpetually cold hands are handed out with the diploma.*

She could use that chill for another purpose. Leaning back in her chair, she closed her eyes. She imagined a crisp fall day, walking with Brick in one of the patches of woods near her home. He backed her against a tree, pushed her sweater up over her breasts, his big hands pulling down her bra cups...

She slid her hands under her sleep shirt, curving them around her breasts. They were his hands, fingers cold from the weather. He drew her breasts together and angled her nipples upward under his gaze, so intense the look stabbed her low in the belly. His voice was in her ear. Capable of bellowing over dancing flames, or dropping to a soothing rumble, offering authority as he calmed whomever he held in a world of fire.

"You'll stay still, warm my hands with your flesh."

Not a question. A command.

She pulled her hands away from herself. An orgasm inspired by thoughts of Brick would hamper what she needed to get done tonight, tempting her to let her mind wander into far more distracting places.

But tonight it wasn't the *fantasy* of him she was denying herself. It was the too-tempting reality.

He'd said he looked forward to expanding the scope of her reality. His version of that would differ from hers. Because expanding her reality would incorporate another fear. What if it didn't change at that finish line? What if she had to sacrifice every personal relationship to become the best doctor she was capable of being? Or worse, it took all she had just to be a halfway decent one?

What if she always had to work twice as hard as anyone else, checking and rechecking things a dozen times, to ensure she was giving her patient the absolute best care? While losing sleep to the worry and anxiety that she might have missed something.

If she let herself have a life, divided her attention, she would stumble and fail. She'd let everyone down.

There was no finish line. She wouldn't ever be able to have him.

She moved to sit on her bed, her bare foot on the braided rug beside it. Her mother had made it for her, a mix of white, yellow and purple. She'd chosen the color of Les's favorite fall pansies, growing in the nooks and crannies around the farmhouse. A motherly reminder of where she came from, a visual path she could follow home whenever she needed it, even if she only had time for the visit in her head.

The box *had* included the zucchini bread. She should have opened and shared it with Brick, though she had no doubt her mother had provided him with his own loaf. It had likely been inhaled by the firefighters at the training class.

The cheerful letter she'd expected offered news of how Rory and Daralyn were doing at the store, plus the activities in her mother's garden and community groups. Clippings about topics of shared interest from the nearest big city newspaper were in the envelope, plus a couple cartoons. Her mother enjoyed sitting at the kitchen table with her coffee and going through the Sunday edition, just the way she had with Les's father.

Brick's gift, the slim red box bound in silver curly ribbon, sat on her desk. She'd played with those curls as she studied, letting them wrap and unwrap over her fingers.

He'd said not to open it until her birthday. She'd obey him because... Because.

After another mental struggle, she rose from the bed and verified her door was locked. When she returned to her tablet, she opened the file she only viewed when she was alone.

What would he think of the photos? Deep inside, she thought she knew. It was in his touch, his kiss, the way he spoke to her. She doubted she'd ever be brave enough to ask him straight out.

She'd saved them in a password protected file, using a jumble of numbers, letters and symbols that meant nothing. Except to her, since she'd come up with it. Something I Don't Want My Mother To Find Until I'm 112 Years Old. Or Dead.

SIDWMMTFUI@112YOOD.

The erotic photos showed males restraining, spanking and psychologically topping attractive females. There were only five pictures, but each one took her into a world of expanded possibilities, a galaxy of stars and planets rotating around a fiercely burning sun.

A woman bent over a spanking bench as the man administered punishment to her raised ass with a gloved hand. Les's attention lingered on that glove, stretched like a supple second skin over his broad palm. He was a big man, with muscles and dark hair. No need to guess why that appealed to her.

Wait until you actually put it in your mouth.

The image Brick's comment had triggered hadn't come out of a vacuum. The next picture was a woman on her knees, servicing the male's cock with her mouth. His leather pants were open but clinging to his ass. Her wet eyes were raised to his in adoration as he gripped her hair in a tight fist, her lips stretched over his sizeable organ. A coiled whip was held in his other hand, resting on his hip.

Third photo. The woman was restrained on a tilted table while a man had his mouth between her legs. Her body was bowed up to him, her mouth open on a scream, part anguish, part overwhelming pleasure.

For the fourth picture, a woman squatted gracefully in high heels, her wrists cuffed and fingers resting on the edge of a table. The man sitting at it drank coffee and read his paper. Except for the restraints and shoes, she was naked. He had his free hand in her hair, stroking it idly. It suggested Dominance and submission as something that permeated everything in the private life of the couple, not just beginning and ending with actual sex.

The last one was a black and white still. A long-haired, naked girl knelt in profile, her head dropped down and arms braced. The caption said *Waiting on Him.*

She didn't explore too deeply why the pictures captivated her. All she knew was when she looked through them, in a meditative, one-after-another fashion, it calmed her anxieties. Centered her. Even as it turned her on so much, she'd shift restlessly in her chair, feeling the throb of her engorged sex.

She'd resisted the urge to collect more. Everything in moderation. If she was killed in a freak lightning storm, and that password was miraculously cracked, she didn't want to have more porn on her computer than a teenage boy.

Les closed the file. Time to get back to her studying. As she rotated in her desk chair, she saw herself in her dresser mirror, and the words printed on her sleep shirt, an oversized T-shirt.

I'm the smart one.

It had a cute caricature of a girl with messy hair and oversized glasses perched on her nose. Marcus had given each of the Wilder siblings a similar shirt. Thomas's said *I'm Mom's favorite*, because they always teased him about being the favored firstborn son. Rory's said, *I'm the dickhead*, because that was the relationship he and Marcus had. After putting it on, Rory smoothed it over his chest and bared his teeth in a grin. "I'll wear it with pride," he informed Marcus. "It'll be my Pride Day shirt."

She shook her head, a slight smile on her face. She wrapped her fists in the excess cloth, holding it over the dull ache in her stomach. The word *smart* was distended by her knuckles. She was getting into dangerous territory. She knew better than to spend too much time thinking when she was by herself.

She settled back with her tablet, one knee propped against the desk, the other leg stretched out by her laptop, bracing herself for a couple hours of exam study for the Psych rotation. She wasn't too worried about the essay portion, but the oral exam was a different matter. Beulah would help test her. She'd probably make Les laugh with her imitation of a strict German Dr. Freud, firing off questions.

After she passed that exam, she'd start the ER rotation.

She gave herself one more lingering second to imagine Brick's face, feel the touch of his mouth on hers, his broad shoulders and powerful arms under her hands. Then she banished all of that. She wouldn't think about him again tonight.

Denial. It was the only way to achieve an impossible goal.

CHAPTER FOUR

Present Day

I'm not with the woman I want to be with tonight.
    I shouldn't have agreed to give her this much space.
  She needs me. Something's wrong. I know it. I knew it when I drove away from her, four weeks ago. Fuck.

No matter how emphatic that internal voice was, right now wasn't the time to deal with it. Brick needed to take care of Tish, and make sure this experience was everything she wanted it to be.

"What are you thinking?" Tish's voice cracked.

For the past couple months she'd been exploring submission with him and others, under his close supervision. She could do a credible job of staying calm. Even when naked and stretched out on a table while he stood over her, preparing to set her on fire.

But it didn't matter how strong a woman was, and he'd had some of the most kickass under his control. He knew when they needed reassurance. The challenge was knowing what kind. He took her hand, holding it in a sure grip.

An ADA with an unflappable reputation, she was still grappling with letting go of control. Especially when venturing into a form of play she hadn't yet tried.

Fireplay.

In her normal armor of trim suits and sensible heels, he teased her about looking like she walked off the set of a crime show, but she was damn good at her job. She had a methodical mind, lining up the information she needed to win a case, preparing for all contingencies.

A lot like someone else he was thinking about too much tonight. "Did you follow my direction?" he asked Tish. "No lotions, perfumes, fancy soaps?"

"Yes. I rinsed off again in the changing room, just to be sure. Will it leave any marks?"

"It's always possible, but we've done what's needed to avoid it." He'd checked her over to confirm she had no cuts or abrasions that could make the skin more susceptible to deeper marks from the fireplay's effect. "You'll have some redness. You might feel a little rawness under your bra straps for a couple days, like from a sunburn."

Despite her nervousness, she batted her lashes. "Will that turn you on if you see me at work? Knowing I'm feeling that sunburn under my clothes?"

Even before her decision to explore her sub side, they'd been on-and-off friends-with-benefits, no hold on each other. So he took the flirting in the spirit it was intended. "I'll be hard as my name, baby. How're you doing?"

"Wondering if I'm nuts. But wanting this." A breathless half-laugh, her hand flexing in his. "I'm crazy hot right now."

Thanks to the dividers set up around this space, the main play area noise was muted. Mick, the building's owner, held monthly dungeon parties here for their private group. Tish hadn't wanted to do this in front of a big audience, so Brick chose a form of fireplay he could do indoors, and reserved this spot.

It was still open to viewing, but there was limited access. People could filter in to watch, but only the quantity that could hug two sides of the dividers one row deep, staying behind the tape that maintained a fifteen-foot-wide perimeter around the table and Brick's staging area.

Tish could block them out of her field of vision by turning her head toward him, or looking up at the high ceiling. But once they got started, Brick knew it wouldn't be an issue. The shudder of her breath, the quiver in her breasts and long thighs, held sensual anticipation.

He pried opened her fingers, patting her palm and giving her a reproving glance. He bent down, capturing her attention. "Do you trust me?"

Her expression steadied, eyes full of affection and personal need. "You know I do."

"Then don't be scared. Not in the wrong way." He shot her a wicked look that made her chuckle. She had a rusty laugh that could stiffen a man's cock with only a few notes.

Brick put his hand under her elbow and guided her arm so it was stretched out above her head, knuckles resting on the table. At his nod, she did the same with the other.

He'd laid out everything he might need as the scene progressed, and he checked that over one more time. Fire suppression blanket, wet towels, his jump medical bag with a few items added specifically for burns. He'd rarely had to make use of those items, but he'd mentored under an experienced fireplay Dom. That, plus Brick's knowledge of what fire could do, and just how fast it could do it, meant he *never* cut corners.

However, because he liked fireplay and experimenting with it, he was always ready for it to go south. The woman under his care was his top priority.

"No restraints?" she asked.

"Is that disappointment I hear?" he teased her. Initially, she'd stayed with psychological forms of submission and easy-to-slip restraint scenarios. But true to a submissive getting more confident with her desires, her interests were expanding. She'd asked him to do the fireplay with her, because his reputed skill with it intrigued her. But he suspected the more restrictive bondage situations, where she had to relinquish all physical control, connected to her deeper cravings.

It was part of why he was using Richard as a spotter tonight. Richard was a firefighter, too, and routinely offered Brick the back-up, so Brick trusted him to do his job. However, since ropes and restraints were Richard's thing, Brick was also using this as an introduction between him and Tish. When she laughed, he noted the flicker in Richard's blue eyes. Yeah, she had his attention.

Brick liked bondage plenty, but not with fireplay. "No restraints," he told her. "If something goes wrong, you have the ability to help douse the flames, the way you and I went over together."

That said, he always made sure his spotter was someone strong enough to hold the sub down, if she forgot all that and panicked. Richard could do that.

The reminder that things could go wrong increased Tish's apprehension again, but Brick knew how to dispel that. He braced a palm at her side, putting a firm hand to her face. "I don't need any fucking restraints, do I?" he asked silkily. "You'll keep your hands where I tell you to."

She pressed her lips together, that little aroused gesture he loved from subs. "Yes."

He softened his touch, a light tap to her cheek. "You can get lost in this. It's okay. I know what I'm doing. On this table, everything you are rests in my hands. While this is happening, you're the most important thing in the world to me."

Banter was the way they maintained the boundaries of their day-to-day relationship. But for this, he used a tone that reminded her he was in charge, and she was giving him that control.

He preferred his fire bottom to be naked. Sometimes he stripped down to nothing but shorts or jeans himself, but it was chilly outside. It made the building cooler, especially in their cordoned off area. The dividers helped to control air currents from the ceiling fans, but it also blocked the warmer air they were circulating from the various free-standing heat lamps. As well as the body heat from the hundred people engaging in multiple scenes.

He'd take the trade-off. He'd witnessed at least one fireplay scene where an audience member, feeling stuffy, had taken a cardboard fan out of her purse, the kind used in a church revival. The resulting gust of wind had passed over the sub and the fire flared higher than expected, a flame jumping to her hair. Quick use of wet towels had doused the fire and avoided injury, but the top and bottom's immersion in the experience was decidedly disrupted.

To keep her warm, he'd put Tish under a blanket until it was time to get started. Now he removed and folded it, tucking it out of the way.

"You won't be cold long," he promised her.

That tremor passed through her again. He also loved watching what happened to a woman when a Dom and her own submission gave her the safe space not just to take off her clothes, but to become naked.

41

His gut tightened, his thoughts again taking him elsewhere. He imagined serious hazel eyes watching him the way Tish was watching him. Trusting him.

He dipped the wand's rolled cotton tip into the alcohol solution, then set the handle in the horizontal rack above the cup, letting the excess drip back into the container. He treated every movement like a tea ceremony, precise and significant. All of it was sensory input that would intensify the experience for her.

When he was satisfied the tip had the right saturation, no drips, he picked it up and turned to Tish. He gripped her wrist, brought one arm back down so she could watch him run the wand over her palm, spreading the alcohol, which he'd dyed purple. If any excess liquid ran to other places, he or Richard would see it. With the deftness of long practice, he shifted his grip to trigger the long-necked lighter he held in the same hand.

Her breath drew in as flame bloomed in her palm. The blue line between the flesh and the flame was the alcohol barrier. He ticked off the seconds for her to register the heat, then his hand clasped hers, dousing the fire and sealing in the warmth. A first demonstration, proving to her what he meant about trust.

Her fingers tangled with his and her eyes flicked up to his face. "Wow," she breathed. Her lovely brown eyes had grown wider, her pupils darker. "I'd like to do more."

"I'll start with your back. Then we'll move to your front."

She had some trepidation about the front, so this would give her time to settle over it. Obediently, she turned over, stretching her arms above her again. He put his hand on the back of her neck, beneath the tight French braid he'd done himself. She was a tall woman, coltish and narrow-hipped, with a heart-shaped ass and pert, high breasts. Her fawn-colored flesh came from mixed-race parents. He'd met them, her mother a tall black woman from Gulfport, Mississippi, her father a bullish Venezuelan who played a brutal game of soccer with Brick in their backyard, when he'd been invited over for dinner.

Tish's nipples were so sensitive he could bring her to climax by suckling them. When she'd wanted to explore the psychological side of submission, he'd done that a few times, ordering her to straddle him and stay absolutely still—as much as she could—while he did it.

He rarely hooked up with a woman who didn't respond to his Dom

42

side, even if she didn't realize she had the bottom or sub vibes to mesh with it. He enjoyed introducing them to it, opening those doors and seeing what rooms they ended up wanting to visit.

Tish was a better than pleasurable fit. She'd admitted to those cravings early in their relationship. Their agreement to stay friends, not lovers, had helped with that. No deep emotional drama associated with exploring the urges she'd had long before she knew what they were.

He drew the wand in a zigzag fashion, traveling from between the dimples over her hips to her shoulder blades. The flame followed. His hand swept over it, the alternating movement of wand and palm creating blue and gold ripples across her back before he smothered them. Fleshing was one of the simpler forms of fireplay, but it was also one of the most intimate. He'd had bottoms tell him it felt like being petted. It could be soothing, but depending on how the heat built in the more sensitive areas, how he applied and manipulated it, it could also stimulate and arouse.

With Tish's sensitive nipples, he expected applying fire around them was going to be a memorable experience for them both, if they got that far tonight.

His one-row-deep audience were elbow to elbow. But they only held the part of his attention needed to maintain the integrity of his space. If anyone crossed the taped line, the watchful Dungeon Monitor, who'd joined them when Richard let her know Brick was about to start, would get them to step back. But because Brick didn't abdicate that responsibility, he stayed aware.

When he did demos, his bottom was co-instructor and visual aid, so he could talk and do this at the same time. But tonight he was giving a good friend her first fire experience. She deserved his full attention.

There were people comfortable holding the lives of others in their hands and those who weren't. He cherished every bit of control a sub gave him. And while his mind tried once more to take him back to the sub he most wanted to give him that trust, this time he stayed fully in the here and now.

Just as he intended, she was starting to feel the heat and its sensations more intensely. Tish was digging her fingers into the table's flame-resistant pad, her thighs and ass starting to flex. Little sounds were breaking from her lips, and sometimes she jerked when the heat gave her a more noticeable kiss. Brick had done scenes where the sensations overwhelmed the sub, enough she would have rolled off the table if they hadn't been there to hold and protect her.

This probably wouldn't reach that level of intensity, but Richard shifted closer, just in case. When she was making soft sounds of arousal, and those jerking motions were getting more noticeable, Brick decided that was enough for the back.

He set aside his tools, and clasped her arm and hand. "Turn over now. Arms up, legs spread, so your ankles are at the corners of the table pad."

As she did it, he noted the hesitation, the slight hitch to her chest, the puckered nipples. Fuck, if she ever bonded with one Dom, she'd be treasure to him. From Richard's expression, Brick suspected she was close to winning a lead contender for the honor. He'd shoulder himself to the front of the line.

"What is it you want to say, Tish?" Brick asked.

She looked surprised that he'd picked up on it. He'd been called a mind reader, but it wasn't that. The world outside didn't often slow down for moments like this, where everything about a woman drew him in like a book he couldn't, didn't want to put down. One he didn't want to rush, absorbing every possible meaning of the words.

If a man took the time and prioritized it, practiced it in a place like this, he could do it when it counted in the day-to-day world.

When he had the submissive he wanted to keep, to bind to him, he'd fight for the right to read and hold her soul forever. The things he learned here would let him do that, giving her all she needed, both under his control and when he stood at her side. Or at her back, if that was where she needed him to be.

Shit. Focus.

"Can I be blindfolded?" Tish said. "I want to feel it, but if I see it, I think I'll be too...worried."

In their earlier discussions, she'd admitted to having a little fear of fire. Not a phobia, just what was to be expected from any sane person.

"All right. No blindfold, though. Close your eyes."

When she complied, he kissed her temple. "Just like where I put your arms, counselor. Your blindfold is my command. Your eyes don't open until I say so. Understand?"

"Yes. Why do I keep shaking? I thought I was past that."

"Does it feel bad?" She shook her head. "There are a lot of different rooms to submission, and every one of them you enter can turn you into a newborn again, shivering with that first touch of a different, bigger world. Ready to explore it?"

At her nod, Brick gestured to Richard. The man came closer to the table. Brick picked up the damp wand again. This time, she shuddered immediately, a mix of physical and mental reaction, as he passed it over her upper thighs, her navel, the arch of her rib cage. Circled her nipples, painted the curves of her breasts.

He'd told her to remove her pubic hair if she wanted to experience fire close to her sex, and she had. Some subs liked the unique sensation of letting a fire top burn the hair off, but he preferred it this way for his own fireplay. For tonight, it also kept things simpler.

He slid his hand over her smooth cunt, a firm pressure against her clit that had her arching. Now he picked up the other wand and lit it. The flame caught the track he'd laid out and flew eagerly over the new terrain. His hand followed, dousing, sealing in the heat. The blue meeting point between the flame and the alcohol was burned into his gaze, mixing with the hue of her flesh, the way she moved.

She sucked in another breath as he sent flame over her upper thighs again. As he smothered it, his thumb grazed the crease at her groin. He returned to her breasts. A low moan broke from her throat as the fire licked over them, his hands cupping them to seal in the heat. He did her belly again, but this time, he leaned in and blew gently on the flame, sending a wave of heat over her swollen clit.

"Oh...God." Her thighs jerked.

"Stay still, counselor." She made a concentrated effort, which always gave his Dom side a satisfying tweak. He did the circuit once more. Thighs, stomach, breasts. A wash of heated sensation over her nipples from his breath had a sharp cry coming from her.

Yep, he'd been right about that.

He also sent more heat across her clit the same way, first from the fire on her thighs, then from her belly again.

His cock had gotten uncomfortable in his jeans, but fireplay was a delayed gratification, one he'd allow to build to a conflagration and consume him later, in the privacy of his own bedroom.

He hadn't put his cock in anything but his own hand for months now. Even though Tish had been more than willing.

He played over Tish's nipples, giving them a rub and squeeze after he quenched the flame. She cried out again, her eyelids fluttering but staying shut. She was getting close, her body writhing in a contained way, her mind fighting to keep it still, the arousal wanting to take over.

Richard was right across from him. Her eyes being shut had allowed him to close the final gap without being a distraction. Brick's pattern became more complicated, and he built the flames higher, bathing her in heated air, then he brought the level down again. As the fire streamed and reshaped itself around his touch, he watched the flames dance and flow, showing their colors. He worked with them, directing them where he wanted them to go.

When Brick leaned in and breathed on her clit this time, the moist heat took her perilously close to the edge. The strangled sound of her moan warned him of it.

Getting her off in front of people was one of her limits. But as he quenched the flames, the hand he'd first kissed with fire closed into a fist, her arm jerking as if she'd wanted to lower it and reach for him. She might have forgotten herself enough to do it against his command, because he was her friend, not her Master, but he'd warned her of the dangers of unexpected movement.

"Do it," she gritted.

"I'm a Dom, Tish," he said quietly. "You want something from me here, you ask."

She nodded, eyes still squeezed shut. "Please, I want to climax with you touching me. Not because I..."

"That's all I need. No explanation." He wound his hand in that French braid he'd done tight, because she liked to have her hair pulled, just a little. Most women he did fireplay with seemed to feel that way.

Brick put his other hand in one of hers, letting her circle his wrist with slim but strong fingers. Then he prompted her, guiding her to move his hand down between her legs. He slid his arm around her back to support her, letting her set the rhythm and pace of his touch against her clit and pussy.

He felt the ripple of her cunt against his fingers and pushed them in enough to add to the stimulus as she shattered, her head falling to his biceps. She buried her cries against his chest, her back rounding and twitching, body pushing against his. He braced his feet and held her easily. Being his size had its advantages.

As she shuddered through it, Brick twitched his fingers between her legs, a massage that took her through the last satisfying aftershock. Following his instincts, he tilted his head toward Richard, an unspoken direction. Understanding, the man wrapped his arm over Brick's across her back. The two of them held her together, sealing in the warmth around her. When her head tipped back and came forward again, she rested it against Richard's shoulder.

"Oh God," she breathed. "I don't think I can handle any more tonight. That was wild."

Brick agreed. This was enough for the first time. "We've got you. Richard is helping me hold you. Open your eyes."

She looked dazed, a little disoriented. She seemed okay with Richard's proximity, though, so Brick didn't signal him to withdraw.

"You went a little deeper than you've gone before, Tish. Your mind's going to seem wonky. You may or may not experience some volatile emotions when things settle."

So far she'd been a sleepy kind of sub during aftercare, but different types of play could bring forth different emotions from a woman.

"I'm going to keep my eye on you, but Richard is really good at this part. Are you all right with him holding you, taking care of you, bringing you back to earth?"

She'd had her gaze on Brick, amazement and wonder in her expression. No matter that Brick had told her Richard was here, when she looked his way, she started, but not from fear. It was just settling in, realizing another man was this close. Richard smiled, his blue eyes kind, concerned and very in charge.

"Just...aftercare."

"Yep. Just aftercare. If you change your mind, I'll be right over here cleaning up. You won't hurt Richard's feelings if you get uncomfortable. This is all about you. You're my responsibility until your mind's as clear as it is in the courtroom."

"Now I know why you drove. I feel like I'm drunk."

"It's like that. I'm still waiting for your answer, Tish. About Richard."

"Oh...yeah. Yeah. I think that's okay." Then she put both arms around Richard, snuggled up against him and offered a little sigh. She began to hum tunelessly.

Richard shot Brick an amused look. As his arms tightened around her to lift her from the table, Brick mouthed *"You owe me one."*

Richard gave him a thumbs up with one of the hands curved over her back. Brick helped him secure the blanket around her as the DM emptied out the room, clearing Richard's route to an easy chair in one corner. He carried her there and settled in.

As he packed up, Brick kept an eye on Tish as promised, though if her emotions took an unexpected turn, Richard would be the first to give him a heads up.

Brick had no problem with aftercare. He enjoyed it, but when cradling a woman in his arms after giving her this first-time experience, it was harder to keep his thoughts from going right to where they'd wanted to be. Not just since the beginning of this night, or even that visit last month. The desire to think about her had been going on for a long time before that.

Celeste Joy Wilder.

She'd been called Les for as long as he'd known her, which was since his teen years in the small town of Fairhope. She'd been several years younger than him, so should have been entirely out of his sphere of interest. And she had been. Until she wasn't.

Before that visit four weeks ago, he'd held off on acting on his feelings. When a female got into your head in high school, you waited to see if it would change. That was the way these things were supposed to go. As life gave a man more possibilities, those possibilities shaped who he was and wanted to be, molding him into an adult with other needs, not just in work and life, but in relationships.

His best friend's little sister being the end of his rainbow hadn't made any sense. He could have a hell of a satisfying relationship with a woman like Tish. But his heart always pointed him back to one serious, lovely young woman whose needs were more complicated than most suspected.

That suspicion had been confirmed at Rory's wedding a few months back. Even in their far too few interactions there, Les had responded to him in a way he recognized.

She had the heart, mind and soul of a submissive.

She hadn't actively pursued it, he was almost sure of that, and she might not even be aware of it herself, but everything about her broadcast it to him. The vibes were so strong he'd had to restrain himself from finding more blatant ways to test it, then and there.

In his early days exploring his Dom side, he'd made the mistakes a young guy with those desires but no good sense would make. He'd eventually acquired a mentor, a sixty-year-old Dom who'd been in the lifestyle for forty years. He'd set Brick straight on a lot of it.

Subs were allowed their stumbles from overeagerness, the euphoria and sometimes manic needs that came to the surface as they discovered that side of themselves. It was a Dom's job to help them manage that. Yes, Doms had similar issues, but because they were the one in charge of the sub's welfare, they had to have better control over it.

So Brick had put in the time, knowing he wanted to be ready and experienced before he directed those desires toward the woman he wanted most.

He was ready.

Ever since he'd returned from the wedding, he'd had zero interest in sex with anyone else. He'd taken a pass on the standing friends-with-benefits offer with Tish, and hadn't allowed any sub he played with to give him sexual relief. His visit with Les at her college had made that resolve non-negotiable. She'd admitted she wanted him, and now she had his commitment, whether she was aware of it or not.

Brick's attention snapped back to his immediate surroundings. Tish had shifted against Richard, and tears were slipping down her cheeks. As Richard spoke to her soothingly and rubbed her back, rocking her, he gave Brick a nod. All good. Just all those places deep inside a woman that could open up from a good session.

Tish not needing him specifically in this instance, just a responsible and caring Dom, reinforced his thoughts. Brick let himself imagine it had been Les on the table, him touching fire to her skin, arousing her, making her body lift to his touch, his attention keeping her safe and warm at the same time.

Les was too busy to be active on social media, but their mothers were friends who chatted regularly. Over the past couple years, whenever he'd talked to his mother, he'd always asked after Les's wellbeing and what she was up to. Somewhere along the way his mom had gotten wise to the fact his interest wasn't casual. Now when they touched base, she always had a "Les update." She didn't take it beyond that, exercising that maternal caginess that told him she liked the match, and was smart enough not to push it and turn him away from it.

He wasn't going to encourage her by telling her there didn't seem to be any chance of that. Rory had always yanked his chain about Brick's enduring interest in his sister, either because Rory wasn't sure what to make of it, or just because he liked to yank Brick's chain.

But Brick wanted to wrap that chain around Les and make her cry out for him, shudder under his touch and flame.

Crazy? Maybe. But if he looked at his life, his certainty made a lot more sense. He'd known he was going to be a firefighter from the time he was twelve. When he discovered an aptitude for football, he used it to gain a modest scholarship to a school where he could get a degree in fire sciences. While continuing to work for the local fire department where he went to college, he discovered his interest in arson and tailored the degree's coursework accordingly.

He was a patient and decisive man. Brick never rushed anything, because if he wanted something, he would earn and obtain it when the time was right, an unknowable factor he left to powers bigger than himself.

He'd gone to see her, and turned a spark to a flame. He'd agreed to turn it down, keep it simmering and waiting until she was ready, and had been ready to respect that. Because of the age difference, she was in a far more transitional time of her life than he was. A third-year med student's life was total chaos.

All reasonable considerations. She'd sent him an enthusiastic thank you for her birthday gift, but lighthearted. Heart emojis. Hug gifs. He hadn't taken that as a dismissal, or that she didn't understand the significance of the gift. Just the opposite. He'd seen what she was struggling with that day. Her desire had been as strong as his, but it had been struggling under a crap ton of responsibilities.

That was why he hadn't given in to the desire to call her every damn day since. Though the response he'd sent to her birthday text had reflected his struggle with self-restraint.

Happy birthday, doc. I'm thinking of you every day.

What he wanted from her could be too easily unleashed if he kept trying to communicate with her. Which would put pressure on her.

The lost weight, the shadows in her eyes, said she already had enough of that.

But hell...those things said other stuff, too. Fuck, had he been this much of an idiot? Driving away hadn't felt right. He'd thought it was just the ache of wanting her. But that uneasy feeling had been with him ever since.

He stuck with a resolve as long as he was sure it was the right path, but there were also moments when an experienced firefighter sensed something about a fire's path was about to change. You didn't ignore that instinct.

The size of a fire, its heat and intensity, could double in a matter of minutes.

Les had needed something from him that day. It hadn't been him respecting her need for time and space. The certainty of it sharpened to an edge that cut through his resolve now and reminded him of the Patrick Swayze *Roadhouse* comment, "Be nice until it's time not to be nice."

Fuck it. He was calling her after he got Tish safely home. And if that conversation confirmed that feeling, he'd be back on Les's doorstep this weekend.

Whether in the ways he wanted, or only how she needed them right now, he'd be her Dom.

CHAPTER FIVE

$\mathcal{T}$he rain had followed Les into Virginia, staying with her the way the memory of Brick's visit had. Though she reached Richmond after nightfall, traffic was still busy and nerve-wracking. She had his address, a townhome in the south part of the city, but when she reached the complex and parked her car in a guest spot near his unit, she didn't see his truck, and only the porch light was on.

Les hadn't doubted herself during the couple hours' drive to get here, but with rain hammering her car, and faced with the sudden lack of forward motion, she realized how insane this was. For all she knew, he was out of town.

A shred of rational thought suggested she find a cheap hotel and a shower. In the morning, she'd evaluate what she should do, when her mind was clearer. He never had to know she'd done something this crazy.

But she couldn't move. She needed to be here, until she was sure he wasn't going to be.

She put her hand over her necklace, fingering the two pendants strung upon it. She'd been bad, opening his gift before her birthday, but she'd always had trouble waiting to open gifts. She'd told herself she'd put it back in the box once she knew what it was, so she could truthfully tell him she'd opened it on her birthday—leaving out that it was for the second time.

But she hadn't put it back in the box. Brick had given her a fire charm. The leaves of the Maltese cross were engraved with a crossed pair of axes and the location of his first firehouse, Fairhope, North Carolina. The badge number he carried, 285, was in the center. In high school, she'd doodled that number on the inside cover of her notebooks.

Her thumb passed over its raised silver outline. He'd probably intended it for the charm bracelet Marcus had given her one Christmas. A thoughtful gift giver with deep pockets, her brother-in-law had included a charm subscription from the company that crafted the bracelet. She'd added a paintbrush for Thomas, a football for Rory. A book, to represent Daralyn's love of reading. A caduceus for herself.

Instead of putting Brick's charm on the bracelet, she'd strung it on the necklace she wore most of the time. It held a gold cross her father had given her for her sixteenth birthday. At its center was a tiny, glittering star made of diamond chips.

During the most challenging parts of her day, she'd been clasping those two talismans in her hand. She'd think about her parents' faith in her, and Brick's confidence. He'd told her the more she learned, the better she'd get at her chosen field. She'd considered it a good luck charm.

Thoughts too painful to contemplate now, but she still held the empty comfort in her hand for its physical substance, and a reminder of the inner magnet that had pulled her to him.

She got out of the car. The rain would soak her to the skin in minutes, but she didn't care. It was better than the damning silence in the vehicle, the repetitive drumming against the metal. She couldn't feel the damp or cold anymore. The shaking of her hands that had persisted while she was driving was only mildly interesting to her.

Lights flashed through the parking lot, and she drew in a shuddering breath, the ache in her throat like a knife. It was Brick's truck.

But as she watched, he pulled up in front of a townhome that wasn't his. Had she written the wrong number down?

As he emerged and came around the front of the truck, Les started forward, wanting to get close enough to call out to him. Her voice was raw, hoarse from crying.

She froze as he opened the passenger door and a long, shapely leg emerged. He took the extended manicured hand, opening the umbrella he carried with a quick snap. It sheltered the leggy blonde who slid to the ground, his grasp steadying her on her fashionable heels. She wore a tailored suit with a modestly short skirt.

He tilted the umbrella over her, rain pattering his broad shoulders. He guided her up the steps of the unit several doors down from his. He did it the way he'd shepherded Les into the diner, a hand at the woman's lower back.

Les's heart thudded like the rain, but louder than thunder. She'd had no plan. She'd put something into the vacuum of her despair to keep it from sucking her in, in the hopes that this one act would help her...what? Figure it out? Make it better?

It couldn't be made better, and she found it horribly, wretchedly funny that this made it worse.

When they reached her door, Brick spoke to the woman, holding eye contact until she nodded, a confirmation she'd heard whatever he'd just told her.

Because she was in the mood to lacerate herself, Les didn't look away as he brushed a kiss over the woman's dark pink mouth. She gave him a half smile, then her gaze slid past him, and she stilled.

Les couldn't move as Brick turned, the two of them staring at the figure standing in the parking lot. A person cloaked by the rain, the night and the street light glare off the asphalt, but noticeably ogling them.

Oh God. Go, you idiot, before he recognizes you.

She jerked into motion, turning to walk away, adjusting her heading to direct herself back to her car. Maybe he'd think she was a gawking neighbor. One taking a walk in the rain with no coat, by herself, no dog needing a bathroom break as an excuse.

It was okay. He wouldn't think it was her, showing up like this. Why had she thought this was the right thing to do? He'd said he'd give her time. No promises about either of them not being with someone else. That would have been unreasonable.

Even if everything in her howled that she'd wanted it to mean exactly that.

She would figure it out, she would. She was strong, she could handle everything if she stayed calm and worked it through.

Shut the fuck up. Never use that again. She could be as calm as a glacier, patient as Job, and nothing would be fine. She was stupid to think anything would make it fine.

54

She barely managed not to break into a run, making her look more suspicious. When she chanced a look back, he was saying something to the woman, opening her door and waiting for her to go inside. Les's steps slowed. She was further away, under the dripping trees, safe from being seen.

Brick turned and headed down the steps, probably to relocate his truck to the front of his own townhome.

Instead, he passed it and headed in her direction.

She bolted.

Stupid. If she'd just stayed still, he might have lost her in the dark, but running like a spooked deer...

Reaching the car, she folded herself into the seat with a wet squelch. She fumbled for her keys, while awkwardly trying to shut the door. She yelped, startled, as his hand landed on it, keeping her from closing it.

"It's okay, miss. I'm not going to hurt you. I just want to know if you're all right."

He hadn't recognized her. She'd bought the old beater with a loan from her mother during her second year, to make it easier to get back and forth from the hospital. He'd never seen it. Her head was down, and she hadn't parked under a streetlight.

He also hadn't seen her enough over the past few years to recognize her in these conditions. That cutting knowledge reinforced how crazy she was to have done this.

He clicked on his phone's light and shone it into the interior of the car. First responder, no shyness about evaluating a situation. She didn't look up as he muttered a startled oath.

"Les. What the hell?" He sounded as if he thought she were a figment of his imagination, which was fair.

She was still pulling on the door handle, a move as effective as pulling rebar out of concrete. He detached her hand, putting it back in her lap, and dropped to a knee. He pushed her wet hair out of her face, gripping it at her nape so her face was turned toward him. Hell, his touch felt so good. It penetrated the cold, finally making her realize she was freezing, and shaking even harder.

He followed the damp strands down to her shoulder and then paused, before he let his fingers drift to the necklace resting on her chest. Her father had put the cross around her neck the first time, his strong fingers caressing her with love and affection.

When Brick touched the cross and his badge, she knew luck wasn't the only reason she'd worn it. Not that it mattered.

"What happened, baby?" he asked.

She stared at the wheel. "Nothing. I need—I'm going. I was just... stopping by, like you did, and it's a bad time, and I'm on my way home." Home being the exact opposite direction from school, and in North Carolina, not Virginia. Her lips were stiff, her voice croaky. "I need to go, I'm going."

She was spun out like a car that had careened off the road and turned over, no way to get back on it.

"You need dry clothes. Put your arms around me."

He leaned in, filling up the small space of her car. As she clumsily complied, he slid his arms under her legs and behind her shoulders. He lifted her out of the car as easily as she would have picked up her phone. After rising from the kneeling position, he settled her in his embrace and nudged the car door closed with his knee.

As he carried her to his porch, she wanted to drop her head on his shoulder, but hair was soaked. All of her was, so she guessed it didn't matter. She was going to make his shirt wet. The heavy cotton carried hints of smoke, a touch of incense, and weirdly, isopropyl alcohol, like they used at the hospital. Also something floral she hoped wasn't from the blonde. He hadn't invited her home, and he hadn't gone into her place. None of which changed how intimate they were with one another. They'd obviously had sex before.

The thoughts made her stiffen. She considered trying to leave again when he put her on her feet, but he held her by the arm as he pulled his keys from his pocket and unlocked his door.

The panel was blue, with a silver knocker. White trim, solid black numbers. A mounted flag over them, illuminated by the covered porch light, rippled in the breeze, valiantly shedding drops of rain. It was an American flag tinted red, a firefighter flag.

He'd pushed open the door, but when she didn't move, he eased her inside with a firm touch on her lower back. As he closed the panel and turned the lock, she stared at the floor. The tiled entryway transitioned to a cherry-gold hardwood in the living room. It was covered by a cream-colored area rug and sectional sofa. Directly to her left were steps to the second level. It had a black metal balustrade.

"I didn't see a bag in the car. Did you bring any clothes?"

She hadn't even brought a toothbrush. Her shaking increased again, body responding to the warmth of the apartment. She needed to say something, to explain herself. He was waiting for that, like any person would be. But each time she tried, her throat convulsed, and her body would jerk. She'd swallowed all of it, a poisoned meal too big to go all the way down or come back up. It was stuck high in her chest, making it hurt like she'd been beaten there with a fist.

"Come over here. Hold onto this." He brought her to the sectional sofa and laid one of her cold hands on the top of it. The fleece throw folded there was soft against her icy fingers.

When he dropped to his knees to remove her shoes, peeling the wet socks off her feet, something inside her recoiled. Wrong. This was wrong.

But she couldn't move. He put the footwear aside and untied the drawstring of her scrubs, sliding them off her damp underwear. When he rose to remove her shirt, that wrongness eased. He was standing. She could breathe again.

Her pink bra and panties were a modest cotton. It didn't mean fuck-all, but in a less terrible reality she'd have been glad she coordinated the color before Brick saw them.

He tugged the throw from beneath her grasp and draped it around her. "I'm going to get some towels and find you something to wear. Take off the underwear and add it to the pile. I'll throw it all in the dryer."

He moved away. She swayed and he stopped short, came back. "I'm going to sit you down."

She shook her head. Instead, she took one step back and sank to her knees.

She did it with a deliberate slowness, directed by something that had the force of a conscious decision, though she gave no words to it in her head. This was what she needed to do, for reasons she couldn't articulate but hoped he understood. That same subconscious compulsion said he would.

So did his stillness. If he hadn't understood, he would have lunged to catch her, thinking she'd finally become too weak to stand.

She lifted her head and stared at him.

"I didn't come here for you to be nice to me," she rasped.

CHAPTER SIX

$\mathcal{L}$ es had attended Beulah's Baptist church a couple times in Richmond. In one of the sermons, the theatrical preacher had said sin was burned away. "The soul is purged and cleansed by fire," he'd shouted. The syllables had lifted and fallen, like heavy metal music punctuated by a bass line.

Tension emanated from Brick as she mumbled those words. She wanted to close both hands on that wire of energy and feel it rip through her.

"You don't want me to be nice to you," he said slowly. The words thickened, deepened. Emphasized like the preacher's, they struck answering chords within her. It didn't make sense to her. But hearing him say it, the relief that swept her was so strong, so widespread. He knew. He understood.

At her jerky, shaky nod, a roughness edged his next response. "Why should I be mean to you, Celeste Joy? Tell me."

She stared at the floor. Started to shake again, only unlike it had been on the drive here, this wasn't a cycle that would crest and ebb, pausing before it repeated again. Now it would keep intensifying until it could shake apart a ten-story building.

She stared at his shoes, his long legs and powerful thighs, denim creasing around his hips and groin, holding what was there and making her stomach flipflop. Noticing it made sense, no matter her emotional turmoil. It was part of all of it, what held her still and aching.

Slowly, he reached down and curled his fingers in her hair, twisting it, a gradual pull against her scalp that increased until a sound escaped her, animal-like. Oh God, she couldn't stop it. The crack raced outward, breaking apart the concrete foundation. What it had held clawed its way up the sides of the building, releasing the four damning words that brought it all down.

"I killed a child."

She stuffed a fist against her teeth hard enough to cut her raw knuckles, despising herself for the cry she made on the ragged end of the statement, an outburst that begged for pity, for a forgiveness she didn't deserve.

Brick squatted in front of her. It wasn't like his kneeling to undress her, the cosseting that had disturbed her. This brought the full force of his presence right up into her field of blurred vision. He pulled her hands away from her mouth. His gaze dropped to the bludgeoned knuckles, the blood that had dried there after her fight with the garden wall.

A muttered oath, and he had his arms around her. She fought him, fought herself, seeking movement to escape the truth that invaded too much abhorred stillness.

"No." A single, relentless word, which contained an order to submit. He wouldn't let her go, so she had to surrender to the exhaustion, the tears, let them scald through her.

She knew the body had limits, even for something like this. She'd known the truth would break her a hundred times over when it breached the wall she'd put around it to get her here. Maybe that was why she'd had to get here, because he didn't break. Nothing held in Brick's arms could break apart.

Unless he wanted it broken.

His hand was back in her hair, that tight grip. She buried her face in his neck, breathing wet sobs against him. She'd already doused him with her rain-soaked clothes, so the tears were absorbed into damp cotton.

Even after surrendering to it, she couldn't stop the hard waves of emotion. She'd thump a fist against him, turn it toward herself, and he would recapture and hold it. He was all the way on the floor, his broad back against the sofa, her sprawled between his legs, pressed against his torso. When her body at last gave out, all she could do was lie there.

Only then did he pick her up again, blanket and all. He took her up the stairs to a bedroom. The master bedroom, not a guestroom. He carried her into the bathroom, setting her on the commode as he started up the shower.

He turned and framed her face in both hands. He studied her the way she checked on a patient going through a procedure, to see where they were at. Only his regard penetrated to a different level, looking for different things.

"Shower and then bed," he told her. "You'll sleep, and in the morning, we'll go from there. Does anyone know where you are, Les? Your roommate, your family?"

"No. It doesn't matter."

He leveled her with a stern look. "It sure as hell does. I'll take care of it."

He peeled the blanket off her and stepped back. Steam billowed out of the shower. "Underwear," he said.

When she didn't move, feeling so helpless she couldn't translate his direction into the movement of her limbs, a muscle twitched in his jaw. Her skin prickled with gooseflesh as his gray eyes hardened.

"You're a grown woman. You don't need me to undress and bathe you before you get pneumonia."

It startled her into stumbling to her feet. But she hesitated. Modesty was something med students lost early, but in front of Brick was different.

"I'm not leaving," he said. "You're not steady enough for me to leave you alone. Take off the rest."

Numbly, she unhooked the bra, removed it, pushed her panties down so they fell to her ankles. Hunched over, she picked them up and put them with the bra, on top of the blanket he'd folded up on the counter.

"You're not a beaten dog. Straighten up, Les."

Tears rolled down her cheeks, but she complied. He touched her face again, drawing her attention to his eyes. "Good girl," he murmured, though his gaze remained cool. "Get in the shower."

She'd told him she needed him to be mean to her. Somehow, he'd understood just what that meant, even better than she herself did. No matter the stabbing pain in her chest, the commotion in her mind, she could now move and follow direction. She got into the shower. Caught up in that maelstrom, she didn't notice how he shifted closer, ready to catch her if she fell.

～

When Brick had told her to straighten up, the way she snapped her spine into position reassured him. Though what that move did to her breasts was a pleasure to watch, he sure as hell wasn't indulging himself in it. If she looked any closer to passing out, he was prepared to enter the shower fully clothed. A good wind might knock her out.

Not undressing her like a child and taking over had been harder than he'd ever let her know.

He'd helped trauma victims. He also paid close attention to what helped a sub and what didn't. She was both right now. Someone like her, believing she'd killed a child? If she'd been the sole survivor of a preschool bomb blast, she couldn't be more devastated.

He stepped out only for the time it took to retrieve a sweatshirt from his dresser. It would cover her from neck to knees and would do for tonight.

When he'd visited her, he'd wondered if he'd pushed her too hard. Instead it seemed he'd planted a trigger in her submissive side that had brought her right to him when she didn't know what else to do. The theory, hard to refute after she knelt in his living room, had him reeling. He was pretty certain she lacked any experience as a sub, which meant she'd operated on pure, uninformed instinct, something he'd never seen manifested like this.

Tish had talked about how "hints" of the natural inclination had always been there for her, same as being a Dom was for him, but they'd both pursued and developed that in a structured way.

What also floored him was her wearing that charm around her neck with her cross. Like a mark of ownership, a collar. Yeah, he was probably taking that a couple steps further in his mind than was warranted. But god *damn*. This was a tangle he wasn't yet sure how to unravel.

First things first. After the shower thawed her out, she needed to get some sleep. She was vibrating with an insane amount of fatigue. He wasn't going to dwell on her driving here in that condition, at night and in the rain. He'd be too tempted to blister her pale, cold bottom with his hand.

Though he'd limited himself to a functional evaluation of her physical state, there was no overlooking the small, perfect curves of her breasts, tipped by tight nipples. The curly light brown hair over her sex, the hint of her clit. The delicate bones and small marks unique to her.

He preferred to do his first full perusal when he could order the sub to stand and submit to it, letting her feel the weight of his regard like the stroking of his hands.

If she was a submissive down to her soul, the longer he savored that still moment, the more aroused she'd become, the more committed to the moment. Because she'd be responding to what the Dom inside him was doing, what it meant, what he wanted, she'd start to tremble, and the reaction would increase, the longer he made her wait for actual contact.

He was pretty damn sure Les had that capability, but her current shaking was from a dangerous level of stress. Her knuckles appeared to be her only physical injury. Fortunately, he didn't have to find someone and kill them, because he knew the signs of punching the daylights out of something impervious to pain. You did that because you wanted the pain.

I didn't come here for you to be nice to me.

His girl wanted punishment. He knew how to dish that out, but sure as fuck not for this. Taking submission when it was offered like that wasn't a gift. It was an invitation to fucking up her head worse than it already was.

They'd deal with all of it. Once it was all figured out, then he'd punish her. For driving when she was in an unsafe frame of mind. For asking for the wrong kind of punishment. For...well, he'd just add it all to the list he would tell her about one day, when the time was right.

Which wasn't now.

She'd folded herself onto the bench seat in the shower, and was leaning against the wall. She was half-asleep. Since it was hot enough in the bathroom to make him sweat, he deduced she was warmer. He reached in and shut off the water. When she clumsily tried to stir herself, he wrapped her in a towel and brought her out to dry her before helping her into the sweatshirt.

He'd made his point and deemed it didn't need immediate reinforcement. He wasn't sure he could have summoned the will to do it twice anyway. Not when she looked this vulnerable.

"What's your phone password, Les?"

She blinked at him and seemed to search her mind for the information. "DadTR," she said at last. Her voice was thick, but she cleared it. "@285."

The significance gave him a jolt, but he picked her up and took her to his bed, tucking her in and adding an extra blanket. Her eyes were half open, mouth moving, but no words came out. "Go to sleep," he told her. "That's an order. We'll deal with it, Les. Together, we'll deal with it."

Her face creased with despair. He sat on the edge of the bed, holding one of her hands, rubbing her fingers until her eyes drooped and closed. She subsided in minutes, though there was no smoothing that furrow in her brow, even when he stroked it.

When he was certain she was fully out, he reluctantly released her hand, tucking it under the blanket. A quick trip downstairs and to her car helped him locate her phone and confirm what she'd told him. She hadn't brought anything with her. Hell, she must have left straight from the hospital. No evidence of stopping for a fast-food dinner, not even a bottle of water. He'd put one by her bed so if she roused tonight, she could hydrate. When she woke in the morning, he'd get breakfast into her. He kept a well-stocked kitchen.

He locked up the vehicle, moved his truck to the space in front of his unit, and returned to the bedroom. She hadn't moved, except to burrow more deeply under the covers. Okay. Next step.

He entered the password and found Beulah in her contacts to send a text. *Safe, took a road trip, back in a few days.*

It didn't sit well with him, pretending to be her, no matter how generic the message. That feeling increased when Beulah responded immediately, telling him just how worried Les's roommate was.

U ok? Know u need space, but I'm here if u need 2 talk. Hospital attorney looking for u. Left you vm and texts. Even gave me his digits for u 2 call.

She'd followed the text with a few hug emojis. After thinking it through, Brick hit the call button over Beulah's name. As he did, he moved into the hallway and took a seat on the top of the stairwell. He would hear Les if she woke.

Beulah picked up on the second ring. "Hey, girl, I'm so glad you called." She had a full-bodied voice, Southern bonhomie and feminine confidence. "I was worried, since your car's gone and no one's heard from you since—"

"This isn't Les. This is Brick McGuire." He paused, curious if Les had told her roommate enough about him to stick in Beulah's memory.

"The arson cop. Good. She's with you? She's safe?"

"Yes. She's at my place here in Richmond. She's sleeping now, but she'll reach out to you herself tomorrow." He'd make sure of that. Re-establishing connection after trauma was important, no staying alone in her head.

Her breath rushed out in a relieved sigh. "Okay. Wow. She has such good instincts—even her residents and attendings say so. She's the last of us we'd expect to have something like that happen. I'm worried how she's going to handle it. They tell us all the time it can and will happen, but for the first to be a toddler..."

"Beulah, stop." She was upset, making the info dump understandable. The edge in his order was fueled by his frustrated desire to let her keep going, to find out everything. "She hasn't shared much with me yet, and I don't want to get that information without her consent. Not unless her health is at risk because of it. But is there anything she needs to do right away, to protect her interests or the hospital's?"

Beulah's tone reflected her surprise at his unwillingness to grill her for info, though it also suggested he'd earned an additional measure of her respect. "Okay, yeah. I told Dr. Portland, her advisor, that she was out of town, so no one will expect her to show up for class and stuff right away, but hospital legal wants her to call them as soon as she can. Though the heat will fall mostly on the supervising resident and the on-call attending, they'll want to talk to her. Dr. Jack—Dr. Jack Toll-man, but we all call him Dr. Jack—was the resident. Dr. Redmond was the attending."

"Will they throw her under the bus?" Brick asked bluntly.

"It doesn't exactly work like that. This is a teaching hospital, so there will be an M&M conference where a bunch of the medical staff will go over everything, to determine what should or could have been handled differently. That's not supposed to be a punishment thing, but to map out how to keep something like it from happening again. Legal is different, though. They focus on what to do if the family brings a suit. They can name anybody who was involved. Including Les."

Shit. He could imagine what that would do to Les. So apparently could Beulah.

"It's probably good she's away from campus for a couple days while this first part is happening, but she also needs to come back before it settles in too deep, if that makes sense."

It did. Brick's mind went to the first time—and not the last—the fire had won when he tried to rescue someone caught in it.

"She was really stressed out by the ER rotation," Beulah said. "Honestly? She's probably the best doctor among us third years, but she agonizes over having all the information, afraid of missing something. Which is why this might be even tougher for her. Sorry. I thought it might be helpful to know that."

"It is."

From being at past Wilder family gatherings, Brick had seen that quality in Les himself. Rory had mentioned his own concerns about that aspect of his sister's character, the potential causes that had exacerbated it. The loss of their father, Thomas's struggles, Rory ending up in a wheelchair...

"I'm glad she went somewhere she feels safe," Beulah continued. "Should I call her family?"

"I'll take care of that, but thanks. If they call before then, let them know she's here with me. It's up to you, but I'd recommend not telling them more than that. I think it's her story to tell."

"Agreed. I don't want to second-hand grapevine that shit with her mom or brothers."

The colorful observation offered him a grim spurt of humor. "I better go. Thanks for being a good friend."

"Give her a hug from me. And tell her to remember the 'when not if' thing. Shit is going to happen." A touch of female smugness transmitted over the line. "I'm not surprised she ended up at your place. You've been on her mind. A lot."

Hearing it loosened some of the tightness in his chest. "Glad to hear it. Before I go, I'd like to ask a favor. I'll send you the money to do it..."

After he hung up, Brick considered Beulah's parting words. The problem wasn't that Les didn't know things like this could happen. It was that she did, and she'd likely pushed herself over and above the already taxing demands on her time and brain, to prevent it from happening.

And then it had happened anyway.

Even an experienced, licensed doctor couldn't catch everything. There was a reason they called it practicing medicine. If she'd made a mistake, yes, it was her mistake. But there was a key difference in accepting that and moving forward, versus honing it into a blade and falling on it.

His phone buzzed. Tish had done as he'd told her, letting him know how she was doing. She'd been aware but floaty on the way home. Her text said she'd taken a shower, done some paperwork, and was now going to bed. Mental acuity and physical wellbeing confirmed.

He sent her a sleeping *zzz* happy face. He'd check on her again in the morning.

He didn't want to think about what would have happened if Tish hadn't seen Les, and Les had left, unnoticed by either of them. He would need to help her understand what his and Tish's relationship was, but he'd handle that later. The important thing was she was in his bed, warm and safe.

Next thing. He considered which Wilder family member to contact and settled on Rory for two reasons.

Rory was his best friend, and he was a Dom himself.

It was late, but Rory's day started early. He'd see it in the morning. Using his own phone, Brick typed out the text and sent it. *Your sister is here in Richmond. She lost a patient, a kid, and needs to regroup. Doesn't want to talk about it yet, but she's safe. Unless your mom is looking for her, suggest not saying anything yet. Let her do it when she's ready.*

His phone buzzed in a matter of seconds. Brick grimaced, but it made sense. With his mother right down the road, living alone, Rory would always rouse for a text, even if he and Daralyn had gone to bed.

Shit. Understood. Why'd she come your way?

For the reason you'd expect. She's what I thought she was. Maybe as deep as Daralyn. And before you make me reach through the phone to kick your ass, my first priority is helping her deal with this. I'll take care of her.

Those typing-in-process dots strobed for several minutes, as if Rory was going over a variety of responses. It made Brick a little edgy. Which he squelched. He shouldn't be acting like a possessive Dom before he had the official right to do so.

Make sure she calls me in a couple days. Sooner if she's up to it. Let me know if either of you needs anything.

He acknowledged with a thumbs-up, glad Rory wasn't calling to ride him for more. But he expected Rory had seen and noted the important part.

I'll take care of her.

Daralyn, Rory's wife and submissive, could get close to catatonic when pushed, thanks to a childhood too horrific to contemplate. She'd improved slowly after Rory's family took her in and helped her reclaim her life. But once she and Rory came together, her natural and deep submissive orientation finding the love of the right Master, the progress had accelerated. Her astonishingly strong soul and generous heart had carried her through hell, but now they were also nurtured by genuine happiness.

Les had a strong soul and generous heart, too. Plus she'd been born into a far better support system than Daralyn. She'd be okay. It didn't stop Brick from hating what she was going through.

In his first year doing search and rescue with the Richmond fire department, he'd found a man trapped by fire in his apartment, a video game developer barely in his twenties. Brick was taking him toward the door when the ceiling collapsed. The impact knocked Brick back into the hallway. The kid hadn't been so lucky. Brick would never forget that last look of terror on his face, the outstretched hand as he vanished under a truckload of flaming debris, too much of it, too hot. Not even a remote chance of digging him out alive.

When they sifted through it later, he'd been found, with a desiccated arm still partially outstretched. The ones you almost saved, or felt you could have saved, were the worst.

He returned to the bedroom. She was still out, but her fists were clenched against her chest, and she was making fearful noises in her sleep. He took off his clothes, put on a pair of sleep shorts, and slid under the covers with her. Even with two blankets and the sheet, her skin was cold. She was shivering. Necessary as it had been to touch base with her roommate and family, he cursed himself for taking this long to come to her.

His substantial bulk was a heat magnet, drawing her to him. He wrapped his arms around her, curving his hand over her hair. It was still damp, but that didn't matter to him. He tucked her full against him.

Like any red-blooded male who wanted a woman, there were plenty of things he'd like to do to and for her. He wanted to hear her scream herself hoarse from her orgasms. He wanted to see all the emotions that went with that kind of surrender cross her face, fill her beautiful hazel eyes. For good sex, he could find and give pleasure with moderate effort. But bliss took spiritual commitment to the act.

He wanted to give her that commitment. This moment connected to that, his woman resting unafraid in his arms. Her trust for that came from the same well as what would allow him to put flame to her skin, spank her ass, or restrain her. Get her to kneel to him, compel her to call him Master or Sir.

The kneeling part had happened a little sooner than expected. The grim smile at that died away as his mind went to other things. It was as Beulah said. All medical students were told to expect this. While it would pull the rug out from under anyone, he thought there was more to Les's reaction.

His job started with the end results of a fire, working backwards toward the origin, cause and fuel source. Les had the smarts and commitment to go the distance in medical school, and she wasn't afraid of hard work. Yet those things that had concerned him a few weeks ago, when she talked about her rotations and clinical work, bugged him even more now. Because those warning signs had been evident *before* what had brought her to his door.

She'd been goal-driven since high school, qualifying for early admission to college. Rory had told him if she'd stayed for her senior year, she would have nailed the valedictorian spot. Instead she went to UNC-Charlotte, and met all requirements there to again accelerate her finishing time, obtaining her undergraduate degree in three years and securing a scholarship for a top-notch medical school.

She wanted to do her residency in her hometown. Their population of twenty-five hundred souls had one overworked doctor with two nurses and a part-time PA. Dr. Spring would welcome her with open arms.

Brick doubted it had ever crossed her mind, using her medical degree to earn a six-figure salary, drive a fancy car and set aside her Wednesdays for golf. She was an intelligent woman with a loving heart, with a deep attachment to home and community. Even so, the yearning she'd displayed at her mother's care package had surprised him. After six years of shuttling between home and school, that reaction had gone beyond homesickness. It was a primal longing for that childhood sense of security.

It pissed him off with himself anew. But now that she was here, he'd help give her the space to evaluate the situation and look at the information from the right perspective.

Like the arson case he'd had on his desk recently. When the frustration overwhelmed him, Jed Hamilton, the sergeant of his unit, told him to join him for a weekend outing. He didn't tell Brick what they'd be doing until they were sitting in a hangar and Brick was getting instruction on how to jump out of an airplane.

For the next couple hours, Brick had only one occupation, thinking he'd lost his fucking mind. But he found the courage to do it, leap out into the blue sky and tumble to earth.

Later, smoking a Cuban cigar next to Hamilton, he figured out the case. The smoke and fumes had funneled up a laundry chute system in the building, then gotten hot enough to reignite on the upper floor. That had led to the mistaken idea the source was up there, which was counterintuitive, since lower floors had burned and fire rarely went from up to down.

"I need to check the basement more thoroughly," he'd told Hamilton. Sure enough, using his trusty shovel to carefully shift through the burned and charred debris, he'd found evidence of the accelerant that started the fire.

While Les didn't need to go sky diving, the logic of pulling her out of her own head to help her handle what had driven her to his door, and address what had been causing her problems even before that, made sense.

He had a couple ideas on how to do that. One would involve taking a comp day and reaching out to Rufus, to see if he'd be on board with what Brick had in mind. It was a lot to ask, but he expected Rufus would agree, if he knew the reason for the request.

The other idea had his cock trying to stiffen against the softness of her body. To settle it down, he reminded himself of the perils of wishful thinking.

Yes, Les wanted him. She had also come to him as a sub came to her Dom. But if he was her first, and she only had a nebulous sense of what a power exchange relationship was, he could end up being just that—the first. Not the last.

He'd prefer chewing on glass than facing that reality, but what mattered was what she needed now. Mean or nice. Gentle or demanding. Asshole or hero. He could be all of those things, when he determined a sub needed them.

And right now, she *was* his. He wouldn't make the mistake he'd made a few weeks ago. Whether she officially accepted him as her Dom or it had to stick to a more informal track for now, he would hold her wishes and desires in a gentle hand, but he wouldn't let them interfere with meeting her needs. And right now she needed something from him. Badly.

He let his eyes close and willed his body to sleep. No matter how easy it would be to let his hands wander over her, wake her, and bring her the mindlessness of sex, now was not the time. He'd waited a long time for that. He could wait a little longer.

Or so he thought.

CHAPTER SEVEN

*L*es started awake. She was used to grabbing quick cat naps wherever med students could find a space and break to do that. Her internal clock said this one had gone on too long, with none of the usual interruptions to wake her and get her back to work or studies.

She wasn't at the hospital. She also wasn't in her bedroom, her tablet tucked under her arm where she'd fallen asleep on it, the corner poking into her ribs.

She did have something insistently pressing against her, but it wasn't her tablet.

She was wrapped in Brick's arms, one of the most sheltering places she'd ever been. His breathing was an even flow over her brow. Her face was nestled against his chest and throat. Her hair felt itchy, reminding her she hadn't combed and put it into a twist before bedtime, like she usually did. She'd have to wet it down again to fix it. Preferably before Brick saw it and thought he was in bed with one of those birds who poofed out their ruff to scare off predators.

A mundane thought to balance out her very not mundane reality. Being a medical professional and not a virgin, she knew men got erections in their sleep. But comparing her ex-fiancé Bart to Brick...whoa.

She adjusted, wondering if she was disoriented and one of his arms was between them, pressed at an angle across her stomach.

Nope. The room was dark, the streetlight gleam coming through the pulled curtains telling her it was still nighttime, but she could verify both of his arms were around her. One hand was against her back and shoulder, the other resting over her hip and the rise of her buttock. The third "arm" convulsed in response to her adjustment, confirming it was what she suspected.

A tingle like a bag of SweeTarts on the tongue shot through her belly and thighs.

Brick shifted, and she bit her lip as all that hardness pressed against her mound, a message her clitoris received loud and clear. At the strong ripple through it, a moan hummed in her throat.

Waiting for her attention were thoughts and images that would kill every ounce of desire, so no surprise, her body desperately overrode that part of her mind. Her brain didn't take much convincing, a co-conspirator to the crime.

She opened her fingers on his chest to stroke through the hair and slide over the bump of a nipple, moving down to the layers of muscle over his ribs. She knew the names for all of them, and had an in-depth knowledge of what was beneath them, thanks to Rick, her assigned cadaver.

She'd keep that thought to herself. Medical students tended to view the body and its workings differently from normal humans. It didn't change her female appreciation of what she was touching now.

Using Rick's name helped keep him a real person in her mind. He'd donated his body to her education; he wasn't just a bunch of parts, or an inanimate object like a microscope. But if ever proof of a soul was needed, it was evident in the comparison. Rick had long ago left the husk of his body, while Brick fully inhabited his, taking up every square inch of space with his life energy.

Energy that made her restless and ready. Her thighs were getting slippery, no underwear in the way. She wanted his hands on her under the sweatshirt. She wanted the sweatshirt gone, so she could press her breasts against his wide, bare chest, feel the rough rasp of his hair.

He had given her a place to land, and he wanted her. He was in bed with her, wasn't he? He could have put her in his guest room.

There was no reason they shouldn't, and every reason to reach for that pleasure. He wouldn't deny her. What man would? *I'm here, I'm willing, and there's nothing to stop us.*

"Les. What are you doing?"

Sleep deepened his voice to that husky sound. She'd reached his waist, fingers sliding along his hip and back, to the hint of a very firm ass under the waistband of his shorts.

She tipped her face to his, pushing herself forward to find his mouth. A kiss would answer the question, a kiss like the ones in his truck a few weeks ago. She wanted another.

He moved his hands to her waist. In a motion that expelled a startled gasp from her, he had her on her back. He leaned over her, his knee between her legs, pinning one thigh, that steel bar of his cock pressed against it. She could see the faint outline of his head and shoulders.

"I asked you a question. What are you doing?"

His tone took control of her mind, while his hands took control of her body. "I...I thought you wanted me. And...I'm offering..."

"Do you want me?"

He wasn't asking for a verbal response. He slid his hand under the sweatshirt. She bit her lip on a groan as he grazed her mound, his fingers playing over her clit before shockingly sliding them two knuckles deep inside her wetness. No man had ever touched her with that kind of sure knowledge and sexual skill.

"Yes," he rumbled. "I can feel you do. But that's not up to you, is it?"

Her gaze snapped up to his. With her eyes adjusting, she could detect the set of his face, that firm and soft mouth. Her body shuddered over his thick fingers. Since his knee held her leg down, she was aware of his strength, how easily he could overpower her. She heard expectation in his voice, waiting for her answer, as if he was testing something.

She felt a little ashamed and a lot aroused. When he asked her a question like that, answering him the strange way she wished seemed to be her only choice.

But she licked her lips, shying away from it. She would avoid it, play dumb. "I...I should have asked if you were okay with it. Consent and all. Not molested you in your sleep."

It sounded foolish, with his fingers inside her and his unflagging erection against her thigh. As she spoke in a breathy voice, he grew harder and thicker. Her sex convulsed around his fingers. His other hand was now near her face, fingers sliding along her jaw and throat. A throat still sore from crying, but all she could think about was how it would feel if screams from a climax made it worse. She could handle that kind of pain. Wanted it.

With the way her body liquefied under his command, she thought the reality would be well beyond her expectations. A reminder of what he'd told her that day in his truck, which made her body throb even more.

"Consent is important," he agreed. He added another finger, stretching her and making her grab for his biceps.

"Oh...that's a little...uncomfortable."

"Yeah. I assumed it would be. But does it hurt?"

She shook her head. He was being very gentle. And relentless.

"My dick is bigger than that," he said conversationally. "When you take it, I want you ready and knowing what to expect."

What was against her thigh verified he wasn't bragging. "But that's not going to happen right now," he continued. "You're going to tell me the truth. Why isn't it up to you?"

"Because it's up to you. When...when you..."

"When I fuck you is up to me. You also know why that is. We'll talk about it later. Along with a lot of other things. Go back to sleep. It's just past four o'clock. We'll get up at seven."

She wisely didn't scoff at the likelihood of her being able to return to sleep. His fingers slid from her, pulling another moan from her lips. He brushed her wetness over them as she inhaled her aroused scent. She quaked with need, feeling the burn of his gaze in the murky gloom.

"Wait here."

He slid from the bed and headed for the bathroom. She heard a drawer open, the rush of water from the sink. The bathroom had a green safety light which allowed her to see his profile. A big man, seemingly calm and focused on what he was doing. The shadows and shorts cloaked his erection, but she could imagine it.

She wanted to put her hand between her legs to press against that need, stroke herself to a small, intense orgasm while looking at him. But he was back before she could try to sneak it in.

He put something on the nightstand, and slid into the bed, settling on his back. Curving an arm under her, he guided her to lie between his legs, her head on his chest, her stomach pressed against his rigid cock. With her thighs split over one of his legs, her sex was pressed against firm muscle. She had to make a conscious effort not to rub, though the difficulty sent a shudder through her.

He reached toward the nightstand. She heard something dipped in water, then his fingers were on her hair, smoothing and straightening it before he started using a dampened brush to rewet and comb it. When his hand followed the stroke, he tightened his grip on the strands, a little pull against her scalp. Her heart stuttered.

"Count my heart beats and sleep, doc," he murmured. "I've got you. It's all crazy and messed up in you now. I'm not going to let you fly apart and go down the wrong path."

She stiffened, her pride hurt, as well as something deeper. "You're saying me wanting you is wrong? After you've told me that's exactly what you want?"

He pressed a hand to her shoulder blades, keeping her in place. "Not what I'm saying at all. Shut up and count the heart beats."

His voice was mild, but all those emotions and needs rebelled. She shoved away, sitting up in the bed. She stared holes at him, wishing she could read his face better in the shadows. "Fuck you. Who says you're in charge?"

"You do. Every time you react to me." He sighed. "I told myself I wasn't going to go this way until we can have the right conversation about it, but sometimes you just go with your gut on this shit."

He moved way too fast for a big man. She yelped and scrambled back, but he already had her by the waist. In a blink, he had her turned over his lap, a second before the brush landed against the lower curve of her ass. He'd exposed the bare cheeks by holding the roomy sweatshirt against her lower back. The blow stung, but it shocked more. She tried to struggle, but he had his elbow and forearm against her back, holding her immobile.

That erect cock was pressed beneath her breasts. It didn't flag as he followed up the first blow with four more strikes. He spread out the location so it didn't get to be too much, but she definitely felt them, warning her how much worse he could make it.

"Apologize for what you said to me."

She opened her mouth to offer a double *Fuck You*, but he anticipated it with another swat, this time with his bare hand.

Her body wasn't rejecting the pain. She was craving it. Wanting him to do more. He was right. She was an emotional mess.

As she strangled on a sound mixed between frustration, annoyance, tears, and arousal, he rubbed where he'd hit, sliding over her burning flesh. Her thighs trembled.

"Stop it," she said, but it sounded weak, even to herself.

"You can count heartbeats, or more strikes on your ass. That's the choice I'm giving you. Neither one is wrong. You want more? If you do, I'll give you more."

This might be the most remarkable conversation she'd ever had in her life. He expected her to embrace the spanking, rather than treating it as a punishment to avoid.

"If you want more of the brush, it'll hurt more as I go along. I'll stop when I decide you've had enough. I have a pretty good idea that's how you'd like it. Under the right circumstances, control freaks hand over control like it's a hot potato they can't bear to have burning their palms anymore."

"This is..." She curled her fingers in the bedding, her hair falling around her face as she dropped it to the mattress. The strands were already softer and smoother, thanks to his ministrations. Something else inside her softened, the anger filtering away uncertainly. "I don't know."

A significant pause. "Yeah. I know. Like I said. I wasn't putting you down, baby. Just stating the way it is, where your head seems to be. My first and only job tonight is watching after you. But you still have to make a decision. Heart or ass?"

She couldn't help a strangled chuckle. "Heart...I guess."

The heat that entered his voice took her by surprise, but also reassured her he meant what he said. He wasn't patronizing her. "You don't make it easy, doc."

He helped her up, settling them back in the bed again. He put her in the same position, draped over his body, her leg over one of his, her hand curled on his chest. She closed her eyes as he dipped the brush in water and began again, combing out her tangles with fingers and bristles. Her ass was throbbing a little.

She began to count his heartbeats. As she did, her body and mind settled, surprising her. Even lying on his erection became a reassurance, not a provocation. He wanted her, but he would have her when the time was right.

He was correct. Now wasn't the best time.

When her father died, and all the family dominos fell in the subsequent years, she'd abhorred the helplessness she felt. She'd associated that feeling, not entirely wrongly, with being a child, unable to control her own fate.

Yet there seemed to be a difference between surrendering control and losing it. While it was a toss-up on which of those had just happened, because he had literally wrestled control away from her, he'd also gained her willingness to let them move forward that way.

It was a very different feeling from what she'd experienced as a child. And she wasn't messing things up by pushing them in the wrong direction. Because he wasn't going to be pushed.

Earlier, she'd thought her shaking, her mental state, could take down a building. Being inside Brick's care was being inside a place where the walls couldn't fall down. A stability and surety she desperately needed, when the rest of her world was crumbling.

"Brick...it's not weird, me reacting that way to you." She mumbled it as sleep started to pull her down again, but she took his answer with her.

"No, baby. Not at all."

Sunlight woke her. He'd opened the curtains, showing her the thin strip of woods behind his townhome. Through the tree branches, she could see some of the other units and a blue sky. The rain had passed.

She inhaled coffee and breakfast. Her stomach growled with hunger. Then all of yesterday came back and it recoiled from the idea, feeding on dismay, fear and panic instead. As she sat up, she pushed those responses down, trying to manage them the way she did at the hospital. Distract herself with the first thing on the to-do list. Arrange other thoughts over and around them. Those adverse reactions would eventually slither to the bottom of her uneasy stomach, like rocks in a pond.

The strategy mostly worked, though the first thing on her to-do list, texting Beulah, had her avoiding her phone. She wasn't ready for that.

Unfortunately the next thing that crossed her mind wasn't much better. Last night, she'd had tunnel vision, narrowed to Brick and the shit waiting to collapse that tunnel in on top of her. She'd blocked out everything else.

Including the blonde.

She bit her lip. Talk about being morally compromised. He'd kissed a woman on her doorstep, then Les initiated...what he did to her last night. Which he hadn't allowed to become anything, but still. It might not qualify as cheating on someone, but the intimacy of it...

Oh, fuck it, she wasn't giving herself that out.

He had a five-panel canvas mural mounted over the bed. Since the rest of her brain was a swamp, what she might have given a passing glance held her attention.

The flames in the largest center panel swirled upward, an awe-inspiring tornado, the colors dancing. The smaller panel, farthest to the left, showed only a single lick of flame, spouting from a glossy puddle of blue-tinged gas. The second was an amorphous cloud of whitish smoke, dense enough to look silky to the touch. On the other side of the center panel was black smoke. The final picture was a maze of embers amid blowing ash.

Shades of gold, yellow and red, white, gray and blue. Even some green. Though photographs, they'd captured the complexity of the element like a painter. Her mother would say there was no greater artist than God, and fire was one of His elements.

His master bedroom doubled as a home office, a desk and chair in one corner by a window. Folders were arranged in a stand beside his laptop. A notebook was open to show ballpoint scribblings. The pen lay across the page. It was the other pen she'd had in her hair, that day he took her to dinner.

When she moved to his desk to touch it, she noted a stress toy shaped like a football. It required a strong grip to squeeze it, which she was sure Brick's hand was capable of doing.

The wall behind his desk was painted a light brown sugar color, a contrast to the other white walls, though the curtain picked up that sandy color. A bookshelf to the right of the window was crammed with fire and building code texts, plus volumes on arson investigation.

Framed photos were on the brown wall above the shelves. A group firefighter shot in front of the Richmond firehouse, probably the station he'd served before he became an arson investigator. He also had one of him posing with her town's fire department. They stood in front of their pride and joy, a glossy red fire engine. Fairhope, North Carolina was printed in gold and black letters on the door.

Her fingers closed over the cool metal of the badge charm on her neck, and the cross with it. He was a teenager in the picture, but at the age she'd been then, there was no denying a romance with him had been a child's fantasy.

Yet it had survived, to become far more adult and real.

She was surprised to see a picture of her own family. Her heart lurched, recognizing the scene.

A few months before it was taken, her father had taken them to the Georgetown Wooden Boat Show. He'd brought home the plans to build one of the boats. The photo showed the sunny summer day when he, Rory and Thomas had worked on it in the backyard. Brick and a couple of other boys had come over to watch and help.

Mrs. Carlton had taken the picture, Les remembered. A friend of Les's mother, she'd stopped in to chat and see what they were up to that lazy Saturday afternoon.

Her mother had brought out a pitcher of iced tea and a pyramid of cold ham biscuits left over from breakfast, to feed the always hungry boys. Les remembered her patiently listening to her dad's enthusiastic explanation of what they were doing. Thomas had been leaning against the back porch stoop. He had his arms crossed over his chest as Rory worked next to their father, chiming in on the explanations.

Thomas had often done that, giving Rory the opportunity to learn what their father had already taught him about tools and building. Even in this picture she could see the growing isolation in his eyes. Already knowing he was different, standing apart, not sure how to reconcile what he knew about himself with what his parents thought he was or expected him to be.

Les sat on the other side of the stoop, her finger holding her place in a book. She'd paid close attention, wanting to learn about boat building, too. When she asked to help, Rory had scoffed. "Girls don't need to know how to build things. That's what boys are for."

Before she could retort and set off one of their many squabbles, her father had given them the look that pretty much put an end to it. At least in his presence.

He showed her how to use the drill, carefully instructing her in its use. "Men are better at some things, women are better at others. That's why they can form such good partnerships. But *both* of you can do something like this."

A twinkle went through the gray-green-gold eyes she'd inherited. "So if you do ask a man to do something you can do, let it be because you want to give him the opportunity to do something for and with you. That's pretty important to men who love their women."

The look he'd directed toward her mother was one Les hadn't been old enough to understand, but she remembered Elaine's face softening under his attention.

Les brushed her fingers over the picture. Only a few years later, so many things would change. The loving look in her mother's eyes would be replaced by the lost and grieving expression that hit a kid hard, the first time they saw their parent that vulnerable. Despite Thomas's private struggle with being gay, in this picture he didn't have the careworn look he'd had in the months after their father had passed, the weight of the family on his shoulders. And Rory was walking. Soon to become a popular high school athlete, as well as routinely outmatching her in the wrestling matches his jerk-face behavior so often initiated. In her opinion.

It had been a good day. They hadn't known how good.

Things were much better now, she reminded herself. After trying to deny the most important parts of who he was, her oldest brother was now a successful artist, and married to the man he loved. Her other brother was in a wheelchair, yes, but Rory no longer let that be an excuse to keep him from pursuing his own desires. He was devoted to Daralyn, who helped him operate the farm supply store business their parents had started. Rory had taken over its management so well their small community had given him a citizenship award for it.

Their mother had grieved hard for the man she'd built their family with, but now Elaine had a full and satisfying life, well knitted into the community. She loved her three children and was proud and supportive of them.

Why did she let herself get so bogged down in the past? She should be well past it, too. Pushing the sad feelings away, Les slid her gaze to Brick in the picture. He'd been standing near Thomas, but looking toward her. Though the profile told her nothing about what he was thinking, and the direction of his glance was likely inconsequential, she wondered why he'd framed this particular photo.

Maybe because it showed his best friend before a tractor rolling over him put him in a wheelchair? Or because it was time spent with her family, Brick's home away from home, before his family moved back to Virginia?

She went into the bathroom. She didn't meet her gaze in the mirror. Her first look of the day was when she usually spoke her mantra. She wasn't up for that, either.

Then she thought of Brick's stern admonishment to straighten up. He was right. She shouldn't hide from herself. She lifted her gaze and chose a new affirmation. "I'm a grown woman. Act like one. Get dressed, brush your teeth. Eat some breakfast, even if you have to choke it down. You don't get to stop functioning. You haven't earned the right to fall apart."

That last part was an awful truth to face. But because she didn't deserve the luxury of falling apart—any more than she already had—she also didn't deserve to wallow. Life had to go on, and she had to live up to what it required of her.

She wasn't sure about facing Brick after...everything, but short of escaping through the second floor window and hot wiring her car, there was no getting around it. She'd eat breakfast, have a cup of coffee, offer a dignified thank you, and head back to school, to handle whatever she had to.

No matter that the thought made her want to throw up the lining of her empty stomach.

He'd set out toothpaste and an unopened toothbrush, plus the comb and brush. She ran an experimental hand over her buttock. No hint of soreness. Lifting the hem of the sweatshirt and twisting around, she looked for marks, wondering why she was disappointed not to find any.

He really hadn't hit her that hard. Just a light sting at the time. It had merely stayed in her mind like a whole hive had descended on her backside. She had a strange desire to bend over the sink and give herself a thwack with the brush, imagining him doing it again, while she put her fingers between her thighs and...

Clearly her emotional state wasn't hampering the flare of arousal, strong enough to remind her how difficult it had been to tamp it down last night, especially when his leg had been pressed against her core. A little mortified at how tempted she'd been to rub herself against him, she put those thoughts aside and focused on getting cleaned up.

Her scrubs and underwear, clean and folded, were on the counter. They were beneath a change of clothes, far closer to her size than his sweatshirt. A pair of jeans and a light green T-shirt with a daisy print on it, size small. He'd also left a package of socks and cotton underwear. Her shoes had been dried.

He must have made a quick run out to a dollar store, the tags still on the clothes. The jeans were a little long, not unusual for when she bought them for herself, and a little loose in the butt, but they fit.

After she brushed her hair, she French braided it and used a rubber band from the supplies on his desk to hold the end. It left her bangs framing her temples, the wisps of them falling just above her eyes. Which looked tired, her mouth compressed. A more succinct reinforcement was in order. She bared her teeth at the mirror.

"I'm a grown woman. Act the fuck like it."

But a grown woman took responsibility, didn't she? When he was ten, Rory had broken one of his father's tools. He'd tried to hide it, then pass it off as someone else's doing. Her dad had told him, "You break something, you fix it. If you don't know how, you ask. If it can't be fixed, you figure out the next best thing to make it up to the person you've wronged." He'd then given Rory the rare but effective "scary dad" look. "And you *never* lie about it."

Despair surged through her, because what she'd done, there was no fixing or replacing it, no compensating someone for that kind of loss. But there was accepting responsibility, and facing the consequences, whatever they were. That was what an adult did. Not running away and showing up on the doorstep of her childhood crush so he had no choice but to take her in.

"I can hear you tying your head into knots."

She started. Stepping out of the bathroom, she found herself alone, but before she could decide she was losing her mind, Brick's deep voice spoke again, and she located the intercom beside the open bedroom door.

"Come on down and get some breakfast. We have a full schedule today."

She was going to push the reply button, but he continued in a lazy drawl. "Don't make me come and get you. It's not your job to punish yourself. It's mine. I was only getting warmed up with that brush."

He said outrageous, crazy things, and her insides turned over. Not to mention what it did to the rest of her. He'd said last night they needed to talk about this kind of stuff. She wasn't sure if she was ready for that, but she'd take any conversation over one about why she was here.

As she headed downstairs, and made the turn into the living room, she noted more pictures over the entryway table. His family. His dad had been an American history teacher at her middle school. She hadn't seen Brick's mother much, outside of church or community functions, but they seemed like good and loving parents. He had a brother and a sister, the same sibling make-up as her family. Brick had been the middle child, another thing he and Rory had in common.

The living room had the inevitable big flat screen for Brick to stretch out on his sectional and enjoy a game. He also had an over-loaded bookcase down here. While the one upstairs was work-related, this one held fiction, history and poetry. Classics like Victor Hugo's *Hunchback of Notre Dame,* mysteries and thrillers by authors such as Louise Penny or Jack Carr. There were books of poetry and a section on Civil War history, which included worn volumes of letters compiled from the time period.

His father had done re-enacting, she remembered, and Brick had accompanied him to some of the events when he was younger, before they came to Fairhope. She recalled most things Brick told Rory, when she was in earshot. And if Brick was at the house, she made sure she was. Which was why her hand lingered on a book of poetry by John Donne.

"You a fan?"

Brick leaned in the doorway to the kitchen, one hand in his jeans pocket, the other braced on the frame. She wondered how long he'd been there. He wore a black T-shirt with a red Richmond FD emblem on the pocket. She tried to keep her gaze on his face, rather than giving in to the magnetic pull to peruse his broad shoulders and chest, and the fit of the jeans.

He looked every bit as good as he had last night.

She didn't look like a drowned rat, which was an improvement. But—an unwelcome reminder of what else she needed to handle—she didn't look like a long-legged blonde.

His question about the poetry should have been an easy *yes, no, I-don't-know* answer. Because it wasn't, she couldn't answer that until she got the other out in the open.

"I feel like I owe someone an apology." She cleared her throat. "Or I should hit you for being a jerk. Maybe both."

"You'll have to explain that." His gray eyes didn't falter. Her skin flushed under her clothes, wanting touch.

"The woman you dropped off. You kissed her. Are you involved with her? I mean, that's not my business, but if you are...you should have put me in your guest room."

"Her name is Tish. Short for Leticia. She and I aren't in a relationship. Not that kind."

She met his stare, refusing to back down. "Friends with benefits?"

It didn't matter that she was swamped by that same strange compulsion to kneel when she challenged him like this. Certain things were dealbreakers for her in a relationship, and she would stand on two feet when she faced them.

The slow blink seemed like a courteous acknowledgement of her right to make that decision. "It started that way. But it's not that anymore. I'll explain it if you answer my first question. Are you a fan of John Donne?"

"Yes...or not exactly. I overheard you talking about him once, to Rory and Todd."

He'd been explaining a poem for an English assignment they had to do. She'd crept out of her room to sit on the floor outside Rory's door, hoping to hear Brick's voice, to listen to anything he was saying. They'd jeered at him when he told them to read the poem aloud.

"Sure, laugh it up," he advised, unperturbed. "But if you want to pass Mrs. Moore's class, pay attention. Hearing it read aloud makes it easier to understand."

She clasped her hands tight between her bent knees. He spoke the words as if he knew a girl was listening. One close enough to the brink of womanhood to wonder at her reaction to them.

"Love's mysteries in souls do grow / but yet the body is his book."

"Shit, man." Todd snorted. "Rory, this could get Amanda to toss her pompoms and drop to her knees for you."

The crude way they laughed—typical teenage boy swagger—had made her roll her eyes. But how Brick had lingered over those syllables had stayed with her.

"Hmm." Brick straightened. His look made her wonder if he'd known she'd been outside the door. A ludicrous thought, one that wouldn't have mattered then anyway. "Do you remember what you said to me last night? When you knelt?"

Her blush deepened. "Yes."

"Do you know why you asked me not to be nice to you?"

Upstairs, she'd been afraid of him asking her about the event that had brought her here. Now she thought it might be an easier topic to address. She hated not having the answers.

"I'm a sexual Dominant, Les. Do you know what that means?"

She shook her head. "I mean, I'm familiar with the term, but I don't know anything more than the surface."

"I think you do. Your subconscious sure as hell knows it."

She couldn't deny that. It had responded to him last night in this room, and in his bed, when he'd made it clear he was in charge.

"What Todd said that day," he said, "about getting Amanda on her knees. We laughed, because we were high school assholes making a joke about blowjobs. But it stuck with me, bugged me enough, I shared it with the Dom who mentored me."

He'd just confirmed he'd known she was there. Her heart beat high up in her throat. "He said it bugged me because my Dom side knew if a girl knelt for me, I should honor that gift. Cherish it so much I'd want to stop time on that moment. It's not about her lips being wrapped around my dick. Though that feels damn good, it's like saying what's best about Christmas is the presents."

His gaze flickered. She'd moved several steps toward him, and she hadn't even realized it. The words sounded like the Donne poetry had on his lips, unexpectedly natural. That picture from her computer was rotating in her mind, a flashing carousel. He didn't reach out to touch her, but the energy between them vibrated with the possibility. Then his expression shifted, and he finished answering her question. The question she'd completely forgotten she'd asked.

"Tish has embraced her submissive side, and I've been helping her explore that. I'm a member of a local BDSM group here, so last night I took her to one of their events."

She took a step back. "Oh."

Brick noted it, but his voice remained even. "She's a friend, and yes, in the past, we've occasionally had sex. She's too busy to dedicate time to a relationship, and I had other reasons for not wanting to get myself in too deep with someone. You're welcome to talk to her about it."

At her alarmed look, he lifted a hand. "Not a requirement. I'm just not one of those assholes who tells a woman to take my word for what my relationship is with another one. The sure-as-shit flag that he's lying his ass off."

One of Beulah's undergrad relationships had crashed and burned for that reason. Beulah had ended the relationship, steering the car for the cliff and lighting the match herself. "Got that right."

"I think you and Tish would like each other," Brick said, lips quirking at the edge in her voice. "You're different personalities, but you're both driven, accomplished women, determined to be good at your jobs."

That brought other, less pleasant things back into her head, but he tilted his head toward the kitchen. "Come on and eat. As I said, we've got a busy day."

"Yeah, I figured you did. I should go after breakfast, Brick. Head back to school. I need to deal with things."

"I spoke to Beulah last night. You're good for a couple days."

"What?"

"I'm sure she's texted you. Have you checked?"

"No...I haven't."

"Because you're not ready to, are you? Give yourself a breath, Les. You look in better shape than last night, but that's not saying a lot."

"Again with the compliments." She made a face at him. "I did something with my hair. That's at least an improvement on the last time you saw me."

His attention went to the French braid style she'd chosen. An indefinable emotion crossed his face that intrigued her. Though his next observation killed the curiosity.

"You're tense as a wire, your mouth looks like it couldn't smile if your life depended on it, and your eyes..." He paused, lingering there. "It's all there in your eyes, Les."

She backed up, sinking down on the arm of the sofa. "You haven't asked me about it. Do you not want to know?"

Because it might change how he felt about her? Stupid, she knew, but the thought came to mind anyway.

Though he stayed in the doorway, his expression made him seem closer. "You told me the important part. You'll tell me more when you're ready. I also texted Rory to let him know where you are. He'll handle things on the family front, but he said he wants you to call him, soon as you feel up to it. Or within the next couple days, whichever comes first."

He'd told her last night he would take care of contacting her family and friends and she hadn't told him not to. She took a beat to remind herself of that, and that he hadn't taken any decisions from her, just bought her some breathing time.

The answer wasn't lashing out at him. It was behaving like she could handle her own shit. "When you said today's agenda, what did you mean?"

"I need to drop by a friend's place. He's helping to collect items for a local family who had home damage from storm flooding. Our captain at Major Crimes approved donating some furniture we have in storage."

"If you loaded your truck, picked me up clothes, did my laundry and made me breakfast, I'm checking your closet for a cape and tights."

Humor was a step in the right direction, wasn't it? Except it slammed into the wall of her conscience, which demanded to know why the fuck she thought she was allowed to make a goddamned joke.

"I gave up the tights. They irritate my leg hair. I'm picking up the furniture at a storage place near the office. We can grab some lunch after and have a picnic at the Potterfield bridge, watch the kayakers and tourists."

He straightened from the doorway, his voice remaining casual. "That group event, where I took Tish? They're in the middle of a three-day demo party, and tonight is day two. I'll take you tonight, so you can see what some of it is about."

"What? I can't..."

Panic was replaced far too quickly by a not-so-dormant desire to reach for what he was offering. Which was replaced just as quickly by something else.

The part of the mind that managed stress had no actual conscience. It would do what was needed to move forward, pretending something awful hadn't happened, that the direction she'd chosen for her life wasn't over.

She lurched off the couch like a snapped rubber band and paced to the door. When she turned, her rusty voice cracked. "You do understand what I did, right? I can't go have fun, keep skipping along with my self-absorbed twenty-something life. 'Oh, I messed up, but it's okay, it's all right. It's all about *me* and *my* pain, and not...'"

He moved toward her. She tried to dodge him, but his arms were just too damn long. He held her, his expression resolute. "It's not about that. It's about taking a step back from that pain and figuring it out. So you don't let it mire you down and make you do dangerous things, like you did last night. Driving when you were that upset."

She summoned a glare. "I have roadside assistance and a gun, plus brothers and a father who taught me how to use it. I'm a better shot than Rory, who won ribbons for marksmanship at the county fair. I also know how to change a tire and do basic repairs on my car."

"None of that covers your state of mind. Do you remember anything about the drive at all?"

She started to say of course she did, but defensiveness couldn't override honesty. He crossed his arms. "Right. So it goes on the list."

"What list?"

"The list I've been keeping since I first started thinking about you without clothes."

She blinked. "When was that?"

"How about you guess? I'm betting you know."

"I don't," she said truthfully. "Until you showed up at my condo, it never crossed my mind you were considering anything...like that."

"Even at the wedding? When the two of us were looking at each other during the vows? Walking down the aisle afterward?" He arched a brow. "You bailed the next morning like your tail was on fire."

Her stomach fluttered. "When you've been the little kid mooning after your brother's best friend, it's hard to let go of the idea that you're imagining the way he's looking at you, even as an adult."

"Mooning after me?"

She gave him the finger. He captured it, took it into his mouth. It brought her closer to him, and she couldn't breathe as he tasted her.

"Brick..." The word was a plea, a hope. A need. He didn't respond to it, not with words. Just kept teasing her flesh until her forehead was pressed against his shoulder and she couldn't think beyond the sensation of his mouth, the edge of his teeth on her captured fingers.

When he drew back, her wrist was still manacled in his grasp. "I'll add that to the list, too," he said.

"What list?" she managed.

"All the infractions a Dom tracks on a sub. To punish her later."

CHAPTER EIGHT

*L*ike so many things with him, her brain didn't totally compute what he was talking about, even as her body, suddenly weak-kneed and restless, seemed to know exactly.

In an attempt to gain some balance, she latched onto the most incredulous part of it. From the light smile on his lips, she suspected the attempt would be futile. "You said you've been keeping this list since you first started thinking of me...like that."

"Yep." Those gleaming eyes didn't leave hers, didn't let up a bit.

"Written down, or just in your head?"

"Written down. In a journal with a leather-tooled cover. I'll show it to you sometime. Maybe use it to leave more marks on your ass. According to my men's fitness magazine, journaling helps a man better understand his own needs."

She was leaning against the front door, and he had his hand braced over her head. Somehow his other hand was on her hip. He'd chastised her for having no memory of her drive here. He made her lose her sense of her own body the same way. It moved in alignment with him, no steering or direction required from her own mind.

"Was it the wedding when you started thinking of me...that way?" Her voice was uneven.

"Nope. It was the ice cream shop, after we lost the game with Taylor High. You nipped the top off my cone of soft serve to make me laugh."

"I was fourteen years old."

"Yep. I was sure I was going to hell for the thoughts I had the rest of that night." He touched the charm on her necklace. "This goes on the list, too. You opened it before your birthday, didn't you?"

"I texted you a very nice *thank you* on my birthday."

A flash of teeth. "That's not a no. You get flustered when you're avoiding a direct lie, Celeste Joy."

She closed her hand over it and the cross. "You didn't wrap it well. It fell out."

He stroked her sternum, caressing her cleavage through the T-shirt. Nerve endings awoke in that crevice, spreading over her breasts.

"How did you know?"

"Rory said you hated to wait to open gifts."

"Rory was such a dick."

His grin deepened. "He'd be the first to agree. He'd also be glad you put it in the past tense. I think Daralyn helped smooth out his rough edges."

He touched her hand, still gripping the necklace. "Your password, DadTR@285. Tell me about that. This time, you better not lie."

"You're asking me to crack open a lot of myself. Too much, too soon. It's been a stressful week. Exams pending, discovering this whole Dominant and submissive thing, and..."

She couldn't form the words. It couldn't be part of this. Fortunately, he helped.

"I don't think 'discovering' is accurate. You know a little more than that about it. Even if you haven't pursued it actively." His eyes got a sharper gleam. "Have you?"

She raised her chin. "I'm not a submissive person."

"That answers the question." He nodded, as if to himself. "You're *a* submissive. It's an orientation, not an adjective. Sometimes just sexual, and sometimes far deeper than sexual. People outside the lifestyle mix up the distinction. Same goes for a sexual Dominant. While there might be romance book Doms who are powerful billionaires, a sexual Dominant can be anything, including a secretary or construction worker."

"Or a firefighter."

"Or a firefighter. Tell me about the password."

"A password is supposed to protect what matters," she said.

"So you chose a password that reflects the men in your life who make you feel safe."

"Yes." No surprise that he put that together. Dad, T for Thomas, R for Rory. And Brick's badge number. The embarrassing thing was revealing he was one of the men she felt that way about.

How he looked at her now made it less embarrassing. He drew her closer and kissed her. A thorough, slow spin, his tongue moving in to stroke and play. As her body folded against his, she rose on her toes to fit herself better to him. He murmured approvingly against her mouth, sliding his arms around her to hike her up against the wall. The solid surface pressed her tighter against his aroused body.

She made a little moan in his mouth, arching against him as he rubbed the steel of his cock against her clit with explosive accuracy. The noise he made in his throat soothed and commanded at once, telling her this would happen at his pace. But the thickness of his arousal said his body had its own gratifying opinion. If she doubted how forcefully he was holding onto his own control, that confirmed it.

She curled her hands behind his neck, nails digging in. She wanted him closer, a desperation that went beyond arousal and into darker needs.

He dropped a hand to her buttock, squeezing hard. Now she felt the deeper tissue soreness from the brush spanking. It made her even more aroused. He kept kissing her, that grip on her ass enhancing the blatant possession.

His phone chimed, but he ignored it. He shifted his grip to push his hand into the loose-fitting jeans and clamp his hand over her buttock. Panties were far thinner than denim. He pressed insistently against the crevice between her buttocks, stroking her through the cotton. A ripple of reaction shook her while his thumb dipped to trace the lower part of her buttock. All while he kept working her against his cock. He spoke against her ear, a rumble of sound.

"You'll come for me now, Les. Rub yourself against my cock, the way you wanted to rub your cunt against my leg last night. Do it because I told you to. Do it because you want to please me, give me what I demand."

Each word was as effective as a thrust of his cock, driving her arousal higher. Her head dropped back against the wall, her feverish eyes on his. Her body writhed, lifted and fell. When he went still, watching her obey, not helping as she fought to do as he'd commanded, the resulting surge of arousal shocked her with its strength. It pushed her over the crest.

She convulsed against him, nails still biting into his neck as she gripped the collar of his T-shirt. When she cried out, he at last helped her move against him, offering the additional support his strong arms could provide. A second, shuddering wave carried her, gasping and clinging, all the way to the finish.

When she was twitching in his arms, he tangled his fingers in her hair, holding her with his other arm and the pressure of his body.

"That's how I know you're a submissive, Les. That and a million other things like it, that I've been noting for a long damn time. Things I've filed away, like that list. When I embraced my Dom side, all those pieces about you and me came together, the puzzle turning into a picture. This picture."

She loved his poetic side. She wasn't naïve enough to believe it hadn't shown itself with other women, but she didn't think he used it as a conscious tool in his arsenal. It seemed to be a trait driven by the strength of his emotions. Which made her hope she brought them out from a deeper level. Or at least in a unique way.

He eased her down onto shaky legs, stroking a strand of hair from her face. "Let's see what got dropped off."

At her curious look, he gestured to his phone, resting on the entry table. "The chime was my door camera."

"What are you expecting?" She was impressed she could form coherent sentences, though she was still leaning against him. He kept caressing her neck and shoulders, helping her to settle, pull together her scattered mind.

"Let's find out." But as he adjusted them so he could open the door, she stopped him, her gaze latched onto his very noticeable erection against his jeans. "Shouldn't I...we, do something for you?"

"You will. Tonight. I want the time to have you deal with that properly."

That picture on her tablet came right back into the forefront of her mind. She took another erratic breath. It helped to think of it as he said. A submissive, a woman whose desires fell in the category of that...orientation. Not a submissive woman who would let a man walk all over her. He was cherishing her, caring for her, giving her screaming orgasms, even as he made demands of her.

She cleared her throat. "Okay...um, well, why don't I bring in the package? So *your* package doesn't scare a random dog walker or make nearby women swoon."

Or try to jump him.

His eyes sparked amused fire. "Stroking my ego works about as well as stroking my dick, doc."

"Now who's lying?" She suddenly realized what the delivery person might have heard, with them up against the wall right by the entryway. Brick didn't appear to care. She realized neither did she.

She opened the door to find a medium-sized box there. The return address surprised her. "It's from Beulah."

"Yeah." When she stepped back in, he closed the door. "I asked her to put together some things you might need, and wired her the funds to courier it for morning delivery."

His thoughtfulness floored her. Since he'd talked her into staying, she'd been considering a secondhand clothing store to get another change of clothes, plus replacement toiletries from the dollar store. "I'll need to pay you back. That must have cost a fortune."

"No, you won't. It was my call, so I took care of it." He put the box on the stairs, removed a pocketknife and slit the tape on the top. "You can go through this after breakfast, while I'm working out. There's room in the guestroom closet if you want to hang anything up. But for the record," he pinned her with a look, "that doesn't mean you get to sleep in there. I like you where you were last night."

As the caveat gave her another quiver, he took her hand and drew her into the kitchen. It was well organized, the handful of modern appliances, like an air fryer and pressure cooker, suggesting he cooked for himself regularly. Breakfast was simmering on the stove, the source of the appetizing smells that had drifted into the bedroom. The skillets were covered with glass lids to hold onto heat.

Her gaze slid from that to the refrigerator. The calendar he had tacked onto it had attracted her attention—and spurred her curiosity.

The current month featured a shirtless, redheaded male. He wore brown and yellow fireman trousers, red suspenders dangling around his hips. His vivid blue eyes stared out at the viewer, his muscles strategically smudged with soot. He held a similarly dusted white puppy against his brawny chest.

"Is that one of those firefighter beefcake calendars?"

"It's firefighters with puppies," he said loftily.

"Are you in it?"

He tossed the picture a disgruntled look. "Arson investigators aren't eligible. Firefighters only. The competition is stiff."

"So I can see." She tucked her tongue into her cheek as he gave her a narrow look. "And you have this on your refrigerator, because..."

"It was a charity thing. I need a calendar. Come sit your smartass down and eat." He pointed to the chair next to the one at the head of the table. "I'll bring you a plate."

"Do you need any help?" An automatic courtesy, since the food was ready to serve.

When he shook his head, she slid into the chair. A couple stacks of books had been pushed to the side to make room for the two place settings he'd laid for them. One of the stacks was work-related, more code books and technical manuals related to forensic sciences, focusing on crime scene assessment. The other tower was a mix of fiction and poetry. A well-thumbed romance was on the top.

"One of your favorites?" she asked.

"Tish's," he said. She tried not to show her sudden tension, but the flicker in his gaze said she wasn't successful. "When she admitted she's a big erotic romance reader, I told her to give me a favorite. It gives me more cues about her needs as a submissive, as well as what she might imagine doing."

"Like a manual? You read this and know what fantasies she wants to become a reality?"

"If it was that simple to understand what a woman wants, men everywhere would rejoice. But our fantasies are just window dressing for the deeper things we want in actual relationships." He gestured with a spatula. "If a submissive likes to read capture fantasies, it might just mean she wants to feel safe enough to give up control in a scene. Even that desire has a range, from exploring light restraints and psychological acts of surrender, to going all out, with chase scenes and primal play."

At her quizzical look, he explained. "Primal play is basically fighting, wrestling, with sexual intent involved. It can involve hunting and chasing, depending on the people doing it.'"" He quirked a brow. "Last night, you mentioned you didn't mind a good wrestling match."

"I don't think that's exactly what I said." She was out of her depth. "I'm getting all these strong vibes from you, while we're talking about a woman you were with just last night. There's a part of me saying I need to get in my car and go. That it's the wrong time to even try to do this."

"Or the right one."

He put a plate in front of her. It had scrambled eggs, bacon and three silver dollar pancakes. Dots of whipped cream and chocolate chips on the middle one formed a smiley face. Heart-shaped dark chocolates were in the centers of the two flanking pancakes. The warmth of the food had given the chocolate a soft and melty look.

Tears threatened again. "Hey." Brick's voice was warm and sure as he brought her attention to him. "I have a suggestion, Les. I'm offering it as a suggestion because, while we've played around the edges, you haven't consented to being my submissive."

"I haven't?"

"You know you haven't." He met her gaze. "Though you've given me two damn promising signs in that direction."

"What were those?"

"Kneeling to me in my living room, and not going after my testicles when I spanked you."

"As if I could. You were holding me pinned. You only won that match because you took me by surprise." Not because he outweighed her by a hundred pounds of muscle weight and a foot of height.

"Your *official* consent to be a Dom's submissive," he continued, with a reproving look, "is a choice you make for the right reasons. When you give me that honor, I'll recognize and know you were ready to do it. Because you're brilliant, I know you will, too. So until then, here's what I'm *suggesting* you do."

He slid his fingers along her cheek, her ears, her throat. She became so still under his touch. All her unhappy, darker thoughts disappeared into that abyss she could avoid, if she kept herself from the edge.

His suggestion dragged her right over it.

"After breakfast, call the hospital's attorney, so he knows you aren't avoiding him. Call your advisor for the same reason, and make sure your absence isn't threatening anything you've worked your ass off to get."

He stroked her accelerated wrist pulse. "After that's squared away, for today, let it the fuck go. Not because that child didn't matter, but because of how much he or she did."

"He." The word came out of a clogged throat.

"He, then. If you do that, you're not shirking your responsibility. You're preparing yourself to handle it the way you should. I know what it is to lose someone like that, Les."

He'd told her that in the diner, but his expression offered her a deeper view of it. The pain, the sleepless nights, the agony of wrestling with it. He'd handled it, accepted it. While it was a place she couldn't conceive of ever reaching herself, the possibility helped her give more weight to what he was telling her.

"That may be as much why you came to me as any other reason. Because some part of you knew that." He nudged a fork toward her. "Eat."

She looked at the food. "I want to. It looks great, but maybe I need to call them first. Just thinking about it upsets my stomach."

"You'll handle it better with something on it. Try to eat some of the eggs and a pancake." He reached over to cut the middle one for her. She stopped him, a hand against his. "You'll ruin the face."

His lips curved. He moved to one of the flanking cakes with the chocolate heart in the center, her hand still resting on his wrist. He cut down the middle of it, dividing the pancake, then forked up a piece with the gooey squashed heart on it.

She touched his wrist to steady the utensil and took the bite. As her belly churned, she chewed and swallowed. It did settle a little, proving his point.

"You said making the calls is a suggestion. If you were my Dom, how would it be different?"

"It would have been a 'there'll be hell to pay if you don't listen to me' order."

She made a face at him, mainly to cover the nervous swallow. His gaze went to her throat, telling her she hadn't fooled him. Her fingers still rested on his knuckles and wrist as he reached out with the other hand to brush a thumb over her lip. He took the chocolate melted there, like he'd done with her pie, and tasted it himself.

Then he adjusted their hands so they lay clasped between their two plates.

"Eat your breakfast," he said gruffly. "Christ, you and those big eyes."

That made her smile a little. Looking for a distraction, so she could get those few more bites in, she reached for a folder next to the technical stack of books.

"Don't open that." He placed a hand on it, swiftly enough to startle her.

"Sorry. I didn't mean to pry."

"It's not that. The material is confidential, but I'm not worried about you respecting that. That case involved fatalities, and some of the photos are of the victims."

"Oh." She glanced at it. "I don't think it would be a problem. Me and Rick spend a lot of time together. My cadaver," she supplied at his raised brow. "Plus, mealtime conversation among med students includes words like ooze, fester, rupture, and seep. Exploding diarrhea, running pus. Et cetera."

Amusement filled his gaze, though his hand remained on the folder. "I expect that's true, but this was two kids and a mother. It was a bad one. You probably heard about it on the news."

"Not likely. Armageddon could happen and we'd be grumbling about the electronic patient system being down. Or our access to our practice exams being blocked."

But she left the folder alone. What she saw in his eyes told her he'd seen the actual bodies, not just photos of them. Maybe because of the age of the victims, this one had made an impression, even on an experienced investigator like himself.

"Was it an accident?"

"Still working on that." He bit into some bacon, wiped his fingers on the napkin in his lap. "Sometimes it can take weeks to sift through everything at a fire site and make that determination. Way too often, we can't come to a conclusion because fire can burn up all the evidence. We get the occasional easy ones, though. Like the guy burning up his business to collect the insurance, but thinks all he has to do is toss around some gasoline and light a match. Accelerant leaves a streamer pattern, plus we can detect its presence from lab analysis on the building remains."

A wry smile touched his mouth. "With arson, it pays to hire a professional."

"I'll keep that in mind. Where would I find them listed? Craigslist? Fiverr?"

At his chuckle, she noted his shoulders had eased. It felt good to help someone she *could* help, if only with a listening ear. He consumed his breakfast in a cyclical pattern, a few bites of pancake, then eggs, then bacon, and back to the beginning. She also noted he was keeping a close eye on her rate of consumption, that stern look coming back as she pushed food around the plate. Dutifully, she took a few actual bites, though her stomach continued to gripe at her.

She worried she might be developing an ulcer. Thomas had had trouble with them a while back, though Marcus had gotten on top of that, with their mother providing firm reinforcement to get him the right medical care. A big part of what had caused them was the pressure of following a path he wasn't meant to walk.

She didn't like where that line of thought was headed, so she returned to the topic. "What's making it look like an accident?"

"Space heater was the source and origin point. Right now the best accident hypothesis is a stack of magazines fell off a dresser and landed against it. Some of the kids' toys were also too close. Mom had a drug problem. Needle was found melted into her arm, and it looked like she'd passed out at the kitchen table. Kids were in their beds."

"How horrible." It *was* terrible, but forensic details interested her. Seeing it, Brick put down his fork and drew the folder closer, selecting a photo from the contents. It was a close-up of the heater, surrounded by a border of cleared debris. "See the charring of the wood floor around it? The depth tells us how hot it got there, compared to other areas. That gives us evidence of where it started.

"They lived in a rural area outside Richmond, in a place where houses were spaced out from each other, with lots of tree cover between. As you and I know, burning trash isn't unusual in the country, so the neighbors didn't think anything about the smoke smell, not right away. By the time 911 was called and the first engine arrived, black smoke was coming out multiple windows. Black smoke can indicate man-made stuff, like synthetic building materials, are being consumed and possibly producing carbon monoxide."

Though the subject matter was sobering, watching a serious and intelligent Brick McGuire working a case was undeniably hot. "So it was too late to get the family out?"

"Yes and no." A muscle flexed in Brick's jaw. "When the first engine arrived, the neighbor told them no one was home. The mom, Jasmine Whitfield, had told her they were going on a fishing trip with her boyfriend for the weekend. The neighbor said she saw them leave early that morning."

"Oh my God."

He grimaced. "Yeah. They said she fainted when she found out the mother and kids were in there."

"She'll feel like it's her fault they didn't go in." Les's stomach clenched.

"But she shouldn't. While we go on the information we're given, we don't base it on just one person. The IC, incident commander, noted his guys asked several other neighbors on scene if anyone had witnessed activity at the house that day. None of them had."

He took a breath. "Plus, when they got there, the fire was fully involved. The roof collapsed within seconds of them arriving. The IC wouldn't have authorized anyone to go in to do search and rescue at that point. The boyfriend's actually a volunteer firefighter in the next county over, though he works fulltime as a contractor."

"Poor man," she murmured.

"Yeah. But until we rule out arson, he's also our prime suspect."

Her eyes widened. "Why?"

"He knows about fires, how they burn. Plus, construction guys make the best firefighters, because they know a lot about building materials, electrical systems, that kind of thing."

He put the photo away. "Sample data is being analyzed to verify the source details while me and the investigators in my unit collect witness statements, so for now it's an open case. We want to find out why Jasmine and her kids were back home when they were supposed to be fishing."

She studied him. "You're thinking the boyfriend could have done it deliberately? Put the magazines there, instead of them falling off the dresser?"

"Or the mom did. Like a murder-suicide. Or someone else who might be revealed by the witness statements. I don't make an official decision until I have all that information and see how it impacts my review of the fire site. Or if it gives me additional things to look at there." He shifted his attention to her plate. "The chocolate hearts disappeared."

"Dark chocolate is good for an upset stomach," she replied primly.

With an assessing look, he cut her remaining egg into three bites, next to the untouched bacon. "How about this? Tell me one of your favorite Dom fantasies. If they involve me, *and* you eat this egg, you'll get an extra chocolate heart."

Setting the loaded fork on her plate, he leaned back in his chair, pulled the bag off the counter and put it beside him. The purple foil-wrapped candies tumbled toward the open mouth.

She blinked. "Who says I have any Dom fantasies?"

"That look in your eyes, the second I suggested it."

"Maybe they're not about you."

"If you want the candy, you'll do a cut and paste, kick Joe Jonas to the curb, and put me in his slot."

He startled a laugh out of her. Though he seemed almost prescient on certain things about her, the posters on her teen bedroom wall had been hard to miss. She shot him a mock glare. "Maybe it's about all three Jonas brothers."

He smiled, but his gaze had a more serious light. "Tell me one, Les. If this is a road you want to go down with me, this can start the discussion. Don't think about all the reasons you might not have time to explore it. I have a pretty demanding job, too. But when it matters, two people can do a hell of a lot with ten minutes on the phone a day. Or a weekend here and there. Being in a relationship with someone doesn't have to add to your stress," he pointed out. "It could increase your support network, keep you going, knowing you have a person to fall back on when you need them."

Her experience with boyfriends was they required a lot of work and attention. Girlfriends were better for support.

"Maybe what you need is a person who expects and wants nothing from you but who and what you are," he said, watching her expression. "I want your beautiful, flawed, honest self, at all times. That's not what I'll request from you; it's what I'll demand."

He closed his hand around hers. "I'll cut through the bullshit to get to it, until you believe and trust my expectations are that simple. No more, no less."

Words were cheap, but she believed he might mean them. "So is me telling you my fantasies like Tish's book?"

"Yeah. Safewords and protocols are important, but so is this. A Dom has to understand how to communicate with his sub in a way that maintains a connection with her in some pretty intense moments. He has to be able to bring her back to center, help her relax or respond to stimulus in ways that satisfy you both. That requires getting deeper inside."

Picking up the fork, he leaned in. "Tell me, Les. Last time I ask. Don't go off topic again. Stay in this one with me."

She parted her lips to take the bite. While she chewed and thought it through, he forked up the next. By the time she had an answer, she'd eaten all three bites.

"A lot of it is simple stuff."

"Simple works for me. Go on." He set down the fork.

She dropped her attention to his hand, resting on the table. But looking away from his steady gaze wasn't going to be enough to give her the courage to do this. "Is it okay for me to close my eyes?"

"Yeah. This time." Before she did, he unwrapped a chocolate heart and handed it to her. Her reward.

With a half smile, she shut her eyes. As she let her mind drift, she brought the chocolate up to her nose and inhaled before putting the candy on her tongue. He waited for her, letting her take that time. When it melted down her throat, she was ready.

"You're in my room with me. I'm lying on the bed. You tell me not to move. You're kissing me all over, but I have to stay still, or you'll stop. It becomes more difficult, and I want to squirm. But you get this stern look that makes me...like your look did last night."

As she spoke, it became a little easier. As if she'd been waiting to tell him something exactly like this. With what he'd said about being a Dom, it felt right to tell him.

The pressure of his thumb against her wrist, the way he held her with a hint of male urgency, told her he wasn't unaffected. Sharing that arousal, that simmering tension between them, made her reveal what she hadn't expected.

"Because I won't stop squirming, you spank me."

"I turn you over and spank your ass?" The mild way he said it made her mouth dry. He'd said honesty, but...

She lifted a shoulder, an agreement but not really.

"Les. What did I say my single expectation was?"

"Does saying I'm too embarrassed to answer the question meet the expectation?"

"Yes. Long as it's honest."

She opened her eyes. "But because I sort of lied first, it's going on that list, isn't it?"

The wicked look in his gaze told her he liked adding to that list. "In your fantasy, I told you to spread your legs, hold them open without moving, and I spanked your cunt with my open hand. Didn't I?"

Moisture flooded that part of her body. He brushed his mouth over her trembling, quivering lips. "Answer me, Les."

"Y-yes." Her toes curled against his ankle, where she'd rested her bare foot on top of his shoe.

"Hmm." With his hand still on hers, he leaned back and fished out one more purple foil-wrapped bite and put it in her hand, giving it a firm squeeze. "Good. Make your calls."

CHAPTER NINE

*H*e'd told her if she was still on the phone when he finished cleaning the kitchen, he'd go work out in the utility room next to the kitchen. He also refused her offer to help wash dishes as the procrastination tactic it clearly was. When she dragged her feet, he picked up a slotted metal spatula and twirled it with a threatening flourish.

"This hurts a lot worse than a brush," he informed her.

Her reaction was the opposite of what an intelligent person's would be, given his size and the power in his arm. Regardless, she made herself go into the living room and sit on the sofa with her phone.

The first voicemail she checked was from her advisor, Dr. Leanne Portland. Her tone was brisk as she dealt with school matters first. The M&M, Mortality and Morbidity conference, was set for mid-next week. Les was expected to attend. Dr. Portland asked for confirmation, via text or phone. "As far as where you are in the program, your patients have been re-assigned. We'll get you back in the flow after the conference. Study for your ER rotation exam. Dr. Redmond said you'd covered enough clinical work to be ready for it, especially with your diligent study habits."

She'd been routinely praised for her attention to detail, the questions she asked on rounds. Dr. Jack had told her she operated with a fourth year's maturity.

She wondered what they all thought of her now.

Dr. Portland concluded the message with a marginally warmer tone. "Take a few days, Les. Get your mind off it. You'll remember things better. Write them down when you're ready. That will help you prepare for questions at the conference. If you haven't already, be sure to call the hospital's legal department. Martin Sully wants to speak to you."

...help you prepare for questions at the conference...

Though her fingers trembled, and she wasn't sure if it was true, Les texted she would be at the M&M. She unraveled her French braid and ran her fingers through her hair several times before moving on to the next voicemail.

"Les, I'm Martin Sully with the hospital's legal department." He had a firm, smooth voice. "Call me as soon as you receive this. Talk to me before you discuss the details of the incident with anyone, and that includes your advisor, friends or any other personnel involved."

As she dialed his number, she tapped her thigh with nervous fingers. She nursed a hope he wouldn't be there, though when he picked up, she guessed it was probably a relief that he was. The worst part of an axe falling was waiting for it.

"Martin Sully."

"Hello, Mr. Sully. This is Les Wilder. I apologize for the delay in returning your call. I haven't spoken to anyone about the details of... what I did."

She wasn't counting Brick. He was different. He was like talking to herself. Maybe a currently more objective version of herself. That was probably an exaggeration, based on her vulnerable state, but she couldn't deny her faith in the feeling. She wasn't going to doubt it right now. Not when she was doubting everything else.

"The incident," Martin Sully corrected her.

He asked her a few questions, though he surprised and relieved her by not having her do a play-by-play of what happened that night. "Your chart notes were thorough," he said. "Your resident and attending corroborated them. If you're pulled into any legal hearings, we'll do more in-depth prep. When will you be back?"

"The M&M is next week, so I told Dr. Portland I'd be there for that. That's okay, right?" She hoped he said no. She should be there, but a weakness she despised in herself cringed at the idea.

"In theory, M&Ms are supposed to be private and the information shared at them inaccessible to the plaintiff. For now, plan on being there, but also plan on seeing me that morning. And stick with the advice I left on your voicemail. No talking to anyone about the matter. Not your fellow med students, your roommate, and especially no one who could be involved in the case. Nurses, attending, resident. They've all been given the same guidance, so no one should be initiating discussion with you about it."

He paused. "Under no circumstances are you to have any contact with the patient's family. Let me know right away if they or their attorney reach out to you."

"They have an attorney?"

"Yes. They have secured one."

Her heart roared in her ears. Les forced out the words. "Will she sue the hospital? Mrs. DaCosta."

"That's pending. If so, the attending and resident who were on that day are more likely to be named in the suit than you. Your actions are considered their responsibility. Any other questions?"

Jack and Dr. Redmond would pay for her mistake.

"No." She forced the word through stiff lips.

"All right, I'll stay in touch. Hang in there, Miss Wilder. A lot of doctors face this. Some more than once in their careers."

She barely made it to the downstairs bathroom. Pancakes, chocolate and eggs were not an awesome combination on the return trip.

Halfway through the expulsion, Brick's hands were on her back. Cliché or not, as he collected her loose hair in one hand and held it back, she felt relieved he was here. When she sat back on her heels, he had a cup of tap water for her to rinse her mouth.

Surfing tsunami-sized waves of stress had made her a gold medalist at distraction tactics. His body, clad only in shorts and athletic shoes for his workout, was the most available and useful one.

She'd seen him shirtless plenty of times when he and Rory were in high school. Teenage boys, particularly school jocks who were also farm boys, weren't shy about baring their upper torsos.

Elaine made Rory and his friends wear shirts in the house, but Les spent more than one afternoon watching them practice football plays or shoot hoops behind the house. She'd observe from the cover of her bedroom window, her gaze fixed on the ripple of muscle through

Brick's back and thighs. When they played basketball, they used the rusty hoop screwed to the side of the barn.

Later, she'd relocate to the porch swing with her homework, pretending not to listen as they lounged on the steps, drinking sodas. Brick's hair would be damp at his nape, making her want to touch him there. He'd had a scattering of freckles over his shoulders.

Those had faded away. He'd been big then, but as she'd noted the day he took her to dinner, he'd filled out even more with adulthood. His shoulders and chest had well-defined muscle groups that didn't seem bulky. His sheer masculinity was a blatant, unapologetic thing, yes, but the grace and flow to it were like the poetry he read.

Up close and personal, it couldn't help but raise a woman's sexual awareness to full alert. Les wanted to sample him with tongue, teeth, and anywhere else skin to skin contact could be made. She'd slide her fingers through his chest hair, tangle and tug it.

You just threw up, she reminded herself.

He was stroking her arm, his gray eyes assessing how she was doing. He didn't press her with questions, but she suspected he'd been tracking her side of the conversation, picking up enough to make a rehash unnecessary. She'd been able to hear the clank of weights from the living room.

Brick helped her to her feet, then picked her up off her shaky legs and carried her to the utility room. Unspoken message: *I'm finishing my workout, but keeping my eye on you at the same time.* She shouldn't be okay with leaning on him so much, but his proximity reassured her.

This wasn't a large area, but in addition to the water heater and electric panel, it contained a beat-up sofa, a small flat screen and his weight equipment.

The sofa was covered in an appallingly ugly gold and black plaid. "A college heirloom," he informed her as he put her upon it.

"Do I need a tetanus shot to sit here?"

"Don't be hating on this old girl. It was my favorite study spot in the basement of my college library. When they renovated, Mrs. Wisnet, a librarian with a soft spot for brainy jocks, asked me if I wanted it. Stay there."

He disappeared into the kitchen and returned with ginger ale and saltine crackers. He popped the top of the can for her. "These should help."

He was good at taking care of her. It was a not-unpleasant feeling, but she made a valiant attempt to get it together. "I'm good. You can finish your workout. Sorry I interrupted."

"No apologies needed. Drink the ginger ale." But he did back off, giving her the space to collect herself. As he resumed his reps, she sipped at the fizzy drink.

She dutifully made herself do the cardio and strength regimens recommended during first-year orientation. Those who did them had more energy for their studies, which gave her the reason to prioritize the time.

She expected Brick maintained his physique for his job, too. But their levels were drastically different. Lifting her had been nothing for him, and she could see why. The barbell he was lifting in steady reps over his head held plates well over her own body weight.

"Do arson investigators have to stay in this kind of shape?"

He grunted. "It doesn't hurt. Sifting through debris, crawling into tight spaces. Because of the toxins that can linger after a fire, I still have to wear a lot of protective gear, even though it's not as heavy as turnouts. Plus, like I said, I still occasionally join an engine house on their calls."

"To help them know what to look for on your investigations."

"You remembered." He gave her a half-smile. Though his voice held some strain, he wasn't abbreviating his responses. It was impressive, though she expected he consciously exercised his lungs as much as his muscles. Firefighting, even with breathing gear, would test that capacity.

He hung up the bar with a clang. "Yeah. Firefighters might see evidence before it burns up, or fire patterns while they're happening. They can also remember key info offered by neighbors when they first arrive on site, like the Whitfield fire. So increasing that awareness helps me with my job, while I pitch in and help with theirs."

"Plus you get to fight a fire or two."

A quick flash of teeth. "There's that. The firefighting bug is hard to lose."

He adjusted the plates, adding more weight before he moved to squats. The muscles in his thighs and ass flexed against the stretched fabric of his shorts. From what she could see, if he needed to dead lift an adult human and carry them out of the fire, he was more than up to the task.

A smart man with the body of a god. She was surprised women weren't camped outside his door, throwing their panties on the hood of his truck as he left for work.

What she was feeling wasn't merely lust. It was tangled with a deeper need. Something that would help with the emotions she couldn't seem to control. Her eyes lingered on his grip on the bar, the focus of his eyes and set of his mouth.

She wanted to believe him about Tish. All of this was new to her, yet the things he talked to her about touched her deep cravings, part of who she was. So familiar. But she kept getting snagged on the reality, a world where he could do those things with other women he didn't consider...his.

"So," he said. Down, up. Down up. Like her emotions and thoughts about...everything. "Sounds like you're good to be here for a few days."

"Yes. My advisor said I could use the time to study for my ER rotation exam."

Apparently killing a patient wasn't considered an automatic fail. The thought scalded her insides.

"Our worst mistakes can make us the best at what we do, doc." He was too good at reading her face. Brick put the bar back into the rack, then sat down on the bench and picked up a dumbbell to start bicep curls.

She wanted to fire off an acidic comment about platitudes, but it was a nonstarter with him. He *did* know what their mistakes could cost the people they were trained to help. But that knowledge didn't help her solve anything, so she shifted to a different problem.

"If I wanted to be your submissive...would I be one of them?"

He came to a full halt. "Pardon?"

"Sorry." She bit her lip. "I should have waited until you were done to ask a question like that."

He put the weight down. "You mean would you be *one* of my submissives? What if I said yes? What would your response be?"

"I'd say go to hell."

The vehemence of her answer came up without warning, just like her breakfast. But truthfully, she didn't like to be played with like that. She would have gotten up then and there, but his answer stopped her.

"Good. In a negotiated scene, a submissive is under my care. But that's different from considering her mine. I don't have a sub like that. The moment you tell me you want that, you will have my total and exclusive attention, Les. Got it?"

He held her gaze an extra beat. She returned her attention to the ginger ale and crackers, fingers playing nervously over them.

After a silent moment, he picked up a towel and rose. "I'll grab a shower and we'll go."

Not entirely sure what she was doing or why, she got up and stepped forward. She extended her hand, a mute request for the towel.

He let her take it, his gaze upon her. She approached him, wary and intrigued, like an animal whose responses she was still learning. She just wasn't sure if she was applying that description to him or her. Or both.

She put the towel against his back, drying the sweat there, moving down the valley of his spine, stopping above his waistband. This wasn't about her copping a feel. It was about...

"Do you know the term for what you're doing, Les?" He had his head tilted, keeping her in his peripheral vision.

"No."

"Act of service."

She liked the sound of it. Leaning in, she put her mouth between his shoulder blades. Brick reached around, finding her hand and bringing her in front of him, the towel still clutched in her grasp. As she looked up at him, his expression was so intent she had to look down. Needed to look down. Which was when she saw his erection, pushing insistently against his shorts.

Acts of service could take a lot of forms, and she was smart enough to figure out what one of them would be between a Dom and a sub. His hands tight on her hair, pushing her down on his length...

"Christ." Brick tipped up her chin, held it. "I'm getting a shower," he repeated forcefully. "You are going to go into the living room with your crackers and soda. Watch some TV. Something not about sex."

A silly grin teased her mouth, bringing amusement into his own eyes, but his fingers tightened on her jaw. "You come near that shower while I'm in it, and I will unload that entire list on your ass."

She lowered her lashes. "Yes, sir," she murmured.

He snorted. His wrist snapped and the towel popped against her buttock, with enough force she felt the sting through denim. She yelped and glared at him.

"A smartass is a red ass," he promised, heading toward the living room.

Rubbing the sore spot, she followed him. As he took the first few stairs to the second level, she was betting good money he'd lock that bathroom door.

He paused. The gray in his eyes had turned to steel, pinning her in place. "Les? Next time you call me sir, make damn sure I can hear the capital S."

If she did that, she'd be taking another step toward the decision to be *his* submissive. He didn't have to say that for her to know it.

All she was feeling toward him, exploring with him, was happening during one of the most difficult experiences of her life. She knew the dangers of that, too. But she could truthfully say none of that had anything to do with everything she'd imagined and thought of between them since she was twelve years old.

As their gazes held, she could hear her heart beating in her ears.

"Yes, Sir."

If she thought he might not catch the significance, or not pin her on it, given her fragile emotional state, he thrillingly disabused her of any such wiggle room. No matter how well and chivalrously concealed, she'd affected him. He wasn't in the mood to exercise forbearance.

He came back down the steps and crossed the room, a slow stalk toward her. She caught her lip in her teeth, a gesture of nervousness, of need. His gaze riveted on that.

"How's your stomach feeling?" He asked the question like Dr. Jack or Redmond, wanting to know if she was ready to take the lead on a procedure.

"Like a popcorn machine."

His gaze glittered. "We have a lot to work out, but I want you too damn much to put this off. If you're ready to take another step in this direction, convince me of that. Before I do what I'm planning to do to you next."

She gave him a lopsided smile. "Isn't that sort of like holding out a cookie and saying I can have it if I say I like cookies?"

His chuckle had a male edge to it. Her hands curled at her sides, uncertain and restless. He seemed to see everything vibrating through her, intensifying that electricity. "You're old enough to know when it's best not to take that cookie. And the consequences if you do."

His expression sobered. "If you convince me you're ready for this next step, I'll take over some of your choices, but you get them all back with the use of one word. You know what a safeword is, even if you've only heard it as a party joke. Between a Dom and sub, it's damn serious. You use it, I stop doing what I'm doing, no guilt, no apologies. A protection for you, not a punishment."

Usually when he was in this territory, he gave her little touches, tactile reassurances. His refusal to make contact increased the significance of his words. As well as the strength of her longing for his touch. "I'll stop to make sure you're okay, to see if we need to change track," he continued. "But you don't use it lightly. If you're just scared of the way something is making you feel, you can tell me that without using the safeword."

The laser intensity of his gaze increased. "I'll watch for things you may not see yourself until it's too late. Nothing's more important to me than caring for you when this is happening. Nothing's more important to me than caring for you, period. Not even my own desires or needs. If you don't trust another single thing in this world, you can trust that. The safeword protects you. But so will I. Got it?"

What he made her feel was overwhelming, especially snarled up with everything else. She pushed her more difficult reactions aside, because she wanted to go where he would take her. Needed it.

"Yes. Yes, Sir."

He waited. He wasn't going to ask the question again. He expected an answer.

"I want what you're offering, Brick. I don't know all of what that means, but enough of me does to take the first steps toward it. I trust you enough to do that. I just need to know what you expect of me, how I can be that for you."

"And for yourself," he added. "That's also pretty damn important. I can help you with that. For now, stand just like this. Don't move."

He cupped the side of her neck. One large finger slowly slid behind the shell of her ear, along her neck, beneath the lobe. A touch like that said a man wanted to know a woman, learn her. Use those little gestures to find where her heart was, her soul, the center of what aroused and sheltered her. It reinforced what she'd just said.

She could give him her trust.

"What's your safeword, Les?"

She couldn't think, and looked to him in desperation.

"You can choose your own later. For now, it's my given name. Jefferson. Do you understand?"

"Yes, Sir."

He shifted to a full grip of her throat. His hand was almost big enough to circle it. The change from gentleness to inexorable pressure was startling. "Feel your pulse against my palm. Look into my eyes as I hold you this way, feel what it does to you. Focus on me and what I want from you. Feel your response to that build, like your whole body, heart and soul are answering that demand."

As he maintained that still, stronger-than-firm clasp, sensation speared through her, impaling her and holding her fast. He was doing nothing but staring at her face, gripping her throat, but as the seconds passed, her body became rigid with arousal, paralyzed by the force of her response. She honestly couldn't move. A tiny gasp came from her, a little moan.

Flame flared amid the gray smoke of his eyes. "Yeah, baby. There you are. You know your Master."

A whole civilized world vanished, leaving the two of them, her soul agreeing and surrendering to his with a painful surge of relief. Someone who knew her, who understood her. She didn't have to question that knowledge, because he was demonstrating so well what she'd needed and wanted for so long, but been afraid to grasp.

Except with him.

The reason his badge number was in her password, the reason she'd worn the charm, it was all there in his grip.

He dropped his other hand and opened her jeans with a deft pull. "Get rid of these. Panties, too."

No more barrier between his hand and her flesh. He didn't let go of her throat, making her comply while he held her that way. It kept her from being able to bend as she normally would to remove the clothes. But the awkwardness tightened the screws on that arousal. She was obeying him on his terms.

She toed off her shoes and socks, then removed the jeans and panties. The cool air touched her sex, belly and thighs, her buttocks. Her T-shirt brushed her hip bones. Eyes still on hers, an unspoken requirement that she hold his gaze so he could watch every change in her face, he cupped the side of her breast, fingers following the shape of her bra.

"Take this off. Leave on the shirt."

She reached behind her, which pressed her breast into his palm, and unhooked the garment, then fumbled the straps through the short sleeves, stripping it off. A moan broke from her as his hand closed fully over the curve, thumb stroking the nipple through the cotton.

His command, coupled to his full attention, was the most erotic thing she'd ever experienced. She wasn't sure she'd survive it.

She licked her lips, a new sound escaping them as he dropped the other hand to her thigh again. "Why aren't your legs spread for me?" Thrilling menace lay in the soft words.

All her normal sass was beyond her reach. She couldn't quip, "Because you told me to stay still." She could only shift to comply, her movements still awkward because her body was weighted like deep water by his demands.

When he stroked the tops of her thighs, her mound, she changed her mind about her cause of death. She was going to catch fire. Good thing she was with a fireman, but she suspected he had no interest in quenching her flame. He wanted her to burn hot and hard, leaving nothing but ash.

"That term you used," she said. "About a fire, when it's taken over..."

"Fully involved. It means the structure is already lost to the fire. All we can do is contain and control it."

He brushed a kiss over her ear, following it to her throat, above his grip. He nudged her chin up even higher to press his teeth to it. She inhaled his scent, trembling at the scrape of his jaw against her flesh.

"I contain the fire that consumes you, and I'm the one controlling it. Aren't I, Les?"

"Yes. Yes, Sir. Oh..."

His lower hand moved again, teasing over the silky hair between her legs and finding her clit, stroking the labia with the touch of a man who knew a woman's body.

She wasn't going to dwell there, because everything about him said he was here with her and only her, and he damn well expected her to stay in the here and now, too. Since waves of arousal were roaring even higher, it wasn't as difficult as she feared. His words echoed in her head.

The moment you tell me you want to be my submissive, you will have my total and exclusive attention...

Being a Dom was what he was, a non-negotiable, integral part of his relationship with a woman. If he'd said, "The moment you tell me you're mine, I'm monogamous," it would have meant the same. She knew that, as surely as she knew what had been missing in her earlier relationships. That empty part of her had always noticed the absence, knowing what *should* be there.

He curved his hand over her sex and increased his grip over it, as he had at her throat. He used both holds to bring her onto her toes. A cry strangled out over the rocket of sensation between the two points.

When he began to work the heel of his hand against her clit, she was so close to climax. But Brick knew that, too.

"A submissive doesn't release without her Master's permission, Les." He teased her ear with his mouth. When he moved to the area directly below it, she learned his caress there might destroy her defenses, any chance of self-control.

Then he yanked "might" away from her and replaced it with "would." He began to speak poetry to her.

"From the hungry gnaw that eats me night and day... Singing the true song of the Soul, fitful, at random...

"Singing...

"Of the wet of woods--of the lapping of waves

"Of the mad pushes of waves upon the land..."

A cry came from her, that mad push within, those waves rising. The sensual tone sharpened, pulling her in two directions.

"You hold, doc. You don't come until my cock is inside you."

The thought of him taking her, joining with her, could send her over. Yet offering it as an incentive gave her renewed reasons to fight her own body.

"The overture lightly sounding—
"the strain anticipating..."

The bastard was going to kill her. With damn poetry.

"Please," she whispered. "Please don't make me go without you inside me."

"Is that going to happen?"

"Maybe...yes. With you...saying those things...and touching me. Like this."

He turned her away from him, a pressure on her shoulder directing her to sink down onto trembling knees. Then forward, onto her hands. She couldn't see him in this position. She heard him slide off the shorts, the light rustle as they hit the floor. He dropped to a knee behind her, pressing it against the inside of her calf so she widened her stance, which made her pulse thud more rapidly.

He put a hand on her back and slid up to her nape, under her hair. Slowly, he wrapped his hand in the thick mass of it. He drew her head up so she was staring straight ahead. His other hand molded the curve of her ass, knuckles trailing down the cleft so he could touch her labia again, fingers pressing between them. They were sucked into her wetness. Her hips jerked, her scalp pulling against his hold.

"How long has it been since you've had sex? You were tight on my fingers last night."

He hadn't hurt her, though. His gentleness had astounded her. "It's been...about eight months. One time then. Six months before that, one other time."

"That's all?"

"Bart, during my first year of college. He was my first. But I...do stuff for myself, so I'm okay."

"You're okay if I say you're okay." He eased his fingers in, she couldn't tell how many, but he stretched her with that curious combination of discomfort and pleasure as she shook under his hold.

"You have the most beautiful cunt." He withdrew his touch on the startlingly frank comment. Putting both hands on her ass, he lifted her knees off the ground with that grip. Another rough cry broke from her throat as his mouth closed over her sex, tongue invading to swirl and collect her moisture, flick over her clit.

If he hadn't stopped within seconds, it would have been over, but thank God, he settled her knees back onto the carpet and put his cock at her opening. His broad, blunt head was against her wetness, testing. It took tremendous effort not to push back against him. His hands tightened on her, reinforcing the warning against it.

"You on birth control, Les?"

"Yes." She didn't trust a condom alone, and no matter how infrequently she had sex, no way was she getting derailed from med school by an unplanned pregnancy.

"Those two times you talked about. They use a condom? You tell me otherwise, it goes to the top of my list."

"No, they did."

He put a warm kiss on the center of her back as he squeezed her buttocks, thumbs stroking her upper thighs. "I never have sex without one. Except now, with you. No barriers between us."

"Yes," she whispered. "Please."

He straightened and gripped her hair again, using his other hand to guide himself into her. As she'd seen from his erection, he was bigger than Bart, and more so than her other two partners. But he knew his size, and took his time. Even so, every millimeter seemed designed to test her physical limits while pushing her over the crumbling edge of that climax. If he touched her clit, she would lose the battle.

When he was fully seated, it was the most stretched she'd ever felt, and the most connected to a man during sex. He released her hair to drop down over her, pushing her down on her elbows as he covered her. He put his mouth on her neck, her shoulder, her upper arm. He nuzzled the side of her face with his jaw, heating her skin with his rasping breath. His pelvis pressed firmly against her ass, thighs aligned with hers.

He was staying so still, and yet the ripples inside her were so intense, she was making little moans, short cries. Then he circled her waist with one powerful arm, and started to thrust.

"Oh, God..."

"Let it build. Come for me only when you're sure you can't stop yourself."

It did build. He was in charge of the fire, just as he'd said. It immersed her, blood, bone and muscle, involving all her senses. She screamed as it built beyond what she'd thought was possible. When it happened with a vibrator or one of those other lovers, it had always stopped when she thought the sensations were too much.

Brick wasn't stopping, and yes, those sensations became too much. It was so intense. She was begging for mercy and more in the same breath, in the same cry. He denied her the first and gave her the second, pushing her to her physical limits, taking all he wanted from her.

Another important message. She'd called him Sir, but if she wanted to be his sub, he'd become her Master. He was letting her know what that would feel like.

What it did feel like. Even if she hadn't made the decision yet, she couldn't argue against it. She didn't want to.

He put his hand on her clitoris, her labia, massaging, and she was lost. She went over as he climaxed with her, thrusting deep, his breath harsh and rasping against her hair. She shrieked, pushing her forehead against the brace of his arm next to her as her hips lifted to him, taking him deeper, feeling the power of his thrusts, wanting more, more, more.

She didn't finish so much as she dropped from the sky, a bird who'd flown so high she'd lost oxygen and had to spiral back down to earth. But he kept his vise-like grip on her even as he sheltered her fragile frame with his large body.

"Oh God," she whimpered it, her forehead on the carpet, eyes closed. This was when a man usually rolled off her, though all three of her bedmates had done the cuddling thing, because she didn't tolerate unkind or inconsiderate partners.

When kind and considerate combined with the demanding and relentless qualities of a Dom, one she wanted so much, the experience hit a whole new level. From here forward, she couldn't imagine doing without it.

He didn't withdraw from her right away. He put more kisses on her shoulders. He lifted the weight of her hair from her neck, pushed it forward so it brushed the floor, giving him the access to put his mouth there. He'd realized how much she loved having her neck and shoulders caressed by a man's skillful mouth. As he did it, he put his palm on her hair, holding her forehead to the carpet. He nuzzled, nipped. Bit, as his tongue traced her flesh inside the clamp of his mouth. She was making little moans once more, her sex spasming around his cock. If he kept this up, she might...

He put his hand under them and stroked over her clit again, flicking it roughly with his fingertips. Shock gripped her at the same time another small climax did, rolling up and grabbing her so unexpectedly, she clamped her hand over his braced forearm.

Multiple orgasms. Another first for her.

When that one ebbed, he eased up on her hair. "Thought you had another in you. There's probably a couple more, but I'll save that pleasure for another time." He eased himself from her body, his cock still substantial enough for her to feel the withdrawal and shudder at the loss.

"Stay in this position. We're not done."

He trailed his fingers up her back to her buttocks, pushing in between to do a light tease of her sensitive rim. "You got any hard limits, Celeste Joy? Things you're sure you don't want to do?"

"I haven't really considered...all the choices." There hadn't been a lot of time to get creative, even with Bart. She definitely hadn't explored with him what Brick was offering.

"The party I take you to tonight should help with that. In the meantime, I'm going to give you a sample of one of your fantasies. I'll count it as a punishment, to strike one off the list."

"Are you taking it chronologically? Starting with the ice cream offense?"

She squirmed as he gave her a pinch, but he wouldn't let her up, keeping his other hand on her back so she remained on her elbows, her legs spread and backside up.

"You and that mouth. No. I already know the punishment for that one. I'll put the coldest ice cream I can find on your needy little clit." His fingers stroked over it, making her quiver. "I'll let you writhe a while before I start sucking it off. I won't let you come for a good, long time. I like the idea of watching you completely come apart from orgasm denial."

"Oh," she said faintly. "So...what punishment..."

"This one will be for wearing a bikini at sixteen, so I could see your nipples and the cleft of your ass."

"That was a very modest suit," she protested. "When you get out of the creek, it's really cold and stuff clings."

"Judgment has been passed." Before she could prepare herself, his hand smacked her still vibrating sex.

The fierce sting had her reacting instinctively, trying to roll away and clamp her legs shut. He was ready for that, though. He'd put his hand between her legs, sealing his palm over that sting and holding her almost off her knees again.

"Did I tell you that you could move, Les?"

She shook her head.

"Let it settle. I think you'll find you want more."

The command, the act, spiked the whirl of uncertain feelings inside her. It had stung, it hurt.

Yet beneath his palm, her sex also vibrated.

Wanting more.

He'd told her he'd give her one of her fantasies—spanking her sex. The man paid attention, something as terrifying as it was arousing.

"I'm going to do it four more times. You know your safe word."

"Yes...yes, Sir."

He removed his hand. "Spread your knees wider and lift your ass. Show me your pussy. Don't you fucking move this time."

Oh God. She found herself doing it, even as her fingers curled into the carpet and she pressed her forehead into the fibers. Something... something else was happening. She didn't know if it was right or wrong, if...

Second slap.

She cried out, an aching sound that moved into her chest. At the same time, she fought that very reasonable, very sane urge to close her legs and protect herself.

He was in charge. He wouldn't hurt her past bearing.

Third slap.

The ache moved up into her throat, stayed throbbing in her chest. The reaction, tangled up with the aftermath of the climax, grabbed for the pain. Tears were accumulating behind her eyes.

Fourth.

"Brick..." She wailed it, a cry of need and pain.

"It's all right. I've got you." He turned her around, shifted her into his lap, cradled her in his arms. "You don't have to do anything but listen to me and follow my lead. Put everything in my hands."

Like a child would. The thought came to her, an unwelcome

intruder, but one she couldn't deny. She didn't have the right to keep this separate and sacred from it.

She might not have that right, but she wasn't the one in charge of that decision. He was. "Only me and you in this room." He'd registered the tension that swept through her, the agony boiling up with those emotions. "The world waits outside until I say you can let it in. Got it?"

"Yes."

"Yes what?"

"Yes, Sir."

"Good." He removed her shirt, pulling it gently over her head, so she lay fully naked in his arms. He stroked her body, murmured to her, until that ache eased enough she could make a shaky request. "More... poetry. Please?"

He smiled against her forehead. He rose, taking her to the sectional. When he sat down on the throw he put beneath them, he kept her in his arms, on his lap. He trailed his magical fingers over her face, over her breast, the nipple, the curve of her stomach and upper thighs. He played in the damp hair at her sex.

"The welcome nearness—the sight of the perfect body; the face—the limbs —the index from head to foot, and what it arouses... The mystic deliria—the madness amorous—the utter abandonment."

"Is that from the poem you were quoting earlier?" she mumbled, listening in wonder.

"Yes. Walt Whitman. 'Press Close, Bare Bosom'd Night.'"

She blinked at him. "My mother loves Whitman. I thought his stuff was all about nature and flowers."

"It is nature. Some about flowers. Some about other parts of nature."

"I like how big you are." She looked at his hand upon her, thinking how his body had covered her. How his cock filled her. "Makes me feel safe, I guess. Sounds silly."

"No. It doesn't. Makes me feel good to hear it." He found her hand, meeting her palm to palm, letting her see that difference in size. When she curled her fingers around two of his, he smiled.

"So what went wrong with you and Bart?" he asked. "I know he was a dick about wanting to get married before you two finished school."

The breakup had centered around that, yes. It wasn't until months of reflection had passed she'd realized his insistence on it, how angry he'd become about her refusal, had given her the final straw she needed, plus a long-overdue clarity over how different the two of them were.

"He grew up in a small town, like I did, but he never wanted to do that again. He wanted to live in a big university town, do research, or join an engineering company doing big, important things. Nothing wrong with that, but it wasn't a path we could share. I tried, he tried, but when your heart's not in it..."

She looked down at their clasped hands. "Afterward, for a long time, I felt like I'd failed him. For that first, really intense love, especially if it's also your first sex, you convince yourself that's your forever, no matter how foolish it seems to people who are way past that. I translated my heartache from how he couldn't change, into my inability to love him for who he is."

"Do you still feel like you failed?" His voice was neutral, letting her admit the truth, no judgment.

"Not anymore. Neither of us failed. Even if I could have loved him as he is, and him for who I am, it would be in spite of those things we wouldn't or couldn't change, not in support of them."

"I'm glad you reached that conclusion. But I know it hurt when it happened. I'm sorry." He threaded his fingers through her hair, deep, easy strokes.

"Beulah's mom told her there's no magic other than time that fixes a broken heart. The pain you feel and cope with helps you grow."

"What did Beulah say to that?" His amused expression said he'd had enough exposure to her roommate to anticipate her answer.

"'Momma ain't wrong, but a girl needs some fucking timeouts from the agony.'" Les smiled. "For her, that was going out for drinks and dancing. I preferred the 24/7 work and study schedule until I could draw a deep breath again, though Beulah occasionally talked me into her strategy. Both helped."

"Giving yourself breathing room to deal with bad shit is important."

It pointed things right back to the main reason she was here, but Brick didn't let her go down that dark tunnel. Instead, he squeezed her hip. "As much as I'd like to keep you here naked, we have stuff to do. I better get that shower so we can get going."

"Were you going to lock the door to keep me out?"

A wolfish smile crossed his rugged features. "I'm pretty good at coming up with ways to keep my sub from misbehaving."

Her sex still throbbed from one of them, so she couldn't disagree. Brick, who'd gotten in his share of trouble with her brother and their friends, was now a stickler for the rules. Go figure. He was also strict in their application.

She guessed it all depended on what purpose—and pleasure—those rules served.

CHAPTER TEN

$\mathcal{A}$fter he disappeared up the stairs, she decided to take Beulah's box to the guestroom and unpack the contents. She paused, listening to the rush of the shower water. He'd left the master bedroom open, and from the light, she could tell the bathroom door was open, too. He had a clear shower door. If she crept in and checked the bathroom mirror at just the right angle, maybe she could see...

She rolled her eyes at herself. He brought out the sexually intrigued woman *and* mischievous child in her. Though it took effort, she made the adult decision to stay in the guestroom.

When she opened the box and read the note on top, gratitude came with a sting of tears. *You're not alone, Les. Every* licensed *doctor has lost patients. Every doctor wonders if they could have done more. I love you, serious geek-girl. You've always been there for me; I'm here for you, however you need me.*

She set the note aside. Beulah had included a cosmetic bag full of Les's toiletry items and makeup. She'd also packed several changes of clothing, though what she'd chosen had Les's eyebrows raising.

Instead of the day-to-day jeans and shirts she might wear to the hospital before changing into scrubs, Beulah had excavated things from Les's wardrobe more appropriate for the company of an interested male.

Which included the two pairs of jeans Les had that were snugger and more stylish, riding lower on her hips. The shirts were feminine,

V-neck baby doll tees that contoured her small breasts. The hem would ride up to show her navel and hip bones if she reached for anything above her. Like Brick's shoulders.

Beulah had also included Les's one sexy bra and panty set. During her first year of medical school, they had visited a lingerie shop to buy a gift for a friend's wedding shower. Beulah had talked Les into the satin bra and matching panties for herself, the former lifting and hugging her curves, making them far more noticeable.

"Beulah, I'm a farm girl," Les had protested.

"So's Daisy Duke, and she re-branded cut-off jeans for women everywhere."

"Daisy Duke is a fictional character, and that's an exaggeration. The women in Iran aren't wearing these."

"You don't know what they have on under those robes. Maybe nothing at all." Beulah had winked.

Her roommate's outrageousness aside, Les really was a farm girl. But she was also a woman still vibrating from Brick's touch and feeling out of her depth with him sexually. She was okay with him taking the lead on the stuff she didn't totally understand, but when it came to wanting each other, she didn't mind exercising some power to increase his male hunger toward her.

That bra would create deeper cleavage, an effect that made Les think of Brick's trailing fingers there.

Fine, screw it. She donned the pretty underwear and pulled on a pair of jeans. The light blue denim was stressed at the creases, and hugged her ass in a flattering way, without cutting off her femoral artery. The V-necked tee she chose had white dandelion seeds swirling across the gray fabric, headed for the outstretched hands of a fairy. She was sitting in the cup of a daffodil, her body a white silhouette, her intricately veined wings folded over Les's hip.

When she was little, Les had thought floating dandelion seeds *were* fairies. After she shared that story with Daralyn, her sister-in-law had found and given her the shirt as a Christmas gift.

She was already wearing a small pair of gold and silver toned hoops, pretty much the only earrings she ever wore. Since they worked with all of her outfits, it saved her the time of having to choose.

She also didn't wear a lot of makeup for work, but she did put some on now. Especially after she found Beulah's second note, which had a far different tone from the first.

Put on a booty-hugging pair of jeans, brush out your hair, and set that fireman ablaze. PS, when you get back, we're going makeup shopping. This selection is sad. And ancient. Was Toys R Us having a 'my first makeup kit' sale, and your mother got you this to celebrate puberty?

"Bitch," Les muttered, but her lips tipped at the corners. She hung up the rest of the shirts and put her socks, jeans and underwear in a drawer. He kept his guest room ready for its intended purpose. There wasn't much in the closet, except several file boxes of paperwork. She suspected his primary guests were his family, because a collage frame up on the wall showed pictures of his parents and siblings.

Over the bed was an enlarged photograph of a harvested field at dawn, the fog resting on the browning and broken stalks of corn. It looked like the view from the back porch of his grandfather's house, where the McGuires had lived until he passed.

The Brazinski's oldest boy got married soon after the McGuires left, the newlywed couple then renting the property. They'd produced twin boys eleven months later. Whenever she mentioned them now, Elaine said they were total terrors, but she always said it with fondness.

When Brick checked on the property, she was willing to bet he tossed a football with the boys or told them fireman stories. And shared some lemonade or tea with their parents on the porch.

That pang hit her again, the desire to run home to that world. To her mother's arms.

Maybe Brick had been the next best thing, the thing that helped her resist the urges of a child.

She pivoted away from the picture and headed down the stairs. Brick had finished his shower and was dressed and working at the kitchen table. It looked like he was going over that same case, the Whitfield fire. His mouth was a straight line, his eyes serious. She paused in the doorway, watching as he studied one of the photos, then looked at his laptop screen. He scrolled through the text, and highlighted three lines. Then he called up what looked like some other crime photos and increased the size, leaning in to peer at them more closely. Whatever he saw made his brow crease, his shoulders tighten.

"Everything okay?"

He glanced her way, pausing a beat to look her over. She slid a hand in her back pocket and leaned in the doorway, increasing the interest in his gaze. It felt good to get that attention, even as the shadows that had started to gather around her upstairs tried to pluck at her. *You don't deserve to feel good.*

This isn't about that. He said this is about gaining perspective, taking a step back.

He said it. You don't believe it.

"We've logged two more witness statements, but I need to give them some space in my head, let them process." He eyed her. "You okay?"

"Yeah. Doing the same. If we're picking up furniture near your office, can I see where you work? Maybe go inside?"

"We can do a drive by, but hell no to going inside. You'd end up warming a chair in my office for hours while I get sucked into whatever's happening there."

"I don't mind if you need to work. I've got nothing but time today, and what I need to study is on my tablet. I'll bring it with me. Since I've disrupted your work week, I should at least try to be a low maintenance date."

He closed up the folder and laptop, dropped both into his briefcase and rose from his chair, picking up his keys. "Doc, you are high maintenance and disruptive for all the right reasons." He nodded to a cooler bag on the table. "I put in a bottle of water and a snack for the road, to hold you over until we get lunch."

As she picked it up, he gave her a more blatant perusal. "Looks like you had everything in the box you need."

"Thanks." She told herself she had to stop blushing around him, but her face warmed anyway, which flustered her on other levels. He brushed his knuckles along her cheek.

"Remember to let it go and breathe, doc. Just breathe today."

Easier said than done.

The Major Crimes division was at the Richmond police department headquarters. Once Brick exited and left behind the busy traffic of the beltways that ribboned around and through the city, he brought Les to downtown Richmond, where the building was located.

When she asked why the traffic was so heavy, he told her the beltways were always clogged. A hefty local population shared the throughway with tourists headed toward Virginia Beach, or the Chesapeake Bay Bridge-Tunnel, the New England states and DC. There was also a sizable military base.

Once they got downtown, the roads were much quieter. A dotting of historic buildings and old sprawling trees were scattered around the large police complex and parking deck. She rolled down her window and put her hand out into the cool morning breeze. It held a hint of the heat the weather channel promised it would have later in the day.

As Brick drove around the building, he pointed out the window closest to where his office was. "I'm not important enough to have my own window." He winked at her. "And since we're often out in the field, in the labs, or head-deep into reviewing data, it'd be a waste anyway."

He showed her eating places, coffee shops, green spaces and other downtown features part of his day-to-day working life. When they stopped at the storage place, she helped him load the truck with the chairs and table that had probably been part of a breakroom set. There were also several boxes of kitchen items, clothes, toys and nonperishable foodstuffs, since they'd also collected donations.

As Brick secured the load, Les noticed how competently he worked with the tie-downs. The straps slid over his fingers as he tightened up the slack and pulled on the bonds to ensure the furniture would stay where he'd put it.

Cue the shaky breath. As they pulled out of the storage building lot and headed for the exit from downtown, he glanced her way. "We'll check out my office another day," he promised.

"I'd like that." Her palms were sweaty. From the exertion of helping him, she was sure.

The route he took brought them to the outskirts of the city. The roads wound through open and forested terrain. They passed mobile home neighborhoods, farms, and more widely spaced dwellings. The occasional suburban development marked the exodus of professionals who wanted to live outside the city's growing congestion.

She liked the more widely spaced properties. Wildflowers grew in the drainage ditches. Though the developments might have newer, more expensive homes, the land had been clearcut to build them. The older homes, farms and trailers had the established, old growth trees, branches webbed with Spanish moss spread protectively over the structures.

It made her think of the trees in her backyard at home. Her favorite one had a sturdy branch, four feet off the ground, the perfect height and angle to brace herself against the trunk and read. She'd let her bare feet hang down, or bend her knees to curl her soles against the rough bark.

Brick's phone buzzed. He glanced at the display, then hit the connect button as he pulled the truck onto the shoulder and let it idle. "Jefferson McGuire. Yeah, Sheriff, thanks for returning my call. It's about the Whitfield fire. Your deputy took a witness statement from Tracey Sharone. It was thorough, so thanks for that. But would you mind if I call and talk to him about any impressions he had that might not have made it into his notes or our follow ups?"

He paused, listening. "No, nothing in particular. Just one of those gut things. Okay, appreciate it. Just text me his contact info."

Les eyed him as he disconnected. "Jefferson?"

"It's more official-sounding than Brick." He sent her a half-smile. "I bring out the nickname if I want to build rapport. You remember the neighbor who said Jasmine and the kids were on a fishing trip with the boyfriend?"

"She said she saw them that morning."

"Yeah, but eyewitness accounts are notoriously unreliable. She couldn't remember what the vehicle looked like, and she saw them at a distance. It was early, she was letting the dog out, and there was a fog."

Brick twitched a shoulder. "However, one of the two witness statements I was reviewing this morning now corroborates that. Her statement hadn't been released to the press, so it wasn't the grapevine effect. This guy was loading up his truck to go fishing himself. He noted the boyfriend's pick-up going by, with the pole holder on the front and the cooler on the back. Colin Werther is the boyfriend, the volunteer firefighter I mentioned. They waved at one another. Colin had his window down, his arm on it.

"While the rear windows were tinted, the witness said the kids were back there. Jasmine Whitfield was in the passenger seat. It was really early, and it looked like she was taking a quick nap."

She studied his pensive expression. "Have you gotten a statement from Colin?"

"Yeah. He talked about her drug problem, and how it had eaten him up, worrying about her relapsing. She was working the program, but he was concerned she was trying to do too much, too fast, and the stress was starting to pull her back down again. He was helping out as much as he could with the kids. Could barely get through the interview. Every time he talked about the kids, he broke down."

Brick glanced in his rearview mirror and made another turn. "He was glad she'd agreed to the fishing trip and seemed excited about it. Then he said it kind of went to shit. He had to bring them back early, because the kids weren't feeling good. Jasmine was in a mood, and that made it worse. She was pissed at him, blaming him for the kids getting sick because he brought a bunch of donuts. He offered to help, but she told him no."

"No one saw them come back?"

"No." Brick grimaced. "Rural area, no cameras on the neighbor houses. Fishing spot was accessible by backroads, so that was what he took to go there and come back. We have his receipt from the donut shop and a bait store, for ice."

"Okay." She raised a brow. "So corroboration is good. Right?"

"It's the other witness statement that's bugging me, the one I called the sheriff about. Jasmine worked at Tracey's beauty shop, and Tracey said Jasmine had been clean for a year and was doing really well. Enough she was starting to have some confidence in herself. She'd gone back to school and was taking a computer class."

"Which fits with Colin's concern, about her maybe trying to do too much, too fast. Trying to balance school, her job, the kids."

"Yeah." He pursed his lips. "The part sticking in my head is Tracey said Jasmine was pulling away from Colin. She was starting to see her dependence on him as too connected to her old addict behavior. Said with him knowing her history, it felt like he was always expecting the worst of her, making it harder to leave that behind."

He paused. "She'd told Colin she wanted to stay friends, but had ended the romantic side of their relationship a few weeks ago. He was still doing stuff for her and the kids, but she was trying to keep it on a platonic footing. She did mention the fishing trip to Tracey, and said the kids were excited about it."

"You think he killed them because he could see her drawing away from him? And he killed the kids rather than let her take them from him too?"

"It's a theory, and one with nothing but that witness statement and my instincts to back it up. And my instincts have been wrong before."

Yet his theory meshed with some of the unlikely and terrible things she and her fellow med students had seen during their rotations.

"It's tough with addicts," he mused. "They'll make it sound like things are going great, even if they're not, but it's harder to hide that from close friends who've seen you do the spiral. Like Tracey. Every once in a while, who's lying isn't who you thought. Colin might be playing the martyr, the hero who just wanted to do what's best for his troubled girlfriend and her kids."

He sighed irritably. "Or it could be exactly what it sounds like. It isn't like the crime shows. Usually the one you expect is lying is, and that would be the drug addict. She wasn't doing as well as it seemed. She got pissed, stressed, came back home. Maybe gave the kids medicine which made them too sleepy to wake up and try to escape the fire. She wasn't careful about the space heater in their room, so the fire starts after she shoots up. They die of smoke inhalation."

He met her troubled gaze. "Coroner confirmed that part. They never felt it, so that's one mercy. Fewer people than you think are awake when the fire reaches them."

Though he was reassuring her, and this was part of his job, no one got used to seeing dead children. She thought again of how he'd had to look at those small bodies in their beds, sift through the aftermath after they were removed. Look at the remains of their burned toys and bedding.

She put her hand over his. "You have pretty good instincts. It's good you follow them to the end, to be sure."

He squeezed her hand, and they drove for a few moments in silence. Since she wanted to ease the shadows in his expression, she moved the hand to his thigh. "Just FYI, it's really hot to watch you work."

"Oh yeah? I thought you were looking a little heated. I was going to suggest we turn on the AC."

She elbowed him. "I always prefer the outdoor air unless it's sweltering. But on the topic of your hotness, I've been thinking of that calendar. Maybe we should organize one for the arson investigators. I'm willing to help, purely to fight that kind of discrimination."

"I'm thinking I'd prefer a calendar of *female* firefighters. Strike a blow for feminism. They can pose with kittens, and you can call it Firefighters with Puss—"

He took her punch in the biceps with a laugh and slowed down, turning onto a gravel driveway next to a dented black mailbox. "This is Rufus's place. He's the one collecting things for the family."

As they bumped down the drive, a trailer came into view. Though it had seen better days, the grass around it was mowed, and some spring daffodils sprouted along the cinderblock foundation. A flagpole planted in the front yard flapped with the American flag. The blue-tinted police version, a solid blue stripe in the middle, flew beneath it.

"He's a police officer?"

"Yeah. He works in a different precinct, not downtown, which was why I told him I'd bring him the stuff. Save him the trip."

A burly black man was sitting on the front stoop with a cup of coffee and a newspaper in hand. He had short-cropped hair and beard, and wore a Richmond PD uniform, the dark blue shirt open over his clean white T-shirt.

He lifted a hand, his lips creasing in a smile. When his gaze moved to Les in the passenger seat, his brows lifted in interested speculation, though he didn't seem surprised to see Brick with someone.

Brick had Les wait as he circled around to open her door and hand her out of the vehicle.

"You don't have to do that," she said. "Not every time."

"My mother raised me right. Plus, if I tell you to wait, it gives me a charge when you obey me."

She was glad Rufus wasn't close enough to hear the conversation, or see the hot flush that traveled right from her thighs to her face. Brick sent her a wicked grin. "People are going to think you have a medical condition if you keep turning the color of a tomato," he observed.

"I am going to punch you again. Harder."

Capturing her fist in his hand, he opened it up to lace their fingers together, and then tugged her toward the mobile home. Rufus's knowing glance told her he might have read their body language as easily as if he'd heard the conversation word for word. But his greeting was casual and friendly.

"Well, look at you, bringing me a pretty girl first thing in the morning. A nice change from your ugly face. Either of you want some coffee?" Rufus lifted his mug toward Brick. *World's Biggest Asshole* was printed on it. "I'm drinking out of yours, but I could spit in another and use a shop rag to clean it out."

"Now Rufus, don't lie. You know your momma gave you that mug. It's special." Brick grinned.

"I actually have some nice clean cups," Rufus assured Les. "And a good dark roast blend. Starbuck's Café Verona."

"I'm good, but thank you."

"Rufus, this is my friend, Les Wilder. She's a third-year med student. Les, this is Rufus Cole. He calls himself a sergeant, but that doesn't mean he outranks me."

"Don't pay any attention to him," Rufus returned. "It sticks in this desk jockey's craw that I'm out on the street every day."

"You're a double wide dick."

"That's what the ladies tell me."

"Yeah, yeah." Brick rolled his eyes. "Remind me where you and your big dick were during that downtown structure fire a few years back, when we firefighters were hauling line up twelve flights of stairs. Working the barricade?"

"Protecting civilians from the risk of a collapsing building," Rufus responded, "while you pyromaniacs were playing in your favorite sand box."

He wasn't as tall as Brick, but he was still a big man, like a compact tank. After he tossed Brick another grin, Rufus engulfed her hand in a cordial shake. "So this little slip of a girl is the one who holds our big arson detective's heart."

"He's talked about me?" Les asked.

"Unless there's some other young lady with big hazel eyes studying to be a doctor."

"I told him what a pain in the ass you are," Brick put in.

"Only a woman who means something to a man can drive him insane." Rufus winked at her.

She laughed. "How long have you two known one another?"

"Since we were little kids."

"Really?" When it came to Brick's past before Fairhope, she'd been limited to the information she overheard at their house. "How did you become friends?"

"You remember my dad is an American history teacher," Brick said. "Rufus's was also a big history buff, specifically the Civil War, which was my dad's favorite time period."

"You did re-enacting together," she realized.

Brick nodded. "I wasn't doing as much of it with my dad by the time I moved to Fairhope and discovered football. But Rufus's dad was into reenacting too. They did the battle and living history events. And brought their sons along."

"Some boys went fishing with their dads, did sports or hung out together in a hunting blind," Rufus confirmed. "We did reenacting."

Registering her fascinated expression, he held up a finger and rose. When he disappeared inside his trailer, Brick gave her a look of amused patience.

Rufus returned with two 8x10 framed photographs. The first was a group shot. Several young boys stood in front of a line of men, all in Union uniforms, wearing somber expressions. That and the sepia tint gave it the look of the time period.

"That's my daddy there." Rufus pointed him out, and Les saw a broad man with Rufus's features. "I'm the pudgy kid in the middle. I got to be a drummer, which meant my mama had an excuse to get me away from the TV and outdoors, to practice." He affected an exasperated feminine tone. "'Rufus, baby, go play your drum under that big shade tree there.'"

"One that was about half a mile down the road," Brick quipped. He jerked his thumb at the truck. "Where do you want this stuff? I'll unload it while you tell her lies."

Rufus pointed to a metal storage building in the same shape as the trailer. "I'd help, but you need to impress your girl by flexing your overinflated muscles. Plus I haven't finished my coffee."

Brick shot him the bird. As he strode away, Les indulged a glimpse of his purposeful movements. The look of the man in his jeans and Richmond Fire Department T-shirt was too much to deny herself.

Though she brought her attention back to Rufus quickly, she should have known a cop would notice.

"Yeah, most women can't keep their eyes off his ass. I even look at it every once in a while. It's mesmerizing."

As she chuckled, he handed her the second picture. "This is me and Brick."

"I've never seen pictures of him younger than high school." Delighted, Les held the photo in both hands as she took a closer look. Before puberty, Brick's arms and legs had been long and ungainly. He was also incredibly skinny. Those freckles she'd noted on his back had had more company in his youth, a good scattering of them on his face. Even at this age, his expression said he wasn't afraid of a fight for the right reasons, though his eyes looked ready to laugh.

He and Rufus had their arms around each other's shoulders, Brick uniformed in the Confederate Gray, Rufus in the Union Blue. They'd affected cocky but still unsmiling expressions, chins lifted and thumbs hooked in their belts.

Brick's dad had been almost too good of a teacher. Looking at the picture, some of the more dramatic details he'd taught them about the War Between the States came back to her. Including the death toll on both sides.

She was definitely a little frayed emotionally if she was unsettled by the photograph because it made her imagine Brick dying in a battle over a century ago. She cleared her throat.

"So your dad was on the Union side, and Brick's dad was the Confederate side. That wasn't a problem?"

"I've got no problem with the boys in Gray." Rufus chuckled. "My daddy's a funeral director, not a slave. And Brick's dad wasn't a slave owner. It's re-enacting. It's a great way for kids to learn about history. We had to research everything, from all the different reasons men fought on either side, to what daily life was like in both armies."

He looked toward the storage shed, where Brick was stacking up the boxes. "My man there liked the letters the soldiers wrote home. He even made copies of some the re-enactors had from their own collections. His favorites were the ones the soldiers wrote home to their girls. Still got those love letters, you big softy?"

"Fuck you," Brick said mildly. He'd returned to the truck to pull out the stack of chairs.

"His interest in all that made his daddy hope he'd be a history teacher, too," Rufus told her.

"Until I torpedoed it by joining the fire department." Brick hefted the chairs and headed back toward the shed.

"You had a hero complex," Rufus called after him.

"Oh." Les started as something wet poked her. She looked down —not far—to see a giant, wrinkle-faced bloodhound nosing her hand.

"That's Nose," Rufus said. "Served with distinction in law enforcement, and now enjoys his retirement at my five-star assisted living facility here."

Her family had always had a dog or two, and plenty of barn cats growing up. Except for the occasional community cat, there was a shortage of pets in her life right now. The condo's pet restrictions aside, med students had no time to care for them properly. Delighted to have the chance to connect with a canine, Les rubbed the long, floppy ears.

"Do you have time to tell me more?" she asked Rufus. His uniform suggested he was going to work soon.

"Sure. I set aside the time for...your visit."

Her brows rose at the hesitation, but he covered it with a cough and moved over on the stoop, patting the open spot so she could sit next to him.

Nose laid down next to her with a groan that earned him a belly rub with the toe of her shoe. With the truck empty and the tie-downs stored, Brick propped his hips against the front grill of the truck. His arms were crossed in a relaxed manner over his chest, his bill cap pulled down to shade his eyes, but Les could see the gray gaze trained on her.

There was more to this visit than furniture and friendly conversation, but until the ulterior motive revealed itself, she was content to let Rufus feed her desire for more stories about him and Brick.

"One summer, during his college break, Brick and I did a road trip to see what footprints had been left by our ancestors who fought in the Civil War. His roots took us to the Appalachians in North Carolina. Mine were near Gulfport, Mississippi." He looked toward

Brick again. "How's Tish's momma, by the way? Still as hot as her daughter?"

"Still married to the Venezuelan who will cut your throat if you get near her."

Rufus grinned and jerked a thumb at Brick. "His multi-great grandaddy, Waylon McGuire, fought for the Grays. He was a farmer whose momma taught him to read from the family Bible."

At her lifted brow, Rufus nodded. "Yeah, that surprises a lot of people. Most of the boys in Confederate graves weren't big slave owner Ashley Wilkes types. A lot of them weren't slave owners at all. Men fought in that war for a lot of reasons. The spectrum, from state sovereignty to slavery, had a lot of personal perspectives resting along it, and a lot of tributaries running out from those." Rufus swatted absently at a fly. "Part of what's interesting about digging into history is learning how many answers there are to the same question."

"You would have made a good history teacher," Brick told him.

"Why do you think your daddy told my daddy he thought we were swapped in the nursery at birth?" Rufus nudged Les. "From the information me and Brick found, Waylon didn't see himself, way up in the Appalachians, as having much of a dog in either fight, but he was drafted by the Confederate army. Died on the field at twenty-two, but managed to leave behind two kids. Brick's damn lucky he got busy with Mrs. Waylon early."

"How about your ancestor?" she asked.

"Josiah belonged to a Quaker businessman in Mississippi. The man wanted to free his handful of slaves, all kin to one another, but the structure wasn't there yet, not in Mississippi. There were a few Southern states that allowed blacks to be legally freed and own property, at least up until the war, but that wasn't one of them. So his 'owner' treated him free in every way possible, while keeping him a slave on paper, under his protection, such as it was."

Rufus glanced at the first photo, his father in the line of Union soldiers. "When that Quaker went north for business, he took Josiah and his family with him. He left them up there to 'represent his interests,' which allowed them to live as freedmen until it could become official on paper. George Washington did something similar with his personal aide, after the American Revolution. Anyhow, when the War Between the States came, my ancestor joined up with the Union."

"This is the kind of stuff your dad used to tell us," Les told Brick. "The little behind-the-scenes things."

Brick smiled fondly. "It frustrates the shit out of him, having to cover all of American history in one school year, when he could spend the same amount of time on any pivotal part of it, including the Civil War. But he likes teaching middle school, planting that spark of interest."

"He used to dress up and do reenactments in the classroom," Rufus recalled. "I was a shit student in most subjects, but I aced history."

"That was because you copied off your girlfriend's paper," Brick observed.

"That's beside the point, and hurtful of you to bring up." Rufus sent Les a droll look. "Don't mind him. He gives me shit because we kicked his department's ass on the Uptown Funk competition."

Brick straightened from the truck and leveled a warning finger at his friend. "You say another word, I'll feed you that coffee cup."

"I'll haul you in for assaulting an officer of the law."

"You'd have to get your fat ass off that step to do it. I'm not worried."

"Uptown Funk competition?" Les interjected hopefully.

Despite Brick's look that promised death, Rufus shot her a grin. "Big YouTube thing. Lip-sync battle between fire and police departments across the country."

He shoved his cup into Les's hands with a quick "Protect this, it *was* a gift from my momma," before he jumped off the steps to duck Brick's grab. The speed of the move, the ripple of biceps as he blocked Brick's punch, suggested his stockiness was less fat and more the bulk of muscle carried by a heavy weight boxer. One decidedly lighter on his feet than she would have expected.

"See, this is why your department lost," he told Brick as he danced back. "You lacked the footwork skills."

"Only because you all had Jones," Brick retorted. "He was an LA choreographer before he joined Richmond PD."

"Maybe, but he was also working with a buttload of natural talent." Rufus executed a Michael Jackson worthy spin that had Les laughing. He started a Temptations style stroll back and forth, spinning and snapping his fingers as he continued. "Come do this with me, boy. I told you that you should have worked with me before your sad lumbering knocked your department out of the running."

"He danced?" Les's eyes brightened. "Where can I watch this video?"

"Nowhere and never," Brick informed her. "The Internet has been scrubbed."

Rufus put a hand up to his mouth and mock whispered, "Search on Uptown Funk competition, Richmond fire department."

"You really are a dick." Brick landed a gut punch, which Rufus took manfully before he belched in his face.

"Got your own ham-fisted self to thank for that."

"That you ate liver for breakfast? I don't think so. I may pass out now." Brick's phone buzzed, and he glanced at it. "Sorry, I need to take this. It's about a case."

"Go on inside, so you can talk where it's quiet."

Les noted Rufus gave Brick a slight nod with the suggestion. Brick's answering expression contained an intriguing touch of gratitude.

He also looked toward her, seeking nonverbal confirmation she'd be okay. At her nod, he disappeared into the trailer, using a second entry door at the opposite end.

Rufus returned to the stoop beside her, stepping over Nose. She handed him the mug. "Why would your mother give you a coffee cup that says that?"

"That's a story for another time. Can't give you all my secrets at once. You won't find me sexy and mysterious."

She smiled and leaned down to rub Nose's belly again. "So why am I here, Rufus?"

"He said you're smart." Rufus lifted his cup to her. "Brick told me what brought you to Richmond."

She stiffened, but Rufus shook his head. "Before you get mad at him, let me say the most important thing. You have his heart, Les."

It wasn't what she'd expected to hear, but it kept her from saying something cutting and sharp. All the teasing had disappeared from Rufus's expression.

"Are you ready to hear one more story?" he asked.

CHAPTER ELEVEN

*B*rick's voice was rising and falling. He was on a call; that hadn't been made up. It had just provided the opening for her and Rufus to be alone. What had Brick wanted Rufus to say to her that was easier to say in his absence?

She was too curious not to listen. She could kill Brick later. She nodded.

Rufus acknowledged it, but he didn't start right away. It seemed to take effort for him to gather his thoughts, and maybe more than just thoughts, before he could proceed. When he did, his voice was different from when he'd told her the stories about him and Brick, or given her the impromptu history lesson.

"A few years back, I had a good friend on the force. Bobbi, a woman I cared about a lot. Like a cop does for a partner, which is just as heart and bone deep as the other way. We'd gone through quite a few doors together."

He rotated the mug in his hands. His attention dropped to his wrist. *B.A.* was tattooed in script there. The dates of birth and death were wrapped around it. Though the whole thing was barely bigger than a quarter, its significance to him was obviously much larger.

Before she could tell him not to put himself through this, or feel additional anger at Brick for making him do so, Rufus anticipated her.

"Let me just get it out. We responded to a domestic call. Two men, married. One ran a catering business, the other worked construction.

The catering guy, it was obvious he was scared of his husband, but he told us he was okay. Said his husband had just had a bad day. Doesn't matter if the victim is man or woman, it's the same bullshit they always say." Rufus's lip curled. "He wrapped up some cookies he'd been baking, gave them to Bobbi, told us thanks for coming."

He took a sip of his coffee, rotated the cup again. "A couple hours later, he was dead. Soon after we left, his husband took him to a place out in the sticks, tied him up, splashed gas on him, set him on fire and watched him burn to death. Drank a twelve pack of beer while he watched. He recorded the whole thing on his phone. It wasn't a quick death. Not even close."

Les closed her eyes. Rufus took a breath. "We had back-to-back calls right after stopping at their place. We didn't get lunch, so after the second call, Bobbi opened up the cookies. The catering guy had put a note under them. 'Help me. He has the house wired to blow up.'"

Les's hand flew to her mouth.

"Now, you can say he was protecting himself best he could, but truth is, that kid saved both of our lives. I have no doubt if we'd tried to get him out of the house on that domestic call, this motherfucker would have blown us all up to prove a point. The bomb squad told us the blast zone could have killed or severely injured anyone within a fifty-foot radius around the house."

"Oh, Rufus. That poor man."

"Yeah. Every year at Easter I leave flowers on his grave. And Bobbi's."

She swallowed. "What happened to her?"

A flat look took over his expression. "At first, Bobbi seemed like she was handling it okay. Just another shitty call. We have them, it's part of the job. Maybe that's why I missed some of the signs. We all did, but fuck. She couldn't wrap her mind around that happening on our watch. Or that she'd been the one he handed the cookies to. It festered. A month or so later, she went out to the spot where the kid died, drank a six pack of beer—same brand as that asshole who killed him—and shot herself."

God, no.

Rufus held onto the flat look as firmly as the mug. She'd seen plenty of doctors and nurses do the same. Pull it in, compartmentalize it, put it away. Like them, he'd been trained to deal with a lot of potentially life-threatening variables in a split second. But figuring out how to deal with the consequences of those choices was outside the scope of any training, no matter what anyone said.

She was learning that hard lesson herself. Which now told her why she was here.

"I still have nightmares about that man's death," Rufus said. "He was about your age, and his eyes. Christ, they were this clear blue color. In my nightmares, I remember every emotion I saw in them that day. Fear, pain, sadness. A loss of hope, warring with the chance, the barest chance, that we could get him out of this mess. But at the center of it all was heartbreak, right? Because he'd loved the guy enough to marry him, hoped for a forever life with him."

Rufus blew out a breath. "It weighed on both me and Bobbi, but we took different paths dealing with it. I used it to help me go forward, watch for clues in future calls I might otherwise miss. I've done the same with her death."

"Rufus," she said, her heart breaking. "Brick shouldn't have asked this of you."

He gave her an unexpectedly fierce look. "In all the years we've been together, he's never asked me to talk about it, though he sure as hell sat here plenty of nights, watching over me after I drank myself into a stupor over it. Brick would give me every bit of his soul if I needed it."

His dark eyes met hers. "It's the hardest thing you can ever do, moving forward after something like that. You feel like you should be punished for it, do time, make penance in some giant way that will never be enough."

She stared at him. Telling this story was costing Rufus, but Brick knew what it had cost Bobbi. And now Rufus's words hit her, a sharp ache under her ribs. *You have his heart.*

Rufus's sober expression reflected her thoughts. "He brought you to someone who could give you insight into what you're going through. Because he's that damn worried about you."

"How did you get through it?" she asked quietly.

Rufus's expression eased, and he almost managed a smile. He set aside the coffee cup to take both her hands in his. "I learned there's a really fucking important line between expecting yourself to be God, and living up to the expectations of one. That line is all ego on one side, humility and commitment to service on the other."

He tapped the badge on his shirt. "I get up every day and resolve to do my best. At the end of my shift, I hope I did more good than harm, even knowing I have no guarantee of that. If I fuck it all up today, tomorrow I have to get up with the same resolve."

He glanced at the tattoo above his wrist. "I won't lie, Les. For a while, everything you deal with about it is going to be a kick in the head. It's a constant beat down. When you haven't committed a crime, but you've done something you feel is unforgivable, you set yourself up as the judge, jury and executioner. You see everyone else who weighs in on it the same way. But it's not the Monday morning quarterbacks who keep you up at night. It's the one who's not coming back. And the family left behind."

Mrs. DaCosta rose in her mind. With a spurt of panic, Les banished the scene it called forth before the reel could start. She couldn't handle that here, not in front of someone. Not even Brick.

Nose had raised his head and maneuvered a bony rear leg up to scratch one long ear. The flapping noise, his expression of bliss, would have made her smile in other circumstances. "It's tearing me up inside," she said. "It invades my sleep, makes me imagine I'm back at that moment. Instead of doing it wrong, I do it right. Fix it. Then I wake up."

"Yeah. Those dreams are the fucking worst."

"Does Brick get them...about the ones he couldn't rescue?"

"Yeah. He does. I know it's cold comfort right now, but if being a doctor is what you want and need to be doing, you just have to have faith and stick with it." He nudged her. "Don't be too mad at him. He's a pretty decent guy."

"He's also a bit of an overbearing jerk."

"But you almost smiled when you said it." Warmth returned to his expression. "Take care of that big asshole. If he gets on your nerves too much, you can always come find me. I have a lot to offer a woman."

Brick snorted. Les looked over her shoulder and up to find him at the screen door behind them. From Rufus's wink, she suspected he'd known when Brick arrived there.

"No woman is coming home to this dump of a trailer," Brick said.

"Don't disrespect the trailer. You see *Lethal Weapon*? Mel lived in a trailer, and women found him irresistible. Rene Russo lived with him there."

"A trailer on the beach. Plus, that's a movie. Riggs lived in the trailer with Lorna, not Mel with Rene. As in *not* real life."

"All stories are based on real life," Rufus responded. "Just wait and see. Even the songs say so. I'll find the 'Queen of my Double Wide' eventually."

He glanced at his watch. "Oh, shit, I'm going to be late. Since I'm doing roll call, I better get my ass in gear. Unless I want to abuse my power and use the siren to clear Richmond traffic out of my way."

"Why would today be different from any other day?"

"Fuck off," Rufus told him affably. He stood up with Les and moved off the stoop, letting Brick emerge and join them on the ground. The two men clasped hands and bumped shoulders.

"Go get the bad guys," Brick told him. "And stay safe."

"Same goes, bro. Always."

After they left Rufus's, Brick picked up sandwiches for them and drove her toward the Potterfield bridge. She didn't say much in the truck, and he didn't press her. When Rufus had told her his story, she'd opened her heart to him and his experience, but she'd shut her own tightly, afraid of what might pour out in front of him.

Now she let herself open that door just a little, enough to think about the question she'd asked him. How did she go forward?

She wondered about his partner, those last few seconds when Bobbi had been standing on the edge between life and death. Had it been a quiet spot, a place to hold her breath, her heart, waiting to see if a different answer came? Or had there been no doubt, because what overrode everything else was the roaring pain of a single question.

How do I deserve to live, when that man who pleaded for my help is dead?

Llanzo had been three years old. He was learning to ride a tricycle, had begun to speak in sentences.

When the force of the thought made her tremble, a strong hand closed over hers. Held her. Brick was here. She kept her eyes closed, but gripped back.

Bobbi killing herself had been pouring a glass of water onto sand. A waste, just as much as the man's life she'd been unable to save. But Les couldn't deny she understood the agony that might have driven her to do it. As Rufus had said, no punishment, no penance seemed enough.

She opened her eyes when the truck came to a stop. They'd reached the park. Its central feature, the vast pedestrian bridge spanning the James River between Brown's Island and Manchester, was a popular place. Even from this distance, a few hundred yards away, she could see walkers, bikers, and joggers crossing the metal and wood structure.

As those pedestrians enjoyed the nature and city views, including the 9th Street Manchester bridge that spanned the river further upstream, kayakers paddled on the whitewater below. Herons and seagulls fished along the thick lace of vegetation on the banks, and perched among the rocks planted in the water. Through her open window, she inhaled the scents of the river, and heard the rush of the water. Picnic goers dotted the green spaces flanking the walkway to the bridge.

Brick came around and opened her door. "Hungry, or do you want to do some walking before we find a place to eat our lunch?"

"Let's walk," she said.

He unbuckled her seatbelt, then put his arm around her waist, bringing her out of the truck. She slid to her feet against his resilient body. He didn't back up, continuing to hold her as she found the ground. Placing her hand on his chest, she looked up at him.

"I get why you did it. But you didn't have to set me up. You could have just told me why we were going there."

"Yeah. I would have." She saw regret in his features. "I didn't want to keep it from you. But I was giving Rufus the out. I told him I wasn't going to tell you ahead of time, so there'd be no expectations if he didn't feel like he could talk about it."

Knowing he hadn't "made" Rufus do it helped, and reinforced his staunch defense of Brick. "What do you think about what she did?" she ventured.

Brick's mouth tightened. "She wounded him down to the soul. He had trouble coming back from it, no matter how tough he looks. Though I know the worst thing she did was to herself, I've had a hard time forgiving her for that." He looked away, though his hands remained on her. She put her forehead on his chest.

A moment later, he ran his hands up and down her arms, an easier caress. "Want to think about other things?"

"Yes, please." She tipped her head back, managing a faint smile. "I also want to talk about *you*. You seem to be a step ahead of me, holding the upper hand on so many things."

His look stayed serious. "I hold the upper hand because you give that to me, Les. I respond to your desire, what you need and want. With the right match between Dom and sub, that's how it works."

"So you're saying what I need works for what you need, too."

"Count on it. And there are plenty of things I don't know about you, too. I want to know them all."

"You get nothing else, until I see one of those dance moves."

He considered, those fine lips pursing. "All right. But only for you."

Stepping back, he spread out his arms, a mock gesture to clear the immediate area. With grave concentration, he executed a spin, followed by the steps and finger snaps Rufus had done.

As she'd noted before, Brick had exceptional grace for a big man. Which made his complete lack of rhythm nothing short of astonishing.

"Rufus might be right about you killing your team's chance of winning."

He lunged at her. She tried to dash away, but what he lacked in rhythm he made up for in speed and hand-to-eye coordination. He swung her over his shoulder, threatening to drop her as she shrieked and grabbed onto his belt. Grinning, he put her back on her feet, hands sliding over her sides and hips. "I can't be awesome at everything. Give me a break."

"My apologies," she said gravely. "Modesty and dance skills, both subpar. Check."

"There's my smartass." He offered her a hand and they strolled toward the bridge. "Your turn," he said. "Tell me something I don't know."

"My birth name was almost Celestial Joy Wilder, instead of Celeste Joy Wilder."

"That had to be your dad's idea, and your very practical mom nixed it."

They crossed under an old train trestle to reach the bridge entrance. A historical plaque indicated they were beginning the *Three Days in April 1865* exhibit.

"Markers along the bridge offer eyewitness accounts of the burning and taking of Richmond," Brick explained. "When it was the Confederate capital."

She read the entry plaque. *Follow the timeline of the devastation and of the emotions of defeat for many, and triumph for others, as expressed by witnesses during the evacuation and burning of Richmond...*

In her peripheral vision, she noted Brick reading with her. Watching him go over words he likely knew by heart, she wondered if Brick's father had ever figured out what she had. It wasn't the history that drew Brick. It was the poetry of people's emotions that historic events drew forth, as they suffered and triumphed.

Like her and Rufus, and Brick himself. "I can see why you like coming here."

She remembered at the diner, when talking was so easy between them. Kindred spirits understanding and connecting with one another. He met her gaze, and they started walking again. Their shoes, passing over wood and metal, made soft thuds and tinny echoing noises.

The witness markers were part of the decking beneath their feet, metal engraved plaques fixed to the wood. She thought of how three short days had perpetually changed the direction of so many lives. Hopes, dreams, fears. *Triumph and devastation.* What words could she say about the last two days of her life?

"My mom *is* practical," she said. "But when I hit puberty and she and I went through that rough period that a lot of mothers and daughters do, my father reminded me she hadn't always been so practical. That she'd been a girl once, and that girl was still there, a part of who she is now."

Just like the boy who fell in love with her is always a part of me.

Brick slid an arm around her waist, as if he knew talking about her father meant she needed more support. "There's more to the story about your name, isn't there?"

"Yes. But will you tell me something else about you first?"

His fingers glided along her shoulder, under her neckline, in that distracting way that was part possession, part shelter. All Dom.

"You asked, so yes. I like women with long hair. Before I have a session with a submissive, I French braid it, let them feel the pull as I bind their hair. Before I bind them in other ways."

"That's why you looked at me this morning the way you did, because I'd braided it that way."

After their erotic experience in the living room, she'd decided to leave it down, probably in anticipation of him doing what he was doing now, letting his fingers glide on that track, play in the strands. But thinking of why he'd liked it braided gave her a pleasant shudder of reaction.

"Yes." His gaze passed over it. "I like it this way, but I'd also like to see you react to me braiding it. What happened with the name?"

She couldn't go straight to the answer. Not yet. "Dad *was* a romantic. He was always working, but he also brought her wildflowers a lot. Or he'd stop at a yard sale and find something for her. He'd pick up something to justify the stop, like a rusty tool he'd clean up and use. But she knew. He liked to see her smile, and sometimes smiles were a little tougher to come by for them. But he could get her to do it, no matter what."

She glanced up at him. He was so tall, but when he looked at her like this, he felt so close. "Right after my grandmother died, my mother was having a hard time with it. One day, while we were all sitting on the porch, my father got up from the porch swing. He went out into the yard, looked up at the sun, and talked like he was having a conversation with it, though we couldn't hear what he was saying. He opened his palms, held them like that for a minute."

A trio of joggers passed them, feet thumping in rhythm on the boards. When they swung wide to bypass two women with strollers, Brick drew her closer to his side so Les wasn't in their path. The joggers went past.

"It's hard for oncoming traffic to miss you," she observed. "I'm a moped and you're a cement truck."

He squeezed her shoulder. "Mopeds are cute. And sexy," he added, at her censorious look. "Incredibly sexy. So what was your dad doing?"

It had been a Sunday afternoon, she and Rory on the steps, Thomas sitting on the rail. Her mother had been snapping peas in a metal bowl while sitting next to her father on the swing. Before he'd gotten up, he'd had his long legs stretched out, his arm on the top of the swing behind her.

"Suddenly, Dad brought his hands together, like he'd caught something. When he came back up on the porch, we wanted to crowd around and see, but he told us this was for Mom, and he'd show us in a minute. When he spoke in that voice, we knew to listen."

"I remember. Rory could be a real smartass, too, but he never acted that way around your dad. Or your mom."

"Especially Mom. Dad would have taken a belt to either Thomas or Rory for talking back to her. I never saw him do it, but according to them, once was enough for them to treat the rule as unbreakable as one of the Commandments."

"Did he ever take a belt to you?"

His look took her thoughts in a very non-paternal direction. She cleared her throat, ignoring his grin at her telltale discomfiture. "Dad didn't believe in overkill. I was less hard-headed. All he had to do was speak sharply to me and I'd feel skewered."

"Hmm." Brick moved them to the railing and stopped so they were leaning against it, standing side by side. They watched a skilled kayaker navigate the churning waters below. "So what had he caught?"

"He said, 'Honey, your mama thought you needed a ray of sunshine, and asked the sun to give me one.'" He opened his sun-warmed hands and put them on her face. She gave him this smile like she didn't know what to do with him, but loved him to pieces for it."

As Les turned and laid her hands on Brick's face in illustration, Brick's arm slid around her again, letting her lean into his side, his head bent over hers as she dropped her hands to his chest. "God, I still miss him so much. I can't imagine what it's like for her. But she said she feels him every day. Sometimes, when she's out in her garden, I've seen her take off her gloves, hold them up to the sun and put them on her face. I know she's imagining him doing it."

"So why did he want to name you Celestial Joy?"

She gave a half laugh. "It's so easy to get off topic with you, to talk about everything and anything."

His arm tightened. "You couldn't have given me a better compliment, doc. But you're not being entirely honest. There's something you're avoiding. I don't mind the route you're taking, but if you don't eventually answer the question, I may threaten to take a belt to you, just to see you get all flustered again."

"I never wanted my father to, I mean I never felt..."

"The same act can provoke two very different reactions. Like your father kissing you, a gentle, paternal brush against your cheek, the corner of your mouth," he leaned in and put his lips in those two places, lingering, moist, "and me doing it."

She closed her eyes, feeling his impact in all her senses. "I was early. Way early. The pregnancy didn't go as well as it had for Thomas and Rory. I...I almost didn't make it. I was in the NICU for a month. Paying my hospital bills was when my dad took a job outside the farm, plus doing odd jobs where he could."

Brick drew back to stare at her. "I didn't know any of that. Rory never mentioned it."

"Yeah. He was little when it happened, and by the time you came into our lives, it was long in the past. Things were better, and they'd shifted our primary income source from a working farm to the farm supply store. Plus, you know we're old school South. We don't talk about our own tough times. We help others with theirs and get on with life."

She offered a faint smile. "After I got up to the right weight and everything proved normal, no physical or mental adverse effects, they tried not to let it impact the way they parented me, compared to Thomas and Rory. But I still had a bigger dose of protectiveness, even for being the only girl and the youngest."

"Understandably." He gazed at her. "I could have lost you before I ever had the chance to read poetry to you."

"You really are making it difficult to finish this story." She didn't mind that at all. But he lifted an expectant brow, so she reluctantly continued.

"During my first forty-eight hours, things looked pretty bad. Mom told my dad, 'If she goes back to God, she'll be our eternal celestial joy, even if we only had a few earthly moments with her.'"

She offered a wobbly smile. "They'd intended to name me after my grandmother, but when the nurse needed to fill out the birth certificate, my father told her to put down Celestial Joy Wilder. My mother was still out of it, so the nurse wisely waited to check with her before finalizing it."

Les watched a blue heron land on a cluster of rocks, his feathered crest fluttering. "When she found out what Dad had told them to write, I'd started to improve. You know Mom's pretty religious, so she says Dad's willingness to list my name as Celestial Joy was a message that he'd accepted God's will. And maybe as a gift for that faith, God let them keep me. She also said God expected her to be the sensible one who would give me a less fanciful name. They agreed on Celeste Joy."

Brick's expression was so unfathomable she had to ask the question, a little defensively. "What?"

"I could see you in the hallway mirror," he told her. "Back in high school, when I was reading that poem. I still thought of you as a little kid. And I knew you had an obvious crush on me—"

He blocked her half-hearted punch, catching her fist in his hand. He opened hers back up, stroking her fingers. It took her back to how she'd felt about him then, so beyond her reach, but so deeply wanted and desired.

"When I read those lines to Rory and Todd, I saw the look in your eyes." He shook his head. "It was sort of timeless. As if the woman you'd be was there, and the man I was going to be recognized it. Just a flash, and we were back to being kids again."

He half smiled. "Maybe time has colored that memory, made me the 'fanciful' one, but I could never forget it. As you grew up, I'd see this serious part of you, one that felt things in quiet ways you didn't talk about to anyone. At the wedding, I realized how long I'd been thinking about being the person you shared those parts of yourself with. Maybe since that moment, though the time wasn't right until now."

You have his heart. What kind of message was the universe sending her when a childhood wish, a dream beyond her grasp, came to her just as her world was falling apart?

She'd destroyed someone else's life. How could she possibly allow love to save hers?

Brick stepped back, still gripping her hand. "C'mon, let's walk back. I need to feed you."

CHAPTER TWELVE

*T*hey returned to the green space near the parking area to eat their sandwiches. They sat on the same side of the picnic table so they could watch the James River activity, plus be hip to hip, thigh to thigh. After they ate, Brick put his arm around her, and she laid her head on his shoulder. Her mind turned over the words he'd said to her, what she could accept and allow them to mean right now.

She didn't know the answer to that, but she did want to keep learning more about him. So when they were back in the truck, she had a request.

"Tell me about another case. Maybe one with a happy ending? Do you have those?"

"Sure." As he backed out of the space, he put his hand on the head of her seat to glance behind the truck, his upper body twisting and thigh flexing as his foot moved from the brake to the gas and back.

What was between them had far deeper elements, but her reaction to his body alone could carry her like a cruise ship on a world tour. She gave herself a good mental shake before he caught her staring.

Sheesh. He's not that pretty. He has...big ears.

"This one isn't from our department," he said, "but the good stories get passed around. Remember me mentioning it's a good idea to hire a professional arsonist to set your fires? This is about one of those guys, only he wasn't so smart about who he hired to assist him."

As he bumped out of the park and onto the main road, Brick tossed her an easy smile. "Carl paid Larry to help him set a fire in a bar. When they broke in after closing, he told Larry to start sloshing the acetone around. Larry was nervous about the whole deal, though. He kept complaining about wanting a cigarette, but Carl told him to shut up and get the job done. So Carl starts the egg timer, which will set off the fire once they're clear. But when he turns around to tell Larry to bug out, he sees Larry with a cigarette in one hand, flicking the lighter in the other."

"Oh, no."

"Oh yeah. Carl wakes up on a patch of grass to find the bar surrounded by firefighters, cops and the arson investigator. Who leans over him, asks if he's okay, then proceeds to read him his rights."

As she chuckled, Brick shook his head. "It gets better. This was back when people still smoked in hospitals. Larry's down the hall from Carl, and Carl keeps telling the nurses to make damn sure he doesn't get any cigarettes, because he wants the son of a bitch to *suffer*."

He winked. "That story was so good it made it into a book called *Fire Cops*, by Michael and Charles W. Sasser. They brought real police experience to the stories, but ones like that gave you a breather from the more serious cases."

Which brought to mind the one he was working on. "Was your call at Rufus's about the Whitfield fire?"

"Yeah. One of the other investigators in our team is going to do a second interview with Colin this afternoon. He's getting some of the same vibes I am. I gave him my theories and he'll integrate those angles into his questions."

"Did you want to go with him?"

"Sure, but I've learned to let others do their part of the job. Particularly when I have something important that takes priority." He squeezed her hand. "I'm a workaholic, so making time for other things helps me maintain a balance. Seems like you struggle with that yourself."

She twitched, uncomfortable with the topic. "It's not exactly the same. There's so much to learn in medical school, they call it 'trying to drink from a fire hose.'" She sent him an arch glance. "I expect you get the analogy."

"I do. But Beulah feels you're pretty on top of stuff."

"I feel like I have to work twice as hard as she and the others do to earn that compliment. Thinking fast on my feet, putting that info together in a clinical setting, isn't as easy for me."

"Could that be a self-fulfilling worry?"

At her quizzical look, he pointed to her stomach. "The more anxious you get, the harder you push yourself. You worry so much about having the right answer at the right moment, could you be creating the mental paralysis that's slowing you down? If it's really slowing you down at all. Maybe if you can step back, shift perspective, you'll figure out the underlying reasons you're pushing that hard, or thinking that way about yourself."

"Beulah says I need to shove some Zen up my ass."

"I like your roommate. And just FYI, there are other things that can be put up there to loosen you up."

His teasing look made her anxious in a different, far more pleasurable way. It also told her he might be serious. While her initial reaction was *hell no*, she recalled his fingers stroking her rim, and the aroused reaction she'd had.

"I've never done anything there," she said. "Plus I'm not sure about it. Working an ER rotation, talking to the nurses and doctors about what they've seen come in, makes me pretty leery."

"That's why, if it intrigues you, you explore it with someone who knows what they're doing, and how to keep things safe and consensual. And mostly sane."

"Would you like...to do that with me? Anal sex." She was proud to throw that out there, since even with him driving, it was difficult to say aloud. However, the next light caught them, so his response came with his full attention upon her. Those gray eyes that could become heated steel.

"Yes, Les, I would. I'd like to put my cock in your cunt, your mouth, and your ass. I'd like to come on your body, mark you inside and out as mine."

She reminded herself to breathe, even as her hands curled against her thighs. "Is that part of...is that a Dom thing?"

"It depends on the Dom, and the sub. But the way your pupils dilated and your lips parted, I'd say it's definitely this Dom's thing. The sooner the better."

The light changed. He surprised her by pulling into a strip mall, and parking in front of a clothing store. Party and club dresses were displayed in the front windows, everything from flirty and fun to sparkly and formal. "I thought we'd look at something for you to wear tonight, if you want. Casual is fine, but most women like to dress up a little for these events."

"Oh, well. Yes." She was familiar with the store chain, and knew it had reasonable prices, but she also knew down to the penny what she could spend each semester. The extra gas to get here had blown her weekly budget.

"This one's my treat. Because I'm going to pick it out."

If he'd told her he was going to pick out a dress for *him*, he couldn't have surprised her more. When he came around and opened her door, he braced his hand on it and answered the question she was sure was written on her face. "I like the idea of you in something I picked out, bought and want you to wear. I'm not a 24/7 type Dom, but I've thought a lot about the things I'd enjoy doing with a submissive who's mine."

"So you haven't done this before?" She knew she shouldn't throw the hope out there, but she couldn't stop herself.

"No." He met her gaze. "When you want to know, I'll always tell you the experiences I've had with other women who enjoy submission. I don't follow some step-by-step rule book with each one. For one thing, every woman is different. But what I pursue with them does have clear rules about how far it will go." He gripped her hand. "I have no interest in limiting how far I go with you."

He tugged her out of the truck, bringing her against his side as he closed the door. But then he made her laugh with a startlingly accurate imitation of Beulah's voice, complete with a sassy head toss. "Let's go dress shopping, girl."

"What do *you* usually wear to these things?" she asked.

"The usual. Bare ass leather pants, no shirt, nipple rings."

"I'd give good money to see that."

"There's not enough money in the world to make me pierce my nipples. My mother would find out and Western civilization would collapse."

Her mother would be the same way. Les couldn't imagine what her mother would think about her daughter considering anal sex. Nor would Les ever wish to know.

If it was anyone but Brick, she wouldn't be considering it at all. He made her feel comfortable exploring things she hadn't before. Maybe because he also made it clear if she wasn't comfortable, he wasn't going to let her go too far down that road just to please him.

Despite his insistence that he'd be picking the dress, once inside the store, he encouraged her to browse. She always went to clearance racks first, and found one dress she was okay with there. He looked at it, glanced at her, then put it back and steered her over to the regular section. When she turned over the price tag, he closed a hand over hers.

"No looking. My treat, remember? I want to see what you like."

That presented her with a dilemma. What she considered a sexy dress were classic styles. A skirt a couple inches above the knee, with an attractive but not skin-tight fit. The neckline might show the upper swell of her breasts and create a little cleavage. Or have straps that stayed on her shoulders but revealed the lines of collar bone, neck and upper arms.

There were dresses here like that, but she also saw the kind where the skirt stopped barely south of the ass, with lower necklines and fabric that clung to every curve. Would he prefer those?

What pleased him mattered to her; that was the dilemma. It was kind of exciting, to think of wearing something for him that screamed pure sex, with teetering skinny heels that showed off her legs. Her fingers tightened on one of the tits-and-ass baring dresses. But the reality of wearing such a thing spiked her anxiety again. She'd be acting like something she maybe wasn't.

Like a competent doctor.

Stop that shit.

Her other hand was up, toying with her necklace. She couldn't wear a dress like that with her parents' cross around her neck. Yet she had no problem with wearing it to a kinky party. Being something different for one night wasn't wrong, not if it excited her. Or aroused him. Right? But what did he want her to look like?

Brick's big body brushed against her side. Taking her hand from the dress, he kissed her palm. When he made a discreet, teasing flick on the lifeline with his tongue, a tingle went through her arm, her fingers curling against his jaw. He lowered her hand but kept it in his grasp as he used his other one to flip through several of the dresses.

He pulled one free but also lifted the one she'd been holding. He carried them to the dressing room, drawing her with him.

"I want to see both on you." He put the mega-sexy dress in the front. "This one first. Then the one I picked out. Step out here for each." His eyes held heat. "If it wouldn't give the salesclerk an aneurysm, I'd go in and watch you change. But I'll be right out here."

He threaded his hand through her hair, stroking her scalp with strong fingers. "You're all right, doc. Have fun with it. Leave it alone for today," he reminded her. "You're working the problem by not working the problem."

"And keeping me in 'fun mode' will make me a better date." She didn't know where the bitterness or the less than subtle accusation of his motives came from, but she despised herself as soon as she said it. "I'm sorry, I didn't mean..."

His lips had tightened, but he moved his thumb to her cheek, doing a single stroke that, with the piercing look in his gray stare, stilled her.

"I don't give a shit about whatever mood you bring to this. I intend to take you to this party, watch you get hot and bothered by the stuff you see, and fuck your brains out afterward. I will wear you out until you fall asleep naked in my arms, not thinking of anything. Soon as you start to surface from that, to think and get anxious again, I'm going to spread your legs, put my mouth on your cunt, get you wet and slippery, and fuck you all over again."

Though he kept to a conversational murmur, anyone with eyes in their head could see the erotic vibes pinging between them. But he acted as if they were the only two people on the planet, leaning in to brush his mouth against her ear. "Go try on the dresses like I told you to do."

As she pivoted toward the dressing room, a cauldron of feelings suggested she fire off a smartass reply. She bit them back, but was stopped abruptly because he'd hooked two fingers in the waistband of her jeans. "Didn't hear your response to that," he said.

She looked over her shoulder and up at him. When she met his gaze, that part of her that responded to him in a very different way nixed the snark.

"Yes, Sir."

It could have scared her, that she responded to him that way, even in public. Especially because he seemed to know that. But the spear of lust in his gaze made her glad she'd found the courage to say what she wanted, rather than the evasion or defense she'd been tempted to use.

He released her and she slipped into the dressing room.

Les didn't give herself time to think. She stripped off her jeans and T-shirt and put on the tight dress. She'd been wrong about it barely covering her ass. If she bent over, it wouldn't cover anything. She guessed showing the crotch of her panties was the point. No bra was possible, because it was off the shoulders, a thin horizontal strap the only thing keeping the gathered neckline just above the nipples. The color was a shimmery gold velvet. She bet Beulah would look fantastic in it, filling it out with her more ample curves.

She didn't want to go out there, but she'd promised. She decided to stay barefoot, since her sneakers would look ridiculous with it.

When Les and her mother took Daralyn clothes shopping for her sixteenth birthday, they'd had to encourage her to wear anything that suggested she had an attractive figure. This dress was as far outside Les's comfort zone as a modestly fitted pair of jeans had been out of Daralyn's.

But being sexy wasn't about comfort. If it increased the heat in Brick's gaze, gave him that possessive look, she could rise to the occasion.

Still, she peered out of the dressing room door to see if anyone was nearby. Most the shoppers were female, but in her head, her mother's judging eyes were planted in every face.

Brick leaned against the nearest rounder. She focused on him to find the courage to step out. His gaze covered her top to toe, lingered on the expected areas, but not with any discernible reaction. "Okay. Try on the next one."

She should feel relieved, not hurt or embarrassed. But as she stepped back into the shelter of the dressing room doorway, she fidgeted, rubbing one bare foot on the top of the other. "Maybe going to this thing isn't such a good idea. I mean, if this is the kind of thing they wear."

"Look at me, Les."

She brought her gaze reluctantly back to him. "You are beautiful," he told her. "The dress is shit. You don't like it, and I don't like it. Go try on the other one."

Marginally mollified, but still a little confused, she nevertheless closed the door. She'd removed the dress when a brief spurt of air, followed by a light click of impact, drew her attention to the top of the door.

"Put this on under it," he said from the other side.

The changing rooms were in the lingerie section, and he'd apparently been browsing. The bra had shimmery black mesh cups, outlined with matching satin piping.

She stared at it. "How did you know my size?"

"I dried your clothes, remember?"

It was a reasonable answer, though with his attention to detail, she would have believed he'd accurately guessed. Especially if he'd had practice doing it. Most men weren't this comfortable in a woman's clothing store, let alone in the intimates section. But he'd said he'd never done this with another woman.

She gripped the bra to bring it over to her. When it didn't immediately slide her way, she tugged harder. She heard a chuckle as he let it go. "You're a big jerk," she informed him.

"Nothing you didn't already know, doc."

He moved away from the door. Since with his height he could easily look over the top, she assumed he was reassuring the sales staff they didn't have to worry about him being a peeping tom.

She slipped on the bra, hooked it and turned it around, adjusting her breasts into the cups. The shadowy mesh didn't conceal her nipples, the bra's design lifting and enhancing the size of her breasts. It felt decadent and nice, the silky sheer fabric, the satin edging against her skin. As she imagined Brick looking at her in it, her flesh swelled, the tips hardening. She was still wearing her cotton underwear, but she bet a matching pair of panties was out there. He probably already had them in hand.

She turned her attention to the dress he'd chosen. Black embroidery provided flirty coverage over generous expanses of black translucent netting covering the decolletage, short sleeves and back. Below the waist the dress flared out in a skater skirt that stopped mid-thigh. A gauze overlay matched the embroidered top and gave the illusion of several more inches of length. However, the shortness of the solid black fabric beneath drew the gaze to her thighs.

The hidden zipper in the side molded the dress to her figure. It was a good fit, intended for a skinnier, less curvy girl. She twisted to look at the translucent back, which created delicate shadows around her shoulder blades and revealed the satin bra straps.

If she bent way over, no panties would show. However, an errant breeze might just give Brick a glimpse. Or if he raised the skirt that last inch himself. What if he ordered her to bend over so he could see, or spank her or...take a belt to her? Was it twisted that his question about her father had made her mind jump to him doing that?

Brick didn't seem to feel it was twisted.

The other dress had made her stomach churn. This one produced playful butterflies, just as him holding onto the other end of the bra had done. Mixing sexual intensity between them with the right lighter emotions.

The dress was totally her. Sexy and fun, an undeniable touch of the sweet. With a woman's intuition of what that hint of innocence would do to his senses, the arousal in her lower belly tightened, a better stimulation increased by the most important thought of all.

He'd picked out the dress.

A tap on the top of the door, and she saw his big hand holding strappy black sandals with block three-inch heels. They'd look good with the dress, while the block style would keep her from ending up on her ass.

She reached up to take them, and his fingers overlapped hers. "Do you like the dress?"

"Yes. I do."

"Come out here and let me see."

"Okay. Let me put on the shoes for the full effect."

She slipped them on and, before she turned the door latch, she fluffed out her hair.

He'd moved back a few paces. She could view herself in the trio of mirrors outside the fitting rooms, but instead she merely stepped in front of them, so he could see her from all angles. The choice not to look at herself was done for a deliberate reason she could tell he recognized. And liked.

While wearing the other dress, she thought he'd given her a thorough look. Now she knew that wasn't true, because this was what thorough meant. He covered every inch of flesh exposed or hinted at beneath the sheer parts, as well as her curves molded by the solid fabric. She could feel his awareness of what was beneath, that transparent bra that would show him her taut nipples. When the dress was removed, he would tease her through the mesh with mouth or fingers.

The thinness of the bra and the dress couldn't conceal her physical reaction to the thought. Hunger flashed through his eyes. "It needs one adjustment," he said.

She frowned, suddenly uncertain. But as he approached, he put his hands on her upper arms, caressed her collar bone, and freed the necklace from where it had been left beneath the embroidered bodice. She was used to having it against her skin, but she didn't mind the change. Not when she saw his territorial expression as he made the cross and badge visible. The pressure of his fingers sent a ripple of sensation through her cleavage and lower. She curled her hands over his forearms.

"If you'd liked the other dress," Brick said, "it would have shown, and I would have liked it, too. I don't want you to be anything you don't want to be, Les. You're a good Catholic girl. I like that about you. And I love this dress on you."

When he brought his mouth to hers, he let the kiss spin out a few long seconds. Somewhere she heard a female voice murmur, "Lucky bitch," but it was said in the way Beulah would do it. Good-natured female envy, probably backed by a heartbeat skip, an echo of her much stronger reaction.

When Brick raised his head, he held her gaze. "And an even luckier bastard," he said.

She was able to hold onto the good feeling through the afternoon. Brick stopped to pick up a few groceries, getting her input so he could offer her a better selection of snacks and drinks. Though she insisted anything was fine, he was far better at insisting than she was.

However, even as he was caring for her, she noted how often he was getting texts. He also took a couple phone calls. He'd taken off work for her, at a time when he hadn't planned for that. So when they arrived at his place, she told him she needed to do some studying. Which was true, but would allow him to get some work done, too.

"Sounds good," he agreed. "But you should take a nap if you can. I'll wake you in time to get dressed for the party."

"Maybe. All right." She snagged a nut and fruit snack pack and a soda, and settled on the sofa in the living room. While being able to hear and see him as he worked in the kitchen, the position allowed her to concentrate. In theory.

She'd had a lot of practice tuning out her surroundings when studying. He was far more distracting than the norm. However, eventually the details of his phone conversations blurred to a reassuring background rumble.

Reviewing the ER rotation exam info and not connecting it to what she could have done differently that night was more difficult. Fortunately, her body seemed to be aligned with his suggestion—or maybe it responded to him as a Dom even more than her mind did. Her eyelids kept drooping. As she often did in her room, at length she fell asleep. Her body sank into the hold of the couch, the tablet resting against her side.

She didn't feel him remove it and put it on the table. Or spread the fleece throw over her. Her subconscious did register the press of his mouth, and she kissed him back, with a murmur of pleasure.

As Brick sat by her, stroking her hair, he remembered what she'd said to Rufus. That when she dreamed, she tried to fix what she'd done, and waking to the jarring realization there was no do-over turned it into a nightmare.

He'd seen her concern about his work, but there was always work to do. He'd knocked out a couple reports and handled his email, which was enough for today. He adjusted her so she was lying in his arms, across his lap, and made sure her sleep wasn't disturbed, even by her own mind.

When Brick woke her, as promised, he'd given her plenty of time to do her hair and makeup. As Les laid the dress on the guest room bed, her phone buzzed. Beulah was texting her a few cheerful things, keeping her connected with what was happening on campus. Les thought about sending a text to make her roommate's eyes pop open.

Going to a bondage party with the fireman.

She suppressed a smile, then saw another text had come in while she was napping. Her stomach did a sick flipflop.

It was from Dr. Portland, confirming the exact time for the M&M and reminding her that Legal wanted to meet with her that morning before it. They'd do that in Dr. Portland's office.

Confirm again that you will be there?

No matter that she'd been trying to follow everyone's advice about "giving it time," the war drums inside her hadn't abated. The text broke the sound barrier, and they beat through her senses all over again.

Like a festering cancer, pissed at being ignored.

Go find Brick. Go find him now.

The desperate thought shamed her. She couldn't be a coward. She wouldn't. She moved woodenly toward the bathroom. As she lifted her gaze to the mirror, she saw another woman standing before her, eyes so wounded, so broken, they should have been pouring out blood, not tears.

Panic clawed at Les's throat as she tried to speak. As she had tried to speak then. Hands on her, shaking her, a hand slapping her face. Mrs. DaCosta's wedding ring had cut her forehead. Her hand went to the mark at her brow, hidden under her bangs. Hospital personnel had pulled the mother off of Les, but those staring, anguished eyes had locked onto her, waiting for an answer she couldn't give.

Everyone had the dream where they tried to call out for help to save themselves, but no words came. This had been like that, except it hadn't been a dream, and Les hadn't been the one needing saving. She'd been the villain, the one who'd bolted into the rain-soaked garden. And run to Brick.

"Les?"

Brick was standing behind her. Blocking the doorway, keeping her where all those accusing emotions ricocheted off the walls and struck her. Like being stoned in a public square.

"I can't keep pretending everything is okay. Nothing has changed. I shouldn't have come. I need to go back."

She groped for the washcloth and hit the faucet handle to turn on the water. She would rub this shit off her face, scrub her skin like a wire pad applied to soap scum. Pull her hair back into a practical ponytail rather than letting it float around her face like a fucking fairy princess.

When he closed his hands over her wrists and pulled her hands away, she snarled. "Let me go. I'm not hiding behind you or this Dom/sub bullshit for you to make it better."

"You want a fight, doc? You want that wrestling match here and now? Go for it."

His voice was hard, so when he flipped her around, locked her back against his body, rage erupted from a terrible reservoir deep inside. More than she could control.

She screamed at him, feet lifting to kick at the walls and door. With Rory, she'd learned to wiggle, squirm and shove against things, to break his hold. But Brick moved them into the bedroom. Distantly, she realized he was using a psych hold, one she'd learned about during her Behavioral Medicine rotation. Not the modified version, which was less dependent on upper body strength and more on leverage and pressure points. Brick didn't have to worry about that choice. He could use the whole arsenal of strength and strategy together.

He wasn't the target of her rage. She jerked a hand free. He'd made her drop the cloth, so she'd use her nails to scrape off the makeup. Her swipe at her face opened up the scratch under her bangs before he recaptured her hand.

"Let me go."

"Stop trying to hurt yourself."

"Fuck you."

He nipped at her ear, teeth sharp enough to make her yelp. His voice was a harsh scrape over things too raw not to hurt from the contact. "If that's what you want, baby, that's what you're going to get."

She began to fight as dirty as she knew how. He didn't give an inch, staying in the open space of the bedroom, offering her no fulcrum. She couldn't throw elbows, couldn't grab onto anything. The only thing more frightening than being this out of control was knowing she was, and unable to stop it.

Words she'd give anything not to say, to not be true, overflowed, awful and overwhelming. "I broke her. I took everything from her. I can't fix it. I can't change anything." She shouted it at him, and at the universe.

Brick sat them down on the floor, her thrashing legs out in front of her, her arms pinned against her at the elbows. She was struggling, but couldn't move.

"Easy," he said. "Easy, doc. Let it out."

She kept fighting. Once or twice, she went limp and gasping. It was a wild animal's survival trick, intended to fake him out. He was obviously paying attention to something far deeper inside her. He didn't relax his hold until the limpness was genuine, the fury sliding away, replaced by exhausted, pathetic begging.

"Please let me go back to school, Brick. Don't let me dump any more of this on you. I need to deal with this."

"You are dealing with it." His heat covered her back, his breath against her temple. He had his long fingers wrapped over her fore-head, keeping her against his shoulder. He was rocking her, a soothing motion that was helping, no matter that she didn't want to feel better or be helped.

"Next week, you'll deal with the professional part of it. You're here to deal with the rest of it."

"I don't know what you're talking about."

"Ah, doc, you know better than to lie to me. Or to yourself." He put his teeth against her throat. "Why did you decide to be a doctor?"

"To help people."

"That's the easy answer. I think there's a deeper one. Every damn doctor knows this shit can happen. Why did you think you'd be the exception? Ask yourself that, Les."

Why did it matter? Why was Brick asking her things that threw the snarl of her emotions into a worse tangle?

Still holding her with one arm, Brick reached across the floor and picked up the washcloth. He pressed it to her forehead. She felt the wetness of the blood. "You need to trim your nails," he said.

"I didn't do that. I mean, the original cut. Mrs. DaCosta was hitting me. She was wearing a sharp ring."

"She shouldn't have done that," he said tightly.

"I shouldn't have let her child die. But hey, I get to go to a kinky sex party tonight in a kickass dress, so there's that."

"Les."

She closed her eyes and turned her face away, toward his shoulder. "You act like me freaking out didn't surprise you."

"I know how hard you've been working on managing your emotions. Even in your lighter moments today, it shows. Tell me what happened to set this off."

She couldn't look at him yet, but she could answer the question. "Just a reminder of the M&M time, and that I'm meeting Dr. Portland and Legal that morning. Stuff I already knew. Just seeing the text...I don't know. Please, I need to get up. I'm okay."

He helped her rise on shaky legs, but guided her to the bed so she could sink down on the edge of the mattress. She stared at the floor. "I agree with Rufus, the way he went with it instead of how Bobbi did. But...there are a lot of ways to help others in the world. Maybe I chose the wrong way. The thought that I might do it again..."

She paused. "No. Like you said. I will do it again. Medicine has too much guesswork, too many variables, to believe otherwise. I'm not sure if I can accept that. And if I can't handle that pressure, then it's three years of med school down the toilet. But better to wash out now than to become the kind of doctor who's too hesitant, that second guesses herself at the wrong moment."

She took a breath. "I have enough science credits. I could become a science teacher."

Throwing the idea out there should bring a sense of relief, but all she felt was dull, throbbing pain. "I know," she said, as he sat down next to her, braced an arm behind her. "I need to stop pushing myself to make big decisions when my head's so fucked up on all of this, when it's all just happened. But I can't figure out what the answer is, and the lack of it is unbearable."

Her fingers felt stiff, barely able to move, but he curved them over his palm, his other one on top. "That mother is grieving, Les, but so are you. I'm not putting your pain on the same level as hers, but it's not a competition. When someone dies, especially a kid, everyone who had a part to play asks themselves these questions, feels the loss."

He lifted her chin, not letting her escape his gaze any longer. He wasn't above being a bully, proving he still knew when *not* to be nice to her.

"I'm taking you to this party. As far as kinky sex being in your future tonight, I can almost guarantee that. It doesn't say you don't care, or that you're not hurting. It says your very overbearing Dom is making sure you keep moving forward, and balancing that out with other things, so the right answers *will* eventually come."

"There is no right answer. I was paralyzed that day. She was screaming at me, Brick. I wanted to at least say I'm sorry—no matter how less than nothing that was—and I couldn't even get that out. Now Legal says I *can't* talk to her."

"When you learned your dad had died, do you remember anything about those first few hours, anything anyone said to you?"

The shock and loss had been overwhelming, dulling every other detail. Brick saw the answer in her face and nodded. "Stay here. I'll be right back."

He crossed the hall to his room, returning with a straight-backed chair and his wooden brush.

Her stomach quaked, and she felt her eyes widen. His lips twisted with grim humor. "Tempting. Particularly when I can tell, as much as it worries you, you won't safeword over it. The right part of you centers and gets off on it. But I have something else in mind."

He set the chair down, and pushed the guest room door partly closed, revealing a full-length mirror on the back that framed the chair in its reflection. "Take off your shirt and come sit on the chair."

With the volatility of the past few moments, it took her off guard. Her hands worked in her lap. She'd been naked with him, and had told him things more intimate than she'd talked about with anyone in her life. Even so, as he stood waiting, fully dressed in black jeans, boots and a gray dress shirt that enhanced the color of his eyes—wow, she'd just noticed how he'd dressed for tonight, and it made her oblivious libido skip in place—she was too self-conscious and way more vulnerable.

"It's all right, Les." He gentled his voice and held out his hand. She let herself be drawn to her feet and guided to the chair, but once there, she couldn't figure out what to do.

He lifted the hem of her shirt over her head. He considered the bra she'd put back on in the fitting room while he paid for the dress and underwear. It was the satin one she'd donned this morning, a lifetime ago. "Damn, girl."

"Thanks. Beulah picked it out."

"The bra's nice. But I was talking about how you look standing in it and your jeans, your breasts quivering because you're nervous and worked up."

He slid a fingertip under the cup edge, making her eyes half close. He pushed the straps off her shoulders, one then the other, taking a beat to enjoy the effect before he slipped the button of the jeans. "You have a nice ass, doc. I like these jeans on it, but take them off."

She had to wiggle to get them off her hips, and he seemed to like that, too. She'd forgotten the additional benefit of wearing jeans the right amount of "tighter," particularly when being appraised by a man's avid gaze. The bra straps tickled her elbows, and the panties wanted to come off with the denim. When she hesitated, he gave her the firm order.

"All of it."

She'd forgotten about her shoes. He pressed her into a sitting position on the chair, square with the mirror, but dropped to a knee in front of her so she saw his broad shoulders, the flex of his ass and thighs. He removed her shoes and socks, stroking her feet and ankles as he did so.

"That first night, when you knelt to dry me, it felt so wrong." Her voice was scratchy from her screaming. "I didn't understand it."

"Do you understand it better now?"

"Yes. No. I don't know."

"How does it feel, me on one knee right now?"

"Different. You're taking control. It doesn't matter if you're on your knees or not."

"Good observation." He unclipped her bra and guided the straps fully away from her arms. After he set all her clothes aside, he rose and shifted behind her. Nothing blocked her view of herself in the mirror. "Open your knees, Les. Feet aligned with the legs of the chair."

There was no way she could do that. But maybe if she looked at him... Her eyes lifted to his as she complied. "Back straight," he continued. "Give me a little tilt so I can see your breasts better. Look at that, your nipples getting tighter just from me ordering you to do that."

His attention moved back up. "I'm going to brush your hair. While I do that, you look at yourself, not me."

"I feel funny doing that. Self-conscious."

"I get that. But are you going to obey me or not?"

She dragged her gaze to the mirror and her very naked and exposed self. When she squirmed, he touched her hair. "Look at yourself as I see you. Look at how your body is ready for me, for whatever I want from it."

That did change things. But it was still difficult. He must have realized that, because he added an additional incentive.

"I catch you looking at me, I apply this brush a different way. It'll be my choice if I choose the bristle side or the back. And whether I spank your ass or cunt."

She renewed her efforts. *Look at yourself as I see you.* Her naked body open, displayed for his pleasure. His desires. Her breath drew in at how shaped and pointed her nipples were, the hint of glistening moisture on her labia, dampening her curls. Just from thinking about herself the way he was. How he wanted her.

When he began to brush her hair, she had to resist the urge to close her eyes. Long, easy strokes, his fingers following behind, massaging her scalp. He was fixing how she'd messed it up when she had her emotional outburst, but he lingered over the task, until the strands were loose and silky on her bare shoulders. A few locks fell forward to tickle the tops of her breasts, held at that upward angle because of the arch he wanted in her back.

He set the brush aside and began to French braid her hair. Her stomach clutched, remembering why he said he did it. *Before I have a session with a submissive, I French braid it, let them feel the pull as I bind their hair. Before I bind them in other ways.*

It felt so different to have him do it, with the size, strength and heat of his hands. Each pull had meaning, that sense of restraint in his touch.

He addressed her inevitable dampening thought, that she wasn't the first woman who'd had her hair braided by Brick.

"I've done this to a lot of women, but the reasons aren't what you think. I have certain skills as a Dom, and there are submissives who want that experience. They're not seeking a relationship with me. It's just as likely they're already in committed relationships. To keep them safe during a scene, I reinforce that I expect them to follow my direction exactly. Braiding their hair is a ritual, me taking that control and them relinquishing it."

She wondered what specific skills he exercised, but she wanted to stay in this moment, feeling his hands upon her. Binding her to him with the act of binding her hair.

He tied it off with a rubber band from his jeans pocket. He put his palms on her shoulders, thumbs sliding over her collar bones. "You can look at me now."

When she complied, her body was quivering. Her tide of explosive emotions had left her in a state that made all of this an odd relief. Being in the chair, naked, no part of her hidden from his eyes. Obeying his will, watching him braid her hair.

He wrapped his hand around her throat as he leaned down and nipped her ear. He stared at her in the mirror. "Though it means a hell of a lot more between us, the reminder that goes with the braiding is the same. You follow my direction at the party tonight. Got it?"

A hard quiver went through her, but she nodded. "God, you have a beautiful cunt. You're gorgeous from head to toe. I'm guessing it's been a while, maybe never, since you relaxed enough to give and receive full pleasure during sex."

Stung, she flinched, but he pressed onward. "It's not a criticism, Les. It's a door I'm opening to let you look in, see what's there."

He straightened and stripped the belt out of his jeans. Though she felt a stomach drop like when she saw the brush, she was more prepared to be punished with the strap than have him do what he did with it instead. He looped it around one wrist, bringing her arm back, before doing the same with the other arm, binding her hands together behind the chair. He'd tied her in a way she couldn't shake loose, at least not quickly.

The actual loss of physical control set off alarm bells. Maybe because he'd been immobilizing her for far different reasons only a few moments before, and the impression was too fresh. "What are you doing?"

"Proving a point."

"I don't like this. Let me go."

He dropped to his heels, his hand on her shoulder. "Use your safe-word, and I will. Do you remember it?"

She did. The word was right there, she could use it. Should use it. But as she paused, he added another thought to the confused mix in her head. "The second you use that word, I untie you. But if you can trust that truth, you can choose to give yourself a few minutes to explore what's making you think you need it. I'm not going to hurt you, Les, in any way you don't want. Or let anything hurt you."

Her heart was rabbiting, her hands clenched over the strap. His covered it, fingers playing and linking with hers. "Go into your busy brain and tell me why you don't like it. While you think about it, I'll occupy myself."

He leaned in and put his lips on her breast. She shuddered as he passed over the areola, nipping gently at the area next to the peak. He began to work his mouth over the curve, teasing and kissing with heated firm lips. When he closed his mouth over the nipple, he cupped her breast, squeezed it to increase the sensation. How did he expect her to think, to answer the question?

"Tell me, Les. Or I'll stop."

He shifted between her spread knees and cupped both breasts, fondling them as he suckled one nipple, then the other. Pulling on it, pulling so much from her. She bit down on a guttural moan.

"I'm out of control. I'm tied up...helpless."

"Is that such a bad thing? To see where letting go, putting yourself fully into my hands, takes you? You have such hard little nipples."

"Brick..." She was gasping. When he slid a finger into the wetness between her spread legs, she jerked on the chair. "Oh God..."

"I love watching you break apart under my touch. I've waited a long time for it, baby."

The spread of her legs, the change of rhythm and pressure of his touch, held the climax out of reach. It astounded her, how aroused he could get her. More than she'd experienced during even actual sex with anyone else.

When he sat back on his heels, bracing his hands on her thighs, his fiery gaze swept her flushed face and trembling legs. Her toes were pressed hard to the floor. "This is exactly how I want you to feel tonight. Off balance, wet, needing what I'll do to you at the end of the night."

He wasn't going to...? He reached around her to loosen the belt and free her hands. He brought them to her lap, rubbing her fingers and wrists before he rose to his feet before her. She had to suppress another groan at the size of his cock against his jeans. Her sex contracted at the sight, as he drew her to her feet and steadied her. Touched her face to bring it to his unrelenting expression.

"Get dressed and fix your makeup if you want. Though I think your face is just as beautiful without it."

He moved toward the door, then turned back. "You going to go home for Easter?"

The fire in his eyes, the stiffness of his gait, told her that erection was aching. Yet the sadist was asking her about her holiday plans.

"Les." That piercing look. "I asked you a question."

It was all part of it, she realized. Commanding her attention contributed to the hardness of his cock, for the same reasons it soaked her cunt. She hadn't realized the power of that by looking at those pictures, but it had been there. The psychological stimulation was as overwhelming—maybe more so—than physical touch.

How Brick made her feel, the things he made her want, weren't about wearing sexy clothes for him. It was about responding to that Dominant side in a way that had his eyes darkening and that circle of need tightening around her, holding her in a way she wanted and needed.

His expression, his arousal, said he wanted and needed it, too.

"I hadn't thought about it." She hadn't realized Easter was that close, though she was sure her mother had mentioned it during their last phone call, a few days before... everything.

Les had told her she wasn't sure if her current rotation would allow her to make the trip. "The M&M is right ahead of Easter weekend, so no matter what happens, I'm guessing my weekend will be free."

But was she really up for that? For explaining to her family, facing them after whatever was decided and discussed...or what she herself would decide to do.

"What if we go together?" His attention sharpened. "Les, I told you that you could get dressed, but as long as you sit in that chair, you sit in it the way I told you."

She'd closed her legs and brought her hands into her lap to wring them nervously on her thighs, which rounded her back and covered her breasts.

Her breath shortened, a hitch lifting her chest. "Brick..."

That gentling to his tone again, the one that brought her back on point. "Do as I tell you, baby. It will help. Trust me."

She straightened, lifting her breasts to his intent gaze, and slowly shifted her legs open. When he gave her a short nod of approval, it did help. He'd said she was a submissive. Not submissive. Was this proof of it, how obeying his command, assuming this position, miraculously pulled her mind away from the turmoil and centered her?

"You want to go home with me for Easter?" she asked.

"I do. Since I'm taking you to your M&M, we can head for Fairhope right afterward."

Surprise almost switched her back to that defensive posture, but his look kept her still. "They won't let you come into the M&M. That's just for medical..."

"I'll wait outside. But I'm going, Les. I'm not asking your permission to do that. It's my decision. After it's done, after you've held it together, been strong and handled what you need to do, someone's going to be there to hold you. Or take you out for ice cream. You tell me you don't deserve that backup and support, you won't like where that conversation ends up."

His resolute expression, his braced stance, reinforced it. Over the past few years, the words, "I can handle it," or "I'll take care of that" had become as SOP as her now pointless mirror mantra. She was strong-willed and determined. Whenever she spoke those phrases, they were accepted.

She should insist that she do this on her own. But he didn't give a shit. He was going to be there. And if she decided to go home for Easter, he would take her to her family.

"So, you'll follow me in my car..."

He shook his head. "You'll ride with me. I've already talked to one of the guys I work with about it. He and his wife have family in Durham. They'll take your car back there over the holiday and leave it at your condo."

The feelings that swept her were so strong it almost brought back the tears. "Okay. I'll think about Easter."

His gaze slid back over her, slow. His lips tightened as she straightened further, lifting her chin, feeling her heart thud and her sex throb under his appraisal. God, she wanted him. So badly.

"We leave in fifteen minutes," he said. "And Les, before tonight is over, I *will* be inside you. I like making you wait and want that so much you'll beg me for it. I like the idea of being the one who gives you something you want that badly. Do you like that idea, too?"

"Yes," she whispered. "Yes, Sir."

CHAPTER THIRTEEN

"*D*on't worry, you're not going to be mugged."

As he pulled into the parking lot, she was glad Brick offered that reassurance. They'd reached a much seedier looking part of Richmond, and rather than passing through it, he'd pulled into the parking lot of a dingy, large building. The tall neon sign by the road was unlit, no lettering and a couple jagged holes in the plastic face.

The building looked like an abandoned nightclub. Perhaps during the disco era.

On closer inspection, she did note the lot's paving was black and smooth, and three tall security lights illuminated the entire area, currently occupied by about a hundred vehicles. She also saw two people at the double doors, with watchful expressions and dark suits, upscale security for arriving patrons.

The women approaching the entrance wore provocative clubwear, but she didn't feel out of place in her dress. Brick's jeans and button-down seemed to match what most the men were wearing, though some had gone more formal, with slacks and jackets over an open-necked shirt.

He handed her out of the truck. "Okay?"

Facing the new environment, her feelings were back on a roller coaster. "It was easier in the chair, to stay focused. When..."

He gave her an interested look. "When what?"

"I think you know."

He turned her to him. "I'm sure I do. But you're going to say it out loud."

"When you were in total control."

"I'm still in total control." He laid his hands on her shoulders, thumbs against her pulsing throat. "Put your hands on my chest, Les."

She spread her fingers over the wide expanse, feeling his heartbeat against her palms. "There are no expectations here," he said. "You experience this how you wish to experience it. Ask whatever questions you want. Of me, or of the other people here."

"I can do that?"

"If they're not in the middle of a scene, yeah. Most welcome them from people who have a genuine interest." He pointed a finger at her. "No flirting with the other Doms, though."

She chuckled. "I feel so crazy inside. Afraid I'm going to mess something up."

He put a hand under her chin, bringing her up on her toes so she had to hold onto him as he kissed her. "That's not possible. You know why? I've already told you."

"Because you're in control." Just saying and believing it stabilized something inside her.

Then he pressed another kiss against her lips, resurrecting all those aroused feelings he'd stirred at his place. "Exactly. You're under my supervision. You're safe within that protection. Everything you feel and do within that circle is okay. Long as you're letting yourself feel and react honestly, you can't mess anything up here, Les. I promise."

"Brick... What if my reaction to you, to this, is just another way of escaping what's going on in my life? I want to be honest with you, too. I don't want to hurt you by immersing myself just to get away, and then, on the other side of this..."

When his gaze flickered, she swallowed. "You've thought of that, haven't you?"

"Yeah. I have. But you have a total submissive's response to my Dom side. You're not playing at it. It's part of you. How long you want to pursue that feeling with me, well...that's no different from any other relationship. I may only be your first Dom."

She hated that idea. Hated that he could even put it out there, like he could learn to accept it. Then she took a closer look at his expression, the effort to control what was behind it. "That's not what you want."

"It sure as hell isn't." His jaw eased a fraction. "But it's a question only you and time will be able to answer. It's a question we'll explore in everything we do. The answer will come when it comes. It won't be tonight."

Brick slid an arm around her to move them toward the door. A lot of the women on those skinny tall heels she'd thought about were using the arm of their escorts for balance, but Les thought the contact was about more than stability. It was reinforcing connection.

The security people recognized Brick and let him pass. Inside, the foyer was crowded as people milled and greeted one another, but they all seemed to be pressing forward toward a wide opening like a loading dock door, screened with dark rubber curtains. She was walking on cement flooring. The walls had chipped sheetrock. Fluorescent lighting gave things an unattractive greenish glow and she caught a faint scent of mold and old cigarettes.

"You're right." She rose on her toes to speak in Brick's ear. "We're not getting mugged in the parking lot. It'll be in here."

He grinned and held back a section of the curtains so she could pass through their barrier. When she saw what was on the other side, she was so surprised, she stopped in her tracks. He had to nudge her forward and off to the right, so they weren't blocking incoming foot traffic.

She expected all of those new to the club tonight, like herself, would be easily identified by their gaping trout reaction.

The warehouse-sized space before her was broken up by a series of Ionic columns. Beyond being functional, they were wrapped with screens. Erotic videos and images flowed across the curved surfaces. The columns were protected and decorated by slim spirals of glossy black iron that circled them from the bases to the high ceiling.

The floor was a liquid epoxy, swirls of purple and gold complimenting interior walls painted dark purple and mapped with velvety fleur-de-lis. Mounted wall sconces threw light through multifaceted gold-edged glass.

Other lights hung from the rafters on poles. They had various illumination levels, suggesting individual wiring to provide more or less light, depending on the activity happening beneath their scope.

Three bartenders were busy behind a polished wood and brass bar along the wall to her left. Beyond it, an illuminated gold sign directed people to changing rooms and restroom facilities. Music played over hidden speakers, a thrumming instrumental with an edgy rock-n-roll sound to it.

"Holy shit," she murmured.

The deep rumble of Brick's chuckle rippled through her. The scents were definitely far more pleasant and provocative than what she'd tried not to smell in the foyer. Every sound, fragrance and visual in this space was infused with erotic possibilities. The thought sent tingles up her spine, like the trail of his fingers there.

"Mick bought this building a few years back and retrofitted and renovated the inside. He intentionally kept the outside and foyer looking like shit. We're a private BDSM group, with approved membership requirements. Guests are allowed, but only those accompanied by a member who vouches for them."

Brick's gaze swept over the open area. "Regardless, Mick always sets a limit of three hundred and fifty people in here, so there's enough room to play and see everything. When it was a nightclub, the capacity was about a thousand. He does these three-day events once quarterly, and a regular event monthly. Members can also rent it for their own private parties."

"Mick must be loaded. Or the membership fees are astronomical."

"The fees are scaled to income, which is how I'm in here," he said dryly. "He personally approves every membership, and there are rectal exams less thorough than the questions and background checks. Rumor is he was a cop before he was doing this. Or a CIA interrogator. But yeah, you're right. He's either loaded or has backers he doesn't talk about. He claims this place is a hobby, like a backyard garden or woodworking."

She looked around her. "It's a hobby he takes pretty seriously."

"He takes everything seriously. I better not introduce you to him. You're kindred spirits."

"I heard rich. Is he good-looking?" When he grabbed for her, she laughed and let herself be caught. Then gasped when he lifted the back of her skirt and gave her a slap, right against the silky panties he'd bought.

He'd hit the lower part of her buttocks. The sting had maximum effect, sending a crazy ripple through sensitive nerve endings. He'd done that in front of people, their environment making it totally acceptable. If he'd done such a thing in a grocery store she would have reacted with embarrassment and dismay, and slugged him. Instead, arousal claimed her response. Much as his gesture had claimed her, for all to see.

As he rubbed the offended part, her fingers were tight on his fore-arm. "Better behave in here, doc." His eyes glowed. "Let's wander. See what everyone's doing."

But as they moved further from the curtained entrance, the music faded away. Signs that had been darkened now lit up with one word, in a glowing purple the color of phlox.

Quiet. Quiet. Quiet.

Conversation magically died away. Brick bent back to her ear to whisper an explanation. "This happens about once every hour. For five minutes, they play sounds from the play spaces right now, mixed with what's been recorded earlier in the evening and at previous events."

He shifted behind her. They were next to one of the pillars, the lights from the images flickering over her skin. He leaned against the iron spiral as he gripped her waist. "Close your eyes. Open them slow when I tell you."

The mashup hadn't yet started, so she could hear what the music had covered. The movement of people was like a wave, the rustle of their clothing, their hushed whispers. She jumped a little as a sharp crack split through that wave, followed by a gasp, a moan. More cracks. Rhythmic thuds. The clank of chains. Then the speakers started to fill in the composition. With words.

"Lift your ass. Don't hide that beauty from me. It hurts, doesn't it?"

"Yes...yes, Master."

"Tell me you want more."

"Please..."

More gasps and sighs. A tearful plea for more, for mercy. Followed by a teasing reminder that only a safeword brought mercy.

More spoken commands. *Listen. Bend over. Spread for me. Take it. Give this to me.* Loving reassurances. *You please me. I love seeing you like this. Love seeing you beg.*

Whenever she became apprehensive, unsure about the noises or cries, her body communicated it to Brick. He gave her the whispered reassurance she needed, the information to fill in the blanks.

"That snap is a single tail whip... that thud is a paddle or an impact toy like it. The whistling sound is a cane. That's the one causing the shriek. It stings."

He paused at a smacking sound, measured out like a precise drumbeat. Her hand tightened over his at her waist. "That's a bare hand," she said, her throat dry.

"Yes, it is. It tells me a lot, that you recognize it."

He slid his other hand under the skirt, his thumb passing over the crease between thigh and sex. She started to shift into the touch, but he held her fast.

"You don't direct me. I direct you," he said. "When you hear submissives moaning, crying out, gasping, they're telling their Doms if they're okay, or if they need a minute. That clank of chains is when they pull against their restraints. If you listen hard, you can hear the vibrator as a Dom treats his sub to forced orgasms..."

As he drifted off, she detected the grinding buzz, the staccato wailing cries of a woman getting closer to climax. The desperate plea escalated into a hoarse, full-bodied scream, giving it center stage over the rushing undercurrent of all the other sounds.

Les's hands white-knuckled Brick's forearm, his arm banded high on her waist. He was cupping her breast. When he ran an easy fingertip over a nipple, it was so aroused beneath her thin bra the reaction zinged through her chest and lower belly like a weighted pinball. He kissed her shoulder, then pushed her neckline down with a thumb, reaching under the bra cup to bring flesh to flesh.

"Oh..." She leaned against him, pulse pounding between her legs and in her throat. Her body was shuddering.

"I bet if I put my hand between your legs, you'd come right here, wouldn't you?"

Her throat worked as she nodded against his rough jaw. What she was hearing was threatening to spark her reaction to pure flame. A shocked little moan came from her as a mic somewhere picked up his voice, making the question reverberate through the club. The echo of her moan was overlapped by other words, cries and sounds of pleasure, coming from elsewhere in the building.

"Oh my God."

"Open your eyes. Look at what the world around you has become."

She saw people rooted to the spots they'd been when the signs lit up. Many were doing intimate things like she and Brick were. It was a primitive forest of sexual response, swaying with the winds of need.

"How can someone...force an orgasm?"

"In this case, he's using a vibrator. He puts it against her cunt, binds her so she can't stop or adjust it, do anything to mitigate the sensation. You know how you stop when the vibration gets so over-whelming? She can't do that. It's excruciating, a sensual torture. He might leave it on her for a while, so it will take her up as many times as he wants her to endure it."

She thought she could still hear the hum. Though the woman's cries had died away, a quiet keening amid the currents of noise might be her, her Dom keeping her strapped to that relentless vibration.

"Will he grant her mercy when she begs for it? Even if she doesn't safeword?"

"Depends on what he knows about what she really wants and needs. He'll push her to a certain point beyond when she begs for mercy, just to remind her he's calling the shots, unless she safewords. Because she wants that reminder, too."

The Quiet lights went dark, the music returning. She was glad for Brick's arm around her, the time he gave her to steady herself after he took his hands away from her most flammable points. When he did move her forward, he did it at a slow stroll. While it was intended to let her take in all she was experiencing at an easy pace, it was still...so much.

The people who seemed to be milling in groups were actually grouped around stations, the source of some of the sounds she'd heard. Les saw a metal frame at one, big enough to hold a man and a woman. They were bound in rope and suspended in the air a few feet away from one another. Her ropes were purple, his black.

The woman's rope Dom or top—Brick murmured that either term could be true—was still adding to the design. He adjusted the woman's foot so her heel was bound more securely against her buttock, her arm behind her, back arched. She looked like the figure-head on a boat's prow.

Les's knowledge of joints, ligaments and muscles told her, even with the toned and flexible body the woman had, the position had to be uncomfortable.

She posed the whispered question to Brick. Other people were talking, but she still felt hushed, like she was in a church. "Extreme suspension can be uncomfortable, even painful at first," he responded. "But those who love being rope bottoms say you settle into it. Many even reach a deep subspace trance."

The woman did look almost dreamy. The other rope top was female. She was leisurely rotating her bound male on a hook while walking around him. Her absorbed appreciation was as compelling a part of the view as the bound man himself. She had a tasseled whip in her hand. She flicked it over reddened areas of his flesh, exposed between wraps she'd arranged like a sun beam along his torso and hips.

He was an older man, but still in good shape for the workout the suspension would give him. He had a silver cage on his cock and balls, and the cage had a padlock. The female Dominant wore a silver key around her neck. It gleamed against her white blouse. Beneath a leather skirt she wore polished black army boots.

When the Domme noticed Les's astounded expression, her lips curved. She gave Brick a courteous acknowledgment before turning back to her sub. After she stroked his whipped flank, she reached between the cage bars to tease his erect length with her nails. His cock was pressed uncomfortably against the confinement.

"Okay?" Brick asked her. Les realized she was shaking, though she knew it wasn't fear. Maybe something more unsettling.

"Yeah. Yes. I...Can we see more?"

"We sure can. Keep breathing, though."

They passed a female sub tied to a wooden X, her Dom using a flogger on her bare back. The black and silver strands look electrified under the spotlight. Her back and ass were streaked with a red flush, but his strikes didn't seem overly hard.

"The repetition can do that," Brick explained. "Just because a sub likes impact play, doesn't mean she likes lots of pain. Sometimes the biggest turn on is the restraint, the idea of being punished, or serving the Dom's desires. The longer they've been playing together, the deeper the trust, the more likely they might investigate more extreme levels together. But not always."

They'd reached the station with the submissive enduring the

forced orgasms. As she gazed upon the scene, Les became even more aware of Brick's touch, the press of his body against her.

The spiraling iron around the pillars had a use other than protecting the video screens. The woman was bound to it, her arms behind her, a web of ropes holding her fast from just her shoulders to her upper thighs. Her bare breasts were held between two wooden bars screwed down to distend the curves. Her nipples, darkened from the blood pressure, jutted forward. The vibrator had been fitted into the wraps of rope over her thighs, keeping it against her clit. Though she struggled from her arousal, the ropes wouldn't allow her any relief from the stimulation. Tracks of fluid dampened the rope around the vibrator head.

Her Dom, a husky, bearded man with bright blue eyes, wore a utility kilt, chain belt and black T-shirt. He had his hand on her face. When he pushed his thumb between her lips, she sucked frantically on it, her gaze feverish. "One more time, baby. Then Daddy will hold his good girl and rock her to sleep. Tell her a story."

Her eyes pleaded with him, but something in the agonized gaze said she also wanted to do what he said, be a "good girl." The two words were tattooed on her neck, along with a tiny blue teddy bear.

Les understood that push-pull between what you could endure and what you wanted to give, to someone you would give everything to... It burrowed into her head, made her heart and body ache. Her sex was throbbing. What did Brick like to call it, the word that heightened her arousal every time he used it? Her cunt. Her cunt was throbbing.

She didn't know if she wanted Brick to do to her what this man was doing to his submissive, but she definitely wanted something that felt like just as much, just as intense, just as...everything. How could she explain that? She wasn't even sure she could explain it to herself.

"Let's keep going," Brick said. "You're getting a little over-whelmed."

Could he tell the strength of what she was feeling here could disrupt the darker things inside her? The emotions were too similar, too connected to all the things that mattered to her, to her sense of herself. They could rise up and tear her to pieces.

They were already there, like wolves snapping at the heels of a fleeing deer.

She let herself be led onward. Though the girl's eyes rolled in her direction, Les doubted she was seeing anything, not in her current feral state.

They passed partygoers on vinyl sofas and easy chairs, watching the scenes closest to them as they enjoyed drinks and conversation. One of the submissives, a plump woman with blond hair and nipple piercings, was on her knees, on the floor next to her seated Dom. Her slim collar was attached to a leash wrapped around his hand. She sat on her heels, back straight, hands clasped behind her back.

Brick had required her to sit like that, back straight, breasts on display and knees parted. All of her available to his gaze and touch. Even when they'd been talking about difficult things in his bedroom, that reminder had kept her intently focused on whatever he demanded. As well as so aroused, she couldn't think about anything else.

Another sub sat in her Dom's lap. They had their hands laced together, playing finger games. The sub was mostly clothed, but her knees were spread, the Dom's other hand beneath the skirt, knuckles pushing up against the cloth as he stroked her in a relaxed manner. Her skin was flushed, showing he was keeping her worked up, even as they smiled and whispered to one another.

Intimacy, teasing, straight out physical demands. Love, liking, lust. Even controlled violence, and the passion that broke open every secret. It was all here.

She hadn't known all the possibilities, hadn't realized how far they could stretch beyond her own imaginings. Some of it seemed much more extreme than she'd ever want to go, even as it fascinated her.

The emotions surged again, and she realized she wasn't breathing. Couldn't breathe. Or she could, but it wasn't going right or well.

"Brick..." She clutched at him. "I can't..."

Instantly, he shepherded her into a less populated corner. He sat her down in a chair and angled it toward the wall, so she was gazing at velvet fleur-de-lis and gold-faceted lights. As she started to hyperventilate, his hand was on her neck, gently propelling her forward. Air starvation was a terrible, panicky feeling.

She gripped his other hand, feeling mortified, which made the sensation worse. "I can't...I'm so sorry..."

"Not a thing to be sorry for. Just take it easy. Breathe. It's a lot. Remember, nothing is wrong. No expectations."

He wouldn't let her talk, just having her breathe and calm down. When she was able to sit back, she was still holding his hands tight, but she could draw a normal breath. He sat on his heels next to her, stroking her bangs, touching her ear and cheek. Stroking that healing cut.

"I like all of it, but it's so much. I don't know if I can do anything but look tonight. I'm so sorry..."

"Well, fuck. I signed us up for forced orgasm play as soon as that station opens up."

Panic stabbed her, and she started to stammer out a *what the hell* comment. When she noted the amusement in his gaze, mortification grabbed her. "I'm an idiot." A total unsophisticated idiot, nothing like Tish or anyone else he'd played with here.

"Hey." The amusement disappeared. He put his knuckles against her cheek, a tender pressure. "That's the last thing you are, and I better not ever hear you say that again. I shouldn't have teased you like that. This is a world I'm pretty used to, so it made me say something stupid. Too soon."

"That's the problem." She hiccuped, stammered. "You know this world, this is your world, but how can this be my world, and if I want to be with you..."

"Why do you do that? You immediately assume I want something from you that you can't deliver."

"But this..."

"This is a bunch of people with a common interest, but a whole lot of different needs going on. You're smart enough to see that. Don't mess up your enjoyment of the view by clouding it with what you think I'll expect from you."

His tone told her he wanted her out of her head, paying attention to what he was telling her. "Here's what I noticed. You have some interest in being restrained, but not necessarily suspended, which is good, because I don't do rope suspension. Unless it becomes a big interest for you, I don't like the idea of letting any other Dom do stuff with you, even under my supervision. Spanking and some impact play is really intriguing to you. You like the sensation, the idea of marking, but not hardcore welts and bruising. How am I doing so far?"

She hadn't realized how closely he'd been watching her at the stations. Which was good, because it might have made her self-conscious. Or not. "I...yes. But—"

"You're just listening right now. And breathing. Especially breathing." He tapped her hand once before continuing. "The forced orgasm really sucked you in. It's an edge play that emphasizes a complete loss of self-control. The deep part of you that responds to that need is tied to a bunch of other shit. That's where the panic attack started, and I should have seen it."

His jaw flexed. "You were also looking at Jace and Millie. They're sitting on the couch, him with his hand between her legs. That intuitive part of you picked up on the trust between them. Every time she's surrendered control and he's proven he'll protect the parts of herself that surrender has revealed, they've reached deeper levels of trust. Trust that goes so far down there's nothing hidden. He sees her, knows her. Loves her. She does the same with him."

He held her gaze. "Whatever we choose to do together, whatever interests us, I suspect we both want that to be our ultimate goal. Tell me if I got anything wrong."

Instead of being able to reply, she had to put her hand to her chest as it hitched with a near sob. It came with some pain, an air bubble she had to work around. He closed his arms around her as she shuddered. "It's okay," he said softly. "I get it."

"I'm glad you do," she managed. "Because I don't. I don't understand all these feelings, what they mean, where they're coming from this week."

"You'll figure it out." His lip curled wryly. "Until then, I'm here to create distractions and cause panic attacks."

"The distraction part I agree with. I caused the panic attack myself. I really do like it here."

That was part of why it was so unsettling. She never wanted to leave, never wanted to stop looking, thinking, feeling. In this environment, she'd stopped being mortal, transformed into a being of pure sexual energy.

Until she hyperventilated, that is. Her gaze slid past Brick's shoulder. Though there were people nearby, they had recognized she and Brick were in the middle of something. Averted eyes and keeping their distance had created a cone of privacy that included only the two of them.

Or maybe three. A man was leaning against a pillar a few feet away, watching them closely. When he saw her attention, he dipped his head with respectful courtesy.

"That's Mick." Brick didn't turn, his words telling her he knew the man was there. "In case you passed out, he wanted me to have help close to hand."

Brick rose and shifted to stand at her side. His hand on her shoulder told her he wanted her to stay sitting.

As Mick closed the few strides between them, Les saw startlingly sharp-pupiled eyes with irises that could be brown or blue, the club lighting making it too difficult to determine. His ginger-brown hair, a thick wave of it brushed back from a high forehead and square, strong face, matched the groomed beard. His shoulders and torso under the fitted blue shirt said he was solidly built. While not as tall and broad-shouldered as Brick, that didn't make him a lean or small man, since most men weren't Brick's size.

Mick wore brown slacks with the shirt, which was open at the throat, revealing a silver crucifix. A blade of some kind had left a shiny, mauve scar from his collarbone to a couple inches past the cross's resting place. On closer inspection she realized the figure on the crucifix wasn't Jesus. It was a skeleton, and it was hugging the cross, not crucified on it.

"All right?" he asked Brick.

"Yeah, I think so. Just too much all at once."

Mick squatted in front of her. With a somber look, he produced a fruit and nut bar that included dark chocolate. He also had a juice box, a cheerful-looking kitten printed on it.

"No insult to your age," he told her. "The small straw encourages a submissive in need of hydration or sugar to take small sips. The box keeps her from spilling any on her clothes."

"What about the kitten?"

"That's my own indulgence, I'll admit. Female subs are a basket of kittens, endlessly fascinating, fun and sweet."

"You said that in a very non-condescending way," she managed. "It's impressive."

His mouth had a stronger tug on the right side than the left, when it curved in a near smile. The wistful quality contrasted with the still and focused eyes. "I'm an impressive man. Brick should have told you that."

"Yeah. I didn't." Brick gave him an amused look. "Thanks, Mick. Appreciate the backup."

Mick rose. "My pleasure. You didn't anticipate her reaction to this. You're usually a hundred percent ahead of the curve. Interesting."

Brick's gaze narrowed, but Mick merely nodded to him, then to Les, before he moved away. He slipped through the crowd, a nonintrusive shadow, yet with enough presence people unconsciously shifted out of his path. "Does he supervise the whole event?" she asked.

"He pitches in when he sees the need. There are DMs all over the place. They're the ones in purple shirts with black skirts or slacks. They also have black neon-lit lanyards with DM ID tags, to make them easy to notice and find. Dungeon Monitor," he supplied at her blank look. "They monitor activity in a BDSM play space, which is sometimes called a dungeon, because..."

"The restraints, torture and—" She turned her head, squinted to be sure she was seeing what she was seeing, "people in cages?"

Brick's gaze became amused again. "Yes. But consensual restraints and torture."

"Like forced orgasm. Orgasm and torture in the same sentence. Something I never thought about before." She rubbed her forehead. He took the juice box from her lap where she'd left it and poked the straw in it.

"Sip," he instructed.

"Okay. Can we turn the chair around?" She wanted to see what was going on, but with the steadying buffer of the chair and more distance.

"Sure." He did that without her having to move, then brought another chair so he could sit next to her. She opened the fruit and nut bar, broke it in half and offered it to him. He shook his head. "You have all of it. You got way too pale on me there. He's right. I should have been ready for that. Some of this stuff can seem pretty extreme on first look."

He drew her attention back to the forced orgasm scene. "But watch and see what's happening now."

The submissive must have reached that final orgasm her Dom had told her he wanted her to endure. He'd removed the vibrator and was untying her, even as he kept touching and talking to her.

While Les couldn't hear what was being said, he wasn't detached, even if he'd physically appeared that way for some of it. So much more was happening. They were going through the experience together.

As he released her bonds, she slumped, but he was there to catch her. They'd been doing the scene on a raised platform, so he sank down onto the top step with her on the step below him, but still between his spread thighs. One of her arms was wrapped around his leg, her painted pink nails overlapping the denim. Her head rested on his thigh. If she could climb inside him, Les thought she would. The teddy bear and *good girl* tattoo was a soft blur against her skin.

"Edge play can be incredibly intimate, Les. There are also a lot more casual kinds. Sometimes it's about nothing more than that, everyone going their separate ways at the end of the night. Everything you see, every scene, can be as different as the reasons any two people or more hook up."

"Like you and Tish?" she ventured.

"Yes. I'm not in love with women who want to scene with me. But I take care of them as long as they're my responsibility. That's part of being a good Dom."

"Mick's a Dom, isn't he?"

"I don't know." He shrugged at the surprise in her expression. "He refuses classification, and I've never seen him do anything other than primal play. Though that was with a Domme. She used to be a prison guard, so it was an interesting thing to watch."

She bet it had been. "You're right. I liked Jace and Millie. I love all of this, but I do want romance."

His face creased with a smile. "That's good. I love doing romantic shit for and with my girl."

His girl. She liked the sound of that. But she sobered. "I'm not used to turning this much control over to someone."

"Not used to being able to, maybe. Not without giving up too much. You've worked hard for that autonomy, the right to choose your direction." He met her gaze. "I respect those boundaries. If ever I don't, I expect you to remind me."

She believed him, but... "If I do, will you listen?"

"Because you know I'm every bit the testosterone-poisoned, protective bastard that your brothers are?" When she gave him a guileless look, he chuckled. "You're pleading the fifth."

"Or not seeing the need to repeat what you've stated so brilliantly.

"Remember what I said about a smart ass?"

She smiled, but then sobered. "I like watching a lot of this, Brick. But I worry that I won't be as interested in doing what you want to do, and I'll disappoint you. I know what you said about no expectations, but..." She spread out her hands. "You said it, I'm a submissive. I can already tell pleasing my Dom matters to me. A lot."

"Which is why it's his job to remind you that it will never please him to do something you don't want to do. Even when a sub dreads what a Dom is going to do, there's a stronger part of them that wants to do it. Their desires match."

He nodded toward the Dom and sub at the forced orgasm dais. "All of us know it when we see it. Even if it's a type of play that I'm not interested in doing myself, I'll get turned on by watching it, because that common element is there. It's the same one that makes it work for each of us."

The words reassured her, his obvious sincerity. "I know I'm trying to micromanage something I'm just learning about," she admitted.

"Control the outcome, manage expectations, make sure you aren't letting me down." He touched her face. "It's your habit. Which is exactly why, if you decide to be my submissive, I foresee a lot of spankings in your future until you unlearn that trait with me. And yes, the more difficult it is for you to do that, the more those spankings will be punishments that hurt."

Sometimes she forgot she hadn't officially agreed to be his submissive. She suspected his occasional reminder of it was to let her know he wouldn't take her too deep, too fast. He was looking out for her.

"Even as you know I won't safeword, because some part of me really wants them. And gets turned on by the fact I'm surrendering that punishment decision to you."

"You are a very fast learner."

This extraordinary conversation felt so natural here. It made her curious to learn even more. "You said submissives seek you out for certain skills. What kind? The type of play, I mean. I don't want... details."

He played with her hoop earring. "Fireplay."

She didn't know exactly what that entailed in BDSM practices, but it surprised her. She wouldn't have thought anything with fire would interest him, when he'd seen the terrible things it could do.

"Are they doing that here, tonight?"

"There's an area in the back, because they have to control the air movement. Too many fans and vents in the main space. Want to check it out when you're feeling steadier?"

"Yes. I'd love to see more of everything."

"Then finish your juice box and your snack, doc, and we'll get to it."

CHAPTER FOURTEEN

$\mathcal{H}$e'd given her a lot to think about. But with the emotional overload in better balance, her body decided it was its turn to elude her control.

As they walked toward the back of the building, the sounds, scents and scenes possessed every nerve ending, her pulse, the heating of her blood. She was on a speedy track to wanting and needing Brick to take her over. It was as he'd said. That common undercurrent, the interplay between trust and surrender, a submissive offering herself to a Dom's control, to *his* control, was what she was hungering for. And this environment was saturated with that element.

He was aware of her state, perhaps because it also fed into his own reaction to their surroundings, to being in it with her. His hand on her lower back descended to stroke the upper part of her buttock, often enough to prove the gesture had expanded from protective courtesy to blatant ownership. She was his to direct and command.

Even as she'd been aroused by all she'd witnessed tonight, Brick had anticipated her viewing each scene as a medical person. He'd pointed out how the suspension Doms monitored circulation issues with frequent checks of skin temperature and color, while also being careful of joint strain. The scenes involving full head masks or cocooning tactics required close attention to the subs' ability to breathe. Those doing impact play avoided strikes over the kidneys or other vulnerable bone areas. First aid supplies were always close to hand.

When she witnessed DMs stepping in to courteously point out safety issues to less experienced Doms and tops, that advice was promptly followed, without backtalk or rancor. Mick did an excellent vetting job.

All that information, seeing it in practice, had released her from those concerns and let her fully experience her own reaction. Like now, as they passed a Dom and sub well into a caning scene.

She knew what the marks on the woman's generous thighs and backside would look like tomorrow, the stages of healing. Yet she also knew other things, in that intuitive way Brick had noted. Marking was an act of possession by the Dom, of meeting a yearning need for pain and sacrifice by the sub, proving how much she wanted to bear for her Dom. It could even be considered a sacred act, intertwined with the intensely sexual.

The thought gave her a rueful inner smile. Put a Catholic in a kinky sex party, she'd still be Catholic, latching onto the significance of ritual.

The fireplay area was divided from the rest of the club by more heavy clear curtains. As they stepped through them, she detected the scent of isopropyl alcohol Brick had carried when she arrived at his townhouse. There was also the smell of smoke, scented candles and fragranced incense.

Over a half-dozen separate stations were widely spaced from one another. Brick directed her attention to the tape on the floor around the nearest one. "Those are the boundaries no observer is allowed to cross."

There were also more DMs here. Every station had their own assigned person with a lanyard.

At the first one, a woman was stretched out on her stomach on a table covered with a folded blanket. A damp towel had been placed perpendicular under her torso so the long ends draped down either side. She was naked except for a gold bandanna covering her hair, and a dainty ring in her nostril. Her right arm bore a full sleeve tattoo of roses. The man standing over her looked unremarkable and pleasant. Brown eyes, curly brown hair. A thirty-something she might see anywhere, working in a Starbucks or Office Depot.

From the neck down, his story became more layered. Jeans fell low on his narrow hips, and he had a complementary tattoo sleeve on his left arm, a spiral of thorns ignited with fire. The edge of the flames overlapped the creases between his fingers.

He was rubbing another damp towel over her back.

"The fire top—his scene name is Heatwave—is cooling her skin so she can handle the heat of the fire a little longer," Brick murmured. "The contrast of the two temperatures also heightens the sensation."

When he put the smaller towel down next to her hip, Heatwave turned away to pick up two metal sticks. One came from what looked like an empty jar. The other was lying next to the jar. White cloth wadded up like marshmallows were on the ends of the sticks. He touched the one that hadn't been in the jar to a candle, sitting on a table a few feet behind him.

As he stepped back to the table, he had both sticks in one hand, crossed like an X between his fingers. When he passed the unlit one over the woman's bare back, Les saw a faint trail of moisture, just enough to make her skin glisten. The lit one ignited the substance. Les drew in a breath at the leap of the blue flame, which the man allowed to burn a couple seconds before smothering it with the damp hand towel he'd picked back up.

"That's a fire wand he's using," Brick told her. "This is called fleshing."

"Was that alcohol he put on her?" She kept her voice low. A handful of people stood with them, watching.

"Good nose, doc. 70% isopropyl alcohol is one of the most common fuel types for this kind of play, so you'll smell a lot of it in this area. But Heatwave probably has his own mix."

Heatwave fell into a rhythm, one wand passing over her flesh, the other igniting the alcohol. Then the second wand caught fire and he was drumming both along her buttocks, thighs and back, up to her shoulder blades and back down again. The woman started to lift to his touch, feeling the heat, her arousal intensifying. Sometimes she made a little noise and shuddered, as if she'd felt the burn more acutely before he extinguished it with the towel.

"Skin can be more sensitive to the heat in some places versus others. Like most kinds of play."

Les nodded. She had her hand on Brick's side. Whenever the

woman reacted more strongly, or her hips and body flexed, seeking a coital rhythm with the flame, her fingers tightened on him, held, stroked, tightened again.

Brick was kneading her nape with his strong grip, bringing her closer, pressed against his hip. "A lot of fire tops play with the solution as they get more experienced, using higher percentages for a hotter, longer burn, mixing it, or using other fuel types, like butane bubbles or cheap hair mousse. The cheaper mousse is more flammable."

At her inquisitive look, he nodded toward another station. "They're using some over there."

When they reached that space, she saw another woman lying on a table. The fire top here was a short woman with caramel skin, woolly gray hair and dark eyes. She wore a close-fitting black tank that revealed a left arm pitted with old burn scarring.

"Imelda was in a house fire as a kid," Brick explained at Les's startled expression.

She couldn't imagine why someone who'd been through that would want to do this, same as her curiosity about Brick's interest. Holding that question for now, she gestured toward the damp towel Imelda's fire bottom was lying upon.

"That's a precaution," Brick explained. "If the fire gets out of control, the fire top can wrap the bottom up in it, fast."

"What about the blanket beneath the other woman?"

"It's cotton. Synthetic fibers are far more flammable, though anything can burn. Just different flash points. Some people like to use the fire blankets, but they're scratchy."

"Which do you use?"

"I started with the fire blanket, but over time I grew comfortable enough to use the cotton." He trailed a finger over her upper arm. "I like to take care of my sub's skin. Sometimes after I do fireplay, I rub vitamin E oil on it."

She imagined Brick rubbing the soothing oil into her back, over her buttocks...the slide of his hands over her skin. Her grip on his shirt tightened, though she brought her attention back to the scene in front of her.

This submissive was also naked, her pubic mound shaved bare. Imelda laid another towel over the top part of her face and her long blonde hair, in a thick braided tail draped over the table's edge.

The bottom's lips parted, and she shifted in aroused response. She liked being blindfolded, or she liked the towel the fire top had used. It had a pair of handcuffs and the words *My Mistress loves me* embroidered on it. Les thought it might have been a gift from this submissive.

Imelda applied the mousse around her bottom's nipples, did a loop over her navel and drew a line down to her mound. She added two elegant swirls over the hip bones and connected the design at either side of the navel area, forming a loop. The foam was an inch high. She picked up a long-necked lighter.

"Is my baby hot?" Imelda asked.

The submissive nodded. "I want to be even hotter for you, Mistress." Her voice had a breathless rasp.

"Good." The Domme touched flame to the mousse at the nipple, and the hair care product ignited, bringing the pattern to light. Rather than flashing, it reminded Les of a translucent blue ocean wave, following the line of the mousse around the full track, dancing over her pale skin. The submissive's hand tightened on the table edge, clutching the blanket as Imelda's fascinated yet watchful expression followed what the fire did to her, how it moved. The submissive made little gasps as the fuel burned, Les assumed because she felt the heat build.

"More...please..."

Imelda flicked the lighter to restart the flame's path along the trail of mousse. Each time it completed the circuit and died back, she'd relight it to start the process again.

"It's burning the alcohol in it," Brick murmured to her. "Once the alcohol is used up, the mousse will stop burning."

Watching the graceful movements Imelda had used to apply the mousse, and the other Dom had employed when fleshing, Les recognized the art to it. And not just for this. Whether the medium was wax, whips, rope, or role play, an undeniable creative passion was part of what was happening in the building. It could be playful and sexy, or so intense those involved barely seemed aware of their surroundings.

She shared that observation with Brick. "We come here to get ideas from one another," he agreed, "but also to absorb the vibes. An amusement park wouldn't be half as much fun if you were the only person there. We feed on one another's energy, and expand on our own paths by exploring it together."

"So not exactly performance art."

"It's much more personal. A sharing. You go to a circus, see the fireplay, you're looking at a performance. I'm not saying that the performer isn't feeling and enjoying it at a similar level, but even they know it's different when they're by themselves, just connecting to the fire for their own reasons. Or to connect with another person."

The hint of danger, the watchfulness of the DM and the Domme herself, added an erotic edge to that connection. Les could tell that Brick, while appreciating the sensual picture the two women made, was in the same mode. Fire tops had to be adept at splitting their attention, she surmised. While savoring their own pleasure, the top had to stay vigilant. Ensure the sub trusted she was in safe hands, so she too could experience the pleasure the play offered.

Les suspected that challenge was part of why this appealed to Brick. She visualized herself under his hands, as he touched flame to her skin and made heat prickle along her own flesh.

When the alcohol was burned out, Imelda removed the towel from the blonde's face. She used the cloth to wipe away the mousse. The woman gazed up at her with an adoring expression, one that still craved more.

"I know you want the burn, my beauty, but I want your skin red, not blistered." Imelda had a husky voice like the echo in a wet cave.

Brick drew Les to the edges of the group. "With an alcohol fuel barrier, the fire can evaporate the fuel without causing severe burns," he explained. "But sometimes the heat will burn through in spots."

He gestured to the next scene he'd brought her to view. "This is fire cupping. See how the Dom is wiping the inside of the cup with the wand? In fireplay, you have to guard against excess fuel dripping where you don't want it to be. That's why the Dom just misted the inside of the cup with the alcohol, rather than pouring it in. Some do it that way, and transfer the liquid to another cup, but they're giving themselves an additional risk to monitor.

"You can forget to check the seemingly empty cup for pooled excess at the bottom when you tip the cup over. It can run places you didn't intend it to do. Then you put the next cup down, and that spill catches fire. What you want in the cup is just enough to ignite the vapors."

"Have you done this?" She watched as the flesh was drawn up into the suction of the heated cup, the blue flame dancing.

"It's not my thing, but yeah. Fire cupping has been used for massage therapy and healing for a long time, but doing it this way, it will leave marks on the body. I don't mind that, but I like the more tactile forms of fireplay. Fleshing, drumming or tapping. Fire flogging, caning and spanking."

"Fire spanking?"

"I use a Kevlar glove for it."

He moved his touch from between her shoulder blades to her braid. He put it over the top of his hand, but captured the tip between thumb and palm. He tugged on it, bringing her head back onto his shoulder. With her vision dominated by his heated expression, he put his mouth on hers, traced her lips with his tongue, then hovered there.

"If I have the sub remove all the hair on her pussy," he murmured, "I don't have to limit the spanking to her ass. Unless she wants me to burn her hair off there as part of the experience. Though I prefer to do it on smooth skin."

Even when Brick wasn't actively exercising his Dom side, it was there. Maybe that was why she couldn't stop thinking about that part of him, even if they were doing something mundane. In this case, their surroundings were not at all mundane, and he was actively being a Dom. His sexually charged appeal could reach, well, incendiary levels.

"You like having your cunt spanked," he noted, holding her entranced gaze. "If you wanted me to do it with fire, I'd do the hair removal myself, make you smooth. I'd put my mouth there to test I did the job properly."

He released her hair with a caressing touch. "After the removal, we have to wait at least a day to do the fireplay. The alcohol can burn differently right after the removal, leave deeper marks or cause you the wrong kind of discomfort."

"I think you say things like that just to keep me so weak-kneed I need your help to walk."

"It's a side benefit." He slanted her a smile, but the fire in his gaze didn't abate as the two of them wandered onward.

"Imelda, having those scars. And you...I guess I get some of it, but I still wonder why you like this, with the really awful things you've seen fire do."

"I can't speak to Imelda's motives. She's pretty closed mouthed about that. But firemen have an interesting relationship with fire." Brick shrugged. "It's a living thing, needing oxygen and fuel to sustain it. Like most natural forces, it's impervious to love or hate. I know the awful things it can do, and how unpredictable it can be, how wild. But if you learn to understand and respect it, it also has a rhythm. You can dance with it.

"Being able to spread flame on someone's skin and take it away without causing harm, causing pleasure instead, is something I like," he added. "Having that control, balanced with respect for what fire is, how it allows me to use it? It calls to me."

He touched her cheek. "It's like the gift of submission itself, what a sub offers me when she asks me to touch flame to her flesh. Fire burns but it also warms. It strokes, like the heat in my hand." His fingers slid over her back, up between her shoulder blades, emphasizing the point.

When they reached the next station, he settled the hand back onto her hip. The fire top was placing bits of cotton on the skin that made a quick flash when ignited. Hence the term "flashing," Brick explained. The fire bottom, a slender male, wiggled a little bit, as if the sensation was ticklish.

She'd been doing well on the medical side of things, reassured by Brick's explanations of the safety precautions. But as they reached the next scene, the sudden burst of flame, the cry of the sub, couldn't stop her from lunging forward. Fortunately, Brick's hold kept her behind the taped barrier.

The woman on the table held onto the edges with clenched hands as her breasts and sternum were immersed in purple flame. The reason she'd cried out wasn't because of that. Or just because of that. A vibrator was being applied to her privates. As the fire leaped, she bucked.

Two men worked over her, one holding the vibrator, the other monitoring the fire. He passed his fingers through it, his other hand on the side of her head, stroking her through the tight scarf holding her hair from her strained face. As the flames started to die down, he leaned forward and pursed his lips, to blow a soft puff of air over it. The flame leaped up again.

"They're using butane bubbles," Brick told her. She stared, her body vibrating as the woman's writhed, the two men keeping her on the table as she shuddered into a climax. The top monitoring the fire doused the flames and put his hand between her legs, taking her through the rest of it. Les wondered if her skin would feel damp and steaming, moist within and without.

She was reaching that mental overload again, but no surprise, Brick was ahead of it this time. She suspected he rarely made the same mistake twice, particularly when it involved someone he cared about.

He'd drawn her away from the scene, but came to a halt as she clutched his arm at her waist, pressed her face to his biceps. She kissed him there with teeth, soft lips and questing tongue. She wanted...she knew what she wanted. She would tell him right here and now, felt like she should. But before she could open her mouth, someone else spoke.

"Fireman."

Brick tightened his arm around her, the spark in his eyes and the strength of his arm acknowledging the edge she'd been on. Reluctantly, he turned toward the call. A lean and tall man who looked like a fifty-something rock band guitarist was coming their way. The woman with him, around the same age, had long hair the dun color of a deer's flank. She also had large, thick lashed brown eyes, heavy breasts and wide hips.

"Dirk." Brick shook his hand and nodded to the woman. "Lisa."

"Tish doing okay after her first fireplay?" Dirk asked.

"She is. I'm laying bets you'll see her and Richard do something at the next monthly get-together."

"Really?" Lisa's eyes sparked with female interest. "I thought they made a connection."

As Lisa turned a curious gaze to her, Les sorted what pleasant, nice-to-meet-you expression would work. This was her first casual conversation with someone wearing the almost-nothing Lisa was wearing.

A harness held her from thighs to upper torso. The straps framed her naked breasts, while D-links connected the harness to a collar around her throat. It was stamped with one word. *His.*

The harness below her waist was covered with a clear plastic mini-skirt. Straps ran between and around her plump thighs. Dirk's hand rested on her back, thumb through the strap that connected to the collar so he could apply tension as he desired. At least that was where Les's brain went on it.

When Brick had addressed Lisa, she'd lowered her gaze, an acknowledgement of Brick as a Dom. Brick had reinforced that by shaking Dirk's hand and accepting Lisa's nonverbal response as the appropriate greeting.

Les had seen plenty of evidence of Dom/sub hierarchy tonight, and she assumed the degree of it was the choice of the Doms and subs in question. To see a matter-of-fact display of it up close and personal made that longing in her lower belly get even stronger.

Like Brick said, it might not look just like this, but what was under it? *Yes. This is what I want.*

"This is my friend, Les." Brick introduced her. "She's seeing a lot of this for the first time tonight."

"Does it feel incredibly familiar, yet totally sci-fi?" Lisa asked her, with a friendly smile.

A great description. It was as if Les knew the language being spoken here, though the words were foreign. It was the way it was being spoken that made her heart jump, her palms damp, and fingers nervously clutch.

She wondered how she would have felt if Brick could have introduced her as *his* sub.

Dirk gave Les a faint smile. "She's a Trek fan. Spock was her first Dom fantasy. Are you doing any fire spinning tonight, Brick?"

"No. I want to keep my focus on Les tonight."

"Makes sense. When you have time, reach out to me on the group chat link. Lisa has asked for permission to do a fire flogging experience, and I've said yes, but you're the only one I'll trust with that."

Lisa's face flashed with disappointment when Brick said he wasn't playing tonight. Though she quickly schooled her face otherwise, Dirk had seen it. "My mama here knows when I say she has to wait, that's what we do. Though sometimes she gets her butt whipped for getting impatient."

Lisa's mischievous look was flavored with irony. "Need a beer, Master?"

"I once got my ass handed to me," Dirk told Les. "My beautiful mama showed me she knows the difference between 'obey your Master' and 'bring me a beer, bitch.'"

"Some Doms are a little thick-headed." Brick elbowed Dirk. "They have to learn the difference between requiring acts of service and being a lazy asshole to a woman who's been on her feet all day."

Brick's gaze moved to Les. She knew he was remembering her toweling off his back.

"Yep." Unoffended by the observation, Dirk nevertheless affected a mock sternness as Lisa demurely looked at the floor. A smile played over her full lips. "Damn woman upended the beer on my head," he told Les. "She got a big spanking for it later, but for the right reasons, after we clarified where I'd fucked up."

He stroked her thick hair. The devotion in the gesture tugged Les's heartstrings. It was obvious he'd do anything for her. "Anyhow, we'll leave you to it. But if you change your mind, I know a lot of people would love to see a fire flogging tonight."

"Brick." Les looked up at him. "If you want to do that, I wouldn't mind. I'd find it interesting to watch."

Though Lisa's eyes brightened like stars, Dirk didn't acknowledge it. Instead, he met Brick's gaze. "You know where we'll be if you change your mind," he said, and firmly guided Lisa away.

"Oh." Dismayed, Les watched them go. "Did I say something wrong? I wasn't trying to pressure you into anything. Did I break some kind of rule?"

"No. And you're not pressuring me. The decision is mine. Dirk's not upset. He's just giving us room to discuss it. He doesn't know if what's between us is full-on Dom and sub, or just exploring the fringes." Brick turned her toward him so he could caress her upper arms. "No matter how much we're exploring the reality of what's between us tonight, it's still up in the air. Which is why I want to keep my focus on you."

She wasn't sure how in the air it was, but as he'd made clear only a little while ago, he was never going to be Bart, using guilt or other wrong kinds of pressure to shove her toward something she wasn't sure she was ready for. What she needed and wanted meant more to him than his immediate desires.

Another first for her, when it came to relationships. But with her deep service cravings, what he wanted and needed mattered to her, too. "I respect that. But what you were talking about, the spanking... with fire?" When his smile deepened, she knew she was flushing. "I will hit you."

He held up both hands. "I like watching you struggle with it. The shyness turns me on, even as I want to gather you up like a kitten. Mick's not far off on that."

"Remind me to be really offended later, but right now..." She worked through the words. "As I said earlier, I know I'm interested in having you do fireplay stuff on me. To see what it felt like."

"But not tonight." He wasn't asking a question. He was telling her he wouldn't go there with her. At least not here. She agreed with that. It was too new, too personal between them. But given the almost limitless well of arousal she was experiencing, she thought she could do it in a private venue much sooner.

"I wouldn't mind seeing you do it with someone like Lisa, to get a sense of what it would be like if you were doing it with me."

"Why Lisa? Because she's with someone?"

Exactly. Though Brick had adequately reassured her, she already knew she wouldn't feel the same if it was Tish.

He drew her to a corner. "Before I decide on that, I need to be sure you understand what you're asking. When I'm doing this, my attention has to be a hundred percent focused on the bottom. The scene won't *seem* incredibly intimate. It will be."

Her gaze snapped up to him. She'd interpreted his earlier description of fireplay scenes with those who weren't "his submissive" as the illusion of intimacy. But his words told her she'd misunderstood.

"Lisa isn't my girlfriend or my lover, but she'll put her wellbeing into my hands, trusting I'll take that more seriously than anything else during the scene, beginning to end. To get the full benefit of it, she'll also want to experience it as a sub under the control of a Dom, and all the nuances of what that means to her.

"I can put that a hundred different ways, but until I hear it from you, I don't know that you're understanding me. So tell me what I'm saying. Give it back to me, how you're hearing it, as a submissive yourself."

She took a breath. "You have to make everything about keeping her safe and giving her the experience she's hoping to have. Which means you have to be in her head, maybe even her heart and soul."

That was how it felt when he took Les over. So she said what she dearly hoped was the difference. "But that doesn't mean she has *your* heart and soul. You came with me, and that's who you want to be here with, and who you want to go home with."

Without his hands on her, she wasn't sure she would have found those words inside her. She might have called it wishful thinking on her part. But when she saw the easing of tension in his expression, she knew she'd reached into him, and offered truth. And herself relief.

"Good girl." His gaze slid over her. "I'm glad you realize that. Because you look gorgeous in that dress, but all I can think about is how your nipples look in those bra cups that don't hide anything, and how wet you're making those panties. You're going to look so cute and fucking sexy when I tell you to drop them, bend over and hold your ankles. Right before I lift that skirt and see what's mine to fuck."

His gaze returned to her face. "So if I do this, I damn well expect appreciation for the effort it's going to take me to focus on this the way I should. It goes to the top of the list, doc. You'll pay a steep ticket price for this show."

A handful of hookups, plus her and Bart's completely adolescent explorations, couldn't compare to the level of sexual response he drew out of her, with nothing but words. They rocked her into a state of mindless desire. She wanted to follow him down any road he took her. She'd not only accept any punishment for that, but the punishment would be part of the road she wanted to travel with him.

That truth brought a surge of adrenaline, and the desire to play, too. So she swept her gaze down like Lisa had, giving him the same demure look.

He snorted, caught her throat and brought her up onto her toes, capturing her gasp in a rough kiss before he let her drop back to her feet. "Little tease. You want a taste of what it would be like to be treated like my sub, at a party like this?"

"Yes." *God, yes.*

"Then I'm going to require your help. You're going to get Lisa's hair ready for me. The French braiding I prefer."

Unexpected relief flooded her, and he noted it. "Yeah, I told you that act sets the mood and connects me to the woman I'm with. Though I'll connect to her the way I said, I want to keep it clear in your head you're who I'm with tonight."

He pointed to where Dirk and Lisa were watching the fire cupping. "Tell Dirk I'm having Mick clear the inner courtyard. Give me about ten minutes to get that going, then you, he and Lisa can join me. Tell him once you get there I want you to prepare Lisa's hair. Ask his permission to do that."

"Not hers?"

"No. When Dirk and Lisa are here as Master and sub, consent is a dialogue between him and her alone." The softer light in Brick's eyes made Les suddenly more nervous, in good ways.

"She's his universe, his woman, the mother of his three children. That's why it's called a power exchange relationship. It's different for everyone, but that's what works for them. Some things evolve organically once the foundation stones are set. Others you have to take a beat and talk it out."

Just like any relationship. No matter the trappings. Whether just the man and woman alone, or among a world populated by fire, vibrators, rope and restraints, caning or wax play.

"Dirk will know where the courtyard is. If anyone stops you, asks you if you're interested in playing—"

"I'll say, 'what do you have in mind?'"

He bared his teeth, and she laughed until he twisted his hand in the waistband of her dress, bringing her right up against hard muscle and a male with eyes as lethal as a sword edge.

"What will you tell them?" The sensual menace had her heart pounding, but not with the desire to get away.

"That I'm here with someone, but thank you. That I have a Dom. And...I only want to be with him. For any of it. I only want to explore this with you, Brick," she added honestly.

She'd never had an urge to expose her submissive side to Bart. Maybe because some instinct told her he couldn't understand what a Dom was, and if she gave him an inch to try, he'd take a mile. The difference between a Dom and a dick. She understood Dirk's comment better now.

Brick put a hand under the skirt, tracing the edge of the silky panties over her buttock. He pressed her closer to him. His cock wasn't fully erect, but interested enough to be distractingly noticeable.

"This is a safe place with good people," he told her. "I know you're capable of taking care of yourself. I'm still going to tell you this. Anything you do or don't want to do, all you have to do is say "Not interested.' You don't have to worry about hurting feelings. You just have to be clear and polite. If your wishes aren't respected, Mick or one of the DMs will give that asshole a lesson in manners. If I don't get to him first. Okay?"

When she nodded, he released her, though with a lingering caress. "Go to Lisa and Dirk, and do what I said."

As she made her way toward the couple, she understood better why Brick had told her what he had. As soon as she was on her own, far more glances came her way. But as new as the environment was to her, nothing felt personally threatening. It was as Lisa had said. It all felt so oddly familiar. She might only have a handful of pictures, but those images had pulled things from deep inside her that knew this world, long before she'd stepped into it.

She glanced back, though she assumed Brick would already be gone, looking for Mick. Instead, he was where she'd left him. No matter his reassurance, he wasn't going to look for Mick until she was with Dirk and Lisa, who he'd told her to accompany to the courtyard.

He believed in her ability to take care of herself, but it didn't change his responsibility to care for her. She thought of her father, teaching her the lesson about learning how to build a boat. It wasn't that she had to turn to Brick for help. It was knowing she *could*, having absolute faith in that support and backup.

He'd asked her if she wanted to have a taste of what it was to be a sub, to have him act as her Dom tonight, and she'd said yes. That was what he was giving her. Since the moment she'd driven up to his condo, he'd been giving her that. And she'd been responding to it.

It wasn't a matter of deciding if she wanted to be his submissive. It was a matter of knowing when to acknowledge that it had always been there between them.

Since the first time he'd read her poetry.

CHAPTER FIFTEEN

*L*isa was delighted. While more reserved, Dirk seemed pleased by Brick's decision. He guided the two women to the inner courtyard, where Les found Mick had designed another appealing play space.

The central feature was a large concrete pad, embedded with oyster shell. Lights strung between columns on the outer corners provided romantic illumination, while electric torchlight embellished the flared crowns of the columns.

A low wall created by smooth round stones created a perimeter around the pad. The masonry had a smooth bench top, glazed with the same liquid epoxy as the flooring, only in a marble-like gray and white. It made it safe to sit upon without snagging thin and silky club-wear. A stone path several feet wide around the outside of the wall had bistro tables and chairs. People who didn't want to sit on the wall could have a drink and sit there, watching whatever was happening in the enclosed space. She expected the pad could also be used as a dance floor.

"Fire flogging is best done outside," Dirk told her. "It requires more room to do safely than the types of fireplay you saw in the building. It's also a better option for the splatter from spinning the wicks down."

She wasn't sure what he meant until she saw Brick laying out items on a table that had probably been brought out by one of

Mick's staff. The items were coming from a black bag she had noted behind his driver's seat. He did this enough he had his own fireplay tools.

She would have been content merely watching him do this part, but she'd been assigned a task. She was able to accomplish both by having Lisa sit down on the section of the wall directly across the courtyard from where Brick was setting up. Dirk was talking with him, leaving the two women alone together.

Lisa gave her a conspiratorial smile. "Thanks for letting me appreciate the view. Watching Dirk arrange the things he's going to use in a session with me, a paddle, rope, candles, whatever it is, totally shifts my mind into sub space. That part of me centers and I become like melted wax. If he barely touches me, I'll go off."

She had a comfortable and robust laugh. "Actually, that can happen even if he blindfolds me and won't let me watch. Listening to him prepare, the anticipation, can do it."

Brick had that power, too, making Les even more at ease with the woman. Lisa had retrieved her brush from the changing room lockers for Les to use. As Les stroked the bristles through the woman's thick hair, the gray-white strands mixed in the brown giving it that dun look, she watched Brick prepare.

The flogger he laid out had long white strips. The "wicks" Dirk had referenced, she guessed. The wooden handle was painted black, with a red and gold emblem on it. When he handed it to Dirk to examine, Les saw a pair of crossed axes against a spurt of flame. Beneath that, in a font legible even from this side of the courtyard, she read "Fire Man."

Dirk hadn't said "Fireman." It was a play on words, a nod toward Brick's profession and his interest in fireplay.

She thought of the George Strait song, "Fireman," and its lyrics. They worked for Brick. As did Alan Jackson's tune, "Country Boy." Sexy lyrics delivered in sexy Southern male voices.

"Are you nervous?" As she asked the question, she started threading pieces of Lisa's hair into the French braid.

"Yeah. But it's closer to anticipation. We've known Brick a while. Things can go wrong in any scene that involves edge play, but that's why Dirk chose him. Brick does everything he can to prepare for that. No one in the world works harder to keep me happy and safe than my

Master, but when you're under Brick's care, he comes in a close second."

"How long have you and Dirk been together?"

"Twelve years now. I shot my first husband." She made a face. "Sorry. I like to blurt that out, maybe because it still makes me feel good. Not because I shot someone, but because it was when I became who I really wanted to be."

"Now you're going to have to tell me that story."

Less humorous things gripped Lisa's expression, but her tone remained matter-of-fact. "It was so long ago. I was young and stupid, looking for a Master before I knew I was looking for one. So I chose an abusive asshole instead. He made good money, and I thought I'd married up, so I took the abuse, trying to please him, trying to fix him, trying to forgive him. Then I got pregnant. When he punched me in the face in my sixth month, I fell down the stairs. He tried to grab me, I'll give him that, but he missed."

Lisa's gaze shifted onto Dirk and held, a reminder of the here and now. "When he drove me home from the hospital, I had three cards for domestic abuse shelters in my purse. From the nurse, the doctor, and the EMT. I held onto them, and told my husband, "That's it. You raise a hand against my baby ever again, I will shoot you dead.""

She shook her head. "I know what you're thinking. Why the hell did I go home with him at all? I thought because I'd made a stand and meant it, it would change something. The next time he tried to get rough with me, I ran into our bedroom, and locked the door. He was beating on it, screaming at me to open up or he'd kick my ass. I told him to leave the house, or I'd shoot him through the door with his own gun. He didn't believe me."

She glanced over her shoulder at Les. "I wasn't that great of a shot, but I did get him in the shoulder. He got the hell out of the house."

"Good for you."

"Yeah." Her eyes showed sadness. "But my baby was born with a deformed leg. Sheila is my gem. She's the much older sister to the two I had with Dirk before my ovaries said enough already. She's a middle school teacher. But she was born that way because I didn't act sooner."

She took a breath. "That beer incident with Dirk? That happened early, when we were both learning about the Dom and sub stuff. We wanted it, fiercely, but something about how he told me to get him a beer that day—he'd had a bad day and was cranky—brought some of that dark stuff boiling back up. I was rejecting what I'd once been, everything about myself that had put me in that position with my first husband. Dumping the beer on Dirk's head wasn't so much a message to Dirk as it was to me. Never again. We laugh about it now, but we both learned a lot that day."

Les squeezed her shoulder, the woman's manner making it easy to initiate the contact. "You should work in an ER. The victims they see could get some inspiration from you."

"I volunteer for a domestic abuse shelter. I even lead one of the weekly group discussions." Lisa's gaze changed from sober reflection to pure female speculation, her brown eyes dancing as she aimed them toward Les.

"Brick is a really experienced Dom, but he's never bound himself to a woman. He looks like he's thinking about it pretty hard with you."

At Les's expression, Lisa put a hand to her mouth in comic dismay. "Please tell me you're not shocked to hear that, or Dirk's going to beat me, and Brick's going to help him. But I'm like that. Shooting off my mouth when I know I shouldn't."

"No, you're good. He's told me something similar. I'm still working on digesting it." Les wrapped the band Lisa had provided around the tail of her now braided hair.

"Yeah, I get that. When you see how well known he is in this group, it makes you sort through the whole, 'okay, am I just one of many, or am I special?' thing in your head. It's hard to know how to take, being the latest in line."

Les blinked. She hadn't really thought of it that way, and didn't want to. Not until Lisa squeezed her hand and gave her a direct look. "But there's a big difference between being the latest and being the last. The one he's been waiting for."

"I'm feeling so much tonight, it's consuming all my brain cells. I'm afraid of following that feeling and having to walk it back."

Lisa grinned. "I get that. I remember my first sub experiences. And Dirk is the sexiest man in the universe to me, but I'm not blind or dead. Brick would make any woman's heart trip faster, and he wants you. That said... I love that man of yours to death, and I know, if you don't want the same thing, he'll do nothing but respect that, because that's who he is."

Before Les could reply—though she wasn't sure if Lisa was looking for a response—Brick turned toward them. He gestured at Les. She touched Lisa's shoulder. "You okay for a minute?"

"Oh sure. Go see what he needs."

Dirk was headed toward them, and nodded to Les as they passed one another. "My mama okay?"

"Yes. Anxious, but in the right ways."

When Les reached Brick, he drew her close and kissed her. She gave herself to it, let herself be lost in his mouth and touch, as he gripped her upper arms. When he eased back, he asked Dirk's question a different way. "How's she doing?"

"She's excited, a little nervous." Though Lisa had laughed and chatted, Les had sensed those nerves beneath, revealed by higher notes to her laughter.

"Good job, doc. That information helps." He unbuttoned his shirt and shrugged out it, revealing the tank he'd worn beneath it. He handed her the shirt. "In that dress, you might get a little chilly out here. I want you sitting there." He pointed to the section of wall behind the table. "You okay while I go talk to her?"

"Yes." She slipped into the shirt, liking the heat of his body. "Lisa says you've never committed yourself to a woman here, but you're acting like that's about to change."

His lips quirked. "That sure as hell better not be a news flash to you, but damn that busybody. I love her, but I'm going to have Dirk beat her ass."

"That's what she said you'd say. She also says she loves you to pieces, and you'd respect wherever my feelings went on our relationship."

"I will. But I'll also do my damnedest to get you to agree with mine."

"Fair enough."

He kissed her again, in his thorough, distracting way, before striding across the courtyard. Though he acknowledged Dirk, this time he was there to address Lisa directly.

Les didn't have to hear the conversation to pick up on it. He would care for anyone under his protection and take that job seriously. Something any woman could love about him.

Including the woman moving from childhood crush to full-on falling in love with the man he'd become.

Brick returned to the table a few minutes later. "Okay?" he repeated.

"Better than."

After an approving nod, his face settled into a serious mask of concentration. People were gathering, sitting at the tables on the outside of the wall or on the wall itself. One of the X shaped crosses had been positioned in the center of the courtyard.

From conversations happening nearby, the more experienced explaining to the less experienced what he was going to do, she could pick up the basics. But whatever she missed, she'd ask him later. Right now, watching him took precedence, without the interruption or distraction of technique or terms.

Brick sprayed the flogger's woven wicks from a bottle with "my flogger mix" written on it. With his knowledge of fuel types, it made sense that he experimented with his formula, just like Heatwave.

He gripped the black wooden handle, his palm molded over the red fire logo. The staff had left one corner of the courtyard cleared of people, and he moved there before he began to spin the flogger, the wicks flying out in a fan as he twisted his wrist.

It explained Dirk's term, "fire spinner," and the comment about the splatter. As Brick spun out the excess alcohol solution, it was an appealing thing to watch, him in his jeans and tank, the muscles in his arms and shoulders flexing.

Dirk took Lisa to the cross. He removed the harness as well as the plastic skirt before he had her face the cross and clasp the handles, spreading her legs to position them along the bottom pieces. He threaded the tail of her braided hair over her shoulder, so it lay upon her breasts.

When he handed the harness and skirt to an attendant, he was given a wet hand towel. He started to stroke it with loving care over Lisa's back and rounded ass. He caressed her with his free hand, murmuring to her. Her body relaxed further under his touch, even as there was a drifting kind of stillness to her, that shift in focus she'd told Les about.

When Dirk was done, he draped the towel over her head like a veil and adjusted his position so Lisa could see him. He would serve as a spotter, but not the only one. The assigned DM stood at another angle. Les saw Mick leaning against a wall by an exit door, arms crossed and watching the scene play out.

Brick had finished his spinning. He came to the cross, putting a hand on Lisa's shoulder. In addition to being a reassurance, Les could tell he was using that touch to evaluate her tension and where her head was at.

He nodded to Dirk, an unspoken direction. Dirk cupped Lisa's skull, pressing his forehead to hers. Then he put his hand between the bottom cross pieces, touching her between her legs. Lisa's body quivered as he stroked her, his other hand rising to cup and play with her breast.

When she was quivering twice as hard, and Les could hear the rasp of Lisa's aroused breath, see the twitch of her bare ass, Dirk kissed her once more and stepped back. He didn't go far, staying in her line of sight.

Brick's attention swept over everything once more. The two spotters, the safety measures he'd laid out on the table; fire extinguisher, bucket of water, a stack of damp towels. His fuel bottle was at the opposite corner of the table.

When he paced around Lisa, she thought he was confirming the size of the buffer between him, her and the audience.

He met Les's gaze briefly when he turned in her direction. Belatedly, she wondered if she should have asked if there was anything she should be ready to do, like Dirk and the DM. But when Brick included her in that checklist gaze, she knew what he needed from her. Her medical knowledge. It made her an essential part of Lisa's care team.

She really missed that feeling. Up until now, the enormity of what had brought her here had crushed her awareness of anything else. Dr. Portland had treated the reassignment of her patients as an unremarkable step, necessary due to her absence. But it was difficult not to take it as a no-confidence measure.

She liked having assigned patients, being the person who updated the attending and resident on their status. Remembering that enjoyment, the challenge of it, was her first evidence that the spark of desire to heal and help hadn't been wholly quenched two days ago.

Brick had a jump medical bag as part of his supplies, no surprise since he'd gotten paramedic training when he was a firefighter. She did a quick inventory to confirm she had what might be needed, and she did. The man was thorough.

Brick picked up the lighter and touched the flame to the flogger wicks. They immediately caught, suddenly a dramatic fiery horse's tail dancing below Brick's grip.

Conversation around the stone wall died away. With the area illuminated only by strung lights, the flogger fire became everyone's central focus.

As he moved back to the cross, Brick began spinning the flogger again, in a smooth rotation. When he was close enough to make contact, the first blow hit Lisa's back with the fluidity of a cresting wave.

The power of the movement was in its restraint. The strikes on her back weren't hard, but measured and controlled. From the way Lisa arched at the sensation, a little went a long way. A moan somewhere between rough sexual need and a purr of pleasure came from her. Les suspected the initial strikes delivered the flogger's impact sensation; the heat would build with the greater levels of pain from the blows or increasing temperature, depending on where they made contact.

The green, gold and blue flame was a rush of color Les could see against her lids when she did a slow blink. When Brick cued Dirk a few moments later, he moved closer to Lisa's front and began to stroke her between the legs again. One strong, lean hand gripped her shoulder, the heel of his hand on her breast, the nipple jutting against his wrist. His lips were moving, words Les couldn't hear but knew were a mix of reassurances and demands. They would tell Lisa what he wanted from her, how much he loved watching her like this. How she was the center of his world.

There was no way to say this wasn't sexual, but the erotic intensity vibrating off Brick wasn't targeted toward Lisa. It expanded from him, an energy net that pulled all of those around him into the same sensual spell. It reminded every person watching they were sexual creatures, meant to play, come together, and explore all the ways that they could enjoy one another's bodies, plus the hearts and souls connected to them.

Would Brick be amused to find Les was just as turned on watching him do this, as she was when he was doing his fire cop work? Both passions required his extraordinary level of awareness and concentration. He was tuned in to every detail, everything that mattered.

The rhythm and speed of the flogger, the application of heat, maximized the pulsing response between her own legs. Her hand tightened into a fist on her thigh, that pulse jumping every time Brick's flogger hit. As if it was hitting her, like his hand between her legs. A gloved hand covered in fire.

Les tightened her thighs and rocked forward, trying to conceal her reaction. Even in this environment, she needed Brick touching her to lose her self-consciousness about who might be watching.

"Oh..." The climax grabbed Lisa, wrestling cries from her throat. Dirk moved his knee in between her legs, letting her grind against him as he clasped her hands on the cross's handles, keeping her from making any unsafe movements.

She rocked against his hold, while Brick adjusted accordingly. He continued the flogging but backed off, the wick contact a mere brush against her hips and back before he stopped entirely. It allowed Dirk to put his arm around Lisa's waist, his other hand back between her legs, helping her ride those final aftershocks. Her face was pressed against his bearded jaw through the opening of the upper cross pieces.

Brick moved back to the corner and spun the flogger, this time with a more abrupt snap of his wrist. The move extinguished the remaining flame. He dropped it into a metal bucket he'd left there and returned to Lisa, putting a hand on her back, his other on Dirk's shoulder.

Les couldn't hear the murmured conversation, but when Lisa looked at him, her expression was one Les knew. She'd put herself in Brick's hands, trusting he would care for her, not cause her harm. If something went wrong, she knew he'd be able to get ahead of it.

She'd seen that look on the faces of patients. And their family members. That trust was a gift. Brick deserved that gift.

She didn't.

Nausea boiled in her stomach, the thunder that proceeded the lightning, stabbing pains. Damn it, one freak-out per day was enough.

But to keep it at bay, she needed to find a place she could draw a deep breath.

As unobtrusively as possible, she put her legs over the other side of the wall, threaded between two occupied tables and slipped away with a mumbled, "Excuse me."

She sought the nearest exit door, which brought her into a hallway of locked doors, probably storerooms. Fortunately a turn brought her to another restroom with a lit sign mounted next to it. One arrow pointed her back to the main floor, while another in the opposite direction was labeled "rear patio." The sign was unnecessary for the main floor, since she could hear the thump of the music, and the people coming out of the restroom were mostly headed in that direction.

She paused at the restroom, waiting to see if the fruit and nut bar was going to come up. When her stomach uneasily settled, she headed for the rear patio. She could always throw up into some bushes if needed.

The rear patio had high top tables, attractive potted plants, and another stone wall perimeter, only this one was taller, chest high. When she folded her arms on the surface and inhaled the night air, she saw a landscaped natural area on the other side of the wall. It was planted with gardenias, azaleas, and poles holding metal wind catchers, which caught the patio lights as they spun. Behind the plantings was a chain link fence, topped with razor wire, offering rear lot security for the club.

Past the fence, a downward sloping hill ended at a busy four-lane street. It was lined with a pawn shop, cigarette outlet, deli and adult toy store. Illuminated by random yellow streetlights, the view wasn't pretty. Many of the stories that had played out down there probably weren't either.

Three of the patio tables were occupied, but none were near her. She gazed at the view and tried to calm her stomach, which meant coaxing her mind out of the vat of despair her thoughts had plunged her into once again.

A shift caught her gaze, and she saw Mick. He'd lifted himself up on capable arms to plant himself on the wall a few feet away from her. He was mostly cloaked in shadows, and scrolling through his phone. She had privacy, but he was close enough she could initiate conversation if she wished. Maybe because of her erratic mental state—something she hoped to God wasn't permanent, but she was beginning to wonder—Brick had somehow signaled him a standing request to keep an eye on her.

She wasn't sure how she felt about that, but she appreciated he didn't disturb her. She could stand here, stare into the night and try to empty her mind. She wasn't hugely successful. Her tension didn't loosen enough to give her room for a deep breath. Not until Brick joined her. He leaned against the wall, crossing his arms, his hip brushing hers in companionable contact.

He didn't say anything until she was ready to talk. "It was beautiful," she said at last. "Amazing."

He kissed her hair, rested his chin on top of her head, an affectionate contact. A homeless man was shuffling in front of the pawn shop, pushing a cart of belongings.

"Even if a fire top anticipates, prepares, has experience, really bad things can still happen. Right?"

"Yeah." His breath was warm on her scalp. "But a lot less than without all that."

"When those bottoms get hurt, are the tops, the ones who thought they did all they could, able to keep doing it? How do they find the hubris to believe they won't hurt someone again?"

"Kind of apples and oranges there, doc, the comparison you're trying to make. A doctor has to learn how to handle the mistakes. We need doctors. Fire spinners, not so much."

She turned it over in her mind. "You're right about the question I need to ask myself. About why I decided to be a doctor. But that part of my brain is so tired." She looked up at him. "Will you hold me?"

"Always."

She put her head on his chest as he closed his arms around her. She wound hers around his back and waist. "Where'd your guard dog go?"

At his curious look, she pointed toward the now empty section of patio. "Mick."

"He left once I arrived. I wanted to make sure you had someone nearby if you needed anything."

Putting his hands to her waist, Brick lifted her up on the wall, next to the column that supported the covered roof edge. He leaned against it as she laid her hand on his chest to adjust and remove the heeled sandals. Placing them next to her, she let her bare feet brush his denim-covered thigh as she swung them.

"I can see why the fireplay appeals to you, beyond everything you told me. You're a science guy. The fuel mixes, the understanding of oxygen, air currents."

"Science and sex, baby. Can't beat the combo. If only we'd known all the possibilities in high school."

"Hormonal teens doing fireplay. I'm sure nothing would have gone wrong with that."

"Fortunately, teenage boys are pretty single-minded." He smiled. "Getting a girl out of her clothes somewhere semi-private is about as complicated as sex gets for most of us."

She stroked the warm flesh and chest hair above the scooped neckline of his tank, then paused, her fingers curling. "Is it okay for me to touch you?"

"As in, do you need my permission?"

She met his gaze. "Yes."

"Not right now. You'll know when you do. Or I'll tell you."

She stroked his upper pectoral, his collar bones. Rested the pad of her thumb in the valley between them, feeling the echo of his heart beat there.

"Were you ever concerned about the 'little sister of my best friend' thing?"

"No, not really. I did have to consider the possibility of being beaten to a pulp by two protective brothers, or getting speared by the lethal disapproval of a Catholic mother."

"My brothers could beat you to a pulp?"

"Together, maybe. If they brought a big stick and surprised me."

She smiled. "I guess I had the better end of the deal. My adolescent fantasies were totally safe, because I thought you were way out of my reach. I'd have died with embarrassment if I'd known you knew how I felt about you."

"Good thing I didn't let you know. What were these adolescent fantasies?"

"The usual. Hand holding in the school hallway where everyone could see, kisses against my locker. Right in front of Darcy Childs, a cheerleader with big breasts who liked to call me Flat Stanley. Dying declarations of love. Jumping off bridges for me."

He grinned. "I'm not afraid of heights, so point me to the bridge. But how could I kiss you and hold your hand? I was in high school when you were in middle school."

She gave him a patient, pitying look. "Because you were so slavishly devoted to me, you'd come to see me whenever you had a free period. And high school got out earlier than middle school, so you'd come walk me home. Showing everyone I was dating a high school boy."

"Sorry," he said gravely. "They didn't give us classes on the workings of a teenage girl's mind."

"It's a serious oversight in our educational system."

He stroked her bangs and played with her earring, shifting closer. She lifted her face to him. They stayed that way for a few minutes, just looking into one another's eyes. Nothing uncomfortable about it. Like on a lazy summer day, swimming in the same creek-fed pond together, hands and feet brushing. Bodies getting closer. Anticipation getting sweeter.

"I talked to Rory and Thomas about us, at the wedding."

"What?" She snapped out of that reverie and leaned back. "Say again?"

"I knew I was going to make my move soon." He seemed unfazed by her reaction. "When it got back to them, I didn't want them thinking I was after something casual or quick. They're your brothers, and they stand for your dad."

"They haven't said a word."

"Well, there was no telling what way it would go. You might have told me to fuck off. That's what Rory said you'd probably do."

"I'm going to steal screws off his sport chair. The wheels will come off and dump him in a ditch next time he works out."

Brick grinned. "Initially, I was only going to talk to Thomas, since he's oldest. But soon as I broached the subject, he brought Rory in on it. He said he might be oldest, but Rory runs the family business, so it seemed appropriate I talk to them both."

Thomas was like that. He thought of all of them when a decision was needed. Regardless...

She eyed him. "It's kind of antiquated. Getting permission from the male head of the family to court one of the females."

Brick's eyes twinkled. "I'm an old-fashioned guy. Plus, I figured they could broach the subject with your mother. When I was a few hours away. Calculated cowardice."

She rolled her eyes. "Yeah, right. My mother loves you. She's got the whole Catholic mama thing. Girls are okay, but boys are freaking sacred."

He raised a brow. "Seriously?"

"I know she loves me dearly." She waved the concern away. "I'm just aware, like most daughters are, that mothers see sons differently. If Rory or Thomas get any accolades, it's like Jesus has performed another miracle. She tells everyone at church. I get into a good medical school with a scholarship? 'That's nice, but wouldn't you rather stay in town and date that nice Garvey boy, the one who's getting a law degree?' Because obviously being a lawyer's wife is far better than being a doctor."

"Tell me she didn't really say that to you."

"It was back when I was in high school. Before everything went down with our dad, Thomas, all of that. Rory. She didn't say it directly, but it wasn't hard to pick up from the subtext. At the time, it made me wonder if she thought I wasn't smart enough, strong enough to do it..."

She pushed past that quicksand. "But with time and hindsight, I think it had more to do with those residual worries from my birth. Subconsciously not comfortable with me being too far away or out of reach. Plus, having a good marriage and babies was what she wanted in life, so why wouldn't I be okay with that?"

"So why aren't you?"

When she stiffened, he shook his head. "I'm not agreeing with her. I'm asking the question. You've always seemed like what you most want is a small-town life, close to your family. So why choose being a doctor, when you had to spend so much time and years away, getting the training for it?"

"It seemed right. Felt right." At his look, she shook her head. "You're turning me back toward that question you asked earlier. You told me to give myself breathing room tonight."

She didn't want to jump into that swamp and try to figure out what kind of debris was floating around in it. She preferred to stay in the sun-warmed pond with him.

"You're right, doc. I retract it. How about a different topic? Earlier, when you were watching the forced orgasm, I said it keyed into your deep need to let go. But I want to dig under that. Tell me what you felt."

"My mind got so full. Whirling...but there was a center to it, a still place. Where it was all calm, in an almost painful way."

"Why painful?"

"Because what I want is clear, but it hurts, because there are no words, no way to let it bleed. So it just throbs."

Fuck, she couldn't stay out of the weeds of her own emotions, but she seemed unable to filter or not say what was going on in her head when she was with him.

His response helped, though. His eyes darkened, his mouth getting that firm look before he leaned in and kissed her, hand braced over her head on the column. He took his time, drawing it out, mouth wet and warm, tongue stroking hers. Her hands went to his shoulders, holding on as his other hand flexed on her waist.

He pulled back to look at her. "What do you want right now, Les? Tell me."

"I want you to take me home. I want you to do...everything. Anything you want. I don't want to take it farther than that. Every-thing is uncertain. I might get back to school and not be able to think about any of this."

At his expression, her heart lurched. She forced herself to say the words. "You won't do it that way, will you?"

"No." His tone, the steel gray eyes, were uncompromising. "Earlier, before Dirk called out to us, you were going deeper with it. I won't force that, but I will ask you to be honest. Everything you've shown me tells me what you are to me. You want me to take you home, do everything you're wanting and I'm wanting, then you make it official."

He lifted her chin with two firm fingers, not letting her look away. "You say it, mean it so I believe it? Then we pursue it that way until you don't want me. Not because of school, or whatever else has happened. We'll work that out."

Her heart was thumping, her throat dry. She'd driven through a rainstorm to him, of all people, rather than going home.

The urgency she'd felt before Dirk and Lisa had joined them hadn't been just an in-the-moment thing. Any more than the feelings between them had been born over these two days, or even a few weeks ago. They'd been planted long ago, and had survived. They were even stronger now than they'd been when just the sound of his voice in her family's house had quickened her pulse, and made her heart beat faster.

The part of her that knew who he was to her, who she wanted him to be to her, sent the words out of her heart and soul, offered them to him on her lips.

Words that were the only truth she was sure about.

"Yes. I want to be your submissive."

CHAPTER SIXTEEN

*T*heir drive home was quiet. He held her hand and she watched the road, the streetlights and the passing cars a dark river of light. When they reached his place and he came around to open her door, she put her hands on his shoulders, holding on. He lifted her out, but he didn't put her down. He wrapped his arms around her back and under her bottom. She linked her legs around his body, putting her head on his shoulder.

He carried her to the door. When he put her down in the foyer and turned the lock, she stood where she had when she'd come out of the rain. He didn't turn on lights, so when she looked in his direction, she saw his silhouette, outlined by the parking lot lights, filtering through the sheer curtains.

"Will you do something with fire here, with me? Can you?"

"Yes. I can. When I'm ready. Because I'm setting the pace, aren't I?"

She could feel the weight of his gaze on her. "Yes, Sir." Her stomach tingled, her thighs. She had one hand resting nervously on the back of the couch, worrying the seam.

"Stay there. I'll be right back."

He went up the stairs, taking two at a time. She listened to him moving above. Her hand closed and unclosed. Obeying his commands constricted things in her, but also made everything spiral, become

224

more intense. Made her want him to give her more commands. Take her over.

Maybe that was problematic, but she was giving herself permission to go with it. She wanted to stay immersed in all she'd seen tonight, stay in the space in her head that said it was okay.

He was back, carrying a blue metal chest with silver reinforced corners. He left it by the fireplace before joining her at the couch. She was still wearing his long-sleeved shirt. After peeling it off her, he guided both her hands to the top cushion, over that thick seam. He stroked her upper arms, the short sleeves of the dress.

When he cupped her breasts through her clothes, thumbs passing over the nipples in the mesh bra, the friction had her arching into his touch, pushing her hips into his groin. When she tried to straighten, thinking he wanted her to stay in place, he flicked one peaking nipple, eliciting a gasp, another jerk of her body against him.

"Animal instincts aren't against the rules. Unless I tell you to contain them. Then you'll do it, until I want you to let them go."

He continued to fondle her breasts, taking his time, exploring the hardening nipples, the swelling flesh. "I'm turning on the light now." He kept his hand at her waist, reaching toward the wall to bring the lights back up. Not full strength. Just enough he could see her, because of what he wanted next. He turned her so she was still facing away from him, but looking toward the kitchen. In the roughness of his voice, she could hear what touching her and taking command was doing for him.

"Bend over and hold onto your ankles, just like I told you I wanted you to do. Let's see how high up that skirt goes."

When she obeyed, the skirt rode up, the gauze overlay ticking the backs of her thighs. He put his hand between her legs, sealing heat and pressure against her sensitive flesh.

"The hem barely covers the crotch." He slid his arm around her waist, holding her steady as his stroking made her sway, arousal pushing her like those waves in the poem. "Your cunt is getting nice and wet. Good girl. Straighten up."

After she did, he moved to the fireplace. He folded the area rug back to the couch, moving the coffee table in that direction to clear the space. Opening the chest, he removed a cotton blanket and rolled up mat resting on top. He unrolled the mat and folded the blanket over it.

He returned to her. As she quivered, he lowered the dress's zipper and removed the garment, draping it on the couch. She'd taken her shoes off again in the truck and left them behind when he carried her from it, so her toes curled against the area rug.

"I like it when you tremble for this. It does things to me, knowing you're a little nervous about putting yourself in my hands, but you have the trust to do it. Lie down on your back on the blanket. Feet planted and knees spread. Arms over your head. I want your back arched, showing me how your nipples are pushing against the bra cups. Do it."

She complied, moving around the couch in panties and bra. She was hyperaware of the air touching her skin, the heat of his presence. The lust and arousal were like one of those weighted blankets, a reassuring cocoon threaded with exhilarating anxiety. She moved in a way she never moved, a sultry swing to her hips.

As she lowered herself to the blanket, he came to stand at her feet. He was a long way up, intimidating and large. He had his hands on his hips, feet braced. His erection was a thick bar against his jeans. Under his demanding gaze, her shaking increased, but she put her hands over her head, pressed her heels to the carpet and parted her knees.

"Wider. Don't forget to arch your back."

She complied, a noise catching in her throat. His eyes were storm fire, passing over every part of her, lingering between her legs, on the points of her nipples, her working throat, and moist, parted lips.

Dropping to a knee beside her, he held his palm over her belly, inches above her flesh. He moved it down, between her thighs. Not making contact, just hovering. She could feel compressed energy in the space between his touch and her skin.

"Feel that heat?" he murmured. "The fuel barrier can keep you from getting burned, but through it you can feel how hot that flame is. I've imagined every inch of this skin, taking possession of it."

He passed his hand over her neck, her face. Her eyes fluttered closed as he finally made contact, laying his palm over them. Her lashes brushed his skin. "I'm in control of your sight, your breath. You'll hear what I want you to hear, you'll listen to what I say. Even when I take my hand away, keep your eyes closed until I tell you otherwise."

She licked her lips, and he passed a fingertip over that moisture, stroking the fullness of her bottom lip. He shifted his damp finger to her nipple, the sheer barrier intensifying sensation.

"It's all here, in every cell of your body. Everything here for me to call. Your fear, your joy, your triumphs, your knowledge. Every inch of you is beautiful to me, Les. That rush of feeling as I touch you, I control that rush. I control how you feel. No matter how high those feelings rise, no matter how they take you over, it's all safe with me."

In darkness, the words came easily. "Yes, Sir."

"I love to hear you call me that. It pleases me a lot, Les. Do you know what an ignition sequence is?"

She shook her head.

"Three things are needed for fire to happen. What's between us, that's the source. Our bodies are the fuel. Then there's the oxidizing agent, like your breath, or my breath on you."

He leaned in, and she imagined him pursing his fine lips as a tickle of air passed over her nipple and throat. She whimpered as the next ripple of heated air was over her mound, telling her how close his mouth was to her sex. He gripped her thigh with one strong hand. "I want to consume you, Les. I want to drive my cock into that fire, let it burn in your heat. I also want to breathe fire over both of us, like a dragon. Don't you move."

She went rigid with the effort to obey as his mouth closed over her cunt, his tongue sliding over the thin cloth of the panties, teasing clit and labia, pressing against the silken barrier to entry. Small cries came from her as the spiraling pressure of arousal became a tornado of fire, just as he'd promised.

"Oh..."

He stopped and she made a little squeak as he clamped his hand over her sex again, tight enough to feel the strength in his grip. "You hold onto that climax, doc. You don't get that until I say so. Isn't that right?"

When he gave her a little swat there, she managed to gasp out the words over the rocketing sensation. "Yes, Sir."

"Good. Open your eyes now. You can watch me prepare for this."

She saw him reach into the chest and set things out on the fireplace. Isopropyl alcohol, the wands with their marshmallow tips.

"You showered last night, right?"

"Yes. I can take another if..."

"No. That's good. You didn't put on any perfume or lotion tonight, right?"

"Just deodorant. I washed off with some moisturizing soap I picked up when we were grocery shopping."

"That should be all right. Let's start with a kiss and holding hands, like any relationship should."

Like her childhood fantasy. There was a trio of dark green pillar candles on the fireplace. When he lit the shortest one, the heated scent brought to mind pine trees, majestically swaying on the borders of harvested fields at home. When the winds picked up, it would carry that aroma to her nose, flutter it across her skin.

"Did you ever pass your finger through the flame of a candle?"

"No." Her voice was throaty. "But I saw kids do it at a party once, when I was in middle school."

"That was when I started doing it. And playing with matches." He held out his hand, and she put hers in it. "You're cold. I'll see if I can fix that. Does it worry you, Les? Letting me take care of you?"

"Yes. At first. Always before, when anyone else did it, I'd resist it, prove that I didn't need that. But with you...I want to need it."

"An important difference. What we want and need." He stroked her fingers one by one, traced the lines of her palm and moved to her wrist. His lightest stroke there set off a ripple of reaction through her arm and breast, down to her thighs and everything in between. He could do that, with no more than a grasp of her wrist.

"Sometimes I worried I resisted my family's coddling just because they were so determined to offer it."

A smile appeared. "Hardheadedness is a Wilder family trait. But what if the right guy—not Bart, someone older and capable, well established—told you he wanted to marry you. You wouldn't have to finish your degree. You could get a job as a dog walker, work in a flower shop, be a housewife. Have..."

He stopped himself. He hadn't used himself in the example, but if it was going to be a true test, he was the only one that would fit in that slot.

"Have kids," she said quietly.

He tightened his grip, tacit agreement to let the hypothetical unfold in that direction. "I'd take care of you. You could step away from all the demands and anxiety you've put on yourself. How would that feel?"

She lay before the fireplace, in nothing but sexy underwear, under the shadow of his large body. In his intent expression she saw the unsettling truth. If they were at the point of their relationship where marriage was on the table—which they weren't, they absolutely weren't—he would willingly give her all that. She could accept all that. Except...

"No," she said. "You wouldn't be okay with that."

"Why not? The doting wife, ready with my beer at the end of the day? Which I would very politely ask her to bring to me, if she wasn't busy with the kids. Please and thank you." His gaze twinkled.

"If I truly wanted that, you'd be all for it," she responded. "But if I didn't, you wouldn't."

"How do you know?" His expression gave her no cues, but she didn't need them.

"Because if you were okay with it, you would have helped me bathe that first night. You wouldn't have told me to pick myself up and get my ass in the shower."

That mask over his expression dropped, stunning her with the depth of what it had hidden. "I wanted to tear apart the world to help you feel better. All I wanted to do was hold you."

"I'm sorry I put you through that." She turned her head to kiss the side of his hand, a shy brush of lips. "But I like that you know when to be nice to me...and when not to be."

He touched her face then clasped her wrist. "Curl your hand in a loose fist, but leave two fingers out straight, side by side."

When she did, he extended her arm toward the lit candle. Before she could tense up, he'd passed her fingers through the flame, holding her securely. Heat touched her like he did, feeling like...

"The kiss," she murmured.

"The first kiss," he confirmed. "More?"

At her nod, he did it several more times. Bringing those fingers to his mouth, he kissed them, moisture on the lingering heat, then drew them in to suck on them. He nipped her, the sharpness of the bite bumping sensation through her lower belly.

He guided her hand back to the floor, letting it rest on its knuckles, palm up. "Ready to move on to handholding? Don't move. Resist the instinct to pull back. Trust me."

"I do." Brick was the type of man a person trusted. He projected the competence and skill to do what he said he could do. She had the historic proof; A student, a dedicated football player, a firefighter. Pursuing his fire sciences degree and becoming an arson investigator said he'd carried that same commitment into adulthood.

They had that in common. They didn't ask for anything to be given to them. They wanted to earn it. Which included his desire to have her. He straddled the line between respect for a woman's choices and a resolve to have her that could overwhelm the senses.

He put the wand in one of the cups, misting the cotton roll tip with the alcohol solution. He lifted and brushed it over her palm, leaving cool dampness in its wake. Then he dipped the dry wand into the candle flame. When he brought the fiery end close to her palm, the fumes from the alcohol reached for it, making fire bloom over her flesh before the wand ever made contact.

It startled her, but he had her wrist, steadying her. He curved over her, his heat and strength. He'd ordered her to stay still, stay still, stay still. She could feel the heat of the flame on the other side of that thin barrier. It was more subtle than she expected, allowing her to relax enough to really feel it. It was a suspended warm whisper, a dance over her flesh. Just as she thought it might be getting too hot, he doused the flame between their two palms, his fingers lacing with hers, holding her securely.

Kissing first, then handholding.

She was trembling again, from all of it. Watching him use the fire, watching herself accept it.

"How was that?"

She lifted her other hand to touch his neck, his broad shoulder, and curled her fingers into the ribbed fabric of his tank. "Good," she whispered.

"I want you to roll over. Cross your ankles and hold your thighs together."

As she did, he took a small pillow from the chest and put it under her hips. That, and crossing her ankles, lifted her backside. Reaching back into the blue chest, he removed a glove, the same natural-colored woven fabric as the flogger wicks. Kevlar, she remembered. Her pulse skipped a beat, as she also remembered their discussion about fire spanking. He worked the glove over his hand and flexed his large, capable fingers, shooting a nervous little thrill through her.

His gaze became undeniably wicked. "I promised to warm you up, didn't I?"

The light slap on her ass made her fingers curl against the floor. He rubbed the affected area with his ungloved hand. "Think you should rise up to my hand, doc. Show your Master you're not afraid of some well-deserved punishment."

"I haven't been formally charged," she said over a dry throat.

"Did I say this had anything to do with fairness?" That look of evil mischief increased. "It's all about having the chance to make your ass red. Once this glove is on fire, you'll have to stay still. But you can do your best to get away now."

He leaned in, the move emphasizing his size, how outmatched she was. "You won't be able to, but it will make my cock even harder, having to hold you down."

She wasn't going to dignify that with a response. She would stay still and take the spanking. But that resolve lasted through two swats. She was pretty sure he was trying to make it sting as much as possible to get her to do what she did. When she tried to scramble away, he clamped an arm over her back and held her down. She yelped as he kept smacking her ass, with a force and aim that told her why it was called impact play. She kept squirming and fighting, even as the strikes acted like a battering ram against a fortress of cravings.

He proved it when he put his hand between her legs, caressing her slick folds under the crotch of the panties. "You're right," he observed. "The wetter the skin is, the more things cling."

She groaned as he found his way under the elastic and sank those fingers into her. He gave her another swat with the gloved hand while he was still inside her, thrusting.

"Oh, God..." Her squirming was no longer about getting away. She was trying to find the rhythm her body wanted. He took the fingers away and went back to spanking her, this time sliding his arm under her to hold her up. The pain was increasing, but she couldn't seem to tell him to stop, to reach for that safeword. She wanted him to keep doing it forever, even if it hurt like hell.

"That's a nice glow," he growled, sliding his arm out from beneath her so she was back on the pillow, her sore buttocks raised. "Les, look at me."

She darted glazed eyes to him. He stroked a wisp of hair from her cheek. "For this next part, you stay as still as you can. No big movements. If you need me to stop, use the safeword. Got it? I want to spank your cunt with fire as well as your ass, but I'm not going to do that until I shave you. Cross your ankles again, close your thighs. It will protect areas with more hair. And what's the most important thing?"

"Stay as still as I can."

"Good girl." He rose, holding a towel he'd pulled from the chest, and disappeared into the kitchen. When he came back, he'd wet it down. "I'm working without a spotter, so we're keeping this low key and very controlled. But if fire goes where I don't want it to be, I'll use this to smother it immediately. Don't bolt."

"I won't."

"I know you won't." He trailed his gloved hand over her backside, then gave her a firm rub that had her wanting to spread her legs, rather than keeping them closed. "Did you like the feeling of the fire?"

"When you're doing it, yes." She didn't need to have it done by anyone else to know that was the truth.

He removed the thin tank, in a captivating ripple of muscle and gleaming skin, the stretch of his body revealing his hip bones. Then he sprayed the glove with his fuel solution, and set the bottle on the opposite side of the fireplace. He misted a wand in one of the cups before passing that damp cotton tip over her backside again. She tried to stay still, though the coolness made her wiggle just a little, her toes curling.

"That's a sexy little move. Next time I'll use ice. The contrast between it and the fire creates a nice reaction."

He put the wand back in the cup before holding the palm of his glove to the candle flame. Tongues of gold and blue flame erupted there.

He ran his ungloved hand over her back, pressing his palm to it. "I love spanking your ass, doc," he murmured. "But I will fucking love spanking your cunt, because I know that will unravel you, grab at those dark fantasies of being owned by a Master."

"My fantasy or yours?" she whispered, looking at the flames flicker on his hand.

"You tell me. Turn your head away from me."

When she'd had her eyes closed, he'd made other preparations. A full-sized mirror was propped against the sofa, so she could see the two of them, her lying naked, her hips lifted, him over her with the flaming, gloved hand. Her arousal spiked. And then spiked higher, as he swept his hand down toward her backside, landing a firm strike.

Stinging heat, against flesh already tender from his spanking. Her nails dug into the wood floor, her lips pressed together. She was both voyeur and subject. Her attention clung to the muscles moving across his chest, his shoulders, the concentration in his expression, the crease of his jeans over his thighs. A Master in belted jeans and no shirt, powerful, in control. She wanted to be owned by him in every way.

He'd spanked her without fire. Spanking her with it gave the impact moment an extra bright pop, or spark of warmth, like something was combusting upon contact. All of it added to the heat and sensation, kept them building. "Oh God...please..."

She squealed and jerked when he doused the flames between the glove and her flesh on a particularly strong swat. At the same moment, he pushed ungloved fingers into her, enough of them to give her that uncomfortable but not painful feeling of impalement, a Master's demand that she take him inside. She clamped down on him, held him tight. It felt amazing, but she was gasping, whimpering, and she wanted...

"Yeah," he muttered. "You need my cock, baby, don't you? Say it."

"I need...your cock. Please. Sir."

Her words had a frustrated, needy edge, brought from the place within her that would never say such words aloud. Until he demanded it.

In the mirror she watched him rise to his feet, unbuckle his belt and open his jeans. He stripped off the glove, toed off shoes and socks, then pushed the rest off. He stood fully naked in the view of that mirror, letting her look her fill. His erection was thick and ready.

When he gripped it, that edgy noise became a petulant whimper.

His gaze held hers like steel locked around her throat, his bond every bit as strong as the chains she'd seen holding more than one sub to their Dom tonight.

"You want to know what my fantasy is, doc? Having you as my submissive, able to explore everything I want from you. Down to the parts of your soul that will open up even deeper desires than you ever knew you had. That commitment you made to me tonight, that's the gateway. We've crossed it. Nothing from here forward limits us but us."

He headed toward the mirror without self-consciousness. Her gaze stayed locked on his thighs and stiff cock, the shift of his ass as he repositioned the mirror. On her stomach, with her head turned, she couldn't see herself anymore, but before she could miss that, he was in front of her.

"Up on your knees. You know the position now. Back straight, hands behind you, breasts out."

He was close enough he could cup her skull, his fingers threaded into the overlapping strands of her French braid, digging in. "You've fantasized about taking your Master's cock in your mouth. I saw it that day I took you to dinner, and more than once since you've been here. Tell me. Say it out loud."

She moistened her lips, her gaze on his powerful erection, so close in front of her she could have leaned forward to kiss the tip. If he permitted it.

I'd like to be on my knees, with you in my mouth. I'd like to have your hand in my hair, holding me. Making me serve you.

She'd thought the words when masturbating, when looking at that picture. When she said them aloud now, she stammered over them, but when he gripped himself again, her voice broke with her need.

"Please, Sir."

"Keep your hands behind your back and part your lips."

As she did, he fed his cock in between them. A bliss, a relief, a need fulfilled, took over almost instantly. He cupped her head again, working himself slowly in and out of her lips, her tongue tasting, stroking, cheeks drawing in to suck on him.

"Fucking hell, I can smell how wet you are from up here, but that's the most tranquil I've ever seen you, doc. Good thing I didn't know this was what would calm you down. I'd have had my cock in your mouth from the first time you knelt in my living room."

She wasn't sure how that was a bad thing, but all she wanted right now was to do this. But as always, he reminded her who was in charge. After a couple moments of letting her tease, suckle and convey her deep need to serve, he muttered an oath and tightened his hand on her hair, drawing himself free. She sucked on his substantial girth and length, her jaw and cheeks hurting from the effort, but with a good pain. Like her throbbing backside.

"Not going to come in your mouth tonight, doc. We have other places to go. But you'll get your chance plenty of other times, I can promise you that. Down on your elbows."

When he moved behind her, she saw he'd moved the mirror so she could see him kneel behind her. He pressed a kiss to her backside, tenderized by his hand and flame, and bit her again. She shuddered, a cry breaking from her throat. He did it forcefully enough she suspected marks would be left on her ass. He straightened, meeting her eyes in the mirror.

"This moment will be your reminder, the return to center, whenever you need it. From here forward, from the beginning, middle, and all the way to the end, I'm your Master, and you're my submissive. Friends, lovers, confidantes, combatants, partners, soul mates, wherever this journey takes us, that's still the core of our relationship, now and always."

His gray gaze was fierce. The words were from his heart, she was sure, but she wondered if he'd said them to her in his head, long before he said them now. They came forth with the force of a ritual oath.

"Because that's who I am with you, and who you are with me. Do you understand? I want to hear your response."

"Y-yes. Yes, Sir. Please."

He loosened the band on her braid and then combed his fingers with firm purpose through her hair, removing the layers, letting it fall free around her shoulders and face. At least until he bound it anew, in the grip of his hand. He used the handful of it to pull her head up, chin raised, the angle enough to make her arch her back.

He stroked his other hand over her side, underneath her, to

possess a breast, pinch the nipple. Her body reacted, throwing her hips up higher to him, asking, begging.

Animal instinct.

"Watch me take you, doc," he said. "Fuck you like you're mine forever. Because as long as you want that, you are."

More harsh cries tore from her throat as he thrust into her, holding her hair, his other hand on her hip. He pushed her back to her elbows, which helped her brace herself against his enormous strength, even as she knew he was holding back. To care for her, while letting her feel how thrillingly helpless she was. She had to take what he was going to give her.

It was as he'd said. Their bodies the fuel, their feelings the source. The breath she drew into her was the oxygen that had the fire leaping ever higher, that orgasm coming, irresistible. When he changed his angle, holding her almost off her knees as he drove into her, it was upon her before she could try to stop it.

"Brick..."

"It's all right. Come hard for me. Come loud."

She couldn't stop herself from doing either of those things. His cock rubbed against blood-filled, slick flesh as she clutched down on him. When his hand moved back over her breast, teasing, pinching and flicking her nipple at the height of the climax, the spears of sensation propelled her even higher, as did the slap of his body against her buttocks, another kind of spanking. She wanted his discipline, wanted his punishment, his possession. Her cries became screams, long, needy sounds that echoed into the canyon of everything she wanted to be with and for him.

It wasn't until her climax began to ebb that he let his own take him. He dropped down over her, pushing her further toward the mat, her chin and lips brushing it. His hand came back to her hair, wrapped into it and turned her head forcibly so he could clamp his mouth on her neck for the finish, his teeth pressing cruelly against her flesh. Another place she'd be marked by him. Pain had never felt so good.

He kept going until she'd experienced every possible aftershock, until she had to rely on his strength because she had none to hold herself up.

And when he finally eased out of her, he cared for her fragile, raw state. He brushed kisses between her shoulder blades, along her spine, touching his lips to her buttocks. Her flesh had that glowing, slightly sore feeling, like from a sunburn. When she twitched under the friction between his mouth and her skin, he made a soothing noise. "I'll rub some Vitamin E oil into that to help."

It took a few moments for her to find words, to try to sort her brain cells to tease him. "You better."

"Have I mentioned your pushy brat side makes me want to find my belt?" He chuckled as she tensed. "I like it when you want the pain, want to ride the pleasure that can come with it. But right now your sweet skin needs care, not punishment. Plus..."

He dropped to his hip and elbow next to her, with a thump and a half-groan, before rolling on his back and pulling her onto his chest. "You've worn me out. I need some recuperation time."

She smiled, a deep sigh leaving her. Contentment. A few minutes later, when she thought she should push herself up to a sitting position and find that wet towel to help clean them both up, his arm tightened across her back, holding her. "Unh-unh. You stay right here. I like having you naked and draped on me. Plus, you move away, you'll get cold. Can't have that."

She propped her chin on his chest, tracing his pectoral, making a circular track up to the broad shape of his shoulder and back down again. "Those love letters you collected," she said. "Do you know any by heart, like you do poetry?"

"I collected a lot of correspondence. Not just that kind. Rufus is an ass."

"He's right, though, that you liked them the best? You did say you're a romantic."

"I'm a Renaissance man. I appreciated cannon schematics, demolitions and battle tactics as much as my romantic side appreciated the other." He pushed her head back down against his chest, making her smile.

"You'd have been interested in some of the medical correspondence," he added. "Requests for certain supplies, discussions of field medicine and surgery practices. Though how little resources they had to treat battle injuries and disease will horrify you. Particularly toward the war's end."

"Do you keep all that here?" She stroked his pectoral again, played in his chest hair.

"Some. But a lot of what Rufus and I collected on our trip, plus further research I did, are indexed and with my parents. My dad is using it to write a book. Plus, in addition to teaching at the middle school here, he does a summer course on the Civil War at the college."

"Did you do that for him because you felt bad about deciding not to be a teacher?"

Brick grunted, trailing a hand along her spine, over her hip. "Maybe partly. But he respected my choice, and maybe because he did, I was able to appreciate his, and develop my own interest in it. I like helping him. It's something we can do together as adults, like the re-enacting when I was a kid."

If the two of them were in a relationship together, she'd get the chance to know his parents better. Ask his dad questions and see that passion for history surface, like his son's passion for it from a different direction. Brick was definitely the kind of man who brought a girl home to spend time with his family. What would they think of her?

His eyes had shut again, his breath evening out. She didn't want to go there in her head, but it came to her anyway. *"So, Les, what are you doing with your life? Why do you deserve to be with our son?"*

Stop it.

Brick's arm tightened around her. He started stroking her again, down her sensitive back, over her hip and rise of her buttock. Back up the valley of her spine to her nape. The curve of her shoulder. It never stopped amazing her, how her body responded to his touch, as if his fingers awakened reactions in her that had waited just for him.

"'It is very hard here. There are times the only joy in my day comes from thoughts of you and our young son. Does William play in the vegetable garden while you tend it? Does he exasperate his mother with mischief, the way his father does?'"

He hadn't forgotten her request. And he'd felt her tension. Even without knowing the exact cause, he found a way to pull her back from that edge.

His voice was like the trundling of a wagon over a dirt road, evoking the movement of troops, a soldier grabbing a few minutes to write a letter home. It made it easy to hear the words as they might have been felt by the original author. It was the way he recited poetry as well.

"'Do not misunderstand me when I say this, but the relief I feel

238

that you are not here, dear Constance, could fill all the space in Heaven. I would suffer through this a hundred times to spare you the sights I have seen. When, God willing, we see one another again, I will look to see the things in your beautiful eyes that this war has hidden from my heart.'"

Brick paused. "From there, he went on to talk about mundane things. Instructions on what price she should pay for seed, messages she should convey to his father and mother, either because they couldn't read, or because his correspondence time was limited."

"Who was he?"

"A corporal from Kentucky. He fought for the Confederacy. His older brother was a lieutenant with the Union army. Unmarried. I've never located a letter from him, but I expect they both wrote home. I wondered, if his parents didn't read well, if they both sent their letters to Constance. I thought about his mom and dad, worrying that their two boys would face one another on a battlefield. In the same letter, at the end, the corporal—his name was Samuel—says, 'I often think of Matthew, and the path we followed to reach such an impasse.'"

His hand's movement across her back had become a slow, meditative fan, the sensation like ripples in a pond. "They're buried on the family farm in Kentucky, side by side. Supposedly. Samuel died at Gettysburg, and Matthew died in the prison camp at Andersonville. Most of the dead at Andersonville never left, so it's possible there's no body in Matthew's grave, just a headstone and the wish that he could have been buried there. A stone between their graves says 'Together agin, a-g-i-n.' I expect one of his parents put it there."

"Yet Samuel wrote so well."

"The parents' lack of literacy likely drove their resolve to see their sons well-educated. My maternal great-grandparents had four years of schooling between them, but my grandfather and his brother both graduated from the University of Virginia with business degrees."

"Parents want more for their kids."

"Yeah."

She thought about that, feeling sorrow for people she'd never met. "Where is Constance buried?"

"She's right beside her corporal. She lived to be an old woman. Never married again. Their son, William, had ten kids, though. The land still belongs to his descendants. They run a B&B on it. They claim that sometimes you'll see Samuel and Constance strolling together in the gardens. We can go visit sometime. Stay for a weekend, if you'd like."

She would. She gazed at the still lit candle, flickering and reflecting in the glass fireplace screen. *Parents want more for their kids.* She swallowed. Brick's arm tightened.

"I know you're worried about facing your family," he said, "but that's part of why I want to take you home for Easter."

She braced herself on her elbow again to gaze down at him. Brick threaded a hand through her hair, letting it fall back on his chest. "That letter, it shows how love and family help you deal with stuff. Because of what happened, maybe you think you don't deserve to lean on their support and the strength that connection gives you."

"Samuel lived in a simpler time."

He pressed a hand against her back, holding her to him. "Bullshit. You and I can relate to that letter because he was struggling with the same shit we all do. The paths we take, the mistakes, the things we learn, the losses we experience. That never changes."

He stroked her face, fingertips light against her cheek and jaw. "The other thing that doesn't change is what gets us through. Love. It finds the way through all of the things we fuck up and can't understand."

She wanted it to be true, but it didn't change what she'd done. It could never change what she'd done. And yet...

She lay back down, pressing her face against his throat, his heart under her hand. She had her leg over his thigh, her knee close to his groin, his replete cock. While the intimacy gave her a lingering twinge in the same region of her own body, her mind and heart turned over things just as intimate and vulnerable.

"I miss them," she said, her voice tight.

"I know you do."

"I wonder..."

"What?" he asked when she couldn't immediately go on.

"You know the marry-a-lawyer thing from my mom? I think I transformed the lack of high expectations from her and others into the belief that they didn't think I was up to the task of meeting them. I've been trying to prove them wrong, while believing they might be right. Which in turn makes me way more anxious with the clinical part, and high-pressure decision situations like the ER."

She knew he wouldn't dismiss her concerns with platitudes, though the direction he took twisted her gut like a worn-out garden hose. He touched her brow, the cut under her bangs. "The mom attacking you was bad enough. But there was more to it, wasn't there?"

This was probably what he did in an arson investigation. Noting the clues, documenting the information, narrowing down the problem so he could point to a source buried under debris.

When she sat up again, his hand moved to her hip. Maintaining contact. "She was screaming at me. 'You shouldn't be a doctor. No one like you should be a doctor.'" Her voice hitched over the words, and Les rubbed a hand over face, then up over the cut. She started to rub it harder, but he was already clasping her wrist, taking her hand away. He squeezed it, hard enough to give her a twinge. Giving her the pain she needed to focus.

"I don't know how to find the 'professional' detachment for something like this," she admitted. "It's not less important or horrible if the patient had been an adult, but her whole world has been destroyed. Knowing I contributed to it..."

He sat up and closed his arms around her as her voice broke and tears spilled out, no matter her efforts to contain them. Not as violent as the previous two times, but she'd just had mind and body draining sex. She wasn't optimistic enough to think she was dealing with it better, or getting closer to making decisions about it.

"If I do walk away, decide to something else, it might be a relief, not to cart around all that worry." Her voice was tired, broken. "Even if this haunts me forever, I won't have to worry I'll fail again."

"You don't quit because you're afraid." He spoke against her ear. "You quit because you know it's not the right path for you. So until you resolve this shit in your heart, you don't get to quit."

"Says who?"

"Says me. Says the Master who will put his foot up your ass if you give up on yourself."

She thought about shoving away from him, but when thought translated to action, he just tightened his hold around her. She sighed, the fight going out of her, at least for now. "Brick, I hate being confused and indecisive. It makes me want to scream."

"I get that." He tugged her hair. "In the end, most things boil down to something simple, a truth that was there all along. Once you get to it, it will tell you what to do with your life."

"And who with?" She tried for a smile.

He kissed her nose. "I sure hope so. Though for now, I recommend you defer to my vast insight on that topic. You have enough on your plate to figure out."

She nestled down in his arms with a semi-frustrated sigh. But at least one decision had become clearer.

"I'd like to go home for Easter," she said. "With you."

CHAPTER SEVENTEEN

*O*ver the next couple days, Les resolved not to interfere with the work Brick had to get done. He'd already taken a comp day for her, and would be taking off additional days for the M&M and Easter holiday. He might be a workaholic with plenty of comp days stored up, but still.

She also wanted to shadow him for as much of it as was allowed. Which was why she was in his truck now. He'd reviewed Colin's follow-up witness statement yesterday, and that, plus some of the other lab results he evaluated, were bothering him. He wanted to revisit the site, specifically the kids' room.

When she'd asked to come with him, he'd initially refused her. He'd pointed out that seeing the stark reality of how they'd died was far more sobering than discussing it at Brick's kitchen table. And yes, while she'd faced things like that in the ER, she had to acknowledge she was carrying things inside her right now that could be set off when she wasn't expecting it.

The flip side was the M&M was the day after tomorrow and she didn't want to be alone with her thoughts. She would lose her mind. Balancing the two arguments, Brick eventually relented.

The home was in a section outside the city that reminded her of the area where Rufus lived. Rural, along a narrow two-lane road where the houses were more widely spread out, and mostly mobile homes or smaller, older structures.

When they turned down the Whitfield driveway and Les saw what used to be a home, she understood Brick's reluctance to bring her here. One half of the structure had collapsed. What walls and roof remained were blackened, sagging, or torn up with holes the firefighters had made to vent or contain the fire.

It was impossible to look at the ruins and not imagine the mother and two children who'd died in the blaze.

"I can take you back to that McDonald's we passed," Brick said, watching her closely. "They have wi-fi, and I can come back to get you."

"It's all right." She pulled her tablet out of her bag. "I'm going to sit here and study, just like we talked about, while you go in and double check whatever it is you're double checking for."

Last night, he'd gone over so many variables he was juggling on this case, she'd gotten lost in all the forensic speak. Normally, she drank in details like that, but she'd been sleepy. The diagnosis for her fatigue was four earth-shattering multiple orgasms spread out over the day. In the bedroom, against the wall in the hallway. On the sofa. And on the kitchen table, before he made her dinner.

He told her he was just freeing up her mind to work the problem. Who was the smartass now?

The orgasms hadn't been quick waves of sensation. Brick McGuire was a thorough man, and he didn't believe in half measures. He'd taken her over fully each time, letting her explore just how intense sex could be when linked to a Master's orders. *Kneel. Suck me.*

That was how it had started yesterday. Her reaction to oral had made an impression on him, one he was more than willing to revisit. She'd woken up in the early morning to go to the bathroom. When she returned, he was sitting on the edge of the bed, his hand on an enormous erection. He pointed to the spot between his feet.

"Kneel and suck me. I want to come in your throat first thing this morning."

When he took her into the shower afterward, he wouldn't allow her to wash herself. He did all of it, every crevice. Though she was shuddering with arousal, he let her suffer without a release. He did at least make her breakfast.

Mid-morning, she'd brought some cut fruit to his bedroom office to share. As she put it beside him, he was on his phone, setting up a fire code inspection on a factory in the area. As he went over the details, he scribbled words on a pad at his elbow.

Thank you. Take off your panties and jeans and bend over the end of the bed. Spread your legs.

He ate the fruit and finished his call while she did that. Whenever she looked over her shoulder toward him, she found him leisurely gazing at her backside and sex. Her cunt got wetter and wetter from nothing more than the visual attention.

After he ended the call, he put his thumbs in his mouth, one after the other, to suck the juice off of them. Or so she thought. He pushed back from the desk and came around it, his strides purposeful. Putting both large hands on her ass, he parted the cheeks so he could tease her rim with those damp thumbs. When she was gasping and wiggling, he dropped to a knee and started eating her pussy.

He kept doing it until she screamed through an orgasm so intense it strained her vocal cords and her thigh muscles, from her convulsing against his relentless grip.

She was lucky he was a caring Dom, because after he had her against the hallway wall two hours later, he'd made her a sandwich for lunch and let her take a nap on the sofa. Naked, covered by a blanket. He woke her up by moving her into his lap and kissing her, putting his hand between her legs to stroke her until she was begging. Then he lifted her to a straddle, lowered her on his cock, and had her ride him until they both released.

He made her study after that. Until sex on the table and dinner time.

"Les?"

"Sorry, yes?"

He lifted a brow. "You're sure you're okay?"

"Yes. I'm okay. Really." *You nearly fucking me to death helps me forget I'm at the scene of a family tragedy.* Whether it was something she could admit or not, thinking of him taking her over that way helped her. Except for when she'd slept naked on the sofa, she'd worn one of his T-shirts all day. Nothing beneath it.

"I want you accessible, doc."

Her five pictures had always helped her level out during times of stress. She had a feeling they'd been irrevocably replaced by images of what he'd done to her, and imaginings of what he intended to do to her next.

"All right. I have my phone. If you need me to come back out, text me. Don't follow me in, no matter what. Remember what I told you. Burned materials can still put off bad stuff, days later. That's why I'll wear gear to go inside."

"Understood."

He retrieved a protective suit, hat and face mask from the storage box in the truck bed, donning it in a matter of minutes. She noted he also had turnout gear in there, including an SCBA. Always the ready firefighter, even as an arson investigator.

She settled into her seat, knee against the console as she turned toward him, showing she was comfortable studying there. She pointed to her pack of crackers and soda. "Seriously, I'm good to go. I used to sit in that tree in our backyard for hours reading, with nothing but a Moon Pie and a cherry cola."

"I remember. I could see you from Rory's window."

"And I could see you." She smiled. "I always hoped there would be some reason for you to strip down."

"Your parents should have given you more spankings."

She stuck her tongue out, but she also touched his hand. "Take your time and get done what you need to get done. If this wasn't an accident, I want you to get the asshole who did it."

"You and me both." He grabbed his pack and shovel and headed for the house.

Les watched him head off, wondering how many decades would pass before she wasn't stirred up watching him do his job. But seeing him against the backdrop of this burned home brought a more sobering thought. Every fire he went into exposed him to the risk of serious injury. Or death.

There was no point to that line of thinking. She'd thought being a doctor was a calling for her, something she needed and wanted to do. Now she wasn't sure. But for Brick, there was no doubt how deep it ran for him. She had to accept that worry without resentment or regret, because it was who he was. But she was glad he was an investigator, not always on the front line.

He'd taken the main case folder with him into the house, but he'd left out a family picture of Jasmine and her children. On the way over, he'd tapped the image of the little girl, who was holding a stuffed bear tight against her. "Jasmine told Tracey she wouldn't go to sleep without it."

She expected he'd left that picture behind to help her think of the people they'd been, instead of burned corpses. Before she popped open her soda to take a sip, she tucked the picture inside the front cover of her tablet to protect it. Then she started working on her exam questions.

Despite her mind's wish to wander back to the incredible sex she'd had yesterday, she corralled it enough to start digesting information. Occasionally she'd look up to see if she saw any sign of Brick. By the time a half hour had passed, she'd made herself eat a couple crackers so Brick wouldn't admonish her for her lack of appetite. She was taking another swallow of soda to wash down the last bite when she heard a crunching gravel noise.

A red truck was pulling into the driveway behind her. It had a firefighter vanity plate on the front. Someone who knew Brick, perhaps here for a similar follow up.

She opened her door as the man slid out of the truck. He looked tired, as if he'd been fighting fires for days. He was unshaven, wearing jeans and a dark blue T-shirt, the pocket printed with the logo of a firehouse.

"Ma'am."

"Hi. Are you looking for Brick?"

"Is he inside? I thought they were done with it."

"He was following up on some details. I'm Les." When she extended her hand, the man's eyes slid to the house, then back to her again. He started, as if he was just noticing her courtesy. He shook her hand, his palm dry and chapped, his grip like his expression. Distracted.

"Yeah, sorry. My head's not really right these days. I'm Colin Werther. Um...this was my girlfriend's house."

"Oh. Oh, God. I'm so sorry." She stepped closer and put a hand on his arm. His eyes had a haunted look. Her care skills kicked in, as did her natural desire to ease pain. "Why don't we go sit on that bench over there, under the tree? I'm sure Brick will be out soon. Or we can text him. He said something about there being toxic stuff in there, so you should probably wait out here."

"Yeah." A faint smile touched his face and she grimaced.

"Sorry, you know all that. Do you want a bottle of water? I have some in the car."

He seemed to take her words in slow motion, a beat behind when she said them. She was familiar with grief's widespread path. The shock of the loss could radiate into the subsequent days, miring the person in the echoes.

He'd nodded, so she retrieved the water. As she did, she also brought her tablet. If he wanted to sit without conversation, she could make him feel less self-conscious about that by studying. "Did you want me to text Brick?"

"No...I'm sure he'll be out soon." When she handed him the water, she offered him a peanut butter cracker. Another painful half smile crossed his face as he shook his head. His gaze went back to the house, as if he couldn't look away. "So you and Brick...are you his girlfriend?"

She sat down next to him, clasping the tablet in her lap with both hands. "We're kind of working that out. We've known one another a long time. Since we were kids. It's a recent development, in some ways."

"In some ways?" He looked toward her.

Perhaps because the subject had turned to something else, he looked a little more tuned into the conversation. Because of that, she decided to be more forthcoming than she normally would be with a stranger.

"I think there's always been something between us."

"Yeah. It can be like that. Even when Jasmine and I had our problems, it was still there. It's inevitable, being with someone you're meant to be with. No getting away from it. The kids weren't mine, you know. Two different fathers, and she didn't really know either one, because of the drugs. But that didn't mean anything. I told her I'd be a dad to those kids. She was trying. She tried really hard..."

He trailed off. "Sorry."

"No reason to be. Substance abuse is hard to kick," Les said tentatively.

"Yeah." A wealth of turbulent emotions was in the red-rimmed, weary gaze. "What do you do?"

"I'm studying to be a doctor. Third year med student."

She hesitated before she said it. She didn't know if that was still true, but a simple answer was best for a man already dealing with too much in his head.

Confirming it, he hadn't noticed her hesitation. He'd fallen into a brooding silence and was watching the house again. Following the intuition that had compelled her to bring it, she opened the tablet, to make it clear he didn't have to talk to her if he didn't feel up to it.

She'd forgotten about the photo. Colin's attention was drawn to her movement, and his gaze snapped right to it. "How do you have this?" He reached out and lifted it from the tablet pocket. Though she wished she hadn't revealed it, it was just a copy of what they'd printed in the local paper, not detailed crime scene photos. She assumed it was okay for him to see it.

"It's in the file. Brick showed it to me."

"He talked to you about the case?"

"Only the high-level stuff." He'd shared more than that, because he could trust her with the info. Just like he could trust her not to mention that. Even so, Colin's unfathomable expression made her uneasy. Would Brick get into trouble if Colin told someone he'd talked to her about it?

"Weird to have that in the official file." Colin stared at it, his thumb moving over Jasmine's face. Then over the boy, and the little girl with the bear.

"Were you there the day it was taken?" Les ventured.

He didn't answer. He rose, still clutching the picture, and moved toward the house.

"Colin, I don't think..."

"It's okay. I'm not going in. I'll see if he's somewhere visible from the kitchen entry point. I need to talk to him."

Cursing herself for letting him see the photo, Les stood, watching him uncertainly. Then she pulled out her phone and texted Brick.

Brick crouched next to the space heater. During the earlier part of the investigation, he'd had to remove pounds of debris from on top of it. When the firefighters had done the post-fire overhaul to verify it was completely out, they'd torn down portions of the wall behind it and the ceiling above it.

He could still see the cone pattern traces along the wall, though, where the smoke and fire had climbed from that ignition source. Most of the dresser was a crumbling hulk, particularly the side nearest the heater. Paper burned up fast, but the chemical residue around the heater had supported the falling magazine theory. Probably older editions of the slick-paged women's magazines Jasmine had taken from the hair salon. Tracey said she liked to look through them.

So she'd come to tuck the kids in, and maybe her elbow had hit the stack of magazines, putting them close to the edge. They'd fallen later, after she walked out and headed to the kitchen. Or maybe while she was there. If she was angry, worked up or already high, she would have paid them little attention.

Like any crime, it was putting together a story, but it required a rigorous application of the scientific method. The aim wasn't to prove and support a hypothesis. It was to do your best to *disprove* it. The hypothesis you couldn't disprove was closest to the truth, though that could also simply mean he hadn't found the evidence to invalidate *that* hypothesis. As the saying went, every fact was just a theory that hadn't yet been disproven.

The plastic toys scattered over the floor had melted and warped. Any stuffed animals in the fire's path would have been obliterated. Even so...

He shifted the space heater. He'd pulled samples from what was around and beneath it to get lab confirmation on the magazines. Now he used his tweezers to prod and poke through the debris. Looking for what he'd remembered seeing there.

There. The light from his head lamp reflected off a melted piece of plastic. He cleared the area around it before picking it up in the tweezers. The space heater had covered and protected it enough he could still identify it.

A plastic eye from a stuffed toy.

He'd found other things like it, which was why he'd left it. But now he was thinking about the bear Jasmine's daughter held in the picture. Its eyes had been purple. Though soot coated it, he used the fingertip of his glove to see a glimmer of what could be that color.

He'd take it back to the lab to be sure, though his gut told him this was it. This was an eye from that bear.

He recalled the deputy's notes from Tracey Sharone's interview. Jasmine had the family photo tucked into the mirror at her salon station, and Tracey had gazed at it with tears in her eyes.

"Candy wouldn't go to sleep without that bear. She'd clutch it like it was her own baby. Jasmine could come into her room in the middle of the night, and she'd be holding it as if it was the only thing she was sure of. Jasmine blamed herself for that, but said it helped her, every time she was tempted to fall off the wagon. She was sure she was going to make it this time. I believed it."

Jasmine had kept the space heater across the room from the children, well out of range of anything falling from the bed. Maybe Candy had started to feel more secure about things, such that her hand had loosened on the bear in her sleep. Her mother, zoned out on drugs, had picked it up off of the floor and put the bear on top of the magazines after the child fell asleep.

Yet all the details were playing through his mind. *We saw him leave that morning. Mom looked asleep, kids in back...*

Tracey said Jasmine had moved from doing shampoos and sweeping up to getting her own station, doing coloring under Tracey's supervision. She was gaining confidence. Had told Colin she wanted to be friends.

"She was considering a date with a guy who'd asked her, from one of her classes."

He could have the eye tested for any accelerant traces, but they hadn't found any anywhere else. It was why they were leaning toward an accident. That and the seemingly obvious negligence of a mother who'd been found with a syringe in her arm and traces of the drug paraphernalia around her.

A competent arsonist wouldn't have needed an accelerant. The house had old wood floors with some termite rot beneath an even older carpet. All a good fire would have required was privacy and time —their rural location provided those—and a fast-burning ignition source. Grabbing up a pile of stuffed animals and tossing the magazines on top of an old space heater with few safety features would have qualified.

"Shit," Brick muttered. No investigator wanted it to point toward one of their own. But all those details jumbled in his mind were sorting, revolving around a center point.

A point that turned ice-cold and speared him as he read Les's text.

Brick swiftly put the plastic eye in an evidence bag and tucked it away. When he headed toward the exit point, he shouldered the short-handled shovel.

Colin stood silhouetted in the opening. Brick still had the face shield down, covering his expression. He had a damn good poker face, but it gave him more time to set it. Colin's gaunt features, the tangled, sick emotions in his eyes, didn't dissolve that cold feeling. It took it right to glacier ice.

No matter how much Brick wanted to be wrong, he wasn't.

Colin stepped back so Brick could emerge and stand on the cracked and scorched concrete porch stoop. Les wasn't far. She had her hips against the front bumper of Brick's truck, and she looked worried. Though he didn't know why, he was sure it wasn't for the same reasons he was.

That was a good thing. As he stripped off the white coveralls, now stained black, he lifted a hand to her, the casual "give me a minute" sign. In the next few minutes, he had to do the best acting job of his life. With Les only a stone's throw away, he had zero confusion about his priorities.

"Colin, man, you shouldn't be here." Removing the helmet and mask, he rumpled his hair. He injected compassion and firmness in his tone, a fellow firefighter concerned for the man's wellbeing, and an arson investigator doing his job.

"Yeah, well, you know. I can't seem to keep myself away."

"You haven't been inside, right? You know that messes with our investigation."

"No, man. Just outside, like this." Colin's eyes slid away from his, then came back. "I just wish I'd been able to help her. That I hadn't pissed her off that day. I feel like I did something to set her off, even knowing she'd relapsed before."

"Yeah. It's a shame. Her boss at the hair place said she'd been doing so good."

"You talked to Tracey?"

"We talk to everyone. You know that."

Colin gazed at the charred kitchen behind Brick, as if he could see

Jasmine sitting at the table that had been there. Was he remembering sticking the needle in her arm? Had he tied her up? There'd been no evidence of restraints, but a burned body, all the fluids sucked from it by the heat, was severely reduced in size, losing a lot of details. Coroners, just like detectives, often didn't dig past a certain point. Not if they had a plausible reason for a fire and they felt they'd crosschecked and investigated enough. They all had caseloads.

Colin's firehouse had been one of those trained on what to look for, to help Brick's department determine accident or arson.

Every good intention could be twisted for the wrong purpose.

Brick took a couple steps toward the truck and met Les's gaze. *Get in the damn truck. Get in the truck.* He'd left the keys in it, so she could conceivably drive away, go get help if something went bad here.

Shit, she'd picked up that something was off. Her gaze became puzzled. Brick schooled his face to a neutral mask as he turned back toward Colin. He shifted casually, but kept himself between her and the fireman. "I'm headed back to the office, but I thought I might stop at your firehouse, since it's on the way. You know I like to shoot the shit with you guys, remind myself of when my job was a lot simpler."

His half-smile wasn't too much for their surroundings, but would look like a reasonable attempt to get Colin away from the site where he'd lost his girlfriend. "Maybe you could do me a solid, let my girl sit in the front seat of an engine and blow the horn."

Colin blinked. "Yeah. Yeah of course. You know, I saw Norman at the diner a couple days ago. He said you still weren't convinced it was an accident."

Fucking hell. Norman was the incident commander from the fire. Brick was going to tear a strip from his ass. But as he knew too well, Colin's own house would be the first to eliminate him from the suspect list. Cops and firefighters were both bad about letting things leak to their own, thinking it was safe, that the information wouldn't get to the wrong people.

Like the top suspect.

Brick shrugged. "I have to be thorough. I'm just going over the details, finalizing the paperwork."

"What do you think happened here, Brick? You think someone did this deliberately? Because..." Colin took a breath. "Did Tracey

253

mention there was a new guy in Jasmine's life? She didn't have the best judgment, particularly when drugs were involved. Maybe it was a guy who used like her."

Brick gave Colin a no-nonsense look, behaving as he would be expected to act. "I know you're going through a bad time. But this is the last time I'm going to say it. I can't talk about witness statements, or any information about the case."

He moved forward to lay a friendly hand on Colin's shoulder, giving it a brief squeeze. The man was tense as a board. His pulse was jumping in his throat. Brick stepped back. "Go home, or follow me to your firehouse. You look like you could use some time with your guys. Not here at this shitshow."

He tilted his head toward their vehicles, an invitation, then moved toward Les. As he carried his gear, he kept his pace measured. He'd guide Les to the passenger door, help her in. Circle around the back, get in, and drive away.

He saw Les's expression freeze a blink before Colin spoke from behind him. "It was me letting myself be seen with them that morning, wasn't it? I knew that could fuck it up, but I didn't want any of the guys trying to go into the house, do an S&R. I knew the condition of the place. I'd set it up so by the time they got here, it would be fully involved."

Brick pivoted, seeing what Les had, the gun Colin held. Trained on Brick's chest, because he'd kept himself in front of Les. He'd never in his life been so glad he was the size of a billboard.

"Why couldn't you just let it go?" Colin's voice was tired. Eyes flat like a walking corpse. "She was a goddamn junkie."

"She was a woman getting her life back on track, and it was looking like you weren't going to be part of that life," Brick said quietly. "It hurt. I get that. But the kids, Colin? What the fuck was that about?"

He could go the placating route, or he could react how Colin might expect any sane person to react. Asking Colin a question might give them extra seconds.

"Couldn't leave the kids without their mama. My mother died young. I know how hard that is. I was protecting them, letting them go with her. They didn't feel a thing. I put the sedative in the donuts and her coffee, so all of them were out like lights when I brought them back. I sat in the kitchen holding her hand, watching the fire build. I didn't leave her alone until I absolutely had to, Brick. She even mumbled my name a few times. Like she did when she needed me to help clean her up, take care of her."

Colin lowered the gun halfway, his expression troubled. "I've been through a bad divorce, Brick. It sucks, to have someone leave you, to pick up the pieces. I didn't want to do that again."

He lifted the gun again. "Move out of the way. I'll do her first, so she doesn't have to see you go."

"Not a chance in hell."

Brick flung the armload of gear at him. He wasn't close enough for the shovel to be used as a weapon, but it could become a projectile. The helmet spun through the air with it, the coveralls a cloud of fabric tumbling to the ground.

He whirled toward Les, grabbed her hand and jerked her into a run. He zigzagged them across the gravel drive and toward the adjacent field and woods beyond it. It was a way-too-fucking-far twenty-five feet, but it was hard to hit a moving target.

If he hadn't had Les with him, he might have charged Colin, risking the odds to knock him down and take the gun from him. But if Colin got in a lucky shot, Les would face a murderer on her own. Not acceptable.

She matched him, two strides to one, no unnecessary questions, following his lead without hesitation. They reached the woods as the bark of a tree splintered next to her head. *Goddamn bastard.* Any sliver of sympathy for Colin evaporated. Brick was going to dismember the fucker if he got the chance, and leave the remains on Jasmine and her children's graves as a sacrificial offering.

He pulled Les in front of him, onto the faint impression of a deer path. "Keep running," he ordered.

A crash in the woods a few strides later told him Colin was following. Unlike them, he'd crossed the field on a straight line. He didn't have to avoid bullets. He also was too damn decent of a shot.

Brick had his weapon in his truck, a 9mm Glock. He'd never again go into a fire scene without wearing the damn thing, even if it was a Captain Obvious kitchen fire accident caused by a senile grandmother. But first he had to make sure he and Les survived his error in judgment.

In his earlier visits, Brick had followed the back roads to the fishing spot Colin had mentioned in his statement. His recollection of what lay ahead might save their lives. If they could get there.

Broad spears of sunlight through the trees announced the biggest obstacle—another open field. As the woods thinned out, he closed the distance between him and Les. "Run like the very devil," he told her. "Run for the bridge."

They burst out of the cover of the trees. Fifty plus feet of open area before they'd reach the dirt road and the truss bridge that spanned a tributary of the James River.

Another shot rang out, bringing the total to five bullets. Whether he had a ten or fifteen bullet magazine, Colin wasn't wasting his shots, but for all Brick knew, he had additional mags. Brick stayed just behind Les, his weaving body blocking hers. Thank God his girl could run. She was giving it her all.

Another shot ran out, and she stumbled. His heart caught in his throat, but Brick wrapped an arm around her waist to lift her up against his hip. He lengthened his strides. He was terrified she'd been hit, but there was no time to look or determine if she could keep running on her own.

He'd plowed his way through defensive lines. He would ram the gates of heaven if needed. Too many hard heartbeats later, his shoes slammed down on the metal grating of the bridge. He ran for the middle, where the water would be deepest. He didn't look, but he'd know when Colin had reached the bridge, too. They were hemmed in by the two sides, forming an optimal target chute.

The current was swift and strong, but the danger of that was the lesser evil. He swung her over the rail, setting her on her feet on the narrow ledge. The metal support structure gave them some cover. "Grab the railing."

She obeyed as he came over it. She was scared, but—fuck, he loved her—her hand was on him, steadying him as he positioned himself next to her. Their time was measured in half-seconds. He met her wide hazel eyes.

"Let yourself get swept downstream. Make for the bank as soon as you can't see the bridge. There will be a road somewhere nearby."

He heard the hammering of feet on the bridge. The next bullet hit a vertical member beside him, setting off a shower of sparks. Blood bloomed on Les's cheek, a ricochet.

Brick grabbed her hand and jumped. They fell toward the swift-moving water twenty feet below.

~

No. No! Brick's grip was torn from hers as they landed. Les swallowed a cry and water as she went under, the latter cold enough to drive the breath from her.

She thrashed to the surface to find herself going downstream fast. Which meant she was likely out of Colin's range for anything but a really lucky shot, but that was no longer her primary concern.

She couldn't see Brick. *Oh God. Please let him be okay.* Right before they'd jumped, she'd noticed he was bleeding. Wet blood stained his shirt at his lower set of ribs and the upper abdominal area. He could be shot, in an area that would impact his spleen, the stomach or any of the complex surrounding areas. She needed to see, needed to check. Oh, God, where was he?

She gasped as she bounced off rocks hidden beneath the surface. Pain rocketed through her thigh. If she didn't focus on swimming, she'd end up injured enough to drown.

He'd told her to get to the bank as soon as she couldn't see the bridge. The strength of the current that helped put the bridge out of sight made that difficult. Adrenaline helped, but the waters were ruthless, cold and tumbling, driving her on their own path. She couldn't touch bottom, only scrabble against rocks determined to tear skin and clothing. The current wanted to break bones against them.

Panic from the threat of drowning tried to grab her, but she refused to let it have her. She'd grown up swimming in creeks and rivers. Plus countless North and South Carolina beaches, on summer breaks with friends and family. Thomas had taught her to swim.

She conserved her strength, using his lessons on riptides. She stroked along with the current, gradually working toward the bank, wincing when she hit more rocks, was stabbed by underwater tree branches, but rolling away from them.

To keep the fear at bay, she imagined giving herself over to Brick's control, applying herself to the direction they both wanted and needed to go. She could hear him telling her to get to that bank, or he'd go after her with his brush. Or that fascinating, fire-lit glove.

She kept scouring the area for him, but the eddies splashing into her eyes made it hard to see.

When her feet finally found the bottom, she was on her last energy reserves. The relief of solid ground made her sob. But as the water became shallower, it also became rockier. She fell several more times as she struggled toward the slope of damp clay and scrubby grass. Using handholds of vegetation to pull herself onto the bank, she collapsed, breathing hard.

She fumbled for the phone miraculously still in her back pocket, but the stubbornly dark screen told her its water-resistance feature hadn't survived immersion in a river and bouncing down it like a pinball.

Colin might have jumped off the bridge, she realized. Or be running along the banks of the tributary, trying to catch up. Who could predict what a man insane enough to kill his girlfriend and her kids would do? She forced herself to her feet and struggled to a clump of brush and rocks, dropping down within its cover.

She forgot all of those precautions when she saw a person in the water, bobbing in the current like a lifeless doll. Or an unconscious man. *"Brick."*

She scrambled out and was up to her thighs in the tributary, heedless of risking the current once more, when the body rolled in her direction. Her heart jumped into her throat, and she scrambled backward in pure survival instinct.

But her mind caught up, making sense of what she was seeing. She sat on the bank, legs sprawled before her, and stared into Colin's lifeless eyes. She saw the bullet hole marking his temple. Then he was face down again and being carried away, at the mercy of the river.

"Les. *Les!*"

Thank God. She forced her vocal cords to work. "Here. I'm here."

Brick emerged from the woods, clothes plastered to him, eyes wild and fierce. Those superhero arms would have helped him reach the bank faster than her. He'd probably been charging downstream like a bull, trying to catch up to her, to help her get to shore.

It was an incredible relief to see him, so much that her knees buckled when she tried to run to him. But he caught her, going to his knees to hold her in a powerful, life-affirming embrace before he pulled her away from him. His gaze was all over her, fingertips on what felt like a messy scalp laceration as he cradled her head in big hands.

She confirmed it, her fingers following his. The worst she had were scrapes and bruises. Head wounds liked to bleed, even if they weren't serious.

"It's okay, it's superficial," she told him, even as she dropped her hands to pull up his shirt. He was still bleeding, his run through the woods making that no big surprise. Adrenaline could carry someone far too long past serious injury.

"Brick, let me see. Stay still."

He seemed surprised to find he was hurt. He hadn't even noticed, or if he had, none of it had slowed him down. Keeping her safe had been his total focus. Not once had he allowed her to be fully exposed to Colin's aim. All of that crowded into her mind, like panicked family in the waiting room. She told them all to shut up. She was suddenly scared shitless, and needed to fall back on her training, not get caught up in who he was to her or how serious his injury could be.

It was okay. Relief flooded her. The bullet had taken a chunk of flesh out of his side, but hadn't penetrated where the organs could have been adversely affected. The wound would need tending, but a cursory examination showed it was the worst he'd incurred. Like her, he had some cuts, some torn clothing from the rocks, and would probably have impressive bruising patterns by tomorrow. But they were both okay.

She said a prayer of thanks, then lifted her gaze to his. "It wasn't just girlish fantasy."

"What?"

"You *would* jump off a bridge for me."

"Apparently, so would you." He was holding her tight against him again, her examination and his strength reassuring her enough she could afford a gentle tease.

"That doesn't count. You yanked me off."

He snorted out a half-laugh, but she noted his tension and realized he was scouring the river.

"He's dead. I saw his body go past. I think he shot himself."

"Fucking hell." Brick's chest expanded and contracted, an expression of relief that transformed into something else as he lifted her face to his, his hands on her now more insistent. His kiss was flavored with the taste of the water, his heat, and hers. She was aware of the friction between their shuddering bodies, plastered against one another as close as they could get with their clothes on.

In the same moment she had that thought, he had his hands on the button of her jeans, wrenching it open, shoving down the zipper. She answered the aggression with her own, her arms wrapping around his shoulders, nails digging into his back.

It was a primal response to the threat of death. Even as she recognized it, the strength of their mutual response shocked her. Overwhelmed her. She gave herself to it, clinging to him as Brick devoured her mouth, his tongue all over the inside of it, her tongue, teeth, cheeks, tasting her, sucking on her. Biting. He gripped her hair like a caveman might.

"Push the jeans down, Les. Get them to your knees, because you're going to need to spread your legs to take how big I am right now. I'm sorry, baby, I have to. I can't...I need to feel you."

"Your side, it needs..."

"I don't give a damn. Hold onto me."

She made a noise of total understanding and the same need against his mouth. As he pushed her back against the earth, she begged for more. "Please, I need to feel your skin."

He pulled his bloody shirt over his head, her helping him to get it out of the way. Despite his order, he pushed her hands away and worked her wet jeans to her knees himself. He tore away her soaked panties with a rip of the seams. Her hands were over his when they went to his jeans, offering fumbling help he didn't need but which broadcast her matching impatience as he unbuckled his belt, pulled open the zipper.

He was right. He was enormous, thick as she'd ever seen his already sizeable organ. She'd later appreciate the courtesy as he tested her readiness with his fingers. Though her arousal was obvious, it still stunned her that she was so wet his fingers sank to the last knuckle inside her with barely any pressure. Brick muttered a reverent oath.

"My sweet, good girl."

He could have turned her over, but he planted himself between her knees, his legs pinning her jeans such that it was as if she was spread and restrained for him. That was how he wanted her. Plus he wanted to see her face, as much as she wanted to see his.

His thrust into her was savage. The act was at odds with how gentle his hands were on her face, stroking a gash on her cheek, the blood on her temple. He put his mouth on them and any other cut he could reach. As he drove into her, all she could do was hold on, forcibly moved along the bank by his power. She made a feminine noise of acceptance, and he matched it with a male growl.

There were no questions here, no doubts.

I'm yours, yours, yours.

It didn't matter whose mind that was coming from. They were one animal, one mind.

He climaxed in a matter of seconds, her Master who always had such control, but she thought it was deliberate. She didn't need a climax right now, just that marking and affirmation. She held onto him as he shuddered in her arms, and she trembled in his.

When he finally eased back, he rolled over, taking her with him. In the strength of his hold, she sensed his desire to stop the world on its axis, so they could lie like this until the fear of nearly losing one another receded.

She thought it did maybe stop for a few minutes, as they breathed together, bodies pressed so close. When awareness of anything other than each other started to return, as well as sanity and civilized behavior, it wasn't easy to let it in.

"Guess neither one of us has a working phone," Brick said at last. "In a few minutes, we'll get up and make our way to the road to flag down some help."

"How far is it?"

"Not far. Maybe half a mile."

"Better late than never, but we really do need to bandage your side. It's not life-threatening unless it gets infected, and we'll get it tended long before then. But when the adrenaline goes away, you're going to be hurting. I can go to the road and bring back help."

"I can walk. I'm not letting you out of my sight. Don't give yourself shit for it, doc. It's not your fault your patient insisted on fucking you before you could treat him."

A weary chuckle. "That's a problem I've never encountered before."

"Damn glad to hear it."

She paused. "He killed them, then."

"Yeah." He sobered. "Goddamn him."

Les pushed herself up and looked down at him. "You solved it," she said. "You didn't let him get away with it."

"Yeah. Just doesn't feel like enough."

"It never does." She went to her knees to pull up her jeans and refasten them as he did the same. She tore off a cleaner looking strip from his already damaged T-shirt and used it to fashion the bandage high on his waist. She put her hand on the spot. He'd been shot. She couldn't think too much about that. "I'm surprised you have no tattoos."

"Mom feels the same way about tattoos as she does piercings. Put graffiti on her baby? Her finest work?"

"Her giant baby."

"Giant manly baby," he corrected. "Let's get to the road."

She put herself under his arm. No matter that she couldn't take his full weight, she would offer support. His willingness to let her do that, plus the stiffness of his movements, told her he was starting to feel his injuries, like she was. Or he just wanted to be as close as possible to her.

She felt the same about him.

"I'm sorry for putting you in the middle of that," he said.

"I assume suspects popping in to check the status of the investigation isn't a usual occurrence."

"Yeah, but keeping you safe is so important to me, I feel like I should anticipate anything that could mess with that." Though a rueful smile touched his lips, he meant it. It made her heart turn over.

"You did great, doc. Kept calm, ran like a fast-as-hell rabbit. I'm in love with you, you know," he added. "Fully, solidly, head over heels."

As her world tilted on its axis for entirely different, far better reasons, he touched her cheek again, gentle around the wound on her cheek. Belatedly, she recalled it had come from a bullet ricochet before they jumped. No wonder he kept looking at it with such hard eyes.

She blinked. "Wow. I wasn't expecting that, here and now."

"Yeah. Just realized I hadn't made it clear."

Her hand rested over the wound in his side. "I think you have."

CHAPTER EIGHTEEN

*O*nce they reached a road, Brick flagged down the first motorist, a sheetrock contractor, and borrowed his phone to call 911. When several police cars arrived on scene, Brick and Les were told Colin's body had already been found and called in by a group of fishermen.

An EMT unit came with the police. Les insisted that Brick be checked out, his wound dressed. He required she be checked out, too, which was fine since they could sit together at the ambulance.

As what happened sank in, the expected trauma effects started to show. Lightheadedness, conversations happening around her fading in and out, getting fuzzy. Her limbs had occasional spasms. Brick noticed, because he was holding her hand and wouldn't let it go.

"I'm okay," she told him.

"I know. The handholding's for me. Kay might decide to stick a needle in my arm. Sharp stuff scares me."

"He'll faint dead away," Kay agreed dryly. She was a round, compact thirty-something with a bouncy blonde ponytail and tattoos along her neck and arms, peeking out from beneath her EMT shirt.

Despite the banter, when Les gave her an expectant look, Kay offered her professional reassurance. Plus a woman-to-woman tone, her gaze touching their clasped hands. "He's good. With his muscle definition, I'm betting any bullets would have bounced off."

"Especially if he'd aimed for my head. Thanks, Kay. You don't have

an extra scrub top in here, do you? My T-shirt's pretty much a goner."
Brick nodded to Les. "She tore it off of me. You know how you
women are."

Les narrowed her eyes as Kay chuckled. "I don't carry size G for
giant. But we're right up the road from a Dollar General. We can run
you by and take you back to your truck, long as we don't get an urgent
call in the meantime."

"Appreciate it."

It was a few more minutes before they could leave, but Les
could tell Brick expedited it as much as he could. After confirming
he would be at the office in the morning to finish the case report
and fill in any other blanks that needed filling, they were ready
to go.

They picked up a 2XL large blue Hanes T-shirt at the dollar store.
When Kay and her partner left them at Brick's truck, Brick assured
them they were fine from here, and thanked them for their help. After
the ambulance left the driveway, Brick collected the gear he'd flung at
Colin.

The shovel had landed on top of his dropped case folder, so the
contents were intact. Les found the copy of the family picture caught
in the branches of a scorched azalea. After she smoothed it, Brick
tucked it back into the folder and put it in the truck. He slid the
soiled PPE into a bag and stored it with his turnout gear.

By the time he helped her into the passenger seat, the soreness
and fatigue had tripled. She thought Brick was the same, evident in
how heavily he settled into the driver's side before turning the engine
over.

Les moved as near to him as the console allowed, laying her head
on his shoulder. Brick put his arm around her to hold her close. He
backed the truck around Colin's vehicle one-handed.

She saw a Dunkin Donuts coffee cup in Colin's cup holder, and a
saint's medal dangling from his rearview mirror. "St. Florian," Brick
provided, seeing her glance at it. "Patron saint of firefighters."

She closed her hand on his thigh. "Glad he sided with us today,
instead of Colin."

"You and me both."

When they reached his place, by mutual accord, they took a
shower together. Brick removed the bandage, and Les did a quick

inspection, verifying that Kay had done a good job. It would leave a scar, but it would heal.

While she'd have to be dead not to be sexually aware of Brick, she was sure neither of them could do anything with that right now. Until he turned her, coaxing her to lean back against him as he soaped her breasts, caressing the nipples. One hand slid down her front. "I didn't let you finish earlier. I didn't take care of my girl."

Under his skilled fingers, slow and easy waves of need came surging back up. Moans broke from her throat as he massaged her to a spiraling, gradual but powerful climax that had her cries echoing off the shower walls. His erection pushed against her backside, but when she wanted to help with that, he wouldn't let her.

"Later, doc. I appreciate you wanting to serve your Master. But let me take care of you right now."

He helped dry her off as she did the same, the two of them working with the corners of the same towel. Their hands overlapped, and her insistence on drying him made him smile. He set it aside, bent and picked her up. When his breath drew in between his teeth, she protested.

"Put me down. I can walk."

"It's fine. It's just pain. You make me forget all that when you look at me with those big eyes. And when you're naked."

She shook her head at him, but figured it was better to let him get her to the bedroom than argue. Once there he laid her down, putting himself under the covers with her. He wrapped his arms around her. "Sleep, doc."

"You, too."

It didn't take either of them long to follow that direction. She fell right into a deep slumber. The events of the day shadowed her dreams, but whatever lurked within that darkness stayed there.

He'd stood between her and Colin. It was no surprise that his embrace stood between her subconscious and nightmares.

~

Even without serious injury, running for one's life worked out a whole different set of muscle groups. Knowing it, Brick had left her a couple aspirin by the bed, and one of those heart chocolates.

After having both forms of medication, she took another hot shower to loosen up, got dressed, and went looking for him. He was in the kitchen, coffee and breakfast ready.

"You know, you'd make a hell of a house husband."

A flash of teeth, and he drew her to him for a warm kiss. Their hands wandered over one another, reassurance after yesterday's events, plus seeking the pleasure of touching and being touched.

Eventually, he directed her to a stool at his kitchen island, pouring her a cup of coffee and filling a plate for her. "You should take it easy today," he said. "I'll go in, handle the loose ends on Colin, and finish up some other work."

A subtle reminder they would leave for Durham tomorrow, for her M&M. It was absurd that the resulting wave of anxiety was as over-powering as always—maybe even more so.

You might have died yesterday. Enduring an M&M conference is nowhere close to that.

Except that wasn't what made her dread the M&M. It was reliving the events of that night, knowing they could never be changed. She definitely didn't want to sit around Brick's place thinking about it.

"Can I go with you?" She put both hands around her mug. "I can study, like I did yesterday."

"Before a homicidal maniac tried to kill us."

"I got a lot done before that happened."

He came around the island, gripped the stool seat and turned her toward him. He set her coffee cup aside, and nudged her knees apart, putting himself between them. When he framed her face in his hands, he gave her a long, searching look. Her fingers came up to overlap his.

"Why weren't your knees spread the moment I came around this counter?"

He stole her breath when he said things like that. "I hadn't had coffee yet. My reaction time was slow."

"I'll let it go this time."

"Or...you could add it to your list."

His gaze flickered. "Consider it added. Do you really want to go into the office with me?"

"I really do. I like watching you do what you do."

"And it's better than sitting here alone, thinking about tomorrow."

Maybe it was a crutch, using him to keep her from drowning in that well, but it was the truth. She nodded. "Please. Let me go with you."

"All right."

~

He gave her a short tour when they arrived, pointing out where the restrooms and break room were, and introducing her to several of his co-workers. The men were friendly and warm. The women as well, though their speculative looks puzzled her. At least until she reached his office.

The photos on the credenza behind his desk showed his parents and siblings. That same Wilder family picture was there, too, though this one was cropped to show only her, with Brick a few feet away looking toward her.

Gazing at it, she sat down in the guest chair as he took the over-sized chair behind the desk—well, oversized for everyone but him. "You know I'm underage in that picture."

"I don't think there's anything inappropriate implied."

"Except you told me where your mind was starting to go. Predator."

He rolled his eyes, but gave her a pointed look. "You think I won't bend you over my desk and spank you right here?"

For once, it was a bluff she felt safe challenging. She stuck her tongue out at him. He grinned, but the gleam in his eyes told her there were other ways he could follow up on that threat when they weren't at his place of work.

His office was well organized, same as his desk at home, but the stack of files was even larger. Plaques on his wall showed his fire sciences degree, additional certifications and a couple awards. Since Brick wasn't prone to vanity, she suspected it was intended to estab-lish his credentials for any outside visitors, department officials or witnesses he met here.

The first day she'd asked him to take her by his office, he'd told her no, because he'd get sucked in and never be able to leave. Confirming it, within five minutes of him opening his computer and starting to finalize the report on the Whitfield fire, another detective arrived to ask him questions about another case. Brick pulled the file and the investigator braced himself on one fist over it as Brick identified the elements that confirmed the source of the residential fire was cooking oil in a pot, left on a lit stove.

He pulled up the pictures on his computer, showing the detective the destroyed kitchen. Les saw only debris and charred appliances, until Brick pointed out a cone-shaped burn pattern and noted how the stove and wall adjacent had suffered the most damage, indicating the fire's origin point.

"I reviewed the witness statements you sent me, and between that and this, there are no arson indicators."

"Okay. I'll close it down on our end. Expect a call from the insurance adjuster to confirm and grill you some more."

"I already talked to Leo earlier in the week. I'll shoot him an official email for his files."

"Thanks." The detective turned toward the door, giving Les a friendly nod as he departed.

Brick's phone rang again. This time it was their lab, clarifying what he was wanting on a sample he'd given them. Which was followed up by them sending him the gas chromatograph data so he could look at it as they were discussing it. As he stretched back in his chair, forearm resting on the desk, his eyes trained on the screen as he spoke, she couldn't even begin to pretend she was studying.

Yep. It would take years before this didn't make her hot.

When he was done, he noted her interested look and turned his monitor toward her. He clicked open two other files, which looked similar to the data he'd just been reviewing. "Remember what I was telling you, about lemon furniture polish versus diesel fuel? Here are their two element compositions."

"I think I'm going to tell my mom to use a different cleaner."

"Your mom loves that old house. No chance she'd ever sacrifice it for the insurance."

"She'd sacrifice one of us first."

He grinned as his phone rang once more. "Hey, Bob." Brick clicked open another file. "Yeah, the lab verified the traces of accelerant splashed in those areas. We also found the gas can. Guess he thought the plastic would burn up."

He listened to the response. "Well, you know what they say. If criminals were smarter, we'd have to get smarter, too. I'll send those

IGNITION SEQUENCE

results over to you. By the way, just a hunch. One of the witness statements said the perp loves barbecue. Since they think he took off to
Memphis, let the detectives there know that. They'll check the hole-
in-the-wall places, ones the locals know about. If they flash his picture
around, they might get a lead."

Brick paused. "Get this guy, Bob. Bury him under the jail."

As he hung up, he noted her questioning expression. "His fire
killed five homeless people nested up in the building, plus one firefighter was badly injured. Remember what I said, about how insurance
fires aren't victimless crimes?"

When his phone rang again, he glanced at the display. This time he
didn't pick up the receiver. Instead, with an indecipherable look at
Les, he hit the speaker button. "Hey, Tish, how's Richmond's toughest
ADA?"

"Busy as hell, as always. Just needed a quick confirm from you on a
court date."

Les had accepted that Tish and Brick's relationship was nothing to
worry about. Until hearing her sexy, melodious bedroom voice. Was
there anything *not* perfect about her?

The woman also had the take-no-shit tone one would expect from
a successful ADA. An intriguing contrast for a woman exploring her
submissive side.

"We're finally getting the Gettys fire on the docket," Tish was
saying.

"Thank fuck," Brick muttered. "The woman was going to die of
old age before she was put on trial."

"The wheels of justice sometimes grind like sand's been thrown
into them. Can you do Thursday three weeks from now?"

"If I can't, I'm betting Sturgis can."

"I'll take him if I have to, but juries respond better to you on the
technical stuff. The male jurors listen because you look like an action
hero. The female jurors listen because you could read the freaking
phone book and they'd hang onto every word."

"I feel so objectified. I want to be valued for my mind."

"Yeah, yeah. Can you do it?"

"Already marked down."

"Thanks, talk to you later. Gotta fly and lock this in, which is why
I didn't text."

She clicked off before he said anything else, leaving Les blinking. "If I was worried that was going to turn into phone sex, my apprehensions were unfounded."

"Sorry. I was going to introduce you, but when she calls me like that, she's usually walking out of one courtroom and right into another. I seem to have a knack for attracting driven women." His tone was teasing. "You can smooth your hackles, doc."

She sniffed. "I was just waiting for her to mention the only thing more inflated than your muscles. Your ego."

"No inflation, baby. These are solid steel. Remember, Kay said they'd repel bullets." He flexed them.

"That's not backed up by medical science."

"The study results are pending. Yesterday's evidence should land it in the medical journals."

He'd let her check the wounded area this morning, and though, yes, he was healing fine, seeing again how close that bullet had come had given her a bad moment. He'd insisted on checking all of her scrapes and bruises, too, and the look in his eyes, the tightness of his expression as he put gentle fingers and his lips on several of the places, including that spot on her face, told her he felt the same.

Covering her more serious feelings, she rolled her eyes at his teasing and pointedly returned her attention to her screen. The one that had darkened multiple times for lack of activity. But before she could make another pretense at studying, it was her phone's turn to speak. It hummed like a bee, indicating an incoming phone call.

The dread that clutched her stomach—was it Mr. Sully or Dr. Portland?—eased as she saw the caller, though a spike of irritation with herself came right behind it. "Oh shit, it's Rory. I was supposed to call him last night."

"Go ahead and answer. If you need privacy—"

"I'm good, but I'll step out if you get another call."

He gave her a thumbs up, but added, "You can put it on speaker if you want."

She did, accepting the unspoken offer of solidarity it represented. "Hey, Rory. I'm sorry, I meant to call last night, but Brick and I had to escape a homicidal arsonist. Brick got shot, and I had to jump off a bridge."

"I had to pull you off," Brick corrected. "You had a death grip on that railing."

She ignored him. "We were beat when we got home. Didn't even stop for pizza."

"That's tragic. Everyone should treat themselves to pizza after a day like that." Amusement was in Rory's voice. She remembered it cracking and changing when he was in his early teens. In the past several years, the timbre had become even richer and deeper, unmistakably a man's voice. It was as if making peace with the wheelchair and pursuing Daralyn had brought him to full adulthood. "All joking aside, tell me what's going on and how I can help."

"What have you told Mom?"

"Nothing yet. You only talked to her a few days ago, so there hasn't been a need to say anything. I was waiting to hear from you to see how you wanted to go with it."

Thinking of her last phone call with her mother was like seeing the coffee cup in Colin's truck. Something mundane that seemed surreal, seen from the far distant, entirely different place her mind was now.

"I don't want you to lie to her. If she brings up anything that requires the truth, you can tell her the basics."

"She's going to want more than that. To tell the truth, so do I. You're worrying me. You don't sound like you."

"I just...it's...I'm not sure I'm up to talking about it over the phone." As the feelings in her stomach did a sharp twist, poking her like barbed wire, she could feel Brick's gaze upon her. "I know I said on the last call with her I'd be too busy, but my plans have changed. I'm coming home for Easter after all. If that's okay."

Rory's response held relief, but also a gentle rebuke. "If that's okay? What kind of question is that? Mom will be ecstatic. Marcus and Thomas are planning to be here. Julie and Des were going to try to come, too, but it's not looking good. She has a theater performance that weekend. But Mom and Daralyn are already setting up the menu, so bring your appetite."

She put a hand on her sensitive stomach to quiet it. "I'll do that."

Rory paused. "Les, I know we aren't as close as you and Thomas, but we're no longer kids. If you need something, I hope you know I'd do anything to help."

Another surprising reminder of the maturity that, in fairness, she knew had been there for a while now. "I know you would. I really do. I just need to work some things out in my head before I talk about it." She let a little humor slide in to soften the truth. "I don't need anyone trying to solve it for me. You all can be a little overprotective."

"What? Us? I don't know what you're talking about."

"She has all the protection she needs," Brick put in. "From the guy who used to protect your scrawny ass on the football field."

"Scrawny?" Rory snorted. "Are you at your office? I can practically smell the bad coffee."

"Yeah. Les is studying and keeping me company while I'm working. I'll be coming with her for Easter."

Another significant pause. "Okay. I'll tell Mom we need to butcher a whole cow."

"Tell her if she mashes a crop of potatoes for me, that'll be sufficient. Oh, and if Daralyn bakes a bushel of those biscuits she does."

"You'll be in too much of a carb coma to protect anyone."

One of the admins was approaching Brick's office with a handful of paperwork, so Les told Rory to hold on a moment and excused herself, taking the phone off speaker. With a nod to Brick, she headed toward the breakroom. On the way, she noted a TV screen mounted on the wall, a news channel running silent but with subtitles. She paused as the Whitfield family picture came up, followed by a photo of Colin. In the background was the river, a helicopter view of the police units stationed at the spot where the body had been retrieved.

When a formal picture of Brick came up in his dress uniform, she bit back a curse. No mention of her, but that wouldn't matter if the story was picked up outside the local area.

She wanted a copy of that picture, though. Talk about hot.

She paused in the hallway outside the breakroom. "Rory, um, I wasn't kidding about the being shot at thing. You and Mom might see it on TV, so I wanted you to know."

"*What?*"

She briefly explained the series of events. He went silent while she did. When she was done, he had one thing to say.

"I want to talk to Brick again."

"I told you, we're fine. I'm fine."

"Yeah. I heard you. Take Brick the fucking phone."

A disturbing tingle sparked at the base of her spine. She was responding to male command way too easily if she was getting that jolt from her pain-in-the-ass brother. Even so, Brick was his best friend, and she'd told Rory he'd been shot. So she brought the phone back to Brick, who was alone in his office again.

"It's on the news," she said, low, tilting her head toward the main area. "So I told him. He wants to talk to you."

"I figured he would."

Rather than having her put it on speaker again, Brick took the phone. She returned to the guest chair as he explained the situation. She'd thought he'd do damage control, glossing over it. Instead, Brick gave Rory far more detail, sparing him nothing.

When he was done, Brick paused, listening. "Yeah, I know, man. She's okay. The chances of that happening at an investigation site is like a lightning strike. Even so, you know if I'd suspected it, she never would have been with me. But you can be damn proud of her. She ran faster than you ever did on the field."

Les scowled and came around the desk, gesturing. He handed the phone back, but mouthed, "Be kind."

"I didn't tell you so you could beat up on him, Rory. He saved my life. And if you know anything about him, you know he'd never take me anywhere he'd think I'd be in danger."

"I know that," Rory said. "But he's my best friend, and you're my only sister."

What she heard in his voice took away her irritation. She'd felt that way plenty of times herself when he'd had a setback, during the early days of his paralyzing injury.

"I know," she said quietly. "We're okay. I promise. And I'll be home tomorrow night. I'll tell Mom, you, and everyone else, anything you want to know. Promise. In the meantime, you get to give her the news that I'm coming home for Easter."

"With Brick. That will interest her. A lot."

She snorted, but was glad to hear the teasing note. "I just figured Mom needed a testosterone overload at the house. Not."

He chuckled. "Do me a favor and try not to star in any more crime drama episodes up there."

"I'll do my best." She paused. "I love you, dickhead. See you soon."

~

When they left the office late afternoon, Brick assured her he'd covered everything that couldn't wait until after the holiday.

And her M&M tomorrow. Unspoken but there. The barbed wire ball in her lower belly was getting bigger. Basketball sized. She needed to come up with some hefty distractions, but had no idea what would work.

She started with the picture on his credenza. What it meant, how long it had probably been there. "How can you be so certain? Of how you feel about me?"

I'm in love with you, you know. Fully, solidly, head over heels.

Admittedly, she didn't seem to have any certainty problems herself when it came to Brick. Her weak attempts to doubt herself, to suggest false positives were being created by the stress of her life right now, or the euphoria of finally exploring the fantasies of her childhood crush, had come to naught. Most of the fantasies she was exploring with him had to do with far more adult feelings.

"Whenever I think of you, look at you, I'm certain," he responded. "My compass has always pointed to you."

"Is that what we're calling it?" She snorted. "And yet, even with that compass, there've been other women."

He laughed. "I had to practice, doc, so when the time was right, I'd do the job right. Hey, you had Bart. Plus a couple not-Barts."

"I was a virgin until Bart."

His brow rose. "You were a virgin that long?"

"Have you met my brothers? Would I have risked any teenage boy's life by letting him get that far? To say nothing of my father and mother. Plus...I just, we'd get to a certain point, and I'd know what it was about for the boy. I wanted more than that."

"Your mom always said you were exceptionally mature for your age."

She studied him. "Your compass always pointed to me. It's that simple?"

"Sometimes it is." As he accelerated through a light, he cleared his throat to deepen his drawl. "'When I saw you in yer pretty dress at church, I couldn't find the spit to talk at you. But I knew good as anything that I was set to be yer husband and take care of you.'"

In his normal voice, he added, "Even when a soldier didn't have much schooling, there was an eloquence to how he wrote about love in his letters."

"That one reminds me of Rory and Daralyn. His reaction to what happened to us took me by surprise. Sometimes I'm still getting used to him being an adult. A man." She shifted uncomfortably.

Brick glanced at her. "You're a little freaked out by it, aren't you? What you recognized in his voice when he told you to bring me the phone."

"What?" At his significant look, astonishment rippled through her. "Oh no. Not Rory. He's…"

"A Dom."

"No." She shook her head. "If anyone in our family was going to be a Dom, it would be…"

Thomas. Thomas, who—after their father died and Rory's accident—had come home and taken charge of the family…

Yet his name faltered on her lips. Something about it seemed off. *Had* he come home and taken charge? He'd tried to take care of everyone…serve everyone's needs, meet expectations, in a grimly determined way that could be construed as "taking charge." Until his bleeding ulcers said what toll taking that role had cost him.

The subtle difference wasn't so subtle in this light. Especially when that spotlight expanded to shine on who he'd married.

Thomas had strong alpha male traits in plenty of situations. But if triple-uber-alpha was a thing, it applied to his husband, Marcus Stanton. When Marcus had stepped in to help Thomas with their family, there'd been a notable difference in their support. Marcus's had been more about direction and control; Thomas's about service.

Confused, she shifted her thoughts back to her other brother. "So…Rory."

"I'm not outing him," Brick said. "With how you're opening your mind to it, you won't be able to miss it between him and Daralyn."

In one of the painfully shy young woman's rare expressive moments, she'd mentioned to Les that she loved sitting quietly under Rory's touch while he brushed her hair. Probably different from how Brick brushed hers, but still…

Submitting.

"Is Marcus…?"

"Oh yeah. He's actually the unicorn, the Dom that fits the romance novel mold. Rich, successful, in charge in all aspects of his life. He's too goddamn pretty to pull off subtle anything."

She wasn't sure she wanted to know these things about her brothers and their sex lives. However, finding herself on a path they were already traveling was too incredible to keep her from asking questions. "So that means Thomas..."

She couldn't say it, and she didn't know why. It wasn't supposed to be something shameful. It wasn't supposed to be weak. Did she view her own submission that way? It was an avenue that had undeniably helped her cope and find strength, particularly these past few days.

"Yes," Brick said, meeting her gaze. "Thomas doesn't advertise it, but it doesn't get under his skin for people to know it, either. Unless we're talking about your mom." Brick flashed his teeth. "Most kids don't want to swap sex info with their parents."

No disagreement there. Plus, Elaine had had enough of a struggle to understand and accept her eldest son was gay.

"How did you find out about them? I mean, yes, it seems like there's some form of Dom-sub radar, but you know specific details."

He shrugged. "Marcus and Thomas crossed paths with me at a big dungeon event in Atlanta. When Rory got involved with Daralyn and realized how deep her submission ran, and how that might tangle up with her past, he came to Marcus for advice. Marcus asked me if it was okay to let him know what I was, in case I could offer him further support."

A terrifying thought gripped her. "Do they know I'm..."

He closed his hand over hers. "Thomas suspected it for a long time, though he didn't know if you'd ever embrace it the way you've done with me these past few days. Just because someone has a Dominant or submissive orientation doesn't mean they'll decide to take it down that path. It can run in families, you know."

"How do you know he suspected that?"

Brick tugged her hair, brushing a knuckle over her cheek. "At the wedding, because Rory and Thomas know what I am, it was part of the dialogue. Nothing in detail. That's all private between you and me, and that's where it stays unless you prefer otherwise. But they were making sure if you wanted to explore that side with me, I'd take extra care."

"Oh my God."

He chuckled. "It's okay, doc. Look at it this way. You and Thomas outnumber Rory on this side of the whip. Unless you count your mom. If any of us were going to vote on it, we'd all vote for serious Domme there."

"Please don't make me stick a hot poker in my ear to burn that image out of my brain."

But her mind was already moving away from that down another path, the one from her brothers to Julie. Julie was a close friend of Marcus and Thomas's from New York. Julie's passion was community theater, and she'd run one successfully up there. Over the years, she'd become part of the Wilder family, partly because her own was so emotionally distant. Her parents and brother spent more time touring Europe and managing global business concerns than spending time together as a family.

Julie loved them, but routinely claimed she'd been switched at the hospital. Her attachment to Les's family had only increased after she moved to North Carolina to run a community theater outside Charlotte, for a friend who had the capital to get it started, but not the know-how.

The friend, Madison, ran an erotic store called Naughty Bits in Matthews. The theater she'd envisioned was one that celebrated all kinds of erotic performance art.

On the far-too-rare occasions when Julie and Les had managed to be at the farm together, they usually pulled Daralyn into a girls' sleepover. Julie would regale them with scintillating stories of the theater productions. While she exaggerated the details to make them laugh and blush, Julie had also conveyed the theater's more serious intent, to celebrate sexual expression in all its forms. Including Dominant and submissive dynamics.

Initially, Les had suppressed her flood of questions, not wanting to reveal the depth of her fascination. But when she'd recognized Daralyn's curiosity, Les had jumped in and thrown some of those questions out to Julie, under the guise of increasing Daralyn's comfort with asking her own.

Why hadn't she put that together with Daralyn being a submissive? Since Daralyn and her brother had paired up, Daralyn's confidence and ability to express herself had notably improved. It might seem counterintuitive, that embracing a submissive side could result in that. But whereas a folder of pictures had become a moderately successful anxiety management tool for Les with day-to-day challenges, submitting to Brick during one of the most awful experiences of her life had given her an anchor point. From it, she was better able to look at what had happened and ask herself the hard questions about what she was doing with her life.

Belonging to someone, trusting their love and care, helped a person stand on their own two feet.

She went back to Julie. Julie was married to Desmond Hayes, who'd performed at her first community event for Madison's theater. He'd done rope stuff, like the suspension displays she'd seen at Mick's private party.

"So Des is a rope top... Is he also a Dom?"

"Yes. And yes, Julie is a submissive. She'd be totally okay with you knowing that, and talking to her about it if you wanted to." Brick smiled at her expression. "It's not that there are so many active D/s people; we just tend to cluster, the same way most people with common interests find one another."

"Wow." She took a deep breath.

In the resulting companionable silence, those revelations should have given her a sufficient level of distraction, helping reinforce the wall she usually used to function during high stress events. Unfortunately, the invading army was already past the gate, and each one of them looked like a clock, ticking down to tomorrow.

As the thoughts swarmed up again, like ocean water into a footprint left in the sand, she shifted in her seat. She tried to manage it, breathe in and out. Keep herself from wanting to jump out of her skin, get away before the worry constricted her into a fetal position.

"Hey." He looked her way, eyes sharp. "You all right?"

"Yeah. It's a weird mix in my head right now." Her half-laugh sounded hollow, echoing in her chest. "Even being chased by a crazed killer can't seem to derail it. Every hour I'm getting closer to tomorrow's conference, the harder it is to think of anything else."

Brick slowed down for a light and turned his full attention to her. "Then I'll take you home and fix that."

She cleared her throat. "That's a lot to ask of a man who was shot."

"Grazed. But I'm not doing the work, doc. You are. I'm going to push you hard, until you can't think of anything but pleasing me."

Traffic was backed up at the light, so he was able to move the hand on her shoulder to her hair, that tight hold that tipped her head toward his grip and brought her halfway across the seat to him. "What's your response to that?"

Though hearing a "Dom tone" from Rory had given her that startling tingle, it was nowhere close to how she reacted to it from Brick. It set off an EMP among those inner worries, knocking them completely offline in favor of better things. Like in *The Matrix*, the machines floating lifeless.

She was never looking at that movie the same way again. Or her brothers, for that matter.

She met the challenge, offering her own back, with a curve of her lips. "I'd do that for you right here, if you ordered me to."

Humor flitted through his intent gaze. "Rory always said you were a brat. You'll wait until we get to my place. But the second we get through that door, I want you on your knees."

She lowered her eyes, fastening her gaze on where she suspected he'd want her mouth first. Where she wanted it, too. "Yes, Sir."

That hand tightened on her hair again. "Yep," he said. "Definitely a brat."

CHAPTER NINETEEN

*S*he had an irresistible mouth, and he did put it to work first thing. He'd never seen a woman, even a submissive, have the kind of response she did to oral. He couldn't deny it tempted a man to keep his cock in her mouth 24/7, except he couldn't get enough of tasting her body, fucking her, watching her reach her peak and lose control in his arms.

But the shadows were gathering, the fears about what the M&M would unleash. She was still having trouble even thinking about it without a trauma reaction, and tomorrow she'd have to talk about it in front of a roomful of her peers.

She was scared she couldn't handle it. He knew she could, but to do it, she'd tear herself up from the inside out with anxiety. He wasn't going to put up with that.

He wouldn't let her finish him. Instead, he laid her on her stomach and lifted her ass in the air so he could put his mouth between her legs, holding them spread and immobile as he sent one, two orgasms rocketing through her. After that, he turned her back over and lay upon her, surrounding her. He lodged himself deep inside her, in every possible way. He drew another orgasm from her, plus one for him, too.

He'd pushed her as close to the edge of her physical endurance as her still healing bruises could handle. But he knew she'd need more of that. Though he kissed every one of those bruises and let her fall asleep in his arms, he already knew how her morning was going to start. He set the alarm to go off early.

When it started beeping hours later, he was awake. She had slept fitfully, so he'd kept an eye on her. In that merciless way of restless slumber, her deepest sleep came only an hour before the alarm went off. As a result, she started up in bed, struggling to orient herself. He put his hand on her shoulder, reminding her where she was, but he was also watching for that moment where her vision cleared and the realization of what day it was swooped in like a vulture. It would peck and tear at every place that anxiety liked to live.

Not happening. He moved his touch to her hair. As he gathered it up, twisted it in his fist, her attention came right to him. He flipped the covers off himself, revealing his morning erection.

"I think you have a job to finish," he said. "And you better not let a single thought other than serving your Master inside your head. Else I will stripe your ass with my belt and the question you'll be most worried about today is someone asking you to sit down."

Shock crossed her gaze, followed by a tremulous touch of humor. She knew what he was doing, sure, but he also meant every word. The hunger surged forth. Even with an edge of desperation, it was true and real, the same way she responded anytime he took her over and helped her explore her submissive side.

He intended to push that edge until it bled out enough worry that she could think straight. He'd do it by making her totally mindless first.

She braced her hands on either side of him and his grip tightened. "Nope. Clasp your hands behind your back. Hope you know how to relax your gag reflex, or this is going to get tough for you."

Her lips parted, an excited breath escaping, the flare of arousal in her eyes telling him what his words were doing to the rest of her. Her nipples tightened right up. He'd like to suck on them, draw out another orgasm, but he kept himself on target.

He wasn't saying it was selfless—pushing her this hard when she so obviously needed it was something the Dom in him enjoyed the hell out of—but his heart had one goal. He would give her the room to stand up and face this day. Get through it, find herself on the other side of it.

He brought her down on his cock, using his other hand to angle it to her mouth. She was smart enough to wet her lips before she stretched them over his head, and then she made a little noise as he pushed her down on him. About halfway, then drawing her back up. Then back down. He did it slow, but he started to take her lower each time. Her back rounded, her throat convulsed, and he stopped where he was as she choked.

"Relax," he murmured. "Just relax those muscles. You can take me. You will take me. Do it. I know you don't want to find out what a caning is today."

He envisioned using his fire cane on her. Tapping it up and down her back and ass, her upper thighs. He'd make her stand on her toes, stretch out that beautiful body with her hands bound above her. He'd tap, tap, tap, make her jump and yelp as he gave her a fiercer slap with it, that sharp strike sound adding to the sensations as it impacted flesh. Her squirming would increase as the heat built over areas he'd be covering multiple times.

However he used fire upon her, he'd pay close attention to the places she'd be more sensitive. Inner thighs, nipples, the thinner skin over her ribs. Behind her knees. She'd moan in that pleading feminine way. He'd blow on the flame, make it billow over her flesh, bathe her in heat.

His cock convulsed as he watched her mouth work on him. His grip in her hair was what held her up when she overbalanced, her hands no help to her. She was helpless against what he wanted from her. Fuck, she had a blessed mouth. His response was building to the point it was going to short circuit his mind, but he managed to growl out the warning. "Here it comes, baby. Don't you dare stop."

She did her very best in difficult conditions. When his hips bucked against her, semen jetting into her throat, she choked, coughed, but valiantly kept sucking on him, licking, swallowing, trying to take everything as her eyes watered.

Do. Or do not. There is no try. When Yoda said that, he'd never experienced the precious gift of a sub trying to do the impossible for her Master.

That's what he damn well was, too. Because she'd told him that was what she wanted. To be his submissive.

When he finished, he made her sit next to him and picked up the damp hand towel he'd slipped out of bed to retrieve before the alarm went off. He used it on her mouth and streaming eyes. She was crying a little, but it was the good kind. She was lost in the service. He lay back down and folded her onto his chest, held her tight.

"It's going to be fine today," he told her, stroking her hair.

He thought of that caning again. When the heat and pain were enough, he would cool her down with a damp towel like this one. Maybe rub ice over her skin.

He'd hold her while she shook in the aftermath. Just like this. He would take her to subspace again and again, give her that peace, help her learn to let go. So she could be as brilliant as he knew she was, at whatever she truly wanted, her heart's desire.

"There's nothing you can't handle," he told her. "And when you get through it, I'll be there."

Brick didn't press her to eat breakfast at his place. When they headed out, he pulled off at a drive-thru, and got himself a biscuit breakfast, plus a bottle of orange juice. If she was curious why he didn't ask her if she wanted any food, she didn't show it. But when he pulled into a parking space, he retrieved the small cooler he'd stowed behind the seat. It contained a thick piece of wheat toast with a packet of straw-berry jelly, if she wanted a touch of something sweet. Plus a boiled egg. He placed the orange juice in the cup holder near her.

"Try to work on some of that as we drive. You'll do better if you have something on your stomach."

Her look of gratitude was fleeting but sincere. From how deep she was in her head, he suspected she was employing every coping strategy she could. The agony of anticipation could be worse than the event itself, not knowing how or if you could handle what was ahead.

She wore a navy-blue tailored skirt and matching jacket. The lapels had a pink pin stripe. A short sleeved white blouse was beneath the coat. Her cross and his badge rested on the exposed triangle of skin. The outfit made her look thinner than usual. She had her hair down but pulled up on the sides, those hoops she always wore in her ears. She looked very adult. And to him, very vulnerable.

He couldn't stand in front of her, like he had with Colin. He kept reminding himself of what he'd told her. She was strong enough to handle this. But he hated having to watch her do it. One moment at a time. One breath at a time. For both of them.

"Won't your family miss you at Easter?" she asked as she took a careful nibble of the toast.

"We're more about Christmas and Thanksgiving," he said, one-handing the wheel to pull them out of the parking lot as he bit into the biscuit. "I call Mom and Dad at Easter and send them a card. My brother brings his kids over for the egg hunt with Dad, so that holiday is all about the grandbabies."

They talked a little about his family, some about hers. He wasn't sure she heard most of his answers. Eventually, she laid her head back on the seat and closed her eyes, her face pale and drawn. She continued to hold his hand throughout the drive. Whenever he needed it to navigate the truck, he returned it to her as soon as possible. She played with his fingers, stroked them. Sometimes he felt a tremor in hers. They were cold.

Every protective instinct he had told him to turn around, tell all those waiting doctors and legal people to fuck themselves.

When they turned into the hospital parking lot, she opened her eyes. "It's really hard, letting someone go into the fire without you. Isn't it?"

She'd been watching and monitoring him, just as he'd been doing to her. She cared about his state of mind, too. Hell if that didn't make this all the harder. But as he took a second look at her serious and earnest expression, he saw a remarkably evident calm, locked in place like armor.

He expected she'd used some version of this throughout medical school and family tragedy. To cope, to handle whatever pressures she faced, and to conceal whatever worries she had. She had a core of inner strength he'd never doubted, even when she broke down and had to shore it back up again.

If what happened in the hospital destroyed her, they wouldn't know it. He would, when he made her remove that armor, under his touch, under his command. That was how and when she would need him. To help her move forward, and heal.

He needed to say what was in his head and heart. Things he'd held off saying, because he knew she had to come to it on her own, and there was always the chance he was wrong.

Even if he was right, the timing might suck. And he might piss her off. But maybe that was okay. Maybe that would help.

He put his hand on her shoulder, sliding it to her nape to stroke and let her feel his hold there. Her hazel eyes turned in his direction. He felt so damn much for her, he had to steady himself, reach for calm, before he spoke.

"When your dad took that second job to pay your medical bills, that's when his heart problem started, wasn't it?"

As she digested the question, she stiffened a little under his touch and her eyes frosted. "I know what you're implying. It's not my fault, I was a baby, and had no control. I get that. But it was a chain of events that happened *because* of me. Dad died, and Rory tried to take on too much of his work. The tractor turned over on him and that brought Thomas back from New York, where he got bleeding ulcers, trying to be what he wasn't."

"So being a doctor, doing something worthwhile with your life, is a way to make up for some of that?" He spoke quietly. "Prove that their sacrifices were worth it? Because if you're something the world thinks is less important, like a grocery clerk or a pet groomer, why should they have bothered?"

Shock crossed her expression. "That's not what I think. That's not why I chose... Even if it was part of it, that doesn't make it wrong. If it's something I can do and am good at, why shouldn't I do that? And I don't think being a doctor is more important than any other job."

"Glad to hear it. Have you seen the trauma a poorly groomed poodle can wreak?"

"Don't you dare mock me."

Her sudden white-faced anger goaded dark and dangerous things inside him. Like his rage at having to let her stand by herself before a conference she was dreading like a firing squad. "You think that's what I'm fucking doing?"

She shook her head. Closed her eyes. He gripped her upper arms, the sleeves of that trim blue suit creasing under his palms. He turned her toward him. "Look at me, Les."

When she didn't, he made himself let her go and sat back. "Look at me. Right now. It's not a request."

She had her hand on her stomach, kneading it. When he covered her hand with his, pressed his palm there, her gaze rose.

"Every loss, every struggle in your family," he said. "They were going through it while you were the sponge absorbing it. You felt helpless, so helping became the goal. One you sharpened into an arrow, pointing toward being a doctor."

He nodded at the hospital. "Maybe you do love medicine, and healing people. But I think all of that gets in the way of knowing that for sure, one way or another. It also makes it far harder for you to do something that's already really hard. Like understanding that mistakes are a tough but expected part of the job."

Les blinked rapidly before the tears he saw could spill out. "Why are you doing this to me now?"

"Because this M&M thing, the legal stuff—even the terrible thing that happened with this kid—I think it's the catalyst that blew open the door. Maybe you will be a science teacher. Or a great doctor. You have this incredible, analytical mind. Answer why you came here in the first place, why you're here now, and you'll know what you want to do."

He touched her lapel, her earrings, the lipstick on her mouth. "Use this to do whatever you need to do today, but remember at the end of it, I'll be here. Whether it's to let you scream, cry, or have the biggest cone of ice cream I can find for you."

He dropped his hand to their clasped ones. Her fingers were rigid as she looked away, stared at the console. Slowly, they loosened and gripped his. When her eyes shifted his way, he still saw the pain, the nervousness, the anguish, but there was a heartbreaking trace of a smile. "Will you let me nip the top of your cone, without adding it to the list?"

"Baby, you made that one way too easy. You can nip the top of my cone anytime. And it all goes on the list, because you want it there. You want me to take any excuse I can get to put you over my knee and get you writhing and wet."

A shuddering breath. "Don't do that to me right now, either."

He cupped her neck, brought her face to his shoulder and spoke into her hair. "Be true to that big heart and steel backbone I know you have. No matter what shit is going down around you."

"I haven't shown you much of a steel backbone."

"Yes, you sure as hell have. Part of my job is helping you handle the storms. It doesn't mean I don't know and respect how many you've handled on your own. I'm just not going to let you handle more than your share anymore." He eased back to kiss her, tasted the nerves in the vibration of her lips. He squeezed her neck and made himself do what he'd done the night she'd arrived. Be tough.

She'd call it being "not nice." Being a good Dom, a good partner, required that sometimes.

"Get in there and get it done. I'll be waiting."

~

When Les stepped into Dr. Portland's office, her advisor rose from the chair. A mannish-looking woman with solid bone structure, ice-blond hair and brown eyes, she'd always looked to Les like a woman with a Viking warrior in her ancestry. Dr. Portland preferred neat slacks and short sleeved knit shirts. She also had a fingernail-sized tattoo of a sunflower on the curve of one breast. Since it was only revealed when the shirts had a neckline that could gap at the right moment to offer a quick glimpse, no one was brave enough to ask her for the story behind it.

She did smile, but it was tight around the edges. Les expected the tension was due to the occupant of one of her guest chairs, a man in a charcoal-colored suit, reviewing what looked like a detailed document on his phone.

"I'm glad you came in for the M&M today, Les," Dr. Portland told her. "This is Martin Sully, from the hospital's legal department. He wanted a few minutes before you and I talk. I can be present for that conversation, or you can choose to speak to him alone. The choice is yours."

"I'm fine with you being here." She'd prefer it, since Dr. Portland would understand the implications of what Mr. Sully was about to tell her, so that Les didn't inflate—or de-emphasize—the importance.

"Miss Wilder."

She shook Martin Sully's hand, meeting shrewd and intelligent eyes. He had an attractive jaw and thick brown hair. His nails were buffed. His voice was as she'd remembered it, cordial and smooth, not unpleasant.

"Have a seat." He took his chair after she and Dr. Portland did, a gentleman's courtesy. "As Dr. Portland said, it's good you came in for the M&M today. We look forward to you returning to your education and rotation. From what I've reviewed," he gestured with the phone, "you've done strong academic and clinical work. Your evaluations prior to this incident have emphasized your work ethic and attention to detail, as well as how prudent you are about verifying courses of treatment with your residents or attendings. You make cautious, intuitive leaps, but you never go rogue. That's useful for us in proceeding with the family."

"Has it gone further than when you left your message?" Though she spoke the words without faltering, she knotted her fingers in her lap at Sully's response.

"Their attorney has filed the preliminary paperwork for the suit. We've confirmed you will not be named, but your attending and resident for the incident are. As is the hospital, of course."

Her heart thundered in her ears, her pulse rabbiting. But noting what she was sure was a paler expression, Martin Sully shook his head. "It's a serious matter, Miss Wilder, but one we routinely deal with. People grieving often seek someone to blame. Not just in an unfortunate tragedy like this, but even when their loved one was suffering a terminal illness with an inevitable outcome. There are plenty of attorneys who search for people in these circumstances."

He glanced at Dr. Portland, then back at Les. "I also want to make you aware a family member, an aunt, has contacted the media. A story about the incident was released on local networks. It hasn't been picked up more widely, but if a suit does proceed, it's possible that story may get more exposure. If it does, news outlets may bring your name into it."

"Les, here. Drink." Dr. Portland put a bottle of water on the desk before her.

While Les was embarrassed her distress was that obvious, she took a couple sips, trying to keep her hands from shaking. "What do I need to do?"

"Nothing," Martin said firmly. "Or rather, what you've already been doing. Outside of the M&M, you speak to no one about the matter. We will keep you advised. Dr. Portland is suggesting you resume your rotation and normal class schedule next week, after the holiday. It gives you a little time but confirms no fault has been found with your performance."

She didn't know how to say, "I'm not sure I can come back," no matter if they were saying she could. But she knew now wasn't the time to say that.

She hated this. But when she met Dr. Portland's gaze, she remembered what Beulah had said, what Brick had echoed. Every doctor dealt with this. All of them made mistakes.

All of them hated it.

She focused on what the lawyer was saying. "The Mortality and Morbidity conference, as you know, is not open to outside legal representation. In a court case, an attendee cannot be forced to reveal what's discussed there. However, determined attorneys have sometimes obtained notes taken in those conferences."

"Martin," Dr. Portland said. "You might as well be telling her to censor her responses to the questions she'll get."

"I'm telling her the reality, Anne," he said evenly. He brought his attention back to Les. "I meant what I said about your evaluations. The only real concern I've heard from your professors, attendings and residents is how deeply you take things to heart. How it affects your stress management, and the realities of becoming a doctor."

While she supposed it was good that those overseeing her education were paying attention, it unnerved her to hear those things hadn't escaped their notice. Sully's sharp gaze remained on her. "When you're in the M&M, my recommendation is short, precise answers on what you did or did not do, and listening attentively to feedback on what could have been done instead. Not making statements about what you feel like was your fault. Not being emotional. Do you understand?"

"Yes. I do."

"All right." He rose. "Dr. Portland's point is valid. My intention isn't to impact the M&M's ability to improve patient care. But I also can't gloss over the legal aspects. Here's my card, should you have any future questions. Dr. Portland and I are the two people with whom you can safely discuss the details of this situation and case. It's reasonable that you will want to share your emotions with someone, but I would be very selective in doing that. No one directly or incidentally involved in the situation, only with someone you trust, and only when your privacy is insured. Not the local college pub."

He tagged a serious smile on that no-brainer, but she couldn't summon one in return. Les looked at his card, turning it over in her fingers. "Have you...have you had any contact with the family? Like Mrs. DaCosta?"

"Not yet. You haven't attempted to make contact with her, have you?"

His piercing regard was joined by Dr. Portland's, her brown eyes fixed on Les. Les shifted uncomfortably. "I haven't. But I wondered if, at some future time, there might be that opportunity? The night it happened, I didn't express myself as well as I could have."

"Is that a real question?" he asked, his tone incredulous.

When she flinched, he sighed, pinching the bridge of his nose. While he looked like he was having some kind of internal dialogue about dealing with medical students, when he spoke, his tone was even again. "Ask yourself this, Miss Wilder. Do you really think there's anything you can say that would make a difference? It's human to want to absolve ourselves, to seek forgiveness. Unfortunately, offering an apology isn't typically useful for the dismissal of a lawsuit."

She wasn't sure if she agreed with that, but the hospital had more to lose from this than her. She nodded her understanding, rose and shook his offered hand. He glanced toward Dr. Portland. "Anne." Then he left the office.

"So that's done." Dr. Portland nudged the bottle toward her. "Les, take another drink so I'll know you're not going to fall out on me."

"I'm fine," Les said, but she complied. Could she do this? Yes, she could. Because as nerve wracking as this was, as much as she felt like her heart was being shredded, when she walked out of here today, she knew three things for certain.

She wasn't a mother who'd lost her child.

She would be going home to her family.

Brick would be waiting for her.

Reminding herself first and foremost who'd lost the most in all of this helped. As did revisiting the main purpose of the M&M, which Dr. Portland did now.

"The conference will focus on processes, as much as individual action. It's not to assign specific blame, though often it can feel that way." Dr. Portland tapped her closed laptop. "I appreciate you emailing me the detailed list of the actions you took that night."

"I appreciate the suggestion. Writing it down helped me order my thoughts and remember things I'd forgotten."

"Yes." Dr. Portland laced her hands on the desk. "Everything he said about you is true, Les. You are an excellent medical student, and well thought of. It's a terrible trial by fire, but how you handle this, how you proceed, will determine what kind of doctor you will be."

"And if I have what it takes to be a doctor."

Proving her experience as an advisor, Dr. Portland didn't deny it. "This is a profession that often requires detachment from a patient's suffering as well as extraordinary attention to detail, all to improve their health and well-being. We apply what we learn from every misstep toward that goal. Your caring heart is a big part of what will make you a good doctor, Les. Even as it's the thing that could also make you change your mind about being one. Do you understand?"

"I do." Only too well.

The advisor sat back. "Are you going home to North Carolina for Easter?"

"Yes."

"Good. Spend the holiday with your family. You'll have some ground to make up when you return next week, but I've no doubt you'll manage it." Dr. Portland checked her watch. "We should head in that direction."

Blessing that dry toast Brick had made her, absorbing some of the acid in her stomach, Les rose, smoothing her skirt. "Thank you for being in the M&M with me. For supporting me."

Dr. Portland gave her an assessing look. "One last note of advice? After my first M&M, I did tequila shots until I blacked out. I don't recommend it."

Les blinked. "A...friend brought me here. He said he'd take me out for ice cream."

"A much better idea." Dr. Portland's faint smile faded away. "This is no laughing matter. But to keep doing this job well, you have to give yourself breathing room."

"He's an arson investigator. And a fireman. He said something similar."

"I'm glad you have someone like that in your corner. But do go home for Easter, Les. I know how much your family means to you. Let them help you with this. Help you make any big decisions."

Les met her advisor's gaze again. "Yes, ma'am."

~

She'd worried about being in the same room with the resident and attending. But Dr. Jack Tollman and Dr. Arnold Redmond greeted her with no obvious animosity. She envied them their seeming calm. Dr. Redmond was always reserved, just as he was now. Dr. Jack was more friendly, though just like any other day, he had the look of an over-whelmed and busy resident.

She was supposed to sit at the panel table with them. "Once your part of the presenting is done, you'll return to the audience," Dr. Jack told her. "If there are follow-up questions addressed to you at that point, stand up and answer. But after the step-by-step, we should get the bulk of them."

"I'm sorry, Dr. Tollman."

Dr. Redmond was talking to another member of the surgical staff, so she couldn't say it to him at the same time, but she didn't want to wait to say it to Jack now.

"I appreciate that, Les, but you did what you thought was right, and I signed off on it, thinking the same thing. Arnold looked at the notes, and feels the same. The possibility is so rare, and there were no obvious indicators."

"Maybe because you went by my notes. You may have seen something I didn't."

"We trusted your evaluation, which yes, could go two ways." His serious green eyes met hers. "Maybe we would have seen something, or maybe we would have seen the same thing you did."

When he turned to answer an admin's question regarding the slide projector, Dr. Redmond was taking a seat at the table, his conversation done. She offered him the same apology.

His response didn't differ significantly from Jack's, though his was brusquer. "You're here to learn, Les. There's nothing easy about holding people's lives in your hands. So get your head out of your guilt, listen and learn today. And keep doing so, from everyone who's been where you're going."

"Yes, sir."

She understood the logic, the attitudes. But it was still the most horrible thing she'd ever experienced. A child was dead. Would never grow up. Her life, whatever she was going to be, was going to go on. With no official requirement that she make amends, say she was sorry, do...*something*.

As the conference was called to order, that thought kept rolling through her mind, like a boulder crushing glass. The opening remarks, the presentation of the facts of the case, the slides showing the diagnostics and conclusions about them, didn't stop the feeling.

She did her best not to go back to that night, to the faces, the voices and images that could overwhelm her. She had the notes in front of her she'd sent Dr. Portland. She didn't need them, because she'd been through them so often, she knew them all. Not by mindless rote, but because she'd walked through them in her head, over and over.

Llanzo had come to the ER with what his mother thought was a cold virus. However, she was worried enough about it she wanted him evaluated. Les had checked everything she was supposed to check, had listened to his heart. Asked the questions she was supposed to ask. Including questions about honey and home remedies.

She'd confirmed the mother's suspicion it was likely just a cold. She'd sent her home with the usual advice for treating it, plus the instruction to do a follow up with her pediatrician on Monday. She'd made the notation on the chart to email or fax the visit details to that pediatrician. While not required, she called his office and left a message suggesting they contact the mother on Monday to see how he was doing.

After that, she'd moved on to the next patient.

"The patient was brought back to the ER the next night," Dr. Redmond said. "He had developed myocarditis from the virus. He went into cardiac shock and succumbed to it."

Les noticed Beulah and several of her other friends in the back. Their thoughtful but supportive expressions helped when questions started to come in her direction.

What would help them not do what I did? After nearly seven years in an academic mode, she fell into a rhythm of question and response. She thought of what Sully said, and did her best to offer an unembellished report.

Because she'd gone over every step, again and again, the decisions she'd made and could have made, it wasn't difficult to offer thoughtful responses on the questions that weren't covered in her notes. Yet she never lost the dull throb under her heart.

Every word represented Llanzo DaCosta, a toddler who'd played with her stethoscope and looked at her with tired eyes. He'd managed a small smile for her.

When they'd left the ER, she'd gripped Llanzo's fist on his mother's shoulder. He had his head resting next to it, and Les had touched his hair. "You'll feel better soon," she promised him.

Don't go there. *Don't go there.* She divided herself into two people. Every word she spoke as a rational, calm medical professional was a hammer hitting that other person crouched inside her, keening.

While she listened and learned, she hurt and grieved, and wondered if the pain would ever stop. And what it would say about the kind of doctor she was if it ever did.

At the conclusion of the M&M, she made the necessary courtesies, and slipped into the hallway. She saw two things right away.

Beulah, coming out another exit and hurrying her way.

Brick, sitting in a nearby waiting area.

Dismay surged through her, but not because she was mad he was there. She was terrified that seeing him would unleash everything locked down inside her. If he saw how hard her knees were trembling, he might mortify her by picking her up and sweeping her away.

No, he wouldn't. He knew what she needed right now. He also saw Beulah heading her way, so though he rose, he waited for her friend to reach her first.

He would be there, after. At the bottom of the cliff, to cushion her fall.

"Hey, girl." Beulah clasped her in a hard hug. "Damn, I've missed your narrow ass. You and your encyclopedia brain did great in there. You looked as calm as a still pond. Your voice didn't even shake."

That was because all her internal organs had absorbed the vibration. "It was easier once I just focused on the information and didn't think about..." Les lifted a shoulder.

"Yeah." Beulah searched her face. "You headed to our place? I have to finish out the shift, but tonight we could..." She trailed off at Les's expression. "You're not staying."

"I'll go by to pick up some more things, but I'm going home for Easter. Dr. Portland recommended it. Said I should come back next week."

"Are you going to?" The question proved how much Beulah knew about her.

"I'm going to go home, be with my family, and think about it. This was incredibly hard, Beulah."

Beulah's expression showed her dismay over the qualified response, though she nodded reluctantly, squeezing Les's shoulders. "Just promise me you'll call to talk if you need it? Anytime, day or night. I wish you'd hang around for the night at least. Everyone wants to see you."

"I miss them too. But my mom is expecting us. You know she'll be cooking for us." Les managed a weak smile. "Thomas and Marcus will be there."

Beulah rolled her eyes. "Girl, why didn't you say so? I'll pack myself in your suitcase and come along."

"You know Marcus is gay. And married to my brother."

"Thomas can have his heart. I just want his body. Tell him I can suck a golf ball through a straw. A man has a use for that, no matter his sexual orientation. The three of us will do a fun, no-strings-attached orgy."

She had missed her outrageous roommate. Even if the spurt of humor felt like a cherry bomb dropped inside a crystal vase. And Les was the vase.

"Before you get all judgy," Beulah continued, "I'm not the one who brought a hunky-assed fireman as your chauffeur. Like I didn't notice the Henry Cavill lookalike risking the structural integrity of that chair." Beulah didn't turn in Brick's direction as she tweaked a lock of Les's hair. "He was there when we slipped into the back of the auditorium."

"He's pretty determined."

"He doesn't look like much would stand in his way. Unless it wanted to be squashed peas as he rolled over it. Okay, well, let me do this."

Beulah enveloped her in another hug, holding her even longer.

When she drew back, her dark eyes were intent and close. "I know you need to do what's right for you, but I have this selfish dream. We both become doctors, me in DC amid all the crazy fast pace and glamor, and you down in North Carolina, with your backwoods clinic."

She drew a breath. "I call you when I have something I can't figure out, because you'll ask me the right questions. And you'll call me for things, too. We'll confer, we'll be colleagues, and we'll visit each other, drink, hang out, have fun. Be on this journey together, from now until we're old. Become gray-haired role models for the up-and-coming think-they-know-it-alls."

"I like that dream." Les just didn't know if it could be her dream, or if she would end up being the cheering section as Beulah realized it for herself.

The emotions she was bottling up rose with the thought, choking off further reply. Brick saw where she was at. He moved toward her, but she couldn't make herself let go of Beulah until he got there.

"I don't look like Henry Cavill," he told Beulah. "Cavill looks like me."

"Look at you with the superhero nosy hearing," her roommate said, unabashed. She'd shifted to a tight hold of Les's hand, but her shrewd glance moved back to Les. Les expected they could see the cracks forming in her brittle mask. Les kept her gaze on Brick's steady one, trying to use what she saw there as a glue that might hold until she could make it out of here.

"We need to go," Brick told Beulah.

"Yeah, I can see that." Beulah gave Les one more hug, so close the triple studs in her ear, a caduceus, a diamond and a pink quartz, scraped against Les's cheek. "You come back, you hear?" Beulah murmured. "Take the weekend, but come back. I can do this med school stuff without you, but I'd much rather not."

She turned her gaze to Brick. "Take care of my girlfriend."

"Count on it."

Though Beulah looked like she wanted to say more, she squeezed Les's hand and left them. She'd be headed back to the Pediatrics area, her current rotation.

It was a poignant reminder of what it felt like to be a part of this. Not to be standing on the outside. The excitement of meeting new patients, reviewing their information. Feeling a sense of accomplishment when she rose to the challenge of presenting to attendings and residents. All things that had convinced Les she was on a fast track toward graduation and her residency. And ultimately being an attending, capable of instructing students and residents herself.

For one blissful moment, that reminder, the reward at the end of the journey—or its beginning—was stronger than the anxiety and exhaustion, or facing the consequences, the agony of fucking it up. She'd been sculpting herself into someone who would come back to her hometown as the same but also vastly different person who'd left. She'd have more to contribute, more value to give back to the community she loved.

To the family she loved. Even if Brick was right about her motives, so was she. It wasn't wrong to *want* to give back to your life, your community.

But when she went home at Easter, would she abandon that resolve, let the comfort and safety of home convince her to cop out? Take the life her mother had painted for her? Or would it remind her why she'd been trying to paint a different picture for herself?

There was only one way to find out, but it told her why she'd been dragging her feet about going home. Having to talk to her family about what had happened was just the smoke screen. She'd just faced one incredibly difficult thing, but the seemingly less difficult one might hold greater sway on whether she came back or not.

"Les." Brick drew her attention. "What else do you need to do before we head for Fairhope?"

"I need to go to my place and pick up a few things."

"All right." When she didn't immediately move, he added quietly, "I overheard a few comments from the experienced-looking docs who came out of there. Everyone seems to think it could have happened to any of them."

"Yeah."

"Hey." He touched her arm, and she closed her eyes.

"Don't. Not here." The muscles in her shoulders and neck were tight, the steel rod of her will holding her up. "You probably should have stayed in the truck."

"I had a different opinion. I wasn't going to be more than a hundred feet from you while you were dealing with this."

She glanced toward the waiting area. "Based on what I know of the auditorium's square footage and the distance down this hall, I'd say you were about two hundred feet away."

"Smart ass."

A smile tried to reach her lips, but the effect was a rock hitting an already cracked windshield. The breaks started to expand in all directions, not just across the outside, but over what was holding her together inside. "Okay, let's get out of here," she said desperately.

He put a hand to her lower back. "Closest stairwell to the main floor is over here."

Of course a fireman would have scoped the exits. But it wasn't going to be that easy. As they approached the door, she saw a stocky woman with thick and tinted blond hair waiting for them. Agatha Needham. She was an ER nurse, one with special training for pediatric patients, hence her pink scrubs with puppies printed on the top.

She'd been on staff the night Llanzo was brought in. Both times. She was a good nurse, and had provided useful guidance to Les on her rotation.

"Be good to your nurses, because they're your best chance of not killing anyone." Dr. Jack had told Les and her fellow ER rotation students that. The male nurse standing at the duty desk had shot them a *"you know that's right"* look that made them all smile, albeit nervously.

Had Agatha struggled with what happened as much as Les had? She expected Martin or someone else in Legal had talked to her, since they'd interviewed everyone involved.

"Hi, Les." Agatha looked tense.

Les saw flint in Brick's gaze and put a hand on his side. She could handle this, whatever it was. "Did you need to talk to me?"

Agatha seemed to consider the question. Her gaze traveled down the hallway, over the waiting room, and back to Les. She sighed. "Mrs. DaCosta...she lives near me. We're not friends, but since we're neighbors, she recognizes me. The night she brought Llanzo in, you might remember we were chatting when you examined him."

Les hadn't held onto that detail, since there were other far more significant ones about that night. But now she remembered. "I'm not sure what you want to discuss, and I definitely don't want to be rude, but they told me not to talk about any of this."

"I know. That's not what this is about. I've been asked to pass on a message. I've struggled with it. I know what Legal would say, what anyone would say, even myself. But in the end, we're all human, aren't we? Even when they tell us not to react like one."

Les's brow furrowed. Brick's hand had gone from a light touch on her lower back to a firmer, more supportive pressure. If something happened here that required it, she need only give him a sign, and he would extricate her from the conversation with a polite but firm dismissal.

As if she sensed that shift, Agatha glanced at him, then met Les's gaze again. "I'm sorry if this is the wrong thing to do. You don't have to act on it, but I felt like you deserved to make your own choice."

She handed Les a piece of paper. "Mrs. DaCosta wants you to text her. She wants to meet with you, face to face. Just the two of you."

~

"You think it's a setup from the DaCosta's lawyer? Trying to get you to say things outside the M&M they can use?"

Brick opened the passenger door of the truck, steadying Les as she used the strap to pull herself up into the seat. He stayed where he was after he asked the question, resting a loose wrist on the door. He gripped the cushioned head rest near her face, his foot braced on the running board.

He looked nice, she realized. Her mind had been on other things when they prepared for the drive this morning. Firefighter T-shirt tucked into belted jeans, his tan, thick-soled work shoes without scuffs. He'd shaved. He exuded reputable "first responder," enough to have been unhampered by any desk checkpoints between him and the auditorium.

"I guess it's possible. But my gut says no. She's got to be in a terrible state right now. Her lawyer isn't going to use her for some kind of sting operation. That could go just as badly for their side, if she gets emotional and says anything that could be used by the hospital to suggest she might have contributed to the situation. I'd like to say they wouldn't do that, but we all know how court cases can go. I'm surprised she's coherent enough to reach out and ask for something like this."

But there were a lot of stages to grief, including those where the person fixated on things, tasks, anything to keep from drowning in that well of grief and loss. Realizing that thought contradicted what she'd just said, she sighed. "I don't know. I don't know what I'm going to do with the information. Maybe nothing. I'll think about it over Easter."

"If you want, I could run the situation past Tish, see what she says about the risks and what might be going on. We won't use any names, but you can trust her not to take it any further than us."

Les looked at her hands. "Mr. Sully says there's already been local news coverage on it."

"Aw, hell. I'm sorry, Les." He touched her arm, a light stroke over her skin. She'd removed the coat, leaving her in the short-sleeved blouse beneath. "But all the more reason. Before she was an ADA, Tish was a corporate attorney for a pharmaceutical company. She handled her share of liability cases where people were seeking damages for physical or mental harm. You can trust her. I promise."

Hell no was her purely female response to encouraging contact between Brick and the gorgeous attorney. But she pushed aside her reaction for the absurdity it was. "Thank you. I wouldn't mind having that additional insight."

"Okay. Let's go pick up your stuff. I didn't know your mom was making dinner for us. I wouldn't have eaten any breakfast. In fact, I might have fasted since yesterday."

"I'm sure she'll have something in the fridge to heat up if we need it, but I told her I wasn't sure when we'd get there tonight. I just didn't feel up to telling Beulah I don't want to hang around right now."

"Got it." He touched her face, then stepped back to close her door. As he moved around to the driver's side, her thinking about her mother making them dinner, about what had just happened, was apparently a mistake. Because by the time he got in, her chin was trembling.

She turned her head toward the window, and fiercely admonished herself. *Hold your shit together.*

"Hey."

She had to prove she wasn't falling apart. Her breathing was coming short, and she was feeling lightheaded. She'd gotten through some of the toast, none of the egg. She should have eaten more protein. Those cracks ran right into her heart, threatening a full break.

He had his hand on her neck and shoulder, his thumb pressing against her jaw to get her to look up at him. He stroked the sensitive area beneath her ear lobe, a sure way to get her attention. "Breathe, Les. It's okay."

She hooked her fingers over his forearm. He worked the comb free that was holding her hair like a smooth bird's wing. Her eyes fell half shut as he did his soothing, deep scalp stroke, moving down her back and then up, completing the circuit again.

"When I do fire fleshing on you, it will be like this," he told her. "A warm stroke over your skin from the fire, then my hand following behind, a firmer touch. Over and over."

With his rough, strong hands. She liked the thought.

"I don't know what's wrong. I don't fall apart like this. And not this often. I worked in the ER for two weeks. People came in with bad injuries and illnesses, some of them dying from them, right there." Adults. But still. "I handled it. I was anxious about getting things wrong, but it wasn't like this."

"Les, you're a trained medical professional. Look at yourself like a patient. Were any of those injuries a car wreck, where the passenger died, but the driver was okay? No matter whose fault it was, what condition was the driver in?"

"Traumatized." A post-trauma response could go on for a few days after the event. Even longer, depending on the person and the experience. Expected, part of the process.

"Trauma," he confirmed. "So stop beating yourself up over it."

Her chin was trembling again. He muttered something, and moved his hands to her waist.

"I'm okay. I—"

With remarkable ease, he plucked her from her seat and onto his lap. She put her arm around his back, the other over his shoulder to loop it around his neck. He held her as close as she held him. A few tears leaked out of her eyes as she pressed her face against his chest, but ironically, the tighter he held her, the more easily she could breathe. With him holding her, her fears and worries couldn't pull her under.

After a few minutes, the reaction slid away. The ache under her ribs went back to a dull throb, rather than making her feel knifed by a horror show villain.

He pressed his mouth to her temple. "Let's go get your stuff."

"Yeah. That sounds good."

He shifted her back to her seat, and helped fasten her seatbelt. "Your hunky-assed chauffeur will go through the McDonald's drive-thru for a soft serve cone."

"Fudge sundae, with nuts."

At his look, she managed a weak smile. "It's been a tough day. I need the hard stuff."

He squeezed her hand. As they pulled out of the parking lot, Les smoothed her hand over the jacket in her lap, feeling the crackle of the paper in the pocket.

And tried not to think.

CHAPTER TWENTY

*H*er and Beulah's condo was rented out to medical students by a cardiothoracic surgeon, a college alumnus. The two flanking it were as well. Because of that, several of her neighbors had a key to her place and vice versa. Just like undergrad dormmates, they borrowed stuff from one another and, if needed, sought out quieter study corners that shared access provided.

Fortunately, with it being early afternoon, her condo was empty. Like Beulah, most of her neighbors would be in class, working rotations, or studying elsewhere.

Beulah liked her coffee, and drank it several times a day, so the scent lingered in the condo. The condos were furnished. There were rules about damages, but she and Beulah were good tenants. Even so, their landlord was smart enough not to put anything in a student-rented condo he would regret losing. The pieces wouldn't win spots in a home décor magazine, but they were comfortable, sturdy and serviceable. Durham area landscapes and pictures of the university campus broke up the wall space.

A colorful throw her mother had sent her was draped over the beige and gray striped sofa. Whimsical dishes rested in a rack in the kitchen drainer, pretty hand towels hanging on the stove and fridge handles. The comforters and sheets in each of their bedrooms reflected their personal preferences. They didn't have a lot of time for decorating, but touches like that made it their own space.

Les moved toward the steps to the second level. "Help yourself to anything in the kitchen, and there's a remote on the coffee table if you want to channel surf. I shouldn't be long." She paused on the bottom step, her hand on the banister, and looked back at him. "Unless you'd like to see the upstairs."

Brick ignored his surroundings and came to her. With her on the step, they were eye-to-eye. She could hear her pulse pounding in her ears. The quiet in the condo, punctuated by the faint hum of the heating and air unit, the click of the ice maker in the fridge, became more noticeable.

"I'd like to see your room, Les. Take me there."

He offered her his hand, and she closed hers over it. Because of the condo's narrow layout, the staircase was five steps to the landing, then did an about face to the next set of steps to the second floor. On the landing wall was a framed poster of a kitten lying on her back. *Fuck it. It's time to take a nap*, was printed in pink letters beneath it.

"A dorm souvenir?" Brick's gaze sparked with humor.

"The first thing Beulah and I bought together," she confirmed. "It's traveled with us ever since."

They'd joked about fighting for custody over it when graduating. If she didn't graduate...

Les reached the second floor, Brick a silent presence behind her. Her bedroom was on the left. Beulah's was at the end of the hall. They had one guest bedroom, or room for a third roommate, but the rent was reasonable enough they'd decided to stick with two. Third year med school was difficult enough without having to break in the habits of a new permanent roommate.

Textbooks that hadn't been uploaded to the university library system for digital access were on her desk. Next to them were old notebooks from her first two years. She liked to scribble things down, because that helped her remember them. A bookshelf held family photos and two or three figurines she'd brought from home, serving the same purpose as her mother's throw.

As she moved to the closet to pull out her suitcase, intending to fill it with what she'd need for the Easter visit, Brick went to the bookshelf to study the pictures.

He'd see a photo of her family at one of the state parks, from when

Les was in middle school. They were at a picnic table, cutting up watermelon. Dad was chuckling, Mom's hand covering his.

Next to that picture was Rory and Daralyn at their wedding, right before Daralyn threw the bouquet. It hadn't been a large event, because Daralyn still had problems with big groups, especially when she was the center of attention. Rory had his hand around her waist, and she was sitting on his lap in his chair. His attention was all about and on her, making sure she was okay. She had been. She'd radiated love and happiness that day.

Thomas had walked her down the aisle, as Les's father would have done. When her mother's eyes filled with tears, Les knew her thoughts had gone there, and to everything connected to them.

Marcus and Thomas's wedding picture was next. Les had taken the photo, asking them to overlap their hands so she could get the two rings in the shot. As they'd done it, Thomas had looked at Marcus, and that was when Les clicked the image. The photo was almost too intimate, something more appropriate for them to have on their own shelf. They did have one, but she'd made herself a copy. She loved looking at the three pictures, all the romance and love in them. Proof that she and her siblings had been born from love, and confirmation her brothers had found their own, the right person to care for them, and who they could care for.

She also had pictures of herself and Beulah from their undergrad days, group photos with their dormmates. On the wall next to the shelf was a painting of the farm. It was one Thomas had done during her first year, as if he'd known how overwhelming the homesickness had been. When his star rose in the art world, Beulah joked they could sell it to pay a year's rent.

He was most known for gay erotic subject material, haunting and layered pictures of male love, but this landscape held the same undeniable talent. She felt like she could step right into it, like the wardrobe to Narnia, and be home.

The other picture on the bedroom walls had come from Beulah, a birthday gift. She'd found an old window in a vintage store and used one of Les's photos, enlarging and mounting the picture behind the divided lights. The picture was Les's view from her bedroom window at home, the sprawling oak in the back yard she'd told Brick about, the tire swing and fields stretching beyond the lawn. The front corner had caught a section of her mother's vegetable garden.

A window to home, literally.

"What's this?" Brick drew her attention to an empty small peanut butter jar.

She put some jeans in the suitcase. "During my second year, I worked in a downtown clinic. Bugman, a homeless man, was a regular. He was a poorly managed diabetic, and was always coming in for things related to that, like leg ulcers. One day I found him pulling a peanut butter jar out of a dumpster."

She straightened. "He had a plastic knife, and said he could usually get a couple peanut butter sandwiches out of a so-called 'empty jar.' The local grocer gives him out-of-date loaf bread. Bugman told me, 'Laziness and waste can serve a purpose. Even assholes can do good, despite themselves.'"

Brick gave her a curious look. "So is this that jar?"

"No. It's one I kept after Beulah and I finished it. I wanted the reminder. In the clinic, you make assumptions about people just because they're dirty, or strung out. Especially when you're busy or overworked, or frustrated by their unwillingness or inability to take better care of themselves. We're always short on time, so we're already making intuitive leaps that can..." She paused. "Result in the wrong conclusions."

At his concerned expression, she shook her head. She refused to let every damn thought knock her off the seesaw. "'Take a moment. Listen. Learn. Ask the right questions.' One of my first-year professors had that on his wall. Said it applied to everything, not just medicine. Until Bugman, I hadn't internalized it."

"Do you feel like you forgot that with Llanzo?"

"No." She gazed at the jar. "That's what scares me so bad. That even if you think you're doing everything right, listening, paying attention, you can still get it so very wrong."

She returned to packing. "I take Bugman a jar of peanut butter every once in a while. And a bag of apples, so he doesn't get constipated."

"A practical woman." Brick shifted his attention to her mission trip photos, taken at a Navajo reservation in New Mexico. They'd been doing medical screenings for the kids to help them qualify for preschool. In the picture, she was squatting down and surrounded by several children, all of them grinning widely. One cradled a chicken in his arms.

"He was impressed I knew about their feeding and care," she said.

"Rory said you loved that trip." He quirked a brow. "He also said you had the hots for a guy you met there."

She rolled her eyes. "Tsintah. He helped with the mission construction projects. Gorgeous, feathery black hair, dark eyes, great facial bones and lots of muscles. Which we saw plenty of, since he was usually shirtless and wearing a toolbelt. All of us girls were eye-balling him. In hindsight, he was entirely too aware of that. Rory has big ears. I told Daralyn and Julie about him at Christmas that year."

"You have to watch out for those Wilder kids. They like to listen outside of doors."

She made a face at him. "I did love that trip. So much of first year is studying. Second year is where you finally get the chance to apply what you're learning. Doing it for people who really need it makes it more of a charge. Mission trips are an in-your-face reminder of how much value preventive care provides, particularly to people who don't have easy or routine access to doctors and hospital facilities."

She glanced at the photo. "Who gives a shit about being a rockstar when you can give simple nutritional advice to a mother, and keep her kid from becoming a Type II diabetic before he turns eight?"

Brick came to sit on the edge of her bed, on the other side of the suitcase. He picked up a pair of her socks, which she liked to fold over into a ball to keep them together. He passed it from one hand to the other. "No disagreement there. I do school talks to teach kids about fire safety. Plus how to get themselves and their families clear of the house if it catches on fire. They really like that part."

"Of course they do. It's like an action movie or video game challenge. What age?"

"We try to hit them in elementary school and do a revisit at the higher grades. A few months ago, there was an apartment fire. The kid, a fifth grader, couldn't get out of the master bedroom, but he remembered to stay low, and he got into the bathtub with his little sister. He'd covered both their faces and bodies with wet towels. His mom plays handbells for the local church, so he'd snagged a couple of those and was ringing the bejesus out of them. Led the search and rescue guys right to them."

"Those tips came from your talks."

"Well, me and the others who do it. That info saved his life and his sister's, even though that kid's guts, keeping calm and remembering it, made him the real hero."

"But it feels good, to know you helped."

"Sure does. Especially when we deal with the other crap. Like a mom and two kids burned up before there's a damn thing we can do."

Or a toddler dead because of what she hadn't caught. Couldn't anticipate.

She stared down at the suitcase. He put the folded socks back on top of her other clothes, then reached over them to clasp her hand and draw her around the edge of the mattress. As he brought her between his knees, her hands fell onto his shoulders to curl in the fabric of his shirt.

He touched his mouth to her breastbone, below the cross and charm. As he did, he ran his hands down her back, resting them on her hips and smoothing his palms over her backside in the skirt.

"Time to deal with what you're feeling, doc. I want you to unbuckle my belt, pull it free. Offer it to me."

Her heart did a somersault. In a slow blink, his eyes had gone from casual warmth to stern Dom, a look that licked heat between her thighs. The air between their two bodies seemed warmer, more compressed. The ache in her throat and stomach expanded, yet her heart reached for what he was offering, knowing it would help. She knew it would help.

"What are you going to do with it?"

"You don't get to know that yet. But the end result is I'm going to have you here, plow you deep enough to leave a valley in the mattress I'm sitting on. When you come back, you'll remember I was in this bed with you."

If she came back. But she didn't say that. Her voice wasn't working right now, so she didn't have to express that dampening thought. She thought he saw it anyway, because his jaw tightened. "Want to safe-word?" he asked.

She shook her head. She reached for his waist, grazing the hard muscle there. Hooking her fingers in the buckle, she found the tongue of the belt and worked it free. When she tugged it loose, it came smoothly, because of how straight and tall he sat.

"Offer it to me," he reminded her.

His steady expression told her to think about that, what it meant. She took a step back, dropped to her knees, and lifted it.

"Good." He threaded it through his fingers and doubled it over. "Where's your vibrator, Les?"

"What?" When his gaze became more piercing, she fumbled out the answer. "In the nightstand."

"Put it in the suitcase."

"Right now?"

"Yes. I want it within reach, and I don't want you forgetting it. Do that, and then come stand in front of me."

She rose and moved to the nightstand drawer. She had a Hitachi wand, what Beulah called the workhorse champion of all vibrators. "I don't need a vibrator shaped like a boy part," she'd told Les when they were in the adult store. "If I want a boy part, I'll go find one attached to the real thing. This is what gets the job done when I don't have time for more."

For Les, that had been the rule rather than the exception. Until Brick.

She put the toy on top of her clothes, making a mental note *not* to let her mother help her unpack. Under Brick's gaze, which revealed nothing, missed nothing, she returned to stand between his legs. "Take off your skirt and panties," he said.

She unzipped the skirt and pushed down the panties, letting them drop to her feet before she stepped out of them. She picked them up and put them in the suitcase, too.

"Now the shirt and bra."

Her skin heated under his intense regard as she revealed her breasts, the tightening nipples. His gaze slid over her, from neck to feet. "Are you warm enough?"

A quick nod. He'd laid the belt next to him and had his hands on his spread knees, aligned outside her hips. He gave her buttock a firm slap that made her suck in a breath.

"Yes, Sir."

"Good. Turn around, facing away from me, and kneel. Then get on your elbows."

She did, things becoming more wobbly in her mind. How he'd described what he planned to do was a branding, a perpetual reminder he'd been with her in her bed. Which would make her reluctant to take any other man into it.

She suspected that was his intent.

He nudged the inside of her knees with his toe, an unspoken command to spread them out wider. "Raise your ass. Show me your pussy."

Her face heated, though only the floor saw it. He cupped her buttocks, one thumb probing her labia, dipping in to prove to them both how wet she was. Her nipples brushed the carpet, making them tingle.

"I've got you, Les. Don't worry."

He laid the belt across her lower back, then threaded the two ends under her, bringing them out between her spread legs. The straps tightened on either side of her sex and bit into her thighs as he put pressure on that makeshift harness, lifting her lower body and bringing her knees to his thighs. She had to reposition her elbows against his shoes, her nails digging into the carpet. She whimpered as the moist heat of his breath touched her cunt. He took a teasing lick. "Oh God..."

"Best meal in the world. If you come without my permission, I'll take this belt to you. Does that scare you or turn you on?" His lips curved against her inner thigh. "Since your wet pussy just contracted right in front of my eyes, I have my answer. You enjoy some pain, Les."

He put his mouth fully on her. She squealed, the sensation too much, the way he flicked her clitoris and gave it a nip, pushing his tongue against that bundle of nerves. He used his dual-handed hold on the belt ends to move her against his face, draw her in tighter as he fucked her with his tongue. He sucked on her clit, then bit her, holding a clamp on her engorged flesh that had her strangling on a full shriek.

She'd been so emotional at the hospital and in his truck, but she'd contained the feelings. She'd been working on returning them to an even flow, nothing backed up and creating dangerous pressure on her mind or heart.

Belying her efforts, all those emotions surged up. An undeniable force, impossible for her to contain. A sob caught in her chest, her body jerking as he dined on her sex, refused to let her run from that impending flood.

"Brick...Sir... I can't bear it...can't bear it..."

"Safeword or suck it up," he muttered against her flesh. "You're sweet as honey."

"I can't..."

"You can. Let it have you, Les. It's just you and me here."

"I mean...please...it hurts."

"It won't run clear without the pain." He paused as she shook harder, as an incoherent plea came from her throat. "Ask for it. Or safeword."

She pressed her head to her forearms, her hands clutching his shoes. "I need the other kind of pain. This hurts too much. Please. I need it. I need you. Whatever you want. That's what I need."

The belt released and slid away like a brooding snake. He adjusted her so she rested on her elbows and knees again as he rose, bracketing her with his long legs. Her stomach lurched as he slid an arm under her, lifted and turned her so she was face down on the bed, the crook of her hips at the edge of the mattress, feet on the floor to brace herself.

He bit her buttock, likely leaving teeth marks. She could see the belt dangling from his hand. He hadn't put it down, signaling his intent.

"List..." she managed. "What part of the list is this?"

He laid his hand on the upper rise of her buttock, thumb pressing against it, close enough to the crease she felt the nerves in her rectum respond to the pressure. "I still owe you a punishment for driving from here to Richmond in the bad weather. Ten strikes."

"Twenty. At least twenty."

She gasped. In a blink, he'd put his weight full against her back, pinning her on the mattress, his hot breath at her throat. "You never tell me what to do, doc. Now you've earned a worse punishment."

He straightened to draw her arms behind her. He knotted the belt around her wrists deftly enough she couldn't quickly figure out how to get out of it. Especially when any mental skills she could apply to it had disappeared.

She didn't have the same fear of it she'd had in the chair. What she feared right now was far greater than that.

He picked up the vibrator. She hadn't expected him to use it here, but he pushed it under her clit and turned it on. Not the midlevel range, but the highest one, the one that she'd learned would give her an intense, almost painful orgasm in a matter of seconds. She'd always pulled it away before that happened, put it on the slower setting.

He wasn't giving her that option. The way he was holding her, she was like the woman at the party. No ability to avoid the sensations, building so fast, pulsing and grinding against her cunt.

Forced orgasm. This was why forced orgasm was a form of torture. "No," she gasped. "Please, no."

"Let it happen, Les. Or safeword."

"No..." It was too much, tearing into her soul like teeth. It frightened her. "No..."

"Safeword, Les, goddamn it."

She shook her head, her heart pumping painful, poisonous emotions.

"Need to hurt, to suffer..." She never would have put a climax in that category, but he was proving its capabilities.

"Fuck it, I'm doing it for you." The vibrator was pulled away. The jolt to her body had her struggling against him, but she was no match for his determination.

Brick removed the belt, lifted and turned her over. Before she could do anything, he'd knotted it around her wrists again and pushed her arms up above her head. Putting a knee on the bed between her legs, he leveled a hard expression upon her agitated face.

"It's not your job to decide you need to suffer, Les. Is it?"

She brought her hands down in a swift movement, hitting his chest with her bound and clenched fists. He shoved them back over her head, holding them there as he leaned over her. Tears had leaked from her eyes, but she didn't want to be cuddled or comforted. She wanted the poisonous feeling in her gut gone.

He reached between them and freed himself from his jeans. His cock pushed between her labia, teasing the wetness. When she would have defiantly thrust her hips up, he seized her face, fingers against her throat.

"Un-hunh. You lift your hips carefully, slide your cunt over the head of my cock. Tease it, let me know how much you want it without trying to take it."

"I hate you."

"If that's what you need right now, hate me all you want, baby. But you'll also take every inch of me." His voice gentled. "Rub yourself against me, Les. Don't try to put me inside of you. You have to earn that. Let the rest of it go."

"I can't," she whimpered.

"Do what I tell you."

She lifted her hips again, this time under his guidance. She positioned herself so the tip of his erection slid between her labia, up and down, a swirl that put pressure beneath her clit and made her keep her lip tight between her teeth.

"Good. Keep doing it."

She did, her breath turning to a rasp. He'd braced himself on one arm, and him watching her bathe his cock with her juices made her want him even more,

"You're steadier now. Good." The hot flash in his eyes had her biting back an unwise protest as he stood up at the end of the bed. He was still between her knees, his erection mouthwateringly close. He picked up the vibrator again.

"Give me your hands, doc." He slid the handle into the clasp of her bound hands, positioning the toy against her sex. This time when he turned it on, he chose a lower setting, but with how aroused she was, her body immediately stiffened, a groan wresting itself from her lips.

He put his fingers on either side of the wand's bulbous head, stroking and squeezing her labia and clit around the vibration. It varied and intensified it. When her clit was spasming, he shifted the wand's head so it was deeper against her wet opening, those currents of energy teasing and tickling everything directly and indirectly in its reach, all while he continued to stroke her with his own fingers.

She was writhing, lifting to him, him staring down at her, holding her agitated gaze with his own glittering one. He stroked her stomach, her breast, fingers teasing her nipple, plucking it to give a little pain. Back down, over one thigh, then the other. He lifted one of her feet, placing it over his erection, a solid weight under the sole. She licked her lips when he rolled his hips against the pressure.

"You've fantasized about me while using it, haven't you?"

No room for self-consciousness or embarrassment. "Yes, Sir. A lot."

"Hmm. Anything else?"

"Pictures. Some pictures I keep on my computer."

His eyes lit with interest. "You'll be showing me those. But it raises an important question. Do you prefer me or the vibrator? I want to be sure you know the difference."

He clasped her hands, using them to move the wand slowly from one side of the labia to the other, sending pulses through the base of her clit. "Oh..." her voice elevated, broke.

"Which do you prefer, Les?" His voice was even harsher.

It seemed a no-brainer, but then he showed just how diabolical he could be. He made her hold the head in the place most likely to incite an orgasm. His grip kept her there, but otherwise he didn't touch her. "If you prefer me, then you won't come when it's just the wand."

There was *zero* way to stop a purely physical reaction to electric vibration. Even so, looking at his erection, the demand in those gray eyes, the curve of that sinful, firm mouth, he was giving her every incentive in the world to make mind triumph over matter, science over fucking wishful thinking, fantasy and desperate hope.

He intended her to fail. Or he wanted to see how hard she'd try to obey him. Every other thought left her except trying to succeed, to show him how much she wanted...

"You," she gasped, and now those tears had another reason for falling. "Please, Brick, don't let me fail. Please..."

He pulled the vibrator away and pushed her arms back over her head. She was too close, she was going to go over, but he gave her pussy a slap sharp enough to have her squealing. Her legs reflexively started to close, though he stood between them.

It didn't matter. He still barked the admonishment. "Hold them open."

He kept doing it, spanking her cunt. The pain didn't matter. She was so aroused, so under his control, that it shoved her through a narrow door lined with knives, into an orgasm so intense, so wrapped up in her emotions and needs, she knew it really would tear her into pieces.

Heedless of neighbors, she screamed, her vocal cords straining. Her thighs strained against his braced legs when he sealed his hand firmly over her spasming, damp sex, letting her feel the full pressure of his palm and fingers, absorbing the aftershocks. Her blood pulsed against his touch.

She was muttering "Oh God, oh God..." and rocking against his hand. He put his other hand behind her neck, pulling her up so her head dropped back and he took her mouth. It wasn't a kiss. It was that reminder of ownership, that she was his to do with as he pleased. He would keep reinforcing it, she was sure. Until she couldn't ever doubt it.

Proving it, he eased her back down and she saw his cock, hard and thick. She was so sensitive from the spanking, she quaked a little, but he put his fingers in her, confirming all that slippery wetness was still there.

He didn't ram into her. He'd spanked her ruthlessly, but he eased his broad tip inside, bracing himself over her.

"Brick." She stared up at him.

"Hold onto me, baby. Just work me in. I know you can do it. Just like before, you work your cunt over my cock, only this time it's to take me to the hilt."

She did, her breath shallow and fast. It was uncomfortable but not painful, though every inch forward against her sensitive tissues made her whimper little pleas.

"That's my good girl." He crooned it to her throughout, an erotic lullaby. "My sweet girl."

Sensation swirled outward as he seated himself fully and put his hand on her face, fingertips in her hair. Still braced on one arm, he began to stroke, a slow thrust and retreat. She had her legs crossed over his hips, holding him, her heels against his tight ass. Her arms above her head kept her upper body displayed and arched for him. He gazed down at her, watching her, his own face implacable.

He was Brick, someone she'd always known, but something more, that he'd become as an adult. Something her grown-up self wanted with a hunger that eclipsed every other thing she'd ever wanted. He was the center, the core of every need.

He kept going, dipping his head to kiss her breast. He drew the nipple in his mouth to suckle and play. He was feasting on her body, taking his time and pleasure. His hips started to plunge deeper, his thighs and ass flexing under the hold of her legs.

She was gasping with every thrust, wishing her hands were free, but he at last gripped her bound wrists and guided her to drop them over his head. Her fingernails scraped his back as he came with a harsh groan, her hips tilting up and her answering him with a cry as his seed jetted into her.

Oh God. It was too much. But he wasn't done. He slowed down, but he didn't stop. He slid her hands from over his neck, kissed her fingers with lingering touches of lip and tongue, before he pushed her bound wrists over her head yet again. As he gazed with avid male appreciation at her breasts, he eased out of her body.

She was shuddering with need. She hadn't expected to start up the slope toward another orgasm, but as if he'd looped that belt around her throat and tugged on it like a leash, up she'd gone, sensations building so fast, pulsing so she was moving against his thighs and cock, grinding herself shamelessly.

"You're hurting for more, baby, aren't you?" A dangerous light glinted in his eye. "You've proven you prefer me to your toy. But it doesn't mean I can't reward and punish you at the same time, for not giving me the answer as fast I wanted to hear it. Or telling me what kind of punishment you think you deserve."

He reached for his jeans and removed something that looked like a ring from the pocket. He put it over his forefinger, pushing it to the first knuckle. It had a flat base he positioned on the pad of his finger. "Let's see what I can do with this pretty pussy that belongs all to me."

She figured it was a finger vibrator, but finding it had a motor as powerful as the Hitachi startled her. Or maybe he'd just made her so sensitive it felt that way. The result was the same. He caressed her still vibrating labia with it, and then slid his finger inside her, deep and up, finding her G-spot while he stroked her clit with his other fingers.

She would start up toward that pinnacle, and just as she reached it, he would change the position or rhythm, somehow getting her even crazier and hotter, until she was begging him, to stop or keep going, she didn't know which.

She wanted to scream, cry or beg him to hold her, all at once. All the stress, the worries about today, all of it was one big tangled, hot, mess in her belly, her chest, her body. "Brick, please..."

"Please what, baby?"

"I don't know. I just...can't take anymore."

"You'll take this, and then I'll let you rest. That'll be your reward."

"In your arms."

"In my arms."

Her gaze clung to his face, made sure he was telling the truth. She couldn't believe how crazy needy he was making her. Not childlike, but open and more female and yes, possibly more fragile, than she'd ever been in her life.

When he finally let her fly, she did it with harsh, wrenching cries that seemed to go on forever. It all came forth, all the poisoned agony of the day, rushing forth in one volcanic explosion of need, her body bucking, gushing, voice raised in a wailing song.

When she at last spun down, it was from a feathery, drifting world, into the solid world he controlled. He slowly removed his fingers as she twitched and whimpered. He set aside the ring, the Hitachi wand, and took the belt off her wrists. Then he put his arms around her, adjusting them so they were lying in the bed together.

She was feeling some embarrassment about how she'd reacted, how she'd fought him, cried, been unable to control anything. But he wouldn't let her worry about that. "You were everything you needed to be, Les. It's all right. I can handle whatever you are."

He put his mouth to her forehead and spoke against her skin. "Rest awhile. Then you can finish your packing and I'll take you home."

CHAPTER TWENTY-ONE

*A*fter they left the condo, Brick proposed they grab some lunch before hitting the road. He went for comfort food, pulling into a Sonic. After he ordered a double cheeseburger for him, a small burger for her, and a large fries to share, he had another suggestion. "How about I call Tish about Mrs. DaCosta's request? That way if you want to ask her something I haven't thought about, you can jump in."

She was a little worn out after what had happened in the bedroom, so she hadn't said much. But now, after thinking it through, Les nodded, wrapping up her partially eaten burger and drawing her feet up on the edge of the seat. As Brick activated the handsfree, she linked her fingers over her knees and settled on her hip to face him.

She noticed he had Tish programmed into his phone. Fabulous.

Stop it, Les told herself.

"You okay with this?" he asked. He noticed far too much about her sometimes. She made a face at him.

"Of course I'm okay with it. If you were going to have a friends-with-benefits relationship, I'd definitely want it to be with a woman who could be on the cover of Forbes *and* the Sports Illustrated swim-suit issue."

"They want me for the same month, so I'm having a hell of a time choosing," came a female voice through the speakers. "The SI shoot is in Bimini, though, so I'm leaning toward that one."

"Should have warned you," Brick noted. "Tish has a habit of waiting a beat before she talks, because she's usually up to her ass in work when she answers her phone."

Les heard the woman chuckle. The sound belonged to a bedroom in Bimini. She could almost see her tangled in cotton sheets, while a lover, standing before an open-air view of a whispering ocean, would pad back to her side, irresistibly drawn by the throaty invitation.

"Somebody's got to stay on top of justice in our fair city," Tish said. "What's up? You checking on me again? I'm all good now. Plus Richard's checking on me, too."

Under the playful smugness, Les's female ears caught the sound of a woman a little off-balance, in the right ways. That, plus the fond warmth in Brick's eyes, reassured her. It was unfettered pleasure for a good friend's happiness.

"I like hearing that. I've got my friend Les with me on speaker, and I was wondering if you had two minutes for us to run a legal hypothetical by you."

"Who's Les?"

"The drowned rat stalking you in the parking lot," Les said.

"My friend from North Carolina," Brick said, shooting her a look. "The medical student."

"Oh." Tish's tone became noticeably more intrigued. "I've been wanting to meet you. How long are you here?"

"We're heading home to her family's place in North Carolina for Easter. But I hope she'll be visiting again soon. I took her to Mick's party the other night. We had a good time. Didn't see you there."

"Richard took me out for dinner. Decided to negotiate our first session over some sushi. Did I miss anything?"

"Lisa got her first fire flogging."

"Damn. Hopefully Dirk had someone record it on their phone for him. Was this the first time you've been to something like that, Les? Did you enjoy it?"

The direct question took her off guard, but she didn't sense anything catty, just a friendly openness. "Yes. I liked being there with Brick. I think I'd like to do more things like that. With him."

The repetition might seem like she was throwing out territorial markers, but the feelings were honest. Fortunately, Tish seemed to take it that way, and her response surprised Les further.

"If you're up for it next time you visit, we could get together, with Doms or without. If I can help with any questions on the submissive side of things, I'll do it. A lot of this is new to me, too. We can swap what-the-fuck stories. Sound good?"

Les blinked. "You're very hard not to like."

"The defense attorneys I face might not agree. And full disclosure, I have an ulterior motive. I want to learn all the embarrassing teenage stories about Brick."

Brick scoffed. "Ain't happening, counselor. For one thing, there are none. My teen coolness factor was legendary."

"Les is snickering."

Les feigned innocence as Brick shot an exaggerated glare toward her. "You're going to get her into trouble," he said.

Tish laughed. "Trouble with you is the right girl's best dream. Anyhow, lay your 'what if' on me. I've got a conference call in fifteen."

The light moment vanished. Les wasn't sure how to explain the situation without revealing too much or too little, but then she remembered Brick had said she could jump in if *he* missed anything. He proceeded to detail the situation thoroughly and concisely, an investigator used to writing reports.

Tish asked only a couple questions to clarify some points. Les stared at the dash as she listened to them, her hands tight on her shins.

"Give me a moment to think here. And deal with what my admin just brought me. Yeah, Jordan, just courier that over to them. Two-day is fine, but make sure accounting gives you the check to put into the package. Thanks."

Brick's knuckle brushed Les's clenched hand. "Ease up," he murmured. "Relax. It's okay. We're just talking. No decision needed."

He hooked one of her fingers, so she had to let go of her leg and hold his hand instead. She adjusted so their linked hands rested on his denim-covered thigh.

"Okay." Tish was back. "I'm going to state the obvious. Your safest bet is no contact."

"I know," Les responded. "But if it's just us, just talking, no recording, that kind of thing..."

"It would still be admissible, because you said it directly to her. A good attorney would point out it was *he said, she said*, or in this case, *she said, she said*, but under the threat of perjury, neither of you is supposed to lie."

"So it comes down to whether I trust her or not. Play it safe or take the risk."

"Yes and no. You also have to factor in your responsibility to the hospital, and the other parties named in the suit."

Shit. Which was pretty much a deal breaker. Still... "Is there anything that outweighs those considerations?"

"I think that's something only you can answer, Les. I can only tell you what the smart thing is to do legally." A pause. "If you decide to do this, and again, it's not something I'd recommend, don't discuss any medical details. Don't bait that liability hook. If she's there to vent, let her do all the talking. If she wants you to talk, keep it to emotional offerings of support."

Les stared at their linked hands. When Brick squeezed her fingers, a question, she nodded. She knew what she needed to know.

"Thanks, Tish," Brick said. "I'll touch base with you when I get back after Easter."

"Okay. And Les? I'm so sorry you're having to go through this. When someone I know is guilty walks, I always think about tactics or information I should have pursued or anticipated. Those cases keep me up at night, because we won't get another shot at that piece of garbage until he or she hurts someone else. I know it's not the same, but just saying. Living with that kind of thing can be a bitch. We can what-the-fuck about those stories, too. Over tequila."

"Thanks. It doesn't help but it helps, if that makes sense."

"It does. Hang in there."

When Brick clicked off, Les pulled the number out of the pocket of her purse, where she'd carefully tucked it. "So...the smartest thing would be to tear this up."

"Yeah." He offered her the container of fries. "Take a couple more before I finish them."

She dutifully took two and dipped them in the ketchup he'd put between them. "Want a Reese's peanut butter cup freeze for the road?" he asked.

"Will you split it with me?"

"You bet." But he didn't place the order. Instead, as she wiped her

321

hands on her napkin, he touched her face. "What's your heart, your conscience, telling you?"

"This mother lost the worst thing she could lose, and she wants to talk to me. I'm worried about getting Dr. Jack or Dr. Redmond, or the hospital, in trouble. But I feel like I owe her this conversation. We all owe her this conversation."

"Okay." He went back to the fries, but he still didn't order the ice cream. She didn't notice. She was thinking. After a long moment, she picked up her phone, typed in the number and sent a text.

Her hands were shaking as she showed it to him. *Mrs. DaCosta, I understand you want to see me. I'm headed out of town this afternoon for Easter, but please call or text me if you still wish to meet.*

"I guess we should start heading for home," she said.

"Okay. Let me toss the trash."

"I'll do it. It'll be hard for you to slide out your door, close as you are to the menu board."

She dumped the trash in the nearest can and headed back to the truck. He was watching her in the mirror, keeping his eye on her in the busy parking lot. He was like that.

She'd left the door open. As she reached for the strap to lift herself back in, her phone chimed. She stopped, palm braced on the seat, and retrieved the phone from her back pocket. It was probably Rory, or her mom. Beulah. It didn't have to be...

Could you meet now, at the park near my home? I'm texting you the address. Tell me your ETA.

She showed it to Brick. Her heart was pumping too hard. He didn't say anything, just helped her back into her seat.

Les could reasonably put her off until after Easter. Which would give her time to re-think it, back out if she decided to go with Tish's advice. She wasn't mentally prepared. She'd thought it would be hours, days, before she heard from Mrs. DaCosta. If at all.

Brick had waited her thought process out, but now he spoke. "What do you want to do, Les?"

"Go home. Run away." She gave him the ghost of a smile. "I guess we're going to the park. You saw the address. Do you know where it is?"

"Yeah. Tell her it will take us about thirty minutes to get there."

As Les put on her seatbelt and sent the response, Brick backed the vehicle out and returned to the busy road. When he eventually spoke again, his question surprised her. "Feel like you packed everything you need for Easter?"

She marshaled her thoughts. Her voice sounded wooden to her. "I want to stop at that garden statue place on Highway 220 and pick up something for Mom and Daralyn."

"Okay. Sounds good."

"I need to do this alone," she said abruptly. "So when we get there, you can drop me off at the park. I'll text you when we're done."

He made a noncommittal sound. She struggled out of the muck of her thoughts to shoot him a purposeful stare. "I mean it, Brick."

He made a turn at a light. "I'll wait at a distance, like I did for the M&M. But I'm not leaving you."

"I'm not a child. I don't need you to hold my hand."

"Everyone needs someone to hold their hand. The important thing is the timing. Do me the honor, doc?"

He put his hand on the console, palm up, his gray eyes touching hers. "*She smiles gently, seriously, and takes my hand. Leads me out into a night as luminous as noon, more deeply real, simply because of her hand, than any dream Shakespeare or I or anyone ever dreamed.*"

"Modified a bit for my own purposes," he told her. "Anthony Hecht, 'Peripeteia.' I know only two boxers can be in the ring, doc. But at the end of the round, at the end of every round, I'm going to be the one in your corner. Got it?"

She didn't know what her response should be, so she settled for accepting the comfort and strength of his hand. As his fingers closed over hers, she rolled the words of the poem through her mind, a distraction from what lay ahead.

Feeling like this twice in the same day was almost unbearable. Her palms were sweaty, her mind caught in memories of that horrible night. Mrs. DaCosta flying at her, hitting her. Screaming.

Sully was right; there was nothing she could say that would mean anything, which meant there was no rehearsal or practice for this. She'd do as Tish said, be the receptacle for whatever Mrs. DaCosta needed to tell her. She had to believe her gut was right, that this wasn't a legal trap. This was a mother that needed something from her. She needed to do her best to offer it.

The park was a neighborhood amenity, a small playground

surrounded by green space and picnic tables. A square building supplied restrooms and water fountains in adult and child sizes.

Mrs. DaCosta was at the picnic table closest to the pine tree forest skirting the area. Through the branches, Les saw the neighborhood houses. Several mothers were here, their children playing on the equipment. The only vehicle other than Brick's truck was probably Mrs. DaCosta's, since it was in the spot nearest her picnic table. The mothers had strollers, suggesting they'd walked from their homes.

As they parked next to Mrs. DaCosta's blue SUV, Les noted an adhesive stick figure family in the back window. Two parents, a daughter, and a cat. One baby boy. That would have been Llanzo.

Les's mother had displayed steel magnolia stoicism after her husband's death, except for a few key moments. Like when Les had found Elaine standing in the bathroom doorway, staring at her father's razor by the sink. "The big things are a punch in the stomach, taking your air," her mother murmured. "But the little ones are knife blades. You should bleed to death from all the cuts, but they space themselves out, take you by surprise."

A rare poetic insight from a perpetually rational woman. But she was also the woman who'd thought they should name their daughter Celestial Joy, if the angels decided to take her back.

"Les." Brick touched her white-knuckled hand. "You with me?"

She tore her gaze from the car window. "Doctors are prepped in a million ways for losing a patient. But nothing prepares the family for it."

"That's why you're here. It's when the world is at its cruelest that we value kindness the most. Go out there as yourself. No mask, no detachment."

It was the direction of a Dom, but also the other things he'd said. Her partner, her life mate. His words matched where her own mind was on it. She was entering the ring with no gloves, no defenses. She'd give her opponent as many punches as she needed or wanted.

"That said, if I see you've had enough, I'm throwing in the towel and calling it done."

She also knew he'd wait as long as he could, proving his confidence in her, while being ready to catch her before a knockout punch. "Sports analogies are annoyingly useful," she said.

A faint smile touched his face. "Aren't they? Wait there."

This time she suspected he opened her door to show Mrs. DaCosta she wasn't alone, though he nodded courteously in her direction. She could feel the mother's attention on her as she slid out. Brick gripped Les's arm. "Take as long as you need."

She walked toward the picnic table. She vaguely registered birdsong, the children on the playground chattering the way they did. Make-believe games with themselves or the other children, admonitions to their mothers to "watch me."

Had Mrs. DaCosta brought Llanzo here? Of course she had. She would have used the tomato red toddler swings, because he wasn't yet sturdy enough for the other kind. He'd have ducked in and out of the plastic house. Tic-tac-toe blocks in bright, primary colors were mounted on metal poles in the open window spaces, encouraging the push of small hands.

Her tennis shoes scraped over the sidewalk that formed a perimeter around the playground. But Les was back in the hospital again, rubber-soled shoes squeaking on the tile as she hurried toward the cardiac unit. She'd heard Llanzo had been brought back in, was in severe distress. She'd arrived at a near run, her heart pounding and breath short, to find out he'd died two minutes and eleven seconds before her arrival.

When she joined the medical team talking to the family, Mrs. DaCosta's eyes had fixed on her like they did now. As if Les would forever be at the crosshairs of a rifle of emotion she wanted to fire at her heart, obliterating her.

Today, though, Raeni was quiet. Not screaming with rage, tears spilling down her cheeks. Her husband, weeping himself, had helped the orderly pull her back. That night, he'd contained her struggles until she collapsed in his arms, wailing.

Her eyes were dull and quiet, her mouth thin and straight. Her fingers were laced, forearms resting on the picnic table. It had only been a few days since Les had seen her, but she looked like she'd lost ten pounds. It wasn't all physical weight. The part of the soul that made someone seem alive, active, a member of the human race, wasn't there right now.

"They say these things should be acted upon in a timely fashion, while everything is still fresh in our minds," Mrs. DaCosta said, in lieu of a greeting. "I don't want to get out of bed or eat, but I have a daughter, a husband, and now a lawyer, all wanting something from me. They say it's good to have someone to care for, to have a goal, even if it's just to go through the motions."

Les moved to sit on the bench on the other side, careful not to brush Mrs. DaCosta's shoes, a pair of Crocs. She wore jeans and a man's T-shirt, a long open sweater over them. Her hair wasn't combed, just pulled into a messy tail. She wasn't wearing makeup or jewelry.

"My mom said that, too, when my dad died," Les ventured as the silence drew out, as Raeni stared at her, almost vacantly. "She said it the same way, as if it was something you did, not because you believed it, but..."

"Because you don't know what else to do. It's all too soon." Raeni DaCosta's lips twisted. "I expect you want to know if I'm recording this conversation. If I say yes, will you leave?"

Before Les could answer, she reached into the pocket of the sweater, shivering as if moving gave her a chill. She put the credit card-sized recorder between them. It wasn't turned on.

"I came because you asked me to come," Les told her. "And because I didn't get to say I'm sorry that night."

"You think saying it changes anything?" Mrs. DaCosta's voice went up a notch.

"I don't know. I just know not saying it to you is wrong. And..." Les stopped herself. This wasn't about her or her feelings. She waited for the mother to take the lead, but when the silence drew out again, she inserted a gentle prompt. "What do you need, Mrs. DaCosta? Why did you ask me to come?"

"Raeni. Call me Raeni. Not because I want us to be informal, but because it hurts to hear the other. I don't want to be called anything that reminds me I'm supposed to act like an adult."

Les suddenly didn't care about hospitals, legal teams, and all the reasons she shouldn't be here. It didn't even matter that she was responsible for this woman's pain. That couldn't change anything. Assigning blame, everyone thinking about what they should have done differently to help Llanzo and his family, how that impacted any of their lives going forward... All of that was for her to look at another day, in other ways.

Not here and now. She just wanted to help Mrs. DaCosta feel less anguish.

When Raeni had attacked her, she'd dropped a toy on the tile floor. It was the small stuffed rabbit Llanzo had brought into the ER when Les first saw him. He'd likely been clutching it for comfort on the fatal return trip, and the medical team had to hand it to his mother so they could work over him.

After Mrs. DaCosta had been shepherded away by her husband, Les had stood there numbly. She didn't know for how long, but eventually she'd noticed the rabbit. As she'd bent to pick it up, Agatha was talking to her. But when she reached for Les, Les backed away, shaking her head. Then she'd bolted.

On the way to the park, Les had pulled the toy out of her suitcase. During one of the days she'd been at Brick's, she'd found it in her glove compartment and put it with the other items she'd brought back here. She'd intended to leave it in her room at the condo, but after seeing Agatha and receiving Raeni's note, she'd tucked it into the suitcase.

Now she removed it from the pocket of her light jacket. She placed it beside Mrs. DaCosta's laced hands. The mother stared at it. Her fingers opened stiffly, collecting the rabbit so it was sandwiched between her palms.

"The day I examined him, he didn't let it go, not once."

"Yes. It was...originally, it was a pet toy. My sister had come to have dinner with us, and brought her dog. Llanzo wanted that bunny. A few days later, my sister brought him a new one. My husband took the squeaker out, to remove the choking hazard, and to keep us from losing our minds."

A faint smile, tortured though it was, touched her lips. The rabbit was a fleecy white. Blue and pink embroidery provided the eyes and nose.

"He offered to let me hold it." Though it hurt to say it, Les added, "He wanted me to listen to the rabbit's heart after I listened to his."

"And you did." The mother turned it over and over, stroking the fur. Raeni seemed to want her to continue, to speak of a shared memory of her child, so Les did.

"He felt so crappy, but he smiled when I smiled at him. When they're babies, they say that's a reflex, that they're just mimicking us, learning. But you can see when it becomes real."

"Yes."

Raeni's eyes lifted to Les's, locking. It was that gun sight look again, which made her stomach pitch. "I saw you that night. In the garden. Sitting against the wall."

"Oh." Les wasn't sure what to say to that. She'd put her hands back in her lap, fingers tightly knotted. But after a long pause, Raeni continued.

"My husband was taking me...somewhere. I can't remember, just that we were going across the courtyard to get there. Something was blooming, maybe roses. The colors were so vivid, even in the rain. It's odd, isn't it, how everything is the same but looks so different...right after. I saw you. Wet to the skin, crouched against the wall, crying as if you were about to split in two. It made me even more furious with you. How dare you think you have a right to cry? To grieve my child, after you killed him? I would have attacked you again, but Henrique had a firm grip on me."

Les flinched at the harsh tone, but stayed quiet. Raeni's voice became flat again. "They gave me a sedative, a prescription for more. He filled it, but he holds onto them. He won't put them on the bathroom counter or even in a drawer. He keeps them with him."

Her eyes, broken brown glass, met Les's. "He's afraid I'll take too many, succumb to the desire to be lost to darkness, to dreams, where my Llanzo might still play, or be in my arms. I'm glad caring for me keeps his mind off his own grief. It's the only purpose I can see it having. But purpose is defined as accomplishing something, moving toward a desired outcome. And what does that mean to us anymore?"

A chill rippled over Les's skin. She thought of Rufus and Bobbi. Then she thought of her mother. For the first time in her life, she understood why her mother sought prayer for difficult circumstances. Not just for ritual comfort, but as a fervent call for action, focused intent. Some things you couldn't reach in another person. Only something bigger than all of them could go that deep and bring them back.

Raeni brought the toy to her forehead, beat a light tattoo against it. Then she stopped, held it there, her face creasing like crumpled paper. "It smells like him. Everything does. I'm not sure I can ever forgive any of you for sending my child home when his heart was so vulnerable. But I know it wasn't carelessness that caused it."

Her gaze flicked to Les. "I mean a lack of caring. That's the true meaning, right? I saw you sobbing and knew, no matter my anger, your pain was real. Not guilt. Not fear of losing your chance to be a doctor. You grieved for my child. Your anguish, your repentance, was real. When I look in your eyes, I loathe it, but I see some of the same deadness that's in mine, that comes from the shattering of purpose and direction, meaning. An internal car crash you can't figure out how to walk away from, no 911 to call."

Her lips twisted again, an ugly near snarl. "This took something vital from you. I want to be glad for that, that you're being punished for it, but..."

She shook her head, her face smoothing to blankness again. "They say tears don't change or fix anything. Maybe so. I can't feel or think anything on it. But many years ago, my mother told me tears are like water cleansing a wound, allowing it to start to heal, though some wounds take far more tears than others."

Abruptly, Mrs. DaCosta pocketed the unused recorder and rose. She held the rabbit. "What I said that night, about you not being a doctor... I can't forgive, but I can remember. I remember how careful you were, checking your notes. And how you connected to Llanzo, paid attention, took time. How you suggested I take him for a follow up with his doctor on Monday, and said you'd call them yourself, make sure they worked him in."

Her face crumpled again. "They did, you know. Called and left a message, telling me they had an opening early that day. Then called and left another, after they got the update from the hospital. Saying how sorry they were."

She took a breath. "Anyhow, I wanted you to know."

She turned away. Les rose, hitting her knee on the cross piece under the table. She ignored the jolt of pain. "Mrs. DaCosta—Raeni—may I say something to you?"

"You've said you're sorry. I don't want to hear it again. I don't want to hear anything from any of you again." Her gaze landed on the cross around Les's neck. "Tell God you're sorry. Tell Llanzo you're sorry. What penance, what forgiveness you seek, seek your answers from God. I have no answers to give."

The words Les wanted to say froze in her throat. But as Mrs. DaCosta began to walk away, she managed to get them out. "I won't forget him. Not now, not ever."

Raeni didn't turn around. But she did pause long enough to nod her head. Once. Les watched her get in her vehicle, back out and drive away. She entered the neighborhood entrance behind the park. Les hoped her husband and daughter were at the house waiting for her.

Les turned to watch the kids on the playground. One mother was commenting on the leaf her son had brought to show her. The mother closest to them smiled, even as she had that distracted air of mothers everywhere, updating her mental to-do list and handling as much of it on her phone as she could, while keeping an eye on her own child.

Raeni was right. The world was the same but so different. Too bright, too sharp. Too heartbreaking. Mrs. DaCosta's numbness now was a way to mute and buffer it, to make the loss survivable.

Brick was standing at the passenger door when she moved in that direction. Beyond a steadying hand as she pulled herself into the passenger seat, he didn't touch her. She took it as an act of caring, his awareness that the lightest touch would shatter her.

"Please take me home," she whispered.

She said almost nothing for the next two hours. She didn't ask him to stop at the garden place for whimsical lawn art. She was lost in her head, unaware when he sent a couple key texts.

When they reached Fairhope, it was just after dark. Except for the local diner, which closed at eight, the town's few shopkeepers rolled up the sidewalks by six. They passed through Main Street's two stop-lights, then they were back among farmland and rural landscapes, rolling shadows under a crescent moon.

She was only peripherally conscious of that until she felt Brick's hand on hers. He stood by her open door, and they were parked in front of a white farmhouse with black shutters and a wraparound porch. The details of the outbuildings were outside the range of the porch lights, though she could see the gleam of the chicken coop wire. This time of night, the occupants would be peacefully roosting.

"You're home, Les," Brick said.

She'd assumed her mother would be inside waiting, the kitchen and living room lights like welcome beacons. She hadn't expected her to be standing on the bottom porch step.

It was like a lightning strike to her numb state, her jumble of bottled emotions illuminated in one glaring flash. Brick helped her get her feet on the ground, but her legs were half asleep from two hours of stillness.

It didn't matter. She stumbled across the driveway. All of her resolve to act like an adult left her. No judgment or vicious self-admonishment could keep her from breaking into that desperate run. Not with the knowledge she saw on her mother's face.

Brick had told her. She could be mad about it later. Right now, she ran to her mother's arms.

They closed around her like the promise of an afterlife, a place to get past every terrible mistake, every loss beyond bearing. They folded down onto the steps together, her mother continuing to hold her as Les was overwhelmed by the force of her tears.

It was like the night at Brick's, but different. The absorbed grief of Raeni DaCosta poured out for Les's own mother, who might have faced the same kind of loss twenty-four years ago. If her father hadn't called on the heavens with the name of Celestial Joy. If the doctors hadn't been as good as they'd been.

They'd succeeded where Les had failed.

Brick sat down behind her, his leg braced next to her hip. He had his hand on her back and also on her mother's shoulder, offering them both his solid strength.

"It's all right, dear girl," her mother was whispering. "It's all right."

"No...no it's not. No, Mom..."

"Yes, it is." Elaine's voice got fierce as she cupped Les's head, held her closer. "Life is hard, dear baby. That's all. Life is hard to live. It's okay. You're home."

With Brick next to her, her mother's arms around her, and sitting on her front porch, Les didn't know if it was okay or not. But here, she had the best chance of figuring it out, picking herself up, and *making* it be okay.

CHAPTER TWENTY-TWO

*W*hen her crying finally subsided, her mother spoke quietly to Brick. "Did she eat?"

"She had some lunch, but her stomach's been upset a lot. Maybe hold off until tomorrow."

Elaine's fingers tightened on her, but her voice stayed brisk. "Let's get you ready for bed, then. We'll feed you in the morning. You look like a good wind could blow you away."

Les tried to stand up. Whether from lack of food, exhaustion, or the surfeit of emotion, she swayed. Her hand landed on Brick's chest as her mother held her other arm. "I've got her," Brick told Elaine. He picked her up in one matter-of-fact move. "Lead the way."

"Her room's upstairs."

"I know. It's not a problem."

Les caught her mother's surprised but thoughtful look, but she took Brick up the stairs. Les knew she should tell him she could walk, but he gave her *that* look. She bit her lip and put her head against his chest. That telegraphed command, a Dom taking charge, made her decide it was okay to let herself be cared for. At least right now.

When they reached her room, Brick set her down, but held onto her until he was sure she was steady.

"You can use Rory's old room downstairs," Elaine told him. "If you'd like to put your things in there, I'll fix you a plate after I get her settled."

Her mother's way of saying she intended to grill him for more details. Coupled with a not oblique hint she'd be the one with Les while she changed into nightclothes. No matter the obvious physical intimacy between her and Brick, her mother was her mother.

"I'll bring her suitcase up." Brick turned to Les and touched her face. She answered the question in his eyes.

"You can tell her. Tell her everything."

She could wake up in the morning knowing everyone was caught up, and only have to deal with where that left her in her own head.

"You got it, doc." His gray eyes held her. "I won't be far. After I talk to your Mom and eat, I'll go see Rory. I promise to leave you some of her zucchini bread. Maybe."

"If she's put those little chocolate chips in it, you better."

At the spirited response, weak though it was, he kissed her. A surprise, with Elaine there. It was a closed-mouth press of lips, but lingering enough to be a clear mark of ownership. He stepped back with obvious reluctance. "Ma'am."

Les felt her mother's silent evaluation of all of it. Not just Brick, but her lost weight, tired look, her paleness. The guilt knife twisted. She'd never wanted to be a burden to her mother again, and here she was, doing it anyway.

Elaine pulled a nightgown out of the closet, rather than waiting for Brick to bring up her case. It was one of those bulky cotton nightgowns that went to the ankles. One Les wouldn't take to college, but here, she welcomed it like a favorite blanket.

Les went into the bathroom to put it on. She brushed her teeth using the basket of toiletries Elaine kept for guests, and so Les didn't have to pack as many for her brief trips home. When she returned, the suitcase was in a corner and Elaine had turned down the bed. She helped Les in.

"I'll be better in the morning," Les told her. "I'm just tired."

"Don't you worry about anything tonight. Just sleep, baby girl. I'm here."

She guided Les's head to her thigh. As she stroked Les's hair, Les curled her arms around her mother's hips. A little sigh left her. "So tired."

"I know. Sleep. It's all right."

It only took a couple minutes before Les was pulled under, but her subconscious sensed her mother's presence, her touch, for a good bit longer. When fitful anxieties eventually roused her, she was alone, but she had the reassurance of Brick and Elaine's voices, drifting up the stairs.

In the morning she'd stand up and be as strong as she'd taught her family to expect her to be. Even if she still had no answer to the most important question. Would she return to medical school?

The next time she surfaced, the house was quiet and dark. She looked at her phone and found a good night text from Brick, a couple hours old.

Kiss me in your dreams, and my heart will feel it.

She wondered what poem or letter it came from, and looked forward to asking him. She held the thought to her and disappeared back into dreams, seeking that kiss.

When sunrise came, so did the welcoming scent of a homemade breakfast. The house creaked and thumped from people moving around in the kitchen, their familiar voices coming up the stairs. Her phone's text alert had woken her.

Gone to firehouse to visit boys and talk shop. Your mom had me take them a casserole. I'll be back for breakfast. You're on my mind. No worries today, doc. Plenty of time for that later. Be good.

He'd made sure she knew where he was. It brought comfort, she couldn't deny it. As she sat up and rubbed her face, she absorbed the normal, good things home offered.

Daralyn's feminine murmur ribboned around Rory's deep voice. Les had seen their very first kiss, under mistletoe. Despite all the potential packed into that gesture, it had been months later before they acted on their obvious attraction.

"It's so much easier when it's a play," Julie had told Les when they'd commiserated over it. "The director can say, 'Okay, this is the scene where you two get it on, and stop frustrating the fuck out of the rest of us.'"

An extra burst of joy touched her as she heard Thomas's voice, masculine and flowing like river water.

While samples of his erotic work didn't hang on his mother's walls, he had done a trio of portraits for her. Les, reading in her favorite tree. Rory, playing football in the backyard. Thomas, painting in a field at sunset.

Elaine kept them on proud display above the living room sofa. A pencil study of their father, where Thomas had scattered poses and expressions across a wide page, was framed and hanging in her bedroom. He'd told her he'd turn any of them into a painting, but Elaine liked the study.

"It's like him," she'd said. "A man rough and unfinished on the outside, but his soul shining through."

Thomas had done one for himself, though. Les had asked him if she could get a print of it when she had her own place. Thomas had told her no. *I'll paint you an original of it, sis.*

Dropped to a knee next to a piece of farm equipment, her father was looking up as if someone had said something to him that gave his lips the slight tug toward a smile. Laughter simmered in his serious eyes. Thomas had that smile and look as well.

He kept the picture at his and Marcus's place here. Such was her brother's talent, when Les looked at it, she felt like she could touch the sweat-dampened temple under Dad's bill cap, curl her fingers into the collar of his shirt, next to the tanned throat. Brush away the wisp of hay on his shoulder.

He didn't have all the answers, but he'd cared for his family. It was all there. When Elaine asked if he'd painted it from a photo, Thomas had tapped his head. "No. From here."

Elaine rested a hand on Thomas's chest, over his heart. "Or from here."

Les didn't hear Marcus, but wherever her brother was, his husband wasn't far.

"Les?" Daralyn peered in. "Your mom sent me to see if you were up."

"Actually," a raised voice came up the stairs, "We were wondering if you were going to get your butt up so the rest of us could eat."

Daralyn suppressed a smile as Les rolled her eyes. "Is Mom down there?" she called back.

"Yeah, she is."

"So I can't call you a dickhead?"

"No," Elaine said. The tread of feet told Les she'd come to the stairs with Rory. "Stop bothering your sister and come back into the kitchen."

Daralyn's eyes twinkled. She had hazel eyes, too, but the brown, gray and green were a different blend from Les's. Her dark, thick hair was clipped back with a wide barrette, the front part loose around her face, accentuating its prettiness. "Brick went to the fire station, but he should be back soon."

"He let me know. He texted me just a few minutes ago."

"So...he brought you home?" The expectant look on her sister-in-law's face pleased and amused Les at once. Not so long ago, Daralyn would have suppressed the entirely natural female desire to have Les spill all the details.

"He did." Les lifted a shoulder. "I don't know what we are yet, but...we're something. And he's..."

"All over you. I mean how you feel, when you talk about him." Daralyn flushed at Les's raised brow and glanced down the stairs. They could hear pans rattling. "I'll go help your mom. But do you need anything?"

"No, I'm good. I'll be there in a couple minutes. Just a superfast clean-up in the bathroom and I'll change into something that's not pajamas."

"It's all family downstairs. But that's not for us, is it? It's for Brick."

Les crossed her eyes at her. With a quiet note of laughter, Daralyn disappeared.

Brick had been right about the energy one drew from family. Savoring that laugh was part of it. Les had helped Daralyn learn to read, something the bastards who didn't deserve to be called her family had kept her from doing.

It made her think of what she'd told Brick about the mission trip, helping others in simple ways that could mean so much. *Who gives a shit about being a rockstar?*

Though if it meant she could have anticipated the cold virus would invite myocarditis into Llanzo's heart, she'd have given anything for a rock star moment.

She reminded herself of Brick's text. Gripping the cross and fire badge in her hand, she also said a prayer for Llanzo and his family. Both things helped her get out of bed.

Smiling over Daralyn's teasing, Les had to admit it was true. She wanted her appearance to reflect her eagerness to see him. What was between them was too new for her to tolerate being without him for too long.

She put on jeans that hugged her curves, plus a short-sleeved shirt that accentuated her neck, the nip of her waist and flare of her hips. And of course her breasts. She added a little makeup and brushed her hair, creating waves she held in place with a tortoiseshell patterned comb on either side.

The shirt was lettuce green with painted flowers over the sleeves and around the V-neckline. They had a tumbling look, like a close-up picture taken of a covered trellis at the height of spring. Thomas had given it to her, swag Marcus had used to promote another artist. Her brother's trained eye was evident, because the colors in the flowers and the shirt's background brought out the golden brown and green in her eyes.

As she came down the creaky wood steps, she heard Rory and Thomas talking about store stuff, something about local egg production. Her hand trailed along the family photographs on the wall, including one of her maternal great-grandfather. He stood with a violin in hand, the picture a news clipping from when he was in his thirties. He'd been a locally renown fiddler, also known for his peach moonshine recipe. Her mother had it written down and tucked in the back of one of her family scrapbooks.

When Les reached the kitchen, she saw the brief pause, the exchange of glances, that told her she'd been an earlier topic of conversation. But the gazes that turned her way were full of love and care, and the awkward moment was only that, a moment. When Rory started to navigate his chair around the table, she came to him, leaning in to wrap an arm around his shoulders and give him a smacking kiss on the ear.

"Eww, sister cooties." But he hugged her back with a strong arm and brushed her face with a surprisingly firm touch from his callused fingers. Rory had their father's brown eyes and hair, like Thomas.

Though she'd always thought Thomas had more of the look of their father, she was startled to see plenty of him in Rory's concerned expression. He'd embraced the same life as their dad, which had added weathering to his face. That, plus the trim beard her father had also sometimes cultivated, made the similarity more evident. "Good to have you home for Easter," Rory said.

"Good to be here."

Thomas stepped forward. He was built like a man who'd been raised on a farm, but he also had an artist's beauty worked into that, with his dark eyes and hair kept mostly short, though it always had some curl on the ends. He reminded her of a young Colin Farrell.

He enveloped her in another big brother hug, lifting her off her feet as she hid a sudden sting of tears against his broad shoulder.

She was not doing that today. But hell, it was so good to be home. Really home. Not partly here, half of her mind already back in Durham, figuring out how to make up the time she'd stolen for a trip to see family. Which was how she'd managed the past couple years' worth of visits.

"Is Marcus on the porch with his surgically implanted phone?" she asked.

"Yep, but he'll be here to get his hug in a minute. Julie's going to call tonight. It's pissing her off she's going to miss the holiday with us. You know how much she loves getting up for Easter sunrise service."

A chuckle passed through the kitchen. While she did love joining them for holidays, getting Julie out of bed early on a rare day off was like digging Carolina clay out of the ground.

"She said she won't schedule performances on Easter weekend ever again," Elaine said. Thomas intercepted her before she could lift the breakfast casserole, bringing the heavier dish to the table himself. Les suspected the one she'd sent with Brick had been equally large. Elaine gave Thomas a fond look.

"Can I help?" Les asked.

"Go ahead and put ice in the glasses," her mother said. "You know what everyone drinks. The tea and juice pitchers are in the refrigerator."

Daralyn removed biscuits from the oven while Elaine put a covered bowl of milk gravy on the table. Thomas returned to holding up the wall by Rory, staying clear unless they needed help again.

The kitchen table could seat up to a dozen people, evidence of how often her mother anticipated neighbors and family friends dropping in. It was the same size as the one Les had grown up with, though then it had been a large picnic style table with two free standing benches her father had made.

The current table had been made by a local woodworker, Mr. Connelly, in exchange for a year's supply of free eggs. Instead of benches, her mother had found rustic wooden chairs from an estate sale. The new arrangement allowed Rory to bring his wheelchair to the table in a way the benches hadn't.

The sound of a familiar truck pulling up to the house had Les's heart skipping a beat. Rory cocked a brow at Thomas. "She blushed. Did you see that?"

"Shut up," she said. But she slipped out the kitchen screen door. She wanted to take a moment together, just the two of them. Even if they could be seen from the kitchen windows.

Today Brick wore the black Fairhope fire station T-shirt with his jeans. His gaze covered her, lingering on places that made her warmer. She quickened her step. His eyes lit with pleasure at her obvious gladness to see him.

He cupped the back of her head, gripping her waist with the other hand as he kissed her. His restraint showed his awareness of their potential audience, but what she sensed beneath the gesture wasn't restrained at all. He drew back. "You look less tired this morning."

"Someone kissed me in my dreams," she said, shy with the poetry, but glad she'd used it when his gaze warmed further. "Who said that?" She rested her hands on his chest. He had a coffee and new shirt smell, telling her the one he wore wasn't from his high school years.

"Nathaniel Hawthorne. In a letter to his wife, Sophie."

"We. Are. *Starving.*"

Brick grinned as Rory tossed the emphatic comment through the screen door. Brick plucked a shirt out of his truck before they started toward the house. He put his arm around her waist, fingers curved over her hip and through her belt loop. He showed her the shirt, a far more worn version of what he wore.

"In the spirit of nostalgia, I wore my old shirt to the station, but the guys noticed it was a little tight. So they gave me a new shirt."

"They had G-for-giant size?"

"They did." He gave her buttock a discreet pinch, but sharp enough to have her biting back an *ouch*. "But if you don't want the old one..."

She grabbed it from him before he could hold it out of reach, and that sexy smile crossed his face. He opened the screen door for her. As she stepped inside, she discovered Marcus had joined them in the kitchen.

There were no words to adequately describe Marcus Stanton. Mrs. Mayflower, an elderly neighbor who routinely flirted with Marcus, summed it up at a church picnic. "Those looks may come from an angel or a devil, but I don't find myself much caring, long as we get to look at him."

Green eyes, black silky hair to his shoulders, and a body undeniably some god or devil's best work. He was leaner than Thomas and taller by an inch or so. Les had seen him stripped down to jeans, and he had the muscles of a street fighter. When riled—and holy crap, he did have a temper—he had the lethal look of one in his eyes.

If Thomas's well-being was at risk, the wolf crouched beneath Marcus's cynical New York urbanite polish would make itself known. Les had seen that firsthand, during the time Thomas had come home to run the store and farm.

Thomas was just as protective of Marcus. Her brother's anger was far slower to rouse, but when it did, he was a pit bull. Rory was very much the same about Daralyn.

It was what you did when you loved someone. You took care of them, watched out for them. Like Brick had done for her. He'd stayed with her for the M&M and brought her home. That could have made her feel too needy, yet the things he compelled from her, Master to sub, balanced that. She'd given back to him as well. Because she wanted to, and because he demanded it.

She liked that. The crazy little tingle inside just from the thought said so.

Seeing Marcus brought back the conversation she and Brick had had. *It can run in families sometimes...* Her attention brushed over Thomas and Marcus, Rory and Daralyn. Both couples were a part of the world she was discovering, Doms and subs.

Though she couldn't imagine ever talking to Rory about any of this, next time she and Daralyn were alone, or—even better—she, Daralyn and Julie, girls' night was going to get interesting.

Marcus hugged her, bringing her up close and personal to that overwhelming gorgeousness. A targeted smile from him could fluster any woman. It helped that he was family. Somewhat. Les recalled Julie's matter-of-fact comment on it, long before she married Des.

"He's my best friend, so I can usually look past the eye candy stuff and hug him without grabbing his ass. Usually. It is a superlative ass."

"Let's all sit down and say grace so we can eat before things get cold," Elaine said.

"Mom, Daralyn, grab a seat. I've got the biscuits." Thomas directed his mother to the head of the table, holding her chair for her, and snagged the basket of bread. Daralyn was topping off Rory's coffee. She gave Thomas a quick nod, but made a questioning gesture to see if anyone else needed more. She returned the pot to the counter and slid into the chair next to Rory.

Brick sat down with Les, their chairs close enough his knee brushed hers. She noticed a similar proximity between the other couples at the table. Marcus's arm was stretched behind Thomas's chair. Rory took Daralyn's hand in his sun-browned one. At their mother's call for grace, he reached across the table to join his other hand to Les's. Les's to Brick's, Brick's to Elaine's. Marcus was next to her, so he and his mother-in-law joined hands while Thomas took Daralyn's, completing the family circle.

At Thanksgiving, at his mother's request, Thomas sat at the opposite head of the table, which would have been their father's spot. But for informal gatherings, he preferred being next to Marcus. The chair at the end of the table, directly across from their mother, remained empty.

Or to look at it the way Les preferred, it held the spirit of the man who would have sat there.

Elaine spoke the short prayer. She picked them out of selections offered in monthly church bulletins. Les didn't usually pay much attention, but this one made her wonder if her mother had chosen it purposefully.

"We look to you, O Lord, for nourishment for our bodies, grace to build our souls, and love to enhance our lives; through Jesus Christ our Lord. Amen."

Grace to build our souls.

After they raised their heads and started to pass around food, Rory grinned at Brick. "I saw Dillon Welsh at the general store the other day. He's become a semi-decent human being. Has a wife and a kid."

341

"Really?" Nostalgia touched her. At Daralyn's curious look, Les explained, "When I was in ninth grade, he paid attention to me for two glorious weeks. I was sure he was going to ask me to the Valentine's Day dance." She grimaced. "But then he asked another girl and never said another word to me. Boys."

She noticed Brick was studiously cutting his casserole while Thomas and Rory exchanged looks of unmistakable mirth. "What?"

Thomas swallowed a bite of bacon. "Brick's story to tell."

Brick shot Rory a narrow look. "No story at all if you hadn't opened your big mouth."

"So what's the story?" Les pressed.

Brick sighed and put down his fork. "I may be part of the reason he never asked you out."

"What?"

Brick glanced at Elaine, a sign he was choosing appropriate language for family mealtime. "I overheard him in the locker room. You remember JV and varsity shared the gym, and we had overlapping practices that day. He was going to ask you to the dance, but his intentions were to take advantage of your interest in him, for the wrong reasons."

"Oh." Les blinked. "Well, that's mildly hurtful. Though in hindsight, he *was* a flirt. While most the boys couldn't put two words together, he'd show up by your desk and say something charming or tug your hair."

"Then that girl would be moony over him for a month." Rory made a face. "'Did Dillon look at me today?' 'Is Dillon going to talk to me?'"

"Do you really want to go there with the girls you got moony over?" Les said sweetly. She angled a pointed look toward Brick. "So what happened?"

Rory propped an elbow on the table, using the bacon for emphasis. "He told Dillon if he gave in to his baser impulses, he'd snap his 'pale, Rob Pattinson wannabe body into twelve pieces. Not eleven, not thirteen. Twelve precise pieces.' Unquote."

Daralyn muffled a startled chuckle as Elaine's brows rose. "Rory wasn't there to hear it, so I had to step in to defend your honor," Brick told her. "Otherwise I'm sure he would have handled it the same way."

"I would have just punched him in the face. I didn't have the tank

physique and silver tongue combo to terrorize with vocabulary alone."
Rory winked.

"You could have waited until he asked me to the dance to threaten
him," Les pointed out. "Tell him he had to show me a nice, respectful
time, dote on me like I was the most important thing in his world,
and then drop me at my door."

"Oh, heck no. Then it would have been weeks of 'Dillon danced
with me,' 'Will Dillon call me?' 'Was Dillon looking at me in the
hallway today?'" Rory rolled his eyes.

Les ignored him, but Brick sent her a glinting look. "Sorry. At the
time, I didn't think to consult you on strategy." He put a biscuit on
her plate next to her square of casserole. "Shut up and eat that.
Women."

Though she pretended mock offense, it wasn't a bad feeling,
knowing Brick had been looking out for her, even then. From the
delighted female-to-female look Daralyn sent her, her sister-in-law
understood, and agreed.

"After breakfast, want to go see if the old tree house is still standing?" Brick asked her.

"The secret tree house? The one Rory told me never to try and
find, or he'd burn my favorite books?"

"It was a girl-free zone," Brick informed her.

"Until we realized it was a great place to *take* girls," Rory stage
whispered.

Elaine sent him a severe look. "Behave or I will reach across this
table and slap your head. Or tell Marcus to do it for me."

"Ruin his soft, manicured hands?" Rory laughed. "Not a chance."

He ducked his head as Marcus leaned out to swat at him behind
Daralyn and Thomas, then grunted as Marcus proved it was a feint
and punched him in the side. Marcus's hands might be manicured, but
soft they weren't.

Breakfast proceeded with more banter, plus anecdotes from the
store, Marcus's gallery, and Elaine's busy life with neighbors. Les noted
none of them asked her about school. Her family was always interested in what was happening with her in Durham, so she knew it was
intentional, them letting her decide if she wanted to talk about any of
it, even the mundane day-to-day stuff.

Right now, she found she didn't. She listened to what was

happening with all of them, asking questions, drinking in the information as if parched for it. It was frighteningly easy, to imagine never going back to school at all, and letting herself be pulled back into the day-to-day life here. But as what? Doing what?

After helping to clear the table and do dishes, the family went their separate ways. Daralyn needed to work on the vegetable garden at their home, while Rory put the finishing touches on a mantle for their new fireplace. Thomas had a painting in process in his barn studio, and Marcus was going to dedicate himself to clearing his workload. He'd promised Elaine that Easter Sunday would be a work-free zone.

Tomorrow they'd all go to the community, multi-denominational sunrise service. Elaine planned to attend some of the Easter Vigil tonight at the Catholic Church. With the ending of Lent, she and Daralyn already had most things prepared for the Easter Sunday lunch. After that, the family would spend the afternoon on the porch, visiting with one another and any neighbors who stopped by.

As a town made up mostly of farmers and blue-collar workers, a day dedicated to relaxation was rare. *"No-work religious holidays are a way to give the working man a break, and remind him who he's working for."* Her father had told them that, when they'd squirmed about spending Easter with their parents instead of playing with their friends. *"Give your poor dad one day of your teenage lives,"* he'd told them.

Brick had told her he was going out to the garden shed, but he'd meet her out front when she was ready to visit the tree house.

When Les emerged, she saw the unlikely sight of Brick straddling her father's old bicycle. It had mountain bike tires and was front load heavy, thanks to a big rectangular grocer's basket.

"Your mom said I could borrow it," he told her. He'd filled the basket up, though she couldn't tell what was in it. A piece of wood hinged to the basket covered it, a cushion on top of that. "She told me it was the only bike that could handle my weight."

Her father had ridden the modified bike back and forth from the fields. Though it was big for Elaine's short stature, she liked the stability of the wide tires and used the basket to carry food and other things to neighbors.

Brick gestured at the cushioned piece of wood. His gaze met hers. "Better than last time, right?"

CHAPTER TWENTY-THREE

*H*e'd remembered. The memory flapped against the inside of her chest like a freed bird. Though his interest in her was no longer in doubt, it still surprised her that he recalled things that held such significance to her.

She'd been at a middle school basketball game. Afterward, she and her friends Vanessa and Joy had been picked up by Joy's mother. The elementary, middle and high schools were all centrally located on the same tract of land, to serve the population of the county, and the half dozen small towns within it. Which was why JV and varsity sports teams shared locker room facilities.

She and Vanessa had walked home from Joy's house, cutting across the fields. They took the path between the Orbison and Williamson's corn fields, which would come out on the road near Vanessa's house.

While they'd been talking about the usual things, cute boys at the game and who might be interested in who, Brick and Rory had emerged from a thick stand of trees on their bikes.

Les had expected nothing more than Rory tossing annoying comments at them like rotten eggs before they breezed past. But Brick had come to a full stop. He'd asked if they were headed home, and when she said they were—miraculously without stammering her response to his direct question—he'd told her he'd give her a ride on his handlebars. Rory had given Vanessa a ride on his.

She'd made faces when Vanessa called her later to gush over Rory. But while enduring Vanessa's brief malady of puppy love, Les was just as affected.

She'd had to lean back against Brick's chest and shoulder for balance. She'd felt the vibration of his voice, the heat of him, inhaled his scent and dreamed, all while he tossed comments back and forth with Rory. Seemingly oblivious to the girl who could barely breathe for his nearness.

She came down the steps to stand next to the bicycle and tossed him an accusing look. "You acted like you were carting groceries. And Rory would have preferred being dragged through horse manure to spending time with middle school girls. Especially his sister."

"I couldn't act like it was a big deal. But it wasn't too long after the poem. Those serious eyes of yours kept coming back into my head." Brick twined his fingers in her hair, winding the strands over his knuckles for that distracting little tug. "When you were walking with Vanessa, moonlight was reflecting off your hair, making it look silky and thick. Made me wonder what it would feel like, blowing against my face, where I could smell it."

She refused to let herself be tongue-tied, even though it took her a second to respond. Because her tongue wasn't working. "It probably smelled like the gym, a bunch of sweaty hormonal teens watching a basketball game."

He put his nose to her hair, nuzzling her. "They were serving popcorn. I smelled that. Maybe a trace of manure, since you helped milk the cows that day."

"I did not have manure smell in my hair," she said indignantly, pulling away. When he laughed, she thumped his shoulder.

"Jerk."

"No manure." His eyes became more intent, his mouth that firm line. "I smelled the flowery shampoo you were using. Gave me an interesting night, once I was home and alone in my room."

She tried to sound casual, instead of how she felt. "Well, you were a teenage boy. If you saw a tree that looked like it had breasts, the same thing would have happened."

He cupped her jaw, turned her head to him and kissed her. Not an easy brush of lips, either. It involved tongue and teeth, and had her gripping his wrist to balance herself as he took his time.

When he broke the kiss, he stared into her eyes. "I put my hand on my cock, and thought about what you'd look like naked, straddling me, all that hair brushing my chest and face. Tangling my hands in it to pull you down on me."

"Oh," she said faintly.

"Yeah." He caressed her throat. "I was a teenage boy. But there wasn't one damn generic thing about that fantasy. We weren't old enough to do anything about it then. We are now."

He put his hands to her waist and lifted her up onto the cushion. "Lean back against me. It will help with your balance."

It also put her against his chest and shoulder, like it had then. The cushion made it more comfortable, the bar not biting into her ass and thighs. The solid heat of him was the same. He dipped his head, pulling a breath from her as he nipped her throat, giving it a hard suckle, followed by a teasing lick. "Hold on."

As he pushed off, she gripped either side of the basket. By leaning back, she was also inside the brace of his arms. As she kept her legs free of the wheel on either side, she turned her head to brush her mouth against his jaw, his strong throat. Then she tipped her head back, letting her hair stream over his shoulder.

Before college, being young had always been spoiled with the impatience of waiting. Waiting to be old enough to do...anything that seemed worth doing. Fill in the blank.

After the grind of her first two years of medical school, some part of her had gotten tight and grim. The chance to feel young, riding on the front of a bike pedaled by the man holding her heart as well as her body, felt good. He chuckled as he executed the transition to the bumpier terrain of the field paths and made her gasp. She *was* young. Young and in love, a crazy, exhilarating, wonderful feeling.

They'd reached the tree line. "Do I need a blindfold, so I can't reveal the super-secret location of the boys-only treehouse?"

"You won't need a blindfold for that. Maybe for other things."

He nipped her throat again and biked them into the forest. As the trail narrowed, he seemed as comfortable navigating a bike on the uncertain terrain as he'd been back then. When he turned off onto a deer path, he brought them to a halt. He helped her off her perch, removing the cushion and lifting the wood cover to retrieve a cooler and a canvas bag full enough to be lumpy.

As he guided her deeper into the woods, she noticed a blue circle painted on certain trees. "Over the last year or two, I marked it when I came home, so even if the landscape changed, I could find it," he said, noting her interest. "Rory had Thomas bring Daralyn here. Since he built it with Thomas and your dad, she wanted to see it. He wanted to make sure she did."

"Yeah." The thought summoned the usual regret and sadness, but Brick's grip constricted, drawing her out of her head. "Having Daralyn to love and protect has reprioritized a lot of things for him, helped him make peace with stuff like that."

She'd seen evidence of that herself, but hearing it come from a close friend, who had different insights into her brother's state of mind, helped. She moved closer, hooking her fingers over his belt. "Thanks."

"I know you worry about him. He's good, though. Sounds odd, but I think he's at a better place now than he's ever been in his life. Love will do that."

He touched her face, then drew her attention above them. "Here we are."

Her brothers, as many in their county, were skilled at subsistence hunting to supplement the family food supply. It was no surprise they could camouflage a tree house like a hunting blind, making it difficult to find with a casual glance.

Brick took her to one of the trees supporting the structure and revealed a rope tucked into the Georgia creeper on the trunk. "No ladder. You can get on my back and I'll pull us up," he said. "Or you can climb it, if you feel up to it."

Though she worked out, pulling herself up fifteen feet of rope hand-over-hand, even with her feet braced on the trunk, wasn't in her wheelhouse of athletic feats. "I can do twenty-five non-girl pushups," she informed him, just to save face.

He grinned and gave her the bag to hang over her shoulder and threaded the small cooler over his wrist. Then he bent his knees so she could hop on.

She wrapped her arms around his chest and shoulders, but hesitated. "If I put my legs around your waist, it may hurt where you were shot."

"Grazed. And you're good." He reached around to grip her leg, giving her a start on the hop. He hefted her into place as he straightened and grasped the rope. "The bruising from the rocks in the creek did far more damage, and even they've been fine with a few OTC painkillers."

She'd found the same to be true for herself, but she still tried to put her leg where it wasn't directly on the spot. "Is this how Thomas took Daralyn up here?"

"I think he drove an ATV and they brought an extension ladder."

"Sounds like an intelligent decision."

"Yeah, but he wasn't trying to impress her with manly displays of strength."

She chuckled. She didn't mind his manly display of strength. The easy movement of his body under the grip of her arms and legs, the way he took her up toward the treehouse without obvious effort, was definitely impressive. As they reached the deck, he shifted her onto it, handed her the cooler and swung himself up.

"So if getting back down is no easier than up, I expect I'm at your mercy."

"Better be nice to me then." His look prickled heat over her skin and made her very aware of how private and secluded this spot was. For form's sake, she peered over the edge.

"I expect fifteen feet isn't a bad jump."

He brought her away from the edge, but it wasn't to engage in more banter. He pressed her against the outside wall of the treehouse, his arm banding around her waist. Before she could suck in a breath, he had his mouth on hers, his hand gripping her ass. His other palm pressed into her back, thumb caressing her bra strap through her shirt. The hungry, powerful kiss told her he'd been lying in Rory's room last night, thinking about her and this. She hooked her legs around his waist again, to show him she'd been thinking about him just as much. A little noise caught in her throat as he pressed a very solid response between her legs.

"You know," she managed, when he drew back. "I've been reading about firefighting. You're supposed to put your hand on a closed door before opening it, because if there are flames behind it, the wood is hot and the fire might blast you when opened."

His lips curved, sensual promise. "Is that so?"

"Yeah. You're as hot as one of those doors."

"Same goes, doc." Reluctantly, he let her down, to open the latch on the treehouse entry panel. He pushed it inward so she could step inside.

Two windows had been cut into the structure. The screens covering them were in good repair. The interior walls had been painted a forest green and gray color, same as the exterior. But in here, the color was a background for a thick forest of branches painted along the inside walls.

"Stand here." Brick positioned her so she could see the trees outside the windows. The painted branches inside lined up with the live branches outside, as if they were still part of the same forest.

Her delight only deepened as she saw R+D painted in a heart on one of those branches, M+T on another. Her heart twisted as she saw one for her parents. R+E.

In an upper corner, framed by a spray of painted leaves and a perched robin, was a nod to the builders. Robert, Rory and Thomas Wilder.

The painting was done in that texturized way, the signature brand of her brother's work. Thomas had painted the other two walls a blended mix of earth colors, like the tree house on the outside.

"I remember when Thomas and my dad helped Rory build this," Les said.

"Probably why it's remained important to both of them. Though Thomas never spent much time up here when we were kids."

"No." Les shook her head. "He didn't have a lot of close friends in high school. When he wasn't helping my dad on the farm or later, in the store, he was drawing and painting. But he was always there to help me or Rory with homework, or my mom or dad with whatever chores needed doing. It was always about art or family for Thomas."

A polished wooden box was in the corner. She turned away from the window to watch Brick open it. What he pulled out revealed he'd come here earlier to prepare for their visit.

He removed the folded blanket and pillow from Rory's old bed, or rather, the current guestroom. He put the canvas bag beside it, but rather than satisfying her curiosity about its contents, he straightened and looked her way.

He did that thing he knew how to do without words, filling up a space with his intent and energy. When he moved toward her, she backed up a step. Then another, until her back met the wall.

She couldn't tell if he'd compelled her to move that way with his forward progress and portentous gaze, or something inside her had counseled retreat, to show a little trepidation, the kind that inflamed what was swirling between them.

"As much as the past has some nice memories, I prefer the present. Me, having my submissive here, ready to give me what I want. Are you ready to give me what I want, Les?"

That sense of seclusion increased. "Yes, Sir."

"Good. Take off everything you're wearing. Except the necklace."

He dropped to his heels, his fingers tented on the floor, and tilted his head like a focused raptor. Waiting.

She grasped the hem of her shirt and pulled it over her head. Slow, not intending a strip tease, but because when he got like this, her hands and body became a little less coordinated.

"I like to see you tremble for me, Les. The little shivers on your skin, the look in your eyes, anticipation but also a lot of nervousness. The right kind, as you figure out how to let go of control and trust me."

She put the shirt on a brace of hooks, reached behind her and unfastened her bra, letting it slide down her arms. As she turned away to hang it up, she heard him rise, the wood vibrating when he closed the space between them. Her shudder increased as he pulled her hair to the side and kissed her shoulder, then her neck, pressing his body against her. His hands coasted down her sides to the denim at her hips. "Now the rest."

But rather than letting her do it, he slipped the button of her jeans and moved the zipper down with the insertion of his large hand, finding her panties, her mound. He curved his fingers over her clit and labia with a sure, firm pressure, his other hand cupping her ass to knead both her buttocks, rousing the sensitive nerves in the seam between them.

He held her between those two erotic points as she arched back against him, a needy sound coming from her lips. He did that for a while, fondling and squeezing, stroking her as he wished.

"I respect your mother, but it was all I could do last night not to come and hold you, let you sleep in my arms. Wake you up in the middle of the night to drive away any bad dreams."

"Your text did that," she whispered. That was how strong his hold was on her. "But I would have liked your idea, too."

He moved his hands to her waist, a brief, firm hold, before he stepped back. "Take off the shoes and socks, and remove the jeans and panties. Bend over as you do it. Then turn around to face me again."

She removed shoes and socks. Sliding her hands under elastic and denim, she worked the clothes off her hips. As she bent to remove them as he wished, she was aware of the heat of his gaze sliding over the parts of her she was revealing.

Slowly, she pivoted. "Straight back," he murmured with approval. "Chin up. Eyes meeting mine. I didn't even have to tell you. You're learning what your Master wants. I like looking at every inch of your beautiful body. Every inch of what's mine. It is mine, isn't it, Les?"

"Yes, Sir." Her voice cracked. A breeze flitted through the boards, raising gooseflesh on her skin.

"All of it mine to care for." He picked up the blanket. Shaking it out, he wrapped it around her, just off her shoulders, guiding her hand to clasp it at the rise of her breasts. Then he spread out a towel on the floor, opened the draw string of the canvas bag and began removing what was in it.

A black bandanna, big enough to be used as a blindfold. Or a gag. He stripped off his belt and laid it next to the cloth. Though he'd yet to actually use it in the way he'd threatened, her buttocks tingled. Her hands closed at her sides, remembering its hold on her wrists.

Her eyes widened as he took out her vibrator. "How..."

"I transferred it to my suitcase before I brought yours to your room. Saved you and your mother the mutual embarrassment if she unpacked your stuff." He flashed her a feral smile before he withdrew a flogger with a thick fall of red straps. One black leather glove, like a driving glove, that would fit the hand like a second skin. Her pulse accelerated.

The last thing he pulled out was a coiled horse rein.

"Found it in the same shed as the bike," he said. "It had some intriguing possibilities." He pointed to a section of floor to their right. "Drop the blanket. Fold it over once and leave it there, then come here. I'm going to keep you warm another way."

When she reached him, he had another order for her. "Cross your wrists and extend them."

He twisted the rein around them, tightened its hold and wrapped the slack in his hand. "I can use this to bind my sub to me. Bend her over and slap her ass with the end. Or wrap it around her body, over and above her breasts to squeeze them, make her nipples more sensitive. When I lash and tease them with my tongue, she'll cry out and her sweet pussy will cream for me."

If he went through each item and painted a picture like that, she was going to come before he finished the list.

"But the only things I really need to bind you are these." He laid two fingers against her temple, moved the touch to her chest, over the heart pounding inside it. His wrist brushed her nipple, making it tighter. "Your heart and mind require nothing but my command holding you, restraining you. Your desire to submit drives how tough, extreme or tender I'll be."

"What about your desires?"

"I'm going to show those to you."

He loosened the rein, drew one of her hands free, but tied a loose knot around the other wrist. He pushed her to a leaning position against the wall, then looped the slack around one of the ceiling supports, drawing the hand up. He tied the rein off, leaving her held like that, at his mercy.

He was right; she was warm now. He made sure of it, though, running a hand over her arms, the sensitive collar bones and base of her throat. He captured her free hand and drew it down.

"Spread your legs, Les."

He put her hand on her damp sex. "Masturbate in front of me. Do it like you're alone, but lift your chin and look at me. Don't lower your gaze, and don't bring your arm above your waist, because while you do that, I want to flog your breasts."

An intrigued spasm went through her, like a fitful wind skittering over water. "Will you use fire?"

"No. Too many uncontrolled variables here. I'm lacking supplies I need to keep you safe. Even if I had them, I wouldn't flog your breasts with fire, because I won't risk your face. But I'd use the glove I used on you at my place. I'd stroke your breasts and nipples with fire, seal in the heat. Would you like that?"

"Yes, Sir." She saw both things in his gaze, the man she was falling in love with, and the Master whose command she wanted to follow, so naturally and easily. It was miraculous, to discover what had always been waiting inside her, waiting for him to unlock it with her. "Thank you, Sir."

He brushed his knuckles over her face. "You're a gift, doc. I want you to be quiet unless you're worried about something, need to safe-word, or I ask you a question. Focus on what I'm doing and what I want. Understand?"

"Yes, Sir."

"I believe I told you to do something."

When she remembered, she flushed. He liked it when she did that, though. She kept her chin up, but her eyes started to close as she moved her hand into the damp hair and heated flesh between her legs.

"Look at me when you touch yourself, Les. You'll lose that shyness as you arouse yourself and see what it does to me, obeying me to give yourself pleasure."

Her emotions were froth on turbulent ocean waves. "It's difficult."

"You're opening parts of yourself that tend to get shut off as we get older, as we get hurt, disappointed. What lives in those places scares us, because we don't always understand how deep they go, or how they'll manifest if we bring them to the surface. Whatever rises up when you obey me, it will be okay." He held her gaze. "Trust me with whatever is going on."

"May I close my eyes for just a moment, to get into the right head space? I want to touch myself the way you said, like I do when I'm alone, because I know that's what you want, what you'll like seeing, but it's difficult with you watching me."

"No." He stepped closer and settled his hand on her throat, making her chin lift higher. It stirred things in her head, heart and body, cycling around him and that grip. "Start touching yourself, Les. When you trail your fingers over yourself, feel how soft your skin is, do you imagine a man touching you? Think of his hand, what he's touching, feeling?

"Yes...no." Her gaze stayed in the grasp of his, as sure as his hold on her throat. "I think of you touching me. I have, for a long time. I think of what you're touching and feeling."

His voice dropped to a purring rumble. "Then do that, while

looking at me. Don't go away from me in your head. Tell me. Take me on the journey. Start where you would if you were alone. Right now, you can move your hand above your waist."

She imagined it as she would in her bed. Him above her, looking at her. In those fantasies, his face had been blurred, not brought into heart-thudding focus. It took an effort, with him so real and here, but the words came, commanded by his desire that she take him into her mind, her fantasies.

"You play with my breasts." She moved her hand over them, brushing his forearm as she cupped and lifted one, passed her thumb over the nipple. She captured it with two fingers to squeeze it, stroke and shape it into a tighter point.

Her breath escaped in a little puff as his fingers constricted on her neck, his gaze locked on what she was doing. She moved to the other nipple as her hips lifted from the wall, fell back, a sensual invitation to bring his touch lower. "I can't be still. I want you to touch me lower, but you keep touching my breasts, telling me I have to wait...that you want to do things your way. At your pace."

"Damn right."

A little moan escaped her. "The right one is more sensitive than the left," he noted.

"Yes. At first. Eventually the left catches up, but the right is always the most responsive first." She trailed her fingers over his forearm, earning a warning growl that made a smile touch her lips, tense with the stimulation.

She moved her fingers down beneath her ribs, over her stomach and navel, a circle out to the hip bones. His touch slid away, and he stepped back, squaring himself to watch her. A reminder he was commanding her to do this. His eyes swept over her, targeting her movements, but she knew he would keep checking to make sure she was watching him. Right on cue, his gaze flicked up, a stern reinforcement, before he shifted his attention to the track of her hand.

She caressed the tops of her thighs, her mound. She licked her lips and continued. "You stop here, your hand resting on my stomach. You tell me to spread my legs wider, lift my hips to you. I'm dying, needing you to touch me, but your eyes, the way they look...it's like you already are."

"Touch yourself, Les. Spread your feet out wider and keep them that way. As far as you're concerned, I've chained them to the floor. So you can't close them. You can only wait for what I decide to put between them."

She moaned again when she slid her fingers over her clit and labia. As she moved them through that slick, wet valley, every nerve ending ignited. She wanted to remove her hair in that area, wanted to let him put flame there.

"I'll paint it over your smooth skin," he said, and she realized she'd said it out loud. "I'll blow on it with my mouth, let the heat feather over your clit. You'll come before the flame goes out."

A gasp of reaction escaped. She rode the wave of sensation that rippled out from her touch.

"Keep going, Les." He moved to the items he'd laid out and picked up the flogger with its thick tail of straps. "Keep your chin up and your hand down, working between your legs like I told you. Arch your back. Offer those pretty breasts and stiff nipples to me."

She did it. She could trust him. Whatever he offered her, even if it included pain, it would make sense, feel right. If it didn't, he'd want her to use her safeword. Would reward her for doing so. It all meant the same thing.

She was safe with him. Emotionally and physically.

She complied, her fingers playing, stroking, getting wet from the contact. He threw the flogger's tails forward with an easy, economical motion. The sound reminded her of a flock of birds, the cumulative rush of wind that came with their passing. The straps struck her breasts, the base of her throat, her side exposed by her raised and bound arm. The thud had a sting as he pulled it away, but his restraint told her his intent wasn't pain. Her nipples and breasts tingled. She arched further for him, her lower body twisting from the reaction through her cunt, the building need.

"Beautiful," he murmured. He continued to flog her breasts with even, restrained strokes. The pain effect increased, on and around her nipples, on her sensitized flesh, but she leaned into it even as she flinched. Arousal and discomfort together built the intensity, pulling her mind into it. As she worked her hand between her legs and he flogged her, her body turned into a lightning rod, begging for strikes that would electrify everything. She was keenly aware of the rein's hold, keeping her arm raised, stretching and displaying her body for him.

His strokes remained rhythmic, everything under his tight control, until she was gasping, whimpering, making little cries. Her mind was going away, the sting of the flogger hitting her nipples, reddening her breasts, all part of the stimulus that arrowed downward with every strike, a pulse. Her sex rippled in a near orgasmic state. Her fingers were dipping inside and stroking outside, making a wet sound against her flesh.

"God...Sir...I'm so close..."

He ceased. The flogger tails swayed as he held the toy at his side, letting its motion come to a natural stop.

He'd told her he would show her what his desires were. From the size of his erection against his jeans, he had.

"Put your free hand behind your head."

As she did, her arm trembling, he laid the flogger aside and came to her. He untied the strap from her other wrist, but only to tie both wrists together over her head. Before he did, he tasted the hand she'd been using on herself, licking her arousal off her fingers. Then he adjusted the rein so she was pulled up onto her toes, his eyes promising the best kind of sexual torment as he tied that off.

"Sir...Master." She was breathless, mindless, crazed with need.

He ran his hand over her back, then put both along her sides, her ribs and hips. After the stimulation of the flogger, her skin had that same electric reaction to his actual touch. She shuddered and jerked, whimpered.

"Be still, baby." The endearment didn't dilute the severe tone of the command. She could come from that alone. When he pushed two fingers into her mouth, made her suck on them, she almost bit down. His firm touch on her throat helped her recall herself enough not to do that. When they were good and wet, he removed them from her mouth and pushed them inside her.

She screamed. If he'd touched her clit, she would have lost control, but he didn't. He had his other hand on her sternum, holding her against the wall as he played in her wetness and continued to watch her unravel before him, beg without words, only feeling. Except his name. She muttered that like a one-word prayer for mercy.

He captured the necklace in his teeth, pulling on it gently. He released it and used his tongue over her nipples, easing the throbbing rawness the flogger had left. Her cry became a whimper of gratitude, of a need for more.

He stepped back and thank God, removed his shirt. Her gaze slid over the firm flesh, defined pectorals and sectioned stomach. The doctor in her made a note of the healing "graze," confirming he'd told her the truth, that it was fine. The bruising elsewhere was healing the way it should. If she had any doubts, the sex marathon he'd put her through before the M&M said it wasn't slowing him down.

The woman in her needed to feel his upper body against her. He opened his jeans, and pushed the underwear beneath down, scooping out his heavy cock.

She needed that, too.

He left it that way, making her sex throb for what he brought so close.

"Please..."

His cock brushed her thigh as he pressed an almost chaste kiss against her cheek. "Whose pace, Les?"

"Yours."

"When will it happen?"

"When...you say."

She was caught in the powerful storm cloud of demand in his eyes. But he slid his arm around her waist and palmed her ass to lift her up against the wall. He leaned in, putting his cock between her legs. He lowered her onto it slowly, so slowly she decided he really must be sent straight from the most wicked, sinful parts of hell to break apart her soul.

Inch by excruciating inch, he brought her down onto his length. His fingers, still slick with both their fluids, probed between her buttocks, playing with the sensitive nerve endings around her rim.

"Oh God..." She writhed on his cock as he slid all the way home. Sensation slammed into her. She tried to hold on, knowing she needed to wait for his command, even if he built it to a lethal amount of response. He was taking her where he wanted her to go, and she surrendered that to him. Just like her fantasy, that picture. *Waiting on Him.*

"Now, Les."

He wanted her to come. Demanded it, and she was helpless to do anything but what he told her to do.

The orgasm turned the treehouse into a spinning cloud of earth colors as she cried out. Brick's intent gray eyes were at the center, his masculine presence as rooted and firm as the trunks of the trees that held them aloft. His cock was the same, thrusting deep as his thighs and buttocks flexed under her heels, all those muscles committed to what made life worth living. Worth creating. Worth giving and sharing.

He freed the strap with a jerk so her arms could drop over his head. Her nails raked his neck and back, her head pressing against the side of his as she shrieked, as he groaned out his own release against her temple. He pushed her against the treehouse wall, and she felt it creak and groan, absorb their fierce response.

When his seed spewed inside her, the heat of it left one overriding desire. To give him everything.

As they slowed, he was holding her weight against him. He slid from her, but only to turn, drop to a knee and put her on her back on the blanket he'd told her to leave folded on the floor. She was glad the reins still bound her hands, because she didn't want to let him go, and she didn't have the strength to hang on otherwise.

He was still hard enough to put himself back inside her as he lay upon her. Her cunt spasmed, milking out aftershocks that had her clutching him with twitching fingers. He adjusted his hips in small movements, staying as deep as he could, letting her feel him there.

"You make me want to do nothing but fuck you all day long." Her man who loved to quote poetry, speaking raw and plain to her from the primitive pleasure of their joining.

At length, he guided her arms from around his neck to remove the rein. He moved to his knees and checked her circulation, rubbing her wrists and fingers. Her mind was in a drifting, wordless place, so she tugged her hands free to put them on his chest, scraping, asking, pulling. His gaze softened as he lowered himself back upon her, though he held most of his weight on one arm.

He seated his cock against her sex, giving her one more aftershock through her clit. As he pressed a kiss to her cheek, under her ear, he did whisper poetry to her, roughened by the passion still in his voice.

A snippet of the poem he'd quoted to her the first time he fulfilled one of her fantasies, the spanking between her legs.

"The mystic deliria--the madness amorous---the utter abandonment..." He put another lingering kiss on her mouth.

"That Walt was a sex fiend."

"Just a normal man with a poet's soul." Brick chuckled. "He wanted to put the feelings to words."

"For some things, there are no words."

"No." His gaze met hers. "And none needed."

CHAPTER TWENTY-FOUR

*W*as it wrong, to consider that time in the treehouse as sacred as the sunrise service they attended Easter morning?

She hoped not, because it kept coming back into her head as she stood next to her mother on the lawn outside their church. They'd set up an altar for the pastors. Behind it was a cemetery, a field of head-stones planted on a carpet of green grass. Paved pathways wound among them. Hints of the sun were already evident in the sky's rose and gray tones.

Brick stood on Les's left. Thomas was on the other side of their mother, aligned with Marcus and Daralyn. Rory sat in his chair at his wife's side, her hand on his shoulder, his clasped over it.

"Good morning," Reverend Mueller said. Father Antonucci, their Catholic pastor, stood at his right, the town's Methodist pastor, Father Royal, at his left. Father Antonucci looked a little tired, since he'd celebrated the Easter Vigil and Mass, but the smile and warmth he exuded was genuine, appreciative of the many community members who'd left their beds to greet the dawn.

A decade ago, the Baptist church pastor, Reverend West, had passed away suddenly from a heart attack. There was no assistant pastor, and though other church members could step in to provide sermon material while a new pastor was being chosen, Easter was a different matter. Because Fairhope was such a close community, they'd asked Father Antonucci and Father Royal if either of them would be willing to offer a sunrise service, a one-time thing.

They'd decided to do it together and hold it here, behind the Catholic church. While a small church, it had the biggest outside lawn area, plus the east-facing cemetery and forest backdrop made it a serene spot.

The event had been so well-received by the whole town, there'd been a resulting uptick in attendance at all three churches. As such, when the new Baptist pastor, Reverend Mueller, was installed, he and Fathers Antonucci and Royal decided to make it an annual tradition.

"Good morning," Reverend Mueller said. He was in his thirties, with thin blond hair and kind blue eyes. "He is risen."

"He is risen," a wave of voices responded.

Les blinked back unexpected tears. Emotions gripped her, painful and bittersweet.

Brick touched her back, a question. She nodded, confirming she was all right. But as Reverend Mueller started the service, the emphasis on rebirth, renewal and resurrection kept her mind linked to what had brought her home. Including the wound her heart and soul still carried, the shadow of Llanzo's death, his mother's heartbreak.

She couldn't be a good doctor, here or anywhere, if her mind was clouded and dogged by a guilt that sliced her open every time it turned in that direction. Right now, when she couldn't find sufficient distraction, those feelings were a black hole, the gravity of it pulling her in. As long as they did that, she couldn't even consider what moving forward as a medical student would look like.

She could leave school, come home. Work in the community in another way. Help her mother, help Rory and Daralyn at the store. Before entering medical school, she had gushed to Dr. Spring about her desire to work in his medical practice and primary care clinic. His warm but qualified response made more sense now.

"I would welcome you here with open arms, Les. But if things change, don't deny yourself the chance to pursue other opportunities. Just keep me informed."

She hadn't seen him in this assembly today, but since it was one of the largest town get-togethers, just behind the Christmas and Fall

Harvest festivals, it was very likely they wouldn't cross paths. She could avoid the "how are things going" question.

She noticed Rory glancing at her. Her expression must be strained, and Brick's protective body language was reinforcing it. When she offered a reassuring smile, her brother gave her a considering look but nodded back. He returned his gaze to the front.

Father Antonucci was taking his turn at the altar. Gripping Brick's hand at her waist, Les resolved to keep herself in the here and now.

After the service concluded, it was time for another Easter tradition—visiting her father's grave. The church cemetery had been filled some time ago, the most recent headstones dating to the early 1900s. Her father was buried in Fairhope Memorial Garden, a couple miles away.

Marcus held the passenger door for Elaine so she could get into his convertible Mercedes. Thomas got into the back, while Brick and Les rode with Rory and Daralyn in Rory's hand-control operated van.

They didn't say much on the short ride. Daralyn rested a hand on Rory's thigh as he drove. Higher up, because the only sensation Rory had in his legs was toward the tops of his thighs. She touched him where he could feel it.

Les knew the comfort of that. Her hand was firmly clasped in Brick's, resting on the seat between them. After another glance at her, he shifted to put that hand around her shoulder again. As she molded herself naturally to his side, she caught Rory's glance in the rearview mirror, but he didn't tease her.

She was fine. Everything was fine. Even if her stomach got tighter as they pulled into the cemetery.

Rory parked behind the Mercedes. Thomas was holding the door open for his mother. Elaine had brought a bouquet of early spring blooms from her flower garden. The cut stems had been carefully wrapped in a wet towel so there'd be no wilting. Daralyn had done the same with flowers from her own garden.

After Rory came down his ramp, Brick helped pack it away and closed the van door. The family reunited at the cemetery entrance, flanked by lilac bushes. They stayed close together, even as Elaine took the lead, holding Thomas's arm with Marcus just behind. They walked without much conversation along the paved walking path. Old oaks, crepe myrtles, dogwoods and red bud trees were generously scattered across the grounds, most of them budding or flowering, bringing the scents of early spring.

She and Brick followed the procession, her hand folded in the crook of his elbow. The handful of years since her father's passing wasn't enough to dispel the sharpness of the ache, all the memories that crowded in. They invited in thoughts of more recent losses.

A family plot caught her attention, bringing her to an uncertain halt. Ethel Taylor, a mother who'd passed in her fifties. Her husband Joseph died in his seventies. They'd had six children, three who'd died young. Very young. Two before their first birthday, one just after his second.

Llanzo would likely be buried somewhere like this. A hundred years from now, someone would walk by, see the name. Like her looking at the headstones now, they'd feel sad a child died, but could they imagine everything his death had meant, all that it had touched and destroyed?

Her shoulders began to shake. *Oh God, not here.* Not now. Today wasn't about that. But all she could think about was Llanzo's name on a tombstone like this, his mother standing before it each Easter...

Her knees buckled.

But Brick had her, moving her to a nearby contemplation bench and easing her down on it. He pressed a firm hand to her shoulder. "It's okay. Take a breath, doc. Don't move."

He'd injected enough firmness into the order to at least catch her attention, give her pause, but even if he barked at her like a drill sergeant, Brick knew her compulsion to get up, not worry her family, would propel her off the bench.

However, if she stood up, she was going to pass out. Snow had more color than her face. When she wilted, Rory noticed immediately, pivoting his chair in her direction. He'd been watching her during the service almost as closely as Brick had.

Daralyn was already headed toward Les, but Brick moved purposefully up the path toward her and Rory. By the time he'd closed the short distance, Thomas had glanced over his shoulder and murmured to Elaine. When she noted Les on the bench, she began to backtrack.

Brick shook his head, lifting a hand. He intended to be a gateway; he would let them pass if they insisted, but he would do his damnedest to keep that from happening. He could feel Les's agony. She was terrified she would detract from the significance of this ritual because of her own shit. Though no one else would feel like that, it was how she'd be thinking of it in her head, making her lightheadedness even worse, a self-fulfilling prophecy.

"I've got her," he said quietly. "We'll be there in a minute. Please. She's okay."

Thomas and Rory glanced at their mother. Elaine pressed her lips together. Probably surprising them all—even Brick—she took Thomas's arm again. A simple serenity gripped Daralyn's features. "He'll take care of her," she told Rory. "He's the one who's supposed to take care of her."

Brick guessed it made the most sense that Daralyn, a female submissive herself, interpreted and was more reassured by his words and gestures, his body language, than any of the others.

Brick met Rory's gaze. *Yes. I will take care of her. Always.*

After another assessing moment, Rory wheeled his chair around to follow Elaine. Marcus brought up the rear. He gave Brick a confirming look before following the rest of the family.

Brick returned to her. Shit, her shoulders were rising and falling fast, her fists against her chest. She was panicking, fighting herself, and bringing on a worse reaction, just as he'd feared.

He dropped to his heels next to her, putting his hand on her back. "Breathe. Listen to my voice, and breathe."

She'd seemed quiet this morning, and when he'd learned the morning's agenda included a visit to the cemetery, he figured that was the primary cause of her pensiveness. The loss of their father was still a big hit for the Wilder kids. Les herself had likely been focused on that, and not on what had blindsided her.

Of course walking through a graveyard, where there would inevitably be children's graves, would cause her issues. He'd anticipated it, keeping her to the rear, and being prepared to do what he'd just done with her family.

"They'll meet us there," he told her. "We're by ourselves. Just breathe, baby. You're not ruining anything. You're okay. I'm here."

Her breathing was evening out, the hand clutched on his coat sleeve less desperate. When he gauged the timing was right, he drew her to her feet. Her arms slid under his suit jacket, and she held onto him, her face hard against his chest, shoulders trembling.

"I took him away from her. How can I ever...oh God, Brick. It'll never be okay."

"No. It'll never be okay. But other things will be. Life is more than our losses and mistakes, Les." He injected the edge into his voice she needed, and tipped up her chin. "Time. You need time. Llanzo's mother needs time. Life goes on. Simple truths. Hold onto me, and let that be enough for today."

"I'm...we should catch up to them."

"Did you eat anything this morning?"

"No...Easter lunch is huge. End of Lent and all." She gave him that tremulous smile. "I'd throw up if I ate anything right now."

"We'll catch up, but only if you lean on me. Okay, doc?"

They made their way along the path. As they went over a slight rise, a semi-circle of crepe myrtles a couple hundred feet to their left showed their destination. The Wilder family was there, with the exception of Marcus, who had remained on Brick and Les's path. Keeping an eye on them, in case Brick needed backup.

"She's okay," Brick answered his silent look. "Should have eaten something this morning."

"I'm good, Marcus. I'm just being stupid." Les already looked painfully embarrassed. She'd never been comfortable at the center of attention.

Seeing it, knowing it himself, Marcus acted accordingly. "You're not being that at all. Come on, let's head that way." He flanked Les's other side. With each step toward the rest of the family, Brick felt her reclaim her grip on her self-possession, just like she had for the M&M. It was a well that most of the time seemed astonishingly limitless.

Deep enough to drown her when she lost her grip. It was why she had him, though. That was what a Dom was supposed to do. The kind of Dom he wanted to be, at least.

Once they reached the others, she stepped away from Brick and

Marcus, joining her mother and Daralyn. Daralyn had divided her flowers into two small bouquets, and she handed one to Les. As the three men watched, the two younger women placed the bouquets in the smaller containers mounted on either side of the stone.

When Les and Daralyn stepped back, Elaine put her bouquet in the larger middle container, kneeling to arrange and spread it out. "We love you, Robert," she murmured. "I know you're so proud of these wonderful children of ours."

Brick saw Rory swallow, a muscle flexing in Thomas's jaw as Marcus put a hand against his back. Les stood alone, facing her mother. Before Brick could close the distance between them, Elaine's gaze met hers. She turned toward the rest of the family.

"Les and I are going to walk a little bit. We'll meet you at the rotunda."

It was near the entrance to the cemetery, the wood structure surrounded by roses and containing a circle of benches beneath its roof.

After a brief acknowledgment, the others started to move away. Daralyn's hand rested on Rory's shoulder as he pushed the chair wheels. Thomas walked with his hands in his slacks pockets, Marcus's touch still on his back.

Brick noted Marcus gave Elaine a reassuring nod. Thomas was the undisputed male head of the family, but in times like this, Marcus would subtly take those reins, sending Elaine an unspoken message he would look out for her children.

When Marcus glanced toward Brick, it was a pure Dom-to-Dom communication. Brick tilted his head toward Les and Elaine. Though he'd give the women their space to walk and have a private conversation, he'd watch after them.

Satisfied, Marcus followed Rory, Thomas and Daralyn. Brick waited for Elaine and Les to get about twenty steps ahead of him, then followed, at a measured amble.

~

"I'm so sorry, Mom."

"You have nothing to apologize for." Elaine fished a wrapped candy out of her purse and handed it to Les, taking one for herself. It was

367

one of the Atkinson striped peanut butter bar candies they carried in bulk at the store. Her father had loved them. "Eat that. It will help."

As Les dutifully complied, Elaine waited until she'd swallowed to pose her next question. "How are you feeling today?"

They were moving along the path toward the west side of the cemetery. Les made passing note of the different inscriptions, the messages left for loved ones. She wondered what Raeni would put on Llanzo's.

You should be able to bleed to death from all the cuts...

"All right."

"I need honest answers, Les. Not empty reassurances."

Elaine was good at the motherly steel when she needed to make use of it. She'd shaped the same steel in Les, not only to use it in her own life, but to learn how to resist it from others when needed. Even when it came from the woman who'd taught it to her. But she did owe her mother the truth.

"It comes and goes. Sometimes better, sometimes not. When I feel better, I don't feel like I have the right to feel better."

"Hmm." Elaine bent to pull a weed from beside one of the stones for the Mullins family. A great-great grandfather, probably. Edie Mullins worked as a nurse for Dr. Spring.

"I know you're aware Thomas felt responsible for Rory's accident," Elaine said. "He felt if he hadn't gone back to New York that first time, after your father's death, it wouldn't have happened. He might be right, but that doesn't make him responsible, or make it his fault."

"No," Les agreed. "But though I get that Thomas probably wouldn't see it as different, my situation...it feels more direct."

Elaine pursed her lips. "What you may not know is Rory's feelings about his accident. Part of why he was so angry and difficult after he was hurt was guilt. He said 'the worst part was knowing I'd turned over the tractor that day. That I'd done that to my family.'" Elaine's face softened. "To me, his mother.'"

Shock gripped Les. She had known Thomas had felt guilty about Rory, as she had, for different reasons. But she'd never guessed...

"When you love and care for people, and you can't be everything you hoped for them, it's a very difficult thing to live with," Elaine said. "It can turn you away from the path you're meant to walk, obscure it.

368

For those couple years, as you know, Rory was on a bad path. So was Thomas. They both found their way."

She bent and tidied the flowers in another grave's container. "It looks like Sally Winstead has been here, visiting her grandmother. That's good."

She straightened. "Rory realized what he owed me, his family and himself, was to embrace the life he'd been given, to find joy, love and forgiveness for himself. Finding those three things doesn't always take us on the easiest path, but nothing happens as long as our hearts are closed to the truth that God is trying to tell us. About ourselves or our loved ones."

"I don't know if I can be a doctor." The words cut her throat like glass. Yet saying them out loud at last, there was a relief to it, even if nothing else eased.

Elaine gazed at her calmly. "Is that a terrible thing?"

"Maybe not if I'd made the decision before I did what I did. Maybe that's what you were telling me, when you suggested I should stay here and marry a lawyer. But all that time and money, and everyone who expected and depended on me—"

"Stop right there." Elaine guided Les to a bench and took a seat on it, pulling her down next to her. Her hand was firm and cool at once. Her modest wedding set, a single diamond on a gold band, winked in the morning light. She crossed her stockinged ankles and smoothed out the skirt of her peach-colored suit. Her silver crucifix was paired with a longer necklace, an open-faced gold heart threaded with a lily. An Easter gift from her father.

Elaine squeezed her hand. "Parents have dreams, Les. There's no sense denying that. I once dreamed of Thomas running our store. Marrying a girl here, having children that looked like him, grandchildren I could hold."

That had been during Elaine's internal combat over her chosen faith's position on homosexuality, a terrible, ugly battle that had left some painful memories on both sides. But here they were, Marcus escorting her to sunrise service, Thomas happy and married to the fierce, beautiful man who left no doubt he'd tear down the world for him.

Elaine paused, those memories creating shadows and light in her eyes. "It's one thing for parents to say all they really want is for their children to be happy. But when you confront the choices you make, the things you impose on them, knowingly or unknowingly, you realize it's not that simple. You can't keep your dreams from impacting them."

She touched Les's knee. "Certainly I thought of keeping you close, living the kind of life that brought me such joy. I saw how deeply you loved home, and I didn't recognize you could find happiness expressing that love in a different way. Or how proud I would feel, seeing how hard you worked to be your own person, and make your own dreams come true."

Les grimaced. "That sounds so self-serving."

Elaine chuckled, a tender sound. "Oh, my sweet baby. I've known you since that first moment of conception, when God put you inside me. I know your heart. Your dreams, your happiness, will always involve helping others, bringing ease to those in pain, no matter what that pain is."

At Les's troubled look, Elaine met her gaze. "And yes, being a doctor is only one of many ways you can accomplish that. But the one piece of advice I have for you is one you're smart enough to know already. Don't change course because you're afraid of failure. That path is life itself, and the first time you do that, it will become ever easier to do it, until you find you've denied yourself every dream you've ever had. Do you understand?"

"I do." Les brushed away the tears that kept randomly falling, and smiled through them as her mother fished out a tissue from her purse and gave it to her. She blotted her eyes. "I know I'm a control freak. I just wish there was some clear answer in my head right now, something that I could trust isn't from grief over Llanzo, or the anxiety over doing it again."

"It takes time for things to become clear. This only happened a few days ago."

"That's what everyone keeps telling me, especially Brick. I'm just trained to be in a headspace where I have to fix and solve every problem right now." A half smile crossed her face. "Like when we're asked questions in rounds. I need to have the answer, need to study enough the night before, so I don't get tripped up."

Elaine's lips curved. Her gaze moved past Les's shoulder. "He's a good man. Overprotective, but most of the good ones are. Yet I see him giving you the space you need at the right times, respecting your strengths, your need to figure things out for yourself. That's a quality a good man has, too. He's left the boy he was behind, but even in high school, he had an unexpected maturity."

Les had felt Brick's presence without turning to look. She'd known he wouldn't follow the others to the rotunda. He respected her mother, but he made his own decisions about Les's wellbeing, no matter what forces came to bear on that. Elaine was right. He was a man, not a boy.

A twinkle danced through her mother's gaze. "Being easy on the eyes doesn't hurt, either."

"*Mom*." But Les had to smile. "Like we don't have enough eye candy in this family with Thomas and Marcus. And yes, Rory is maybe hot, too. He was a pain in the butt too long for me to admit that anywhere he can hear it."

Elaine chuckled. "You two did rub one another the wrong way when you were younger. Thomas was old enough that you looked up to him and saw him more like you saw your father. You wanted to be involved in what Rory was doing, and he didn't want a little sister tagging after him. But when it was important, he looked after you."

"Yeah, in the 'I'm the only one allowed to torture her' kind of way." Les made a face.

"All my children were born with good looks." Elaine brushed a finger along Les's face. "But that's another good thing about having a man who loves you. He reminds you of your beauty, in the right ways."

Elaine sobered. "A life well lived, as who you are, as the kind of person you aspire to be, is what I want for you. For all of you." That bittersweet look returned. "Thomas taught me that. So did Marcus. Love is about souls, striving to find one another and give each other comfort in the many ups and downs of this life."

She nodded in Brick's direction. "And though you have places to go and things to do before you make any permanent decisions, I'd say he already sees your soul and appreciates everything it is. He's a good person to be at your side at this time of your life."

"He is." Les looked over her shoulder. Brick stood at one of the ponds scattered through the cemetery. A pair of ducks glided across it. His hands were in his slacks pockets, the gesture pulling the suit coat across his shoulders. His legs braced on the bank gave her a hint of the firm backside.

"I understand a doctor isn't a superhero." Her lips twitched. "But I think I might be the girlfriend of one."

Elaine covered Les's hand again. Les felt the touch of the wedding rings. "As formidable as he might be, he needs someone as strong as he is. With what he does for a living, and just the ups and downs of life itself, he'll have his rough days. If you decide you want to be that person, he'll be blessed."

The resolve in her mother's voice, the sincerity in the words, bolstered Les in immeasurable ways. She also remembered when she'd accompanied him to the Whitfield house. Though part of it had been her reluctance to be alone with her thoughts, an intuitive sense had told her he might appreciate the company, even if it was just having someone supportive sitting outside and waiting for him.

Like he had outside the M&M.

For both of them, their first dead child was not going to be their last. She wanted to be there to help him when he had those rough days. Help her superhero feel stronger and more capable of facing his daily challenges.

"I know my desire to be a doctor has to be a dream for me. But is it wrong that at least part of it is for you and Dad?"

"No. That fits with what I said about your big heart." Elaine brushed Les's hair over her shoulder, adjusting the neckline of the dress in a very motherly fashion. "But something isn't right. Your body is acting like it's a prisoner to the choices you're making."

Elaine's gaze slid toward her uneasy stomach, and up over Les's prominent collar bones. "That was what Thomas's stomach ulcers were. Nothing opens a mother's eyes to the dangers of forced expectations like seeing her child destroying his body."

"Mom..."

Elaine held up a hand. "I'm not changing what I said. I'm saying if you are meant to be a doctor, you need to understand what's causing that reaction. Perhaps the loss of this child brought those things more squarely into the light."

Why did you become a doctor?

Her mother's words, Brick's, Beulah's, Dr. Portland's... If she was brave enough, smart enough, to apply her mind to them, they might increase the power of that light, shine it on the tentative connections. Thin strands between ideas, answers, possibilities.

Les looked down at their clasped hands, her mother's wedding ring. "Was he proud of me? Did he think I could do good, strong, important things, like he thought Rory and Thomas could?"

"Les." Her mom's voice was surprised, and she touched Les's chin to lift her face. Les was at a loss to explain it further, but fortunately her mother understood. She was a woman, after all.

Resigned amusement crossed Elaine's features. "It's harder for men sometimes. Lord knows I had to fight Robert on certain things, teach him what I was capable of. I told him I didn't need him to treat me like a bouquet of flowers, but he could bring them to me anytime."

Les smiled tremulously. "He did. Wildflowers from alongside the road."

"Yes. The first time he did it, he told me they were his way of telling me he understood how strong I was, able to thrive wherever I landed. He also said it was his reminder to me, to let him treat me like a flower, delicate and beautiful, whenever I could give him that honor."

Elaine's eyes got a little misty, but when they focused back on Les, they showed her a truth as certain as what she'd said to her daughter about Brick being blessed to have Les in his life. "The answer to your question is yes. Your father knew you were as capable and full of potential as your brothers. He would have done everything to support your decision to be a doctor. Or whatever you decided to be."

Her chin firmed. "I can't tell you if you should be a doctor or not, Les. But I can tell you a doctor should have a heart like yours. So if you decide not to be one, don't let it be because of the words of a heartbroken mother. Let it be because of what your own heart tells you."

The words bounced off the pain, the doubts, the grief. But they added a touch of hope, a glimmer of light, she couldn't deny. Maybe it really wasn't about a different path. Maybe it was as simple as what her mother had just implied. It was about choosing a different approach to it. That was the opportunity that learning and experiencing life brought. Even if the learning and experiencing was so painful the answer was initially lost in seemingly unbearable pain.

Changing her approach might be simple, but it wouldn't be easy.

The way she'd gone about studying, succeeding, she'd built herself a fortress. To dismantle it, open herself to a different way, different forces...deeper vulnerabilities...

But that was what she'd done with Brick, wasn't it? And she'd discovered a place inside her from which she thought anything might be possible.

Except bringing a child back from the dead.

Les swallowed. "Mom... Will you pray with me?"

Elaine's gaze filled with undeniable love. She clasped both of Les's hands. "I will always pray with you, and for you. If you'd like, while you're here, we can go to church and light a candle for that baby, and his grieving family."

Les put her arms around her mother and hugged her tight.

"Oh, dear girl." Elaine hugged her back, and offered the words that were standard motherly gold. "It's going to be okay. You're going to figure it out, and it will be all right."

Brick had told her the same. Both of them believed in her. Now she just had to remember to believe in herself.

As they moved to rejoin the others, Brick caught up and offered an arm to both women. Les hid an amused chuckle as her mother gripped Brick's biceps and shot Les a bouncing eyebrow look at the size of the muscles under her hand. If Brick noticed, he admirably pretended not to do so.

When they reached the rotunda, she discovered a surplus of emotion she needed to expend toward one family member in particular. Since it was difficult to do a full body hug when someone was seated, she slid onto Rory's lap, giving him a fierce embrace.

It almost brought her to tears again when he responded with a "Hey, what's all this about, baby sis," and put his arms around her, holding her even more than she was holding him. His arms were strong and supportive, his chest solid and firm, the brush of his beard soft.

Okay, yeah. She grudgingly accepted it. Her other brother was hot, too.

"You okay?" he murmured.

"Yeah. I am. Thanks to all of you." She pushed herself back to her feet. As he helped her do it, he retained her hand. Though she expected he knew what her hug was about, he brought them back to familiar footing with a gentle tease. "Is Brick upsetting you? I'll kick his ass if you need me to. He's scared of me, you know."

"I'll keep that in mind." When she slanted a glance up at Brick, he offered a solemn nod.

"I hide my fear deep inside where no one can see it."

"Darn right he does." Rory grinned.

The family gathered in the rotunda, each couple taking one of the half-dozen benches arranged in the circle. They accommodated two adults comfortably, but Elaine shooed Thomas away, making him sit with Marcus. While they exchanged memories of a missed father and husband, she smoothed her hand over the empty spot next to her and mostly listened.

They were all keeping a close eye on her. As hard as this loss was for each of them, Elaine's was deeper, affecting every aspect of the life she led without her husband by her side. Les expected that Rory and Thomas, now having their own spouses, better understood how unimaginably difficult that loss could be.

Brick held Les's hand on his thigh. They weren't at that point, but maybe because of the intensity that came with the newness of their relationship, she could still appreciate the depths of that loss.

Eventually the subject went into easier emotional terrain, conversations about day-to-day things, the occasional smatter of their usual banter. Les even talked about medical school, normal things she would share. After her conversation with her mother, and in this serene place, she had some space to think about her studies, Beulah, and her interactions with interesting patients and hospital staff, separate from more volatile recent events.

But the thoughts still stirred uneasiness. Up until now, Llanzo and her own uncertain career future had held the top pennant in her mental loop playlist. She guessed she really was a perennial worrier, but sitting with her two brothers, seeing the people to whom they'd bound their lives, brought something else to mind.

She was a third-year medical student living two hours away from a busy arson investigator. If she went back to med school, she had over a year left to finish that, followed by residency. She still had no doubt she wanted to do that here, with Dr. Spring, but that would put her four and a half hours away from Brick. Then, when she got her license...

Fairhope had a volunteer fire department and no need for a full-time arson investigator.

She'd come to Brick in a moment of crisis. All those submissive longings had found their first expression with him. *I may only be your first Dom.*

How many people stayed with the person they found when they had that many variables to juggle? How did they reconcile wanting to be in two places four hours apart?

Stop it. What was meant to be would happen. She couldn't control or direct it. Like when Brick took over. Things always seemed to end up in a really good place when he did that. Maybe Fate would be just as kind.

Rory was sitting in his chair next to the bench Daralyn was on, which put him within arm's reach of where Les was sitting. At his touch on her arm, she leaned toward him. He pitched his voice low, presumably so he didn't interrupt the current conversation. Thomas was telling his mother about an upcoming art show in California. He and Marcus were encouraging Elaine to go with them, since she'd always wanted to see Monterey and ride along the Pacific Highway.

Rory glanced toward Brick, who was listening to Thomas and Elaine's discussion. "You know," he murmured, "It isn't a surprise to any of us that he became an arson cop. Takes patience, being real methodical and focused."

"I know." She gave him a quizzical look.

"When he wants something bad enough, he's willing to take his time and wait for it. Lot of things you might feel like you have to worry about, Les. That's one you don't. Not if you decide he's the one you want."

Her brother's sudden ability to read her body language was unsettling. But as her gaze slid to Daralyn, she realized it made sense. Daralyn's emotional state had been a minefield for a long time. Under stressors, it sometimes still was. The man who loved her had to stay a couple steps ahead.

Brick's patience wasn't new to her. Discovering that somewhere along the way Rory had found the patience and focus to be the same kind of man for Daralyn? That was proof that miracles existed.

She suppressed a smile. They all grew up. They all learned to wait for what they wanted.

Fate *could* be kind.

Since she'd lately been rocked off her axis by the things she couldn't control, that she thought she could, the words didn't completely settle her. But they helped.

Elaine wound up the California conversation with a promising "maybe," her expression intrigued. But when she glanced at her watch and rose, it was time to return to the house and Easter dinner.

She and Daralyn had wrapped the prepared dishes in foil so they could be re-warmed without much labor. Her mother had also had Les set the table last night with the white china, folding the lavender Easter napkins under gleaming silverware. Marcus had brought Elaine a bouquet of Easter lilies that would grace the center of the table. It would be flanked by a pair of white porcelain rabbits Elaine always brought out for the holiday. They'd belonged to her mother.

Traditions, rituals, patterns. Reassurances that, despite the crises, there were things you could count on. As Brick rose with her, his hand slid to her lower back, a steady pressure. She looked up at him.

No matter what happened, where their relationship went, she could always count on him to have her back if she needed it. Just like her family.

Brick gave her a searching look, so much like Rory's. She was pretty sure she was starting to recognize those "Dom signs." Marcus routinely gave them all that kind of look, though she'd never put it together the way she did now. Now that her "sub zone" had been activated.

Her lips twitched, even as she gave Brick a nod. She was okay. Maybe even a little better than okay.

$\sim$

After an Easter dinner with way too much food, Thomas and Rory gently bullied Elaine and Daralyn into going onto the porch to sit down and relax. The rest of them cleared the table, and handled the dishes. Iced tea was poured and brought out for anyone who wanted it. Dessert would come later, when they had a space for it.

Thomas and Marcus took a seat opposite one another on the steps, their legs stretched out, calves brushing. Rory was beside Daralyn, who sat in a wicker chair, while Elaine was in another one, separated by a small table holding the two women's tea. Rory had his glass sitting on the porch floor next to his chair.

Brick and Les were on the porch swing, Brick's long legs pushing it back and forth as Les folded her legs up beneath her and rested against his side.

There was some talking, but after the heavy meal and the early morning service, they were also content to sit quietly, feeling the touch of the breeze, smelling the scents of spring, watching the sun shine on the world around them. When Thomas caught their attention with a subtle gesture, they were quietly amused to note Marcus was dozing, his head settled against the railing by the porch steps. It was rare to see him that relaxed. From the tender way Thomas looked at his husband, Les suspected he liked those instances that told him Marcus felt comfortable in his surroundings, with Thomas and their family.

Occasionally they waved at neighbors passing in cars or on bicycles. One or two had stopped to chat for a moment before continuing onward.

Les thought about how she would view those familiar faces if she was working here as a doctor. Cue *Doc Hollywood*, the montage of Michael J. Fox's "Dr. Stone" treating his various patients' ailments, from delivering a baby to treating fishhook wounds. It reminded her so much of Fairhope.

"Will you go by to see Dr. Spring while you're here, Les?" Daralyn asked. "He was picking up some lawn seed this week and said he had a book you might want."

"Maybe. Probably."

Considering what she and her mother had talked about at the cemetery, she amended that in her head. Yes, she'd go see him. Maybe even talk to him about what had happened with Llanzo. He'd practiced medicine for thirty years. His perspective would help with her own.

Brick was sliding his fingertips up and down her upper arm. The pacing of it, the rhythm, caught her attention. A slow glide, a sensual intent. She tilted her head his way, and found his gaze on her. The rest of the family was currently in a discussion of...something.

"It's Easter," she whispered. "Don't look at me like that. We'll both go to hell."

"Doug, one of the guys in the Richmond house, has a tattoo of a skull wearing a fire helmet and clasping an axe. The words around it say, 'They won't let me come to Hell. I'll put the fire out.'"

He leaned in and spoke against her ear. "I don't want to put your fire out. I just want to fan the flames higher and hotter. You're beautiful and demure in your church clothes. Gives me all sorts of ideas."

"Hell." She informed him. "Straight to hell."

He grinned. Marcus roused as his phone started buzzing. After he glanced at it, he held up a hand at Elaine's censorious look. "Not work. It's John. Hey, John."

John was Marcus's brother, who lived in Iowa, on the same property as Marcus's widowed mother. Elaine's expression softened as Marcus rose to his feet. "I'll be back," he told her, as he added to his brother, "Let me take you into the house so I'm not interrupting the front porch conversations."

"Tell your mother happy Easter from all of us." Elaine gave his hand a pat as he passed by her. Then her shrewd gaze went to the porch swing. "Brick, how often do you get by to see your mother? I know your job keeps you busy."

Though the question seemed casual, Les noted a trace of reproof, a reminder of the holiday in her expression. As if she'd detected the tone of their exchange, the intimate body language. Rory tossed Brick a knowing humorous look that clearly said, *Busted.*

Les hid a grin, but Brick gave Elaine an easy smile. "The family has a standing lunch date, fourth Sunday of every month. My brother makes the drive down from DC with his family, and my sister in Wyoming videoconferences in."

He kept stroking Les's arm with that distracting rhythm, including the erogenous zone under her wrist. When she had to suppress the overwhelming desire to squirm, she promised herself she was going to kill him. Lent was over. It would be okay.

"Is Willow still not married?" Elaine asked.

"She's way too busy. They have her traveling all over the place for her job." He directed his next words to Thomas. "She's in California next month, not far from where your show will be. Tell Marcus she has a lot of rich, fancy friends with money to blow, and I'm sure he'll send her a personal invitation."

"With encouragement to bring them all," Thomas agreed.

"Does she still have a mean right hook?" Rory asked.

"Still." Brick's gray eyes twinkled. "If only we'd taken video of the day she put down Greta Child."

Elaine tsked, but Daralyn asked, "What happened?" She had her bare feet drawn up on the edge of her chair, her head resting on the top. Her long hair draped over Rory's hand on the arm. He was stroking strands between his work-roughened knuckles.

"Greta was always picking on other girls," Les told her. "One day she went after Brick's sister. Got all her equally worthless friends laughing at her. Which Willow ignored, until Greta tossed a full soda on her motorcycle. A little Indian she'd restored herself. Willow laid her out on the pavement with one punch. Greta never bothered her again."

"No one bothered her again," Rory added. "Even her prom date called her ma'am."

Though the others laughed, Les noticed Brick's attention had moved elsewhere. He'd twisted around in the swing, and was looking out over the side yard, to the fields and homes beyond it. Rising from the swing, he went to the railing and looked down the road in that direction.

A moment later, Les smelled what she expected had caught his attention. Smoke.

"You've gotten used to the city," Rory assured Brick. "A lot of people burn trash around here."

"On Easter Sunday?"

"Could have been left over from yesterday. Picked up when the wind shifted."

"Yeah, maybe. But it smells different."

When he lifted his hand to shade his eyes, squinting them to get more visual range, Les snagged the binoculars off the window ledge. Her mother kept them there for bird watching. She nudged him, drawing his attention.

"Thanks." His look said he appreciated her anticipating his needs, in that act of service way. She might be injecting "Domness" into everything he did, but she wasn't going to squelch the inclination.

Brick scanned the area. Then he stopped. "Where I'm looking. The wood two-story. Is that the old Landry place?"

"Yeah," Rory said.

Brick handed Les the binoculars and met her gaze. The certainty in his gray eyes spiked fear in her chest. "Call 911 and tell them there's black smoke coming out of a first-level window of the house, possibly white smoke on the second level. Tell them to dispatch all available volunteers."

CHAPTER TWENTY-FIVE

$\mathscr{A}$s calm as Brick sounded, Les noted he didn't waste any time leaving the porch and striding to his truck. Thomas was already up and moving with him. She had to break into a near run to catch them, the porch swing bumping against the railing as she bolted out of it. Elaine was dialing 911 to deliver Brick's message.

"What are you doing?" Brick asked as she climbed in the passenger side.

"Going with you," she said. "Alice Shelton lives there. Divorced mom with six kids, ages four to eleven. You may need someone with medical training."

"I'm a certified paramedic." But he'd already turned over the engine.

"Yes, but you can't be and do everything."

The truck bed rocked as Thomas climbed into it. Les opened the back window so Brick could speak to him. "Hold on."

"Tell Marcus," Thomas called out to Rory.

Rory gave him a thumbs up. Les caught the flash of frustration on his face, having to stay behind. However, proving what Brick had told her at the treehouse, it was only a flash. He was already pushing himself into the house to find Marcus, Daralyn opening the screen for him.

Once out of their driveway, Brick glanced in the rearview to confirm Thomas had heard his warning. Then he punched the gas. It told Les how concerned he was about that smoke.

"The fire's coming out an upper and lower window," he told her. "And they're not vertically aligned. It's already spread out from the origin point through a big chunk of the house. White smoke means it's not as involved upstairs yet, but it's going to get there. Visibility inside may already be for shit."

Please God, let nobody be home. Unfortunately, her prayer came too late. As Brick pulled up in front of the house, Les saw four children in the yard, two dogs anxiously milling around them.

As Brick had noted, smoke was coming out of two windows. Jagged glass marked the lower one with the black smoke, perhaps broken from the pressure of the heat. It looked like the upstairs one had been open. She thought she could see flame flickering behind one of the closed and unbroken ground level windows.

"The oldest is Gracie," Thomas told Brick as they exited the truck. "She's eleven."

Gracie was riding herd on the three she had clustered around her, even as she was yelling at the house. Les's blood went cold, not just at the desperation in her voice, but what she was screaming.

"Marty! Josie!"

She turned a frightened face toward them, and ran toward the truck. The two younger girls came right with her, like ducklings keeping close to the mother. She had a firm hold on an eight-year-old boy, who was digging in his heels. "Lemme go! We have to get Marty and Josie and Spud!"

"Hush, Kobe. My phone was inside," she told Thomas, the face most familiar to her. "Momma's at the Lumberton Walmart, doing a shift for the extra holiday money."

"Where'd the fire start, Gracie?" Brick asked.

Despite everything happening, she gave him a coherent answer, used to the responsibility of caring for younger siblings. "I don't know. I saw smoke coming out of what seemed like the living room, but when I went that way, it was burning my eyes. It was too thick going up the stairs, where the twins are." Her voice broke with that desperate thinness again. "I couldn't see, and it was so hot. Kobe was trying to go up with me and I thought..."

She shook her head. "I thought when I called them and they didn't respond, maybe they were already out, so I took everyone outside. Marty and Josie share a room."

"Spud," Kobe shouted. "Gracie, let me the fuck go."

"That's his guinea pig," she said, ignoring the profanity. "Kobe's room is next to theirs."

Brick glanced at his watch again, and Les saw him suppress a curse. He headed back to his truck with a determined stride that had her following. Her heart thudded in trepidation. Thomas stayed behind to help Gracie with Kobe and the girls.

"Carter's a good chief, but he's not as good as Smith was," Brick muttered to her. "The first engine should be on site within fifteen minutes, tops. God damn it."

It had been ten minutes. If a truck was close, they'd be hearing sirens. Brick flipped open the storage box in the bed, revealing the turnout gear.

"Fairhope has an automatic aid call to nearby departments for a structure fire," he told her as he pulled it on. "But they're farther out."

In little more than a minute, he was suited up, the air canister of the SCBA seated on his back, the harness for it tightened down. He checked the gauge and grasped the mask and helmet, turning to stride back toward the children.

"Brick."

Thomas had taken over holding Kobe and had settled him down, but the boy's body language was still mutinous. At the sight of a suited-up fireman, Kobe's angry expression eased a fraction.

Brick pointed to the broken window, drawing Gracie's attention. "That's the living room."

"Yes sir." Tears were in her voice. Brick put a hand on her shoulder.

"Tell me the layout."

In a matter of a few seconds, he'd had her detail what rooms were where, and the most likely places the twins would be on the second level. Then he turned to Les and Thomas.

"I'm going to do a quick perimeter check. If I have a good entry point, I'll try to find the kids and bring them out. Tell Chief Carter everything you've just heard. When he gets here."

The last words had a bite. Les suspected, like her, he hadn't stopped listening for the sirens. She grabbed the sleeve of the coat. "They're on their way. They should be here any minute."

"Those kids are out of time. I know what I'm doing, Les. Don't worry. It's a calculated risk."

"I'll go with you," Thomas said, but Brick shook his head.

"There's no way to determine cause right now. House is in bad shape, so it could be electrical or something else. No telling what chemicals are burning in there. I need you here with the kids and Les. Wait for the others and fill them in."

Les still had her hand on his arm. He met her gaze. "You stay here. As you said, we may need someone on site with medical training."

For the kids. Or him.

He gave her that stern Master's look that something in her had to obey. Unless a deeper, stronger fear ruled her, as it did right now.

"No. You're waiting. You have to wait with us."

"I have to go to work." He bent down, kissed her mouth once, hard, and pulled back. "It'll be all right."

He detached her hand, with strength but also a caressing touch. Then he was striding toward the house.

As he drew closer, obviously studying what was in front of him, he donned the SCBA mask, pulling the hood up and clamping his helmet over the top of it. He did something to check the workings of the canister, or maybe he was turning it on. Then he disappeared around the side of the house.

She balled her hands into fists, and fought what was screaming inside her head. He was damn good at this, she reminded herself.

Like plenty of firefighters who'd died doing it.

She shook that off. It served no purpose.

Instead, she turned her attention to the kids. Gracie had coughed a couple times during her recitation to Brick, and so had the other children. Les retrieved Brick's jump medical bag from his truck, and brought it back. Thomas had moved them across the street, under a big stand of pines. He was talking to Kobe, keeping him calmed down. As she checked Gracie out, she listened with half an ear.

"Why hasn't he come back out?" The boy asked plaintively. "Gracie, what's happening?"

"He'll do everything he can, Kobe," Thomas said, answering for his sister, since Les was examining her. Her oldest brother's brown eyes held the assurance Les remembered from when she was Kobe's age. Whenever anything scared her, Thomas could make her feel better about it.

"I want to be in there, too," Thomas told Kobe. "I hate being out here while they're in there. But the best thing you can do is look after your sisters."

The sincerity in his words, the frustrated gaze he kept flicking toward the house, reflected the emotions raging through Les. She checked Gracie's nostrils and had her open her mouth to see as much of the throat as she could with the flashlight and a tongue depressor. Some soot and inflammation, but not excessive.

She put the stethoscope to the girl's chest. "Take some deep breaths for me." Gracie's responses had been clear, no hesitation or disorientation when Brick asked her questions. So the signs of severe smoke inhalation were absent, though Les still wanted Dr. Spring to check her and the others out at the clinic. She did the same exam of the little girls and then Kobe.

"It's taking too long," Kobe said in a shaky voice. It was raspier than Gracie's. He'd probably been yelling when he tried to bolt up the stairs, and had inhaled more smoke. Les peered into his throat, listened to his chest.

She heard his words, registered his fear, but couldn't let it touch her, because if her mind turned in that direction, she would lose it. Fucking hell, where was he?

Thomas's hand landed on her shoulder, a hard, startling grip. "Siren," he told her.

She'd been so absorbed by her examination and Brick's absence, she'd missed it. But now she registered the wailing rise and fall. A long minute later, a black pick-up pulled in, the red lights flashing on the dash. Two men jumped out of it, already in most of their gear. One of them was the fire chief, Larry Carter.

The Fairhope engine truck pulled up thirty seconds later.

Thomas ran to Carter to give him Gracie and Brick's information. Despite Brick's criticism of their response time, she was relieved to see the men on the engine get right on things with practiced precision. Two lines were dropped off the vehicle and then it accelerated to the hydrant down the road, the hoses flaking out behind it. They were attached by two of the six men who jumped off the engine.

As they were doing that, Carter was circling the two-story house, probably doing the same perimeter check Brick had mentioned. He pedaled back, head tilting up as glass broke on the upper floor. A spout of flame jumped through. Now two of the upper windows were streaming black smoke.

Oh my God. Brick.

Carter barked something at two men who'd donned their SCBAs. They headed for the rear of the building, just as Brick had. Search and rescue.

Thomas jogged back to her. "They've got a couple more engines on their way from Laurel Hill, plus an ambulance en route." He hesitated, his expression grim. The little ones and Kobe were watching the fire, so he put a hand on Gracie, including her in what he told Les. "Carter said to get the kids in Brick's truck and get them out of here. Take them to the clinic."

Gracie's expression whitened. She was old enough to understand the implication. "No," she said, her face crumpling. Les put her hand on her back, Thomas's overlapping it.

"Hope isn't lost," he told her gently, "but we need to get you to the doctor and your mom."

The ambulance he'd mentioned was pulling in, positioning itself behind and clear of the fire truck. Les saw Doyle Williams and Stacie Warrick in the front. Doyle had been in the same grade as Brick and Rory, whereas Stacie was one of her former classmates.

Les turned to her brother. "The kids have mild smoke inhalation symptoms. Kobe's the worst, but they should be fine. Dr. Spring should do a more thorough check, though."

"Les, I'll stay—"

"No. Stacie and Doyle are EMTs, not paramedics. I can help them."

She hadn't been there when her dad had his heart attack. She hadn't been there when Rory got run over by the tractor. She was going to be here, damn it.

And Brick was going to be fine. Anything else was unacceptable.

She spoke to Thomas as she did to patients and their families, creating an oasis amid uncertainty and fear of the worst. "Help me by taking over this part. Chief Carter is right. If those kids are in bad shape"—or worse—"Kobe and his little sisters shouldn't see that."

Neither should Gracie. She'd aged a decade before their eyes. "Go with them, Gracie," Les told her. "Kobe and your sisters need you. We'll take care of Marty and Josie. Help my brother get them to the doctor. I'm sure someone is working on picking up your mom and bringing her home."

Gracie nodded numbly. Thomas gripped Les's shoulder, giving her a steady look. "He's going to be okay."

"He damn well better be."

She saw a trace of his serious smile. "Do you need anything else from Brick's truck?"

"No, we should be okay, now that the ambulance is here."

As her brother and Gracie shepherded the kids into Brick's truck, the EMTs had unloaded the gurney, carrying a jump kit and other things they might need. When Doyle stepped over to speak to Thomas, her brother gestured in Les's direction, likely relaying what she'd done for the kids. Stacie knew Les was in medical school.

As Thomas pulled out with the children, a Laurel Hill fire engine arrived, the sheriff and a deputy not far behind. All hands on deck.

Carter had been back on his radio, but now he shouted and gestured to the driver of the Fairhope truck. "Mayday, *Mayday*."

Les jumped as the engine's air horn blasted, loud enough to make her cover her ears. She swallowed a scream when a portion of the roof collapsed, sagging into the front porch. A more intense wave of heat rolled over her, backing her up a couple steps.

Brick. He's alive. He's fine. It's okay.

How can he be okay?

The firefighters had leaped back at the sound of the airhorn. Showers of sparks billowed and twisted, high into the sky. The firefighters with the charged lines adjusted. One hose was aimed at the upper level while another set of firemen used theirs on the first floor. They stood on the walkway in front of the porch. Still no sign of the search and rescue firefighters.

Les gripped the cross and badge around her neck as Doyle and Stacie came to stand with her, bringing the gurney with them.

"Brick's in there," Les said. "I love him."

Stacie shifted a little closer, arm brushing Les's. "The Laurel Hill guys are setting up the rehab area," Doyle said. "We should head over there."

He was right. Even before the roof collapse, she'd been able to feel the fire's heat all the way to the stand of pines. The men with the hoses must feel like they were roasting.

She shut down the unimaginable things in her head and focused on the things she could do. She could help monitor the firefighters, check vitals, watch for signs of heat exhaustion or eye irritation. There'd be a case of water available on the ambulance to help with those things.

As they started in that direction, she noticed Carter and the sheriff were talking, Carter speaking into his radio. Maybe to the two firefighters who'd disappeared around back. Brick had no radio.

I told my mother you are a bloody fucking superhero. You better come out of that fire.

Yet Carter's tense expression, the grimness around his mouth as he spoke tersely into the radio, told her things weren't good. How could anyone see through all the smoke in the house? The upper level smoke was now mostly black, too. An ache was tightening around her chest, shards of metal in her belly, her thighs numb. This was worse than anything she'd ever felt. Even the night she lost Llanzo.

This can't happen. It can't. Please.

They were halfway across the yard when the chief spun toward them. He made a hand gesture, a rotating motion followed by an emphatic stab of his finger toward the house. "They need you in the back," he shouted.

Les bolted into motion, Stacie and Doyle with her, rolling the gurney over the sparse grass. They moved fast, but though Stacie had been a high school track star, Les still beat her to their destination.

Her heart did a triple gainer when she saw three firefighters, all of them still on their feet, including one particularly tall and broad one. Her gaze latched onto him like a dart hitting a center target.

Brick carried one child, a Fairhope firefighter carrying the other. They laid their precious cargo on the ground as she and Stacie reached them.

Brick was smeared with ash and soot. The residual heat of the inferno the house had become was coming off his gear. But he was alive and seemingly unhurt, so her training snapped toward the most critical patients.

The firefighters, Brick included, moved back as she, Doyle and Stacie evaluated the children. They worked together, handing equipment back and forth.

Neither child was breathing.

Josie was in the worst shape, extensive burns on her back torso and limbs, most of her clothing gone. First step was establishing the airway. While Doyle handled that with Marty, Stacie did it for Josie. Les determined the scope of burn damage.

Rule of nines had to be adjusted for a child, and Les made those calculations quickly in her head. She did it twice to be sure. The third-degree burns were too extensive, and Stacie was having no success with an airway or getting any vital signs. She touched Stacie's hand.

The EMT sat back on her heels and nodded, doing a quick knuckling of her red-rimmed eyes. "The airway is entirely occluded," she said.

Marty's burn coverage was far less, but they still needed a stable airway. "Do you have the equipment to intubate?" Les asked. She was relieved to see Doyle nod.

"We're an ALS unit, and I have the certification, but I've never done it on a kid. I have the right sized tube for it, though."

"I've done it," Les said.

He handed the tube to her. Stacie held Marty's head and neck steady as Les positioned the laryngoscope. Fucking hell, the inflammation was already bad. Really bad.

She felt a hand on her back and recognized it as Brick's, because of the calming strength in it. She took a deep breath, closed her eyes. Shut it all out. The sounds of fire, firefighters, the doubts in her mind, the worries, all of it. She thought of the section in the book, the way she'd practiced it on the rubber simulation mannequin, both adult and child. And on Rick, her cadaver.

Her Pediatrics resident had let her do it once, and Dr. Jack had her do it several times in the ER, once to a six-year-old. Always under supervision. But Marty needed an airway, or he wouldn't make it, not even to the clinic. She opened her eyes, used the light that the scope provided, and found the clearance. She guided the tube in, feeling her way to avoid getting into a lung. Inflated the tube and pulled out the guide. She already had her other hand out for the stethoscope. Someone put it there.

Doyle was there to attach the bag. As he squeezed it, they watched the chest as Les listened. To both lungs for the sounds of air flow, and the stomach for an absence of sounds, so she'd know it wasn't inserted too far.

Both were as they should be.

"All right," Les said. Stacie put sterile dressings on Marty's burns while Doyle drew the gurney closer. He and Stacie lifted the boy onto it as Les stood up. Brick's supporting hand was under her elbow.

"Thanks, Les." Stacie wiped her face with a slightly shaky hand. "Tough with kids."

"Yeah. It is."

Doyle had stepped away to speak on his radio, and now returned to them. "Dr. Spring said to head for the county hospital. He'll meet us at the highway turnoff and ride with us."

"Okay. Do a saline IV—"

"To get him fluids on the ride. Got it." Stacie flashed Les a grim smile, but it faded as her gaze went to Josie.

"I asked Dr. Spring to pronounce her over the radio." Doyle touched her arm. "I told him Les was here. They're sending a transport to take her to the county morgue."

"We'll watch over her," Les told her. Doyle was holding the folded-up body bag, and she took it from him. "Marty's your priority now."

"Okay. Dr. Spring has the other kids with him." Doyle called that out to her as they started to move away, the gurney bumping over the uneven ground. "Marcus and Thomas are riding with them. They'll take over driving the kids once Dr. Spring gets in the ambulance with us. Alice's manager at Walmart is bringing her to the hospital."

"Oh, shit. Almost forgot." Brick removed a plastic tennis ball can from beneath his bulky coat. A brown and white ball of fur inside it came alive with frantic, shifting eyes. As he moved to catch up with Doyle and Stacie, Brick took out a pocketknife and made a couple notches in the rubber lid, allowing air. He handed Doyle the can.

"This is Spud," Brick said over a cough. "Kobe's pet. You might drape something over him to keep him calm. That way he's less likely to chew holes in that rubber lid before they find him a cage. It wouldn't be a bad idea for a vet to check him out, but their systems are so fragile, he'd be dead already if the smoke had gotten a good hold on him."

Though nobody felt like smiling, Doyle managed to inject a wry note into his voice. "You haven't changed, Brick."

"Got lucky. Kobe's room was at the top of the stairs and the cage was right by the door. Found him when I was feeling my way along the walls to keep myself oriented."

The EMTs resumed their swift course toward the ambulance, the tennis ball can tucked under a strap on the gurney. Les turned toward the house. The sky was still lit up by fire, but even with her untrained eyes, Les could tell Carter and his crew were getting it contained. The flames weren't as high, and the smoke was more gray than black.

The heat and her exertions had drenched her with sweat, her clothes sticking to her, but she hadn't noticed until now. Only the need to stabilize Marty, give him an airway, had mattered.

When she looked to see where Brick was, she saw he now stood over Josie. Stripping off his coat, he knelt to cover her. The coat concealed everything but her feet.

She clutched the body bag. They should put her in it. They would put her in it, but for right now...Brick's coat over her felt more right.

Though emotions choked her, when Brick put his fist to his mouth and coughed again, another priority took over. Les brought the jump kit, determined to do the same check on him she'd done for Gracie and the kids.

He held up a hand, seeing her intent. "I was wearing the SCBA. I'm just reacting to the smoke in the yard."

"Whatever. Let me listen and look."

Whether he was humoring her, or he realized she wasn't going to be dissuaded, for once he dutifully followed *her* direction. Yet when she was done, he picked up the end of the stethoscope, as if speaking into a microphone, a trace of grim humor in his gray eyes. "I'm good, doc. The heat was intense. Even with the gear, it can be a little much."

He looked at the covered small figure. "She was lying over her brother, both of them behind the bed. His arm and leg were sticking out, but she protected his most vital parts. The mattress had already caught fire. The smoke was too thick to see anything. I found them by touch. My guess is they got disoriented and overwhelmed by the smoke, so they couldn't find the window. Barry got there in time to help me carry them out."

His gaze moved past her, and she turned to see Chief Carter

approaching them. His brittle gaze touched the covered body, then shifted to Brick. "Fucking hell," he said. Then, "Glad you were on scene fast as you were. Hell of a thing you did, going in there alone without a spotter."

"Gracie gave me a pretty good layout and I stuck to the walls. Just like we're trained." Brick met his gaze. "But if it'd turned out differently, I could have been a case study for what breaking the two-in, two-out rule gets you."

Carter grunted. "Sometimes you have to make a call, and you've always had good instincts. They saved a life today. Actually, two. Gus said you got the guinea pig."

Les didn't hear any derision in the chief's comment. Facing the loss of one sibling and a long and painful recovery for the other, it would mean something to Kobe that his beloved pet was back in his care.

Taking care of someone during grief helped deflect, delay and portion it out. She'd learned that, throwing herself into her studies after her father and Rory. She hadn't been able to be home, helping her mother and Thomas anywhere near as much as she'd desired, so it had left her alone with those terrible losses.

"We could use help with the overhaul if you still want to pitch in," Carter added to Brick. "And you can help me with the report. If the pint-sized doc says it's okay."

"Not a doctor yet. Just a med student." That forced attempt at lightness wasn't what she wanted to say. She wanted to say *no*, it decidedly wasn't okay, that she wanted Brick checked out at the clinic, too. But he knew enough about this stuff to know if he was in any trouble. And he was sleeping with a med student who could keep a close eye on him when the day was done.

"A med student we were glad to have here." Carter glanced at Brick.

"Yeah, I'll be there in a minute."

As Carter retreated, Brick pointed toward the road. Les noted Rory's van pulling up, staying clear of the emergency vehicles. For the first time, she realized at least a dozen trucks and cars were pulled off on the sides of the road beyond the first responder vehicles. Community members responding to the emergency, not to gawk, but to see if there was anything they could do.

Rory was driving, Daralyn next to him and Elaine in the back. Daralyn's hand went to her mouth as she noticed the covered body. Elaine put a hand on her shoulder.

By sundown tonight, a community plan would be in place, rallying around Alice, helping her with a place to stay, food, essentials, babysitting, whatever was needed. Everyone pitching in, according to their resources...or skills.

"So, doc, am I good to go?" Brick touched her hand. He'd removed his gloves when he took off his helmet and mask, so she was able to lace her fingers with his. When she did, she gripped hard and met his gaze.

Before answering, she dug out her phone with her free hand and hit the programmed number she wanted. "Edie? This is Les Wilder. I know Dr. Spring is going to the hospital. I'm going to have my brother drop me off at the clinic after the transport picks up Josie. I can help you however you need until he gets back, if you want. Okay. I'll be there soon."

She disconnected and met Brick's gaze. "Looks like we both have to get back to work."

I'm studying to be a doctor. I want to be a doctor.

It may have started as a way to feel less helpless about her family and her life. It might have been to thank her parents for paying all those hospital bills. But somewhere along the way, it had become real and true. The compass that pointed her toward what she wanted. Who she was.

And who she wanted to be with. A man whose present and future was directed toward helping others, in a way complementary to her own. Never mind the logistics of them doing it in different places, and being at points in that journey that might not align right away. That was a problem to think about later. What mattered was seeing that shared future, understanding the possibilities of it.

Brick put his hand on her neck, thumb along her jaw. "I love you."

"I love you." When he looked toward the body again, Les gripped his forearm.

"It's okay. I meant it. I'll be right here until they come for her. Alice will know she was never alone."

His gaze touched the body bag she held. "I'll help you get her squared away. Before I need my coat back."

"Okay." Then she flung herself at him, held him tight. "Don't you ever do that to me again, or I swear to God, I'll kill you in your sleep."

He held her off her feet, his breath a rasp against her ear. He smelled of smoke, but also like the heated male she loved. "Threatening your Master. That definitely goes on the list."

"It better."

CHAPTER TWENTY-SIX

*O*n Monday, Les called Dr. Portland and told her she would return on Thursday. She'd decided to take an extra day to help Dr. Spring in his practice before heading back to Durham early on Wednesday. She didn't doubt the decision she'd made at the fire. However, dealing with wellness checks and assisting Dr. Spring helped her find her footing again. So did talking to him about the ups and downs he'd had throughout his own journey as a doctor.

Brick spent time at the firehouse. He'd offered to share some of the training he'd had in Richmond to help improve Fairhope's response time. Carter proved he wanted to be a better chief by welcoming the help, rather than drawing territorial lines. All of them felt the loss of Josie.

On Tuesday morning, Les received the write-up of the M&M. It was agreed that Dr. Jack perhaps should have put eyes on the child to verify Les's exam, but they all knew how busy the hospital was. "The medical student in question has good instincts," Les had read, with mixed feelings. "We could not positively conclude that either the resident or attending would have arrived at a different diagnosis. The symptoms presented did not obviously call for the more in-depth diagnostics that might or might not have flagged the patient's vulnerability to the myocarditis."

She would continue to grieve Llanzo. Time wouldn't make her forget, but she would use the experience to give her patients better care. It was all she could do. It was what she *should* do. Most importantly, it was what she *wanted* to do.

Rufus, her mother, Brick, Dr. Portland, Dr. Spring, Beulah...they'd all brought her to the decision. And like her mother had suggested, Les had let her heart tell her it was the right one.

At last Wednesday came. Marcus and Thomas had headed back to New York on Monday. Last night, when Rory and Daralyn came for dinner, Les hugged them good-bye. They'd have gotten up early this morning to have the store open by seven a.m.

So it was just her, Elaine and Brick, standing in the driveway by Brick's truck. Heading back to school had always gripped Les with a bitter homesickness, a reaction that had become far worse on her last few visits. But today was different, more in balance. She looked forward to getting back to her studies and clinical challenges, while equally looking forward to the next time she'd be here.

This was her home, and nothing would change that. She would be back. Again and again, until it was time to stay and be what she wanted to be—a contributing member of the community she loved.

That would be true whether she was a grocery clerk or dog groomer. Or a housewife and active retiree like her mother. But her plan was to be a doctor.

She gave her mother a long hug before drawing back. "I'm all right. Thank you."

"I know you are. I love you," Elaine responded. "Eat something, and reach out if you need to talk."

Then Elaine hugged Brick. Though she was as dwarfed by his size as Les, her grip on his shoulders was strong. When he straightened, she gave him a pointed look. "Take care of my girl."

"You know I will."

He squeezed her hands, and helped Les into the truck. As they pulled out, Les turned and waved to her mother until she was out of sight, then drew a breath.

Brick glanced at her. "Okay?"

"Yeah. Yes. I think I am."

Their clasped hands rested on his thigh. With home receding in the mirror, and feeling the shift of his leg beneath her touch, her mind was drawn to something else important. Possibly even urgent.

Since the treehouse, they hadn't had time to be together...like that.

She'd thought about it plenty, lying in her bed at night. Or sitting next to him at the kitchen table, hips brushing. Talking to her mother in the evening, while watching TV with her and Brick.

Every exchanged look, even the most casual touch of his hand, had her thinking about him. Wanting him.

Fully, solidly, head over heels in love. He wasn't the only one. But there was also a good bit of lust involved in that, especially when a woman's heart was held by a sexual Dominant who could arouse her with no more than a look.

She put her scheduling abilities to work, juggling the variables. If they reached her condo by early afternoon, that would give her a certain amount of time to settle in, field Beulah's questions, prepare herself for rounds tomorrow...

Maybe Brick could stay for the night? No, he'd said he had to be at work tomorrow morning.

She suppressed a sigh. The reassurance Rory had given her at the cemetery had helped, but now it would be tested by reality. She was returning to school, to a grueling study and rotation schedule. Brick would head back to his equally busy job, that stack of cases.

The distance was more unsettling to her now that she knew he might be in active fires to provide firefighters direction on arson investigation. Or maybe he'd face another Colin, lying in wait for him at an investigation site. Or question a witness who wasn't a witness at all, but a suspect who freaked out and...

He'd told Rory the Colin event was a lightning strike kind of thing, but she wasn't buying it. There was a reason Rufus had called them fire "cops," no matter how teasingly, and a reason that Brick had a weapon. Even cops would point out that yes, a great deal of their job was tedium and routine...until it wasn't.

For so long, her feelings for him had been nebulous, based in fantasy. She had to be a grown-up, not act like she would fall apart if she couldn't be with him every moment, like the besotted teenager she'd been.

Even if that was exactly how she felt.

She was a besotted woman, a submissive who craved her Master's touch, his presence, not once every few weeks, but every day. Every moment.

So how would that go over, becoming the clingy girlfriend who wanted him to come see her every weekend? She knew how rarely she'd be able to make that drive and stay on top of her studies.

No matter her wailing and protesting female heart, the relationship needed the freedom to grow. Like wine. It needed to breathe, and be consumed in the appropriate manner and time.

"Um...when you go back, when I go back, I know things are going to get crazy again. I don't want you to feel like you owe me...all the things two people in a committed relationship would. I mean, we're not engaged or anything. I came to you during a bad time, and you were great. But—"

He pulled the truck over onto the side of the highway, cut the engine and turned to look at her. The abrupt act and his expression stopped the words like a hose bent in the middle. He lifted a brow.

"You done?"

Her hackles rose. "Done with what?"

"Worrying. I swear to God, you could squeeze an ounce of worry out of a granite rock."

"I'm just trying to—"

He lifted a finger. When he spoke, his voice was calm. Too calm. "So what are you trying to tell me? While I'm waiting for you to finish school, we go back to the way it was? I keep doing sessions with women like Tish?"

"No," she said, stung. "I mean, well if I can't be available as much as you...I know people like Lisa and Tish need your...skills."

He cocked a brow at her.

"No." She crossed her arms over her chest, which was getting tight. "I don't want that. I'm trying to say..."

"You're trying to manage us like your class schedules or exam studies, because you have to manage things to the nth degree. Maybe that works for that, but not for us."

He held her glare with an implacable look of his own. "We haven't had a lot of time together, Les. Not nearly enough for you to understand how our relationship will work. Only time can do that, and you have to be willing to let time tick without you trying to control it. You said you want to be my submissive. Is that still true? Yes or no."

She stared at him. "So how exactly *does* this relationship work?"

A muscle flexed in his jaw. "I asked you a question. Do you want me, Les?"

"Yes."

"Do you want me to be your Sir? Your Dom. Your Master."

She'd said it during their sessions, but never like this, when her head was clouded with more anger and frustration than arousal. Slightly more. Maybe as much arousal as frustration. But the answer was the same. "Yes."

"Do you know how that will work with the two of us juggling our lives like a circus act?"

"No. Damn it."

"No." His lips curved, though his eyes remained piercing. "So this is how we're going to do it. You're going to be honest with me, about whatever you need from this relationship, and I'm going to be honest right back. And then you're going to let *me* worry about how to solve the roadblocks."

She wasn't sure she'd heard him correctly at first, but he confirmed it. "I'm in charge, Les. That's what's involved in being a Dom. Giving you what you need, caring for you. Hearing what you have to say, responding to that. I'll ask for your input, encourage it, but the only thing that rests in your hands is whether you want me or not. Long as the answer is yes, I'll take care of the rest. When there are things you need to do to help with that, you'll get that direction from me. You have plenty in your life to take care of right now. That won't be one of them."

"So you're saying..."

"I'm saying we belong to each other. We're in a relationship, both as a man and woman, and as a Dom and sub. Which means I won't be doing any sessions with another sub, unless it's a demo thing for Mick or someone that I've told you about first, and made sure you're okay with. I won't be seeking sexual satisfaction, in session or out, with anyone but you."

His teeth bared in what no one would ever safely call a smile. "And every man at your school better be equally aware that you are fully, thoroughly taken."

A flock of birds took off in her chest. "How about women?"

He reached out to grip her behind the neck, bringing her to him like he had that day when he'd showed up at her school. The hard kiss was dizzying. Her hands landed on his chest to grip and steady herself, but he had different ideas.

"Wrong time to be a smartass, doc. Put your hands down to your sides. Keep them out of my way."

Oh, hell. All that arousal swirling around with no outlet for the past few days caught fire. It spread through her thighs and sex as he put his hand on her shoulder. His thumb slid under her bra strap beneath her T-shirt in that erotic gesture he liked to do, but he didn't stop there. She gasped as he pushed his hand into the cup to cradle her breast, caressing her nipple and the flesh around it.

It didn't matter that they were in his truck on the side of the highway. What he wanted was what mattered. As she strained against him, she wanted to prove she'd heard his words, as well as what he was saying to her without them.

"I need you inside me. I can't let you go back to Richmond without that. Please. Sir."

"Good. Because I'm not going back to Richmond without fucking you so deep you'll feel branded."

He bit her throat. As he suckled on her flesh, she leaned into his touch, his hand squeezing and kneading her breast as she whimpered, a crazed plea. When he released her a long moment later, he adjusted and smoothed her neckline with deliberate care, but his gray eyes looked savage. It told her he'd felt the lack of physical intimacy between them as keenly as she had.

It was reassuring. All of it was, enough that she managed to put together a couple brain cells. "May I…"

She'd lifted her hands, needing to touch him again. At his nod, she put her hands on his face. "I will figure out how to accept everything you just said. And try not to micromanage. But I have a really important condition."

He lifted a brow, waiting, his hand resting against her hip. "You have to let me take care of you, too," she said. "I get that Rufus or your co-workers are there for you about work-related stuff, the same way I have Beulah on the medical things. But if you have a really bad day, I want to be the person you call. If I'm insanely busy with exams or whatever, it doesn't matter. I don't want you to spare me."

She curled her fingers against his jaw. "I want to be your person, the way Daralyn and Rory are for each other, and Thomas and

Marcus. The way my mother and father were for each other. If we lost each other, I want it to hurt every bit as badly, because we've done everything they have to become part of each other's hearts, minds and souls. Every honest moment, every stumble and mistake, all of it. We share it together."

He nodded slowly, then touched the badge and cross on her neck. "With one condition of my own."

"What's that?"

Those gray eyes were like the Easter sunrise sky, hints of gold light in the gray. "I want you to belong to me in every conceivable way, doc. I intend to marry you. The day you graduate, I'm bringing you a ring. We get married when you start your residency in Fairhope. Doesn't matter if we're living in the same place yet, that's what's going to happen. Deal?"

How did he know the right question to ask, the right demand to make, to put all her fears to rest? With Brick, it would be okay if they had to be apart until they figured it out. If they belonged to one another, that was all that mattered.

She was trying to speak, which made those gray eyes get fiercer, as if he thought she'd need more convincing. But then she managed a half laugh and wrapped her arms around his back, pressing her face into his neck.

"Yes, yes, yes."

He put a tender kiss on her mouth. "There will be a better proposal when I bring you that ring. But you're a planner. I figured it's good to give you some heads up."

"You're one of the few people whose surprises I like."

"Well that's good. Because I've got another one for you. We're going to make a stop outside Charlotte. At Julie's theater."

"Really? I'd love to see her." She really would, though a guilty part of her calculated how much that would subtract from the thorough-ness of that "branding" once they reached Durham. "Are we having lunch with her and Des?"

"No."

She studied him. "There's something going on."

"Yep." With an enigmatic look, he started the truck again and pulled back onto the highway. He kept his eyes on the road, but laid his hand on the console palm up. A deliberate switch from reaching for her hand, it was a silent requirement that she lay hers in his grip. When she did, his strong fingers closed over hers, sliding along her wrist, teasing her vibrating nerve endings.

"You're just going to have to be patient and wait for it. Because that's what I say you have to do."

As she made a face at him, her phone buzzed. Though everything seemed to have been resolved, she couldn't help the kick of nerves as she saw it was her advisor. She put it to her ear as Brick glanced her way. When she spoke, his hand tightened on hers.

"Hey, Dr. Portland."

"Hello, Les. I'm looking forward to seeing you tomorrow. It is still tomorrow, correct?"

"Yes, we're actually on the way back to Durham now. Is everything okay?"

"Yes." The fist around her stomach loosened at the genuine assurance in Dr. Portland's voice. "I just finished speaking to Martin Sully. The family is asking for any bills related to Llanzo's care be waived, and the hospital to pay the legal costs they've accumulated so far. They've also asked for a sit-down with the ER department head and Dr. Redmond, to talk about what happened, to understand it in an official, off-the-record discussion. That's all they want. If those conditions are met, they're dropping the suit."

"Wow. That's...I'm glad to hear it." Especially that Dr. Jack and Dr. Redmond wouldn't be pulled into a lawsuit.

"Yes. It's a good thing." Dr. Portland paused. "Les, Martin Sully is here with me, and we want to ask you a question. I can assure you this is off the record as well. Did you meet with Mrs. DaCosta?"

Les glanced at Brick. His expression told her he'd support whichever way she went on it, but that he had no doubt what she'd do. She couldn't lie.

"Yes, I did. It wasn't that I didn't care about the hospital, or Dr. Jack and Dr. Redmond. I felt..."

"It's all right. I'm putting you on speaker."

The next voice she heard was Martin Sully's. The man really did have a compelling courtroom voice. She expected if he ever left law, he could read audiobooks. Or become a phone sex worker.

"Hello, Miss Wilder. First, I'll confirm what Dr. Portland said. This is off the record, but given how many cases like these I handle, I was curious. For a long time, the standard operating procedure was to avoid any statements that could be construed as guilt. Including an apology."

"How can we not say we're sorry? It's not about guilt. It's about being a decent human being."

"Out of the mouth of babes." Les assumed Martin had made the wry comment to Dr. Portland, but before she could be offended by the dig at her youth, he continued. "The newer line of thought, though it hasn't completely overcome the other, is there's a fine line between guilt that points to liability, and true remorse. The kind that demonstrates the vital human factor, the weight that doctors and all medical personnel carry in practicing medicine."

That wry tone deepened. "Essentially, what you just said. Expressions of true remorse toward the grieving family sometimes keep these situations from becoming lawsuits, costing the hospital money better spent on patient care."

Les digested that. "So I'm not in trouble for going against what you told me to do?"

"I recommended not doing it. It's not my job to tell you what to do."

"You followed your heart, Les," Dr. Portland said. "While it's my opinion that choice can't always take the lead in practicing medicine, the conscience often follows a different protocol. Do you have any other questions for us?"

"No, ma'am. Thank you. See you tomorrow."

"Look forward to it."

As she pocketed the phone, Brick still had a tight grip on her hand. "He's right, you know."

"On what part?"

"That it's not his job to tell you what to do. That's mine."

"Hmm. Just remember that lesson about assholes versus Doms. I'm sure I can find a beer to pour on your head."

He grinned. "I usually keep a 12-pack of Yuengling in the fridge. Just in case you need one."

She gave his steel biceps a very ineffectual punch, but left her other hand in his. He'd pointed out she had a tendency to try to control things that didn't need her to do that. She had a Dom determined not to let her stress herself out that way. It was part of what she needed. She might not always want him to know it, but on certain things, she was very willing for him to tell her what to do.

She also had a feeling he was about to remind her what kind of reward she could expect for her obedience. And her submission.

~

"Les!"

When they pulled up to the community theater, located on a county property on the outskirts of Matthews and Charlotte, Julie was in the parking lot with Des. They were loading furniture and other stage props into his battered old Ford truck. Hayes Roofing was lettered on the side in faded red and white script.

Julie set down the large white head of a bunny costume—Les didn't want to know how that might have been used in an erotic performance—and bounced over to Brick's vehicle. Her brown eyes shone with delight. A curvaceous brunette in dusty jeans, she wore a form-fitting hot pink T-shirt that had *Yes, I am The Theater Manager* printed over a harried female stick figure, juggling half a dozen theater masks.

"Oh, God, how I hated to miss Easter with you and your family." Julie pressed an enthusiastic kiss to Les's cheek and hugged her tight to her ample bosom. "If you can believe it, in addition to the show itself, my mother and father staged an out-of-the-blue visit. And with them, 'staged' is the operative word." Her voice held resigned fondness.

"You could have brought them. Between the three family houses, we had more than enough guest rooms."

"Oh, hell no. I'd never inflict my parents upon the Wilder clan, especially on a holiday."

Julie had helped introduce Les to her "fun girl" side, as well as joined the Wilder family's efforts to bring Daralyn out of her shell. There was simply no way not to feel better about anything around Julie.

That said, until recently, the theater manager had put a brave face on being single at forty. For a woman who embraced being single, that would have been fine. But Les knew Julie's dramatic personality came with a deeply romantic side.

She'd be the first to admit she didn't have the patience for the maxim "Good things come to those who wait." As such, Les had often heard her say to Des, "Where the hell have you been all this time?"

Which he usually answered with his trademark smile and crooked an arm around her neck to pull her to him. He'd kiss her pursed lips, calming her frenetic vigor with a simple stroke of his hand down her back.

Yes, the Dom vibes were there. Just like with Rory and Marcus, it was in his expression, even in how he hugged Les and shook Brick's hand. Like a private club she hadn't known existed.

Now she was a member of it.

As they exchanged greetings and the expected small talk, she thought of her parting chat with Thomas on Monday. As he'd given her a good-bye hug, he'd glanced toward Brick, who'd stepped away to give them privacy.

"You and Brick are going down a road together that might feel really familiar, but the elements of it are new. If you want to talk to someone about that, I hope..."

He paused, giving her a droll look. "I expect talking to me wouldn't be too comfortable, but you can talk to Julie. She's connected to the more formal aspects of that world. With Daralyn and Rory, it's more private, just between the two of them, but she can be another source. It's in her soul, a lot like it is in yours."

Thomas squeezed her shoulder. "And yes, I'm here, if ever I'm useful for those conversations. It's helpful to have others to talk to. For that, as well as anything else important."

His look held hers a beat, telling her that went beyond the Dom and sub stuff.

She gripped his hand. "You know, when Brick told me, at first, I thought, no way. But that was because I wasn't diving into my own head, thinking about how I react to Brick. What I needed and why. Then it made perfect sense, you and Marcus having that."

It might have a different look and perspective for a gay man, but it was as Brick had said at Mick's party. That undercurrent was recognized by all of them.

A brief mix of emotions crossed Thomas's face, but he didn't seem discomfited by her observation. "Marcus told me there's no formula for it. But sometimes those who demand the most from themselves, and attach that expectation to nurturing and serving, crave submission the most."

"You took care of us, Thomas. You always have."

She saw a raw moment of vulnerability in his dark eyes and put her arms around him, hugging him again. Then she eased back, curious. "What kind of person craves the Dom role, do you think?"

Thomas glanced at his husband, who chose that moment to look right back. The question in Marcus's eyes turned to lazy heat, a promise that spiked Les's own libido, making her wish for Brick's brand of dominance right there and then.

"I'm not sure," Thomas told her. "But something in us sure as hell recognizes it. I'm glad Marcus recognized it in himself." He eyed her, a more playful smile crossing his handsome face. "But tell the truth. Knowing Rory was a Dom gave you a WTF moment, didn't it?"

She chuckled. "That's because of what our relationship has always been. I've been viewing him a different way this trip. Now I can see it, clear as day." Her expression softened as she saw Daralyn smile at something Marcus said to her. She covered her mouth, a habit she'd had difficulty losing. She did it less now, but to help her with it, as he always did, Rory grasped her hand and drew it back, so that smile could warm the world like the sun. A reminder that smiling and laughing was totally okay. Encouraged.

"I'm so glad they found one another," she murmured.

It was the same *and* different, for each of them, she realized. Submission, dominance, sculpted by who they each were. Recognizing one another as trees in the same forest, but with their own root system, their own way of moving with the winds, withstanding the storms. Enduring, no matter the scars that man or nature brought against them.

Thomas put an arm around her as they gazed at their family. "Dad told me things happen in their own way and time, if we just get out of our own way. He and Mom didn't get advice like that off a cereal box. They live it, just like we do. They make the same stumbles and mistakes."

With that thought, Les returned to the present. "What are you guys loading?" she asked Julie. "Can we help?"

"Thanks, but we're good. This was the last stuff from inside. We're putting these props in storage so the set for the next performance can be built." Julie winked at Brick. "The stage is clear, except for what you requested. We added a couple things to expand your options."

"We won't be back today unless you need us," Des added.

"What?" As Les looked between the two Doms, Brick slid his arm around her, hooking his fingers in the belt loop of her jeans, a little tug to quiet her.

"I appreciate it."

Julie captured Les's hand. "I'll drive up to Durham and we'll do lunch next week, since I've got time before I'm ass deep in the next show. We'll also be coming to the family's July 4th picnic, if you can get yourself home for that. Oh, and here."

She trotted back to Des's truck to dig through her purse in the front seat. When she returned, she handed Les a pair of chocolate bars, decorated in purple and gold swirls. "There are two golden tickets in those, like the Willy Wonka invitations. We're having our annual Erotica Gallery performance in June. It's a fundraiser, so that's about five hundred dollars you're holding, not to mention a pretty awesome high grade chocolate. I want you and Brick to come."

"Oh, but maybe Marcus and Thomas..."

Julie snorted. "They can afford their own tickets, and besides, they'll be at their California show. I've invited Rory and Daralyn to come to a more low-key event in May. That's better for her, but more importantly, no brother and sister want to be at an erotica show together." She grinned at Les. "Unless they're a Lannister, or an Egyptian pharaoh."

She glanced at Des, who'd returned to the truck to tie down the load. "I love to watch that man do anything with rope," she sighed, then shot Les a mischievous look. "I'm glad I get to make jokes like that around you now. We are going to have a hell of a time at our next pajama party with Daralyn, aren't we?"

"I had the same thought myself."

Les laughed as Julie hugged her again. Then the theater manager looked toward Brick, watching them with patient amusement. "There's a cozy overnight room at the back of the building. Shower, bed, and fridge. Security code on the theater is 4107. Hang out as long as you need. Text me when you clear out, or if you run into any problems."

Julie blew an air kiss at Les, caught in intrigued confusion. "Have fun."

When she rejoined Des, he had the door open for her. Julie danced up to him with a twirl and a provocative hip wiggle. He shook his head in mock admonishment, but as he helped her into the truck, his hands lingered on her hips.

Les looked up at Brick. "I'd ask, but you're not going to tell me, are you?"

"Nope." He held out a hand. "I'm going to show you. Come with me."

~

He took her into the building through a side door, locked it and engaged the security, then proceeded down a dimly lit hallway.

"You've been here before."

"When the theater isn't preparing for an upcoming performance, Julie rents it out to BDSM groups who want to change up their dungeon nights. Since it's an erotic theater, it already has the set up to handle fireplay, suspension rigging like Des does, that kind of thing."

"Oh." Though Julie's detailed descriptions of the performances here had roused Les's curiosity, sometimes to a near-fever pitch, this was Les's first time in the building. It smelled like a theater. Paint, old wood, heavy, lush fabrics. A hint of smoke, maybe from stage fire effects. Popcorn and cotton candy.

The energy here promised drama, stories. Fantasy. Armchair journeys that transported the mind.

They passed dressing rooms for performers, plus a costume storage area with racks of garments and accessories. Silk, feathers, sequins and leather. When they came upon a room for other kinds of props, Brick slowed his steps, allowing her to take in the impressive and intimidating display.

Coils of rope, floggers, and glinting metal contraptions which made her a little nervous. Not necessarily in a bad way. She'd tucked the chocolate bars in her purse, and made a note to put the date on her calendar. If she could attend, she would. If Brick was available to do the same. She wouldn't want to go without him.

Brick guided her onward, bringing her to the stage wing on this side of the theater. Heavy curtains were drawn back so she could see the auditorium, which held several hundred seats. She noticed that before she saw the stage wasn't empty. What it held caused that good kind of nervousness to increase.

Brick had paused to take it in as well. He appeared to approve of what Julie and Des had done to make the space what it was.

A fantasy for the two of them to share.

At the opposite end of the stage, one of those X-shaped crosses was set up, powder-coated metal arms fitted with handles for the submissive to grasp. Or for the Dominant to tie her to the structure. Rings at the bottom would secure the feet. A table with a mat rolled out on it was in the middle of the stage. Metal slots on the sides would also work as handholds or a way to secure restraints.

Two folding tables, set up in a V-shape a few feet away, displayed everything a fireplay Dom might want or need to convey flame to a submissive's flesh. A fire extinguisher, bucket of water, stack of towels and first aid kit, plus fuel lighters and candles, were on one table. The other held a fire flogger with its white woven wicks, cotton-tipped wands, and a canister of more wadded cotton. Plus a glove, riding crop, and cane. All of them made of or wrapped in Kevlar.

On the table with the fireplay toys was a vase of cut flowers. Bottled water and a few energy snacks were arranged next to it.

A spotlight created a pool of light over the area. It gave the space plenty of illumination, but only there. Shadows clustered outside it, creating a place that seemed separate from everywhere else. Once within that circle of light, she suspected there'd be a hushed, only-the-two-of-us-in-the-world feeling.

She was already feeling that way, just standing in the wings. She also noticed three large mirrors propped around the area. No matter what he was doing to her, unless he blindfolded her, she'd be able to see it.

Brick turned toward Les. He slid his arm around her waist, hand going into the pocket of her jeans to grip her buttock. The firm pressure of his cock was against her belly. "I want to play with fire. With you." His gray eyes were as vivid as the spotlight. "Do you want me to do that?"

"Yes. Very much so."

He brought her closer, so she had to spread her legs and take his thigh between them. She caught her lip in her teeth as he increased his hold on her ass to work her against flexing muscle. As he did, he bent to kiss her parted, moist lips. Her breath was already erratic.

He gripped her hair, a brief tug. Just like that, he confirmed and completed that transition, to full-on Dom and sub. She expected the day would come when a look from him would be all it took. She wasn't all that far from it now.

"Down that last hallway we passed is the room Julie was talking about. Go there, take off everything, and get in the shower. Use only water, and get your hair wet. Rinse yourself thoroughly. I want to make sure there's nothing on your skin that can react to the fuel in a way I don't intend."

He cupped her face, hand on her throat, lifting her chin. "There are oils that will leave a mark. Maybe one day I'll use one, so you can carry my mark on your flesh."

A breath trembled out of her, telegraphing her desire for that, too. In the shadows, his pupils had expanded, making his eyes darker. He took his hand out of her pocket and slid it lower on her buttock, fingers pressing between her legs from behind, so she made another little whimpering sound as arousal rippled out from that touch.

"I wish we'd had a place and time for me to shave you a couple days ago, so I could do more with fire between your legs. But we have all the time in the world."

"Um...when we were at Mick's, you said you'd like to do that. I know you said you wanted to do it, but I thought..."

"Did you remove the hair yourself, Les?"

She moistened her lips. "I did. On Monday. It felt a little wicked to do it on Easter Sunday."

"I don't mind my sub being a little wicked. I don't think God minds, either. Did you remove all of it? Even between these luscious ass cheeks?" He squeezed her, harder this time.

"I did. Is that okay?"

She'd been looking for a Q-tip to apply her makeup when she saw the barely used tube of hair removal cream. It had probably been there since before she left for college. Maybe even from that time she went swimming in the creek in the bikini Brick had talked about.

Seeing it there had planted the idea, and it had helped that she had a half-hour on her own. Brick had been at the firehouse, and her

JOEY W. HILL

mother was with her garden club. Otherwise she might have been too self-conscious about taking the extra time in the bathroom to let the depilatory do its work.

"Yes, it's okay," he said. "Doing it without my permission, when I wanted the pleasure of doing it myself the first time, goes on the list. But it won't be a bad punishment, since you were anticipating your Master's desires."

He nodded toward the hallway again. "Go take care of the shower. Be thorough, but don't linger. I expect you back here, sooner than later. Bring me a brush. I'm the one who will braid your hair."

He caressed a strand between his fingers. "If you think you'll get cold, grab a robe from the prop area. You won't wear anything else, though. Except the necklace."

She felt his gaze on her as she moved down the hallway. While she was gone, she was sure he'd check what Julie had left him, making sure he had what he needed, to play and to keep her safe.

Knowing that made it easy to go out on a ledge with him, trusting he wouldn't lose his footing. He'd never let her fall. Like in *The Greatest Showman*, Phineas and Charity dancing on the rooftops, her leaping onto the ledge and leaning out over empty space, sure that his hand would close around her wrist, hold her suspended like a bird in air before twirling her back into his arms.

Julie had told Les fire was the greatest danger to a theater. One of the biggest start-up expenses for Madison, the owner, had been the fire-treated stage curtains Julie had adamantly insisted upon. It said a great deal about Julie's faith in Brick, and therefore Madison's, that they trusted their beloved theater to him.

When she reached the room, she saw Julie had already been aware of her needs. She'd picked out a robe and left it draped on the bed. The garment suited the occasion perfectly, even as it made Les's cheeks pinken. It was sheer, a shimmering white with lace at the front edges and on the draped sleeves.

She removed her clothes, folding them up and leaving them on a chair by the bed. The little room reflected Julie's personality, with theater photos mounted between hand-applied swirls of blue paint against the white walls. A vanity with a bulb-framed mirror matched the lighting for the room. A dozen round lights were suspended on cables, like bubbles floating in the air.

412

She noted a trio of ropes coiled on crystal doorknob hooks. Each rope was a different color; red, black and purple. She imagined Julie in the bed, Des's hands moving over her, tying intricate designs, binding her...

If she didn't hurry, her Master would come after her. And add to that darn list. Though it was starting to appear that she didn't mind purposefully adding to it.

Brick might be right. She had some brat to her. But if she did, he brought it out in her. It was okay to be naughty and break the rules with him.

After the quick but thorough shower, she dried herself off with the clean towel. It was still a new feeling, her sex being bare. The day after she'd done it, she'd worked at Dr. Spring's clinic. Every movement made her aware of the smoothness of her mound and lips of her sex beneath her panties and scrubs. She'd used a cream to soothe the possibility of abraded skin, then and with last night's shower. She needed to let Brick know, in case that was problematic, even after her thorough rinse.

Using a brush she found on the vanity, she combed out her wet hair, just to smooth it for Brick's ministrations. When she slipped on the robe, all her nerves responded to the silky fabric, her skin eager for touch.

Carrying the brush, she padded back up the hallway, feet bare on polished dark wood. As she predicted, Brick was doing his final checks, arranging things as he wished. She noted something on the cross that hadn't been there before. A set of cuffs, dangling on short chains. There were also tube-like things attached to the table.

Her Master was shirtless, wearing only his jeans, broad shoulders gleaming under the light. Everything inside and out tightened. A feeling that increased as he turned and saw her.

The fabric flowed against her thighs, her peaked nipples. When she reached him, she followed the same compulsion she had only a few days before, only the circumstances now were far different.

She knelt at his feet. When she lifted her head and offered the brush, she drew in a surprised, soft breath.

If there was an expression on a man's face that said, *"You are everything I want, everything I have ever wanted,"* she was certain she was seeing it now.

413

He'd told her she was the submissive he wanted, not just for now, but forever. She would be his wife, no matter how long they needed to wait. Though she had believed him about ninety-nine percent, that last percent now joined the rest. Bringing along a thousand of its friends.

"On your feet," he said, a rough growl.

She obeyed. He took the brush and pointed her to a folding metal chair he'd opened and sat near the table with the mat. A towel was draped over it to keep the seat warm. He knew when to be kind, and when to make her suffer.

After she sat down, he moved behind her. He brushed her damp hair a few more strokes, following it with the blissful massage of his fingers. She was being tended, cherished. Then he set it aside, and a different feeling happened. As he began to French braid her hair, her eyes closed, her throat working as those powerful hands pulled on her hair, bound it. It was as if those coils of rope on Julie's wall were being wound around her limbs, holding her there.

When he was done, he shifted to stand in front of her. "Take off the robe," he said. "Assume the position I like."

She slid it off her shoulders, letting it pool against her back. It wasn't a long robe, so the lower part fell away from her thighs as she straightened her back, arching it so her breasts tilted up, and spread her knees. She arranged her feet on the outside of the two front legs.

His gaze slid down over her breasts, her belly, to the folds of her smooth sex, open for him to see. She was already aroused enough to dampen the towel beneath her.

As he drew out the moment, she started to tremble from the expectations in his eyes, what her obedience meant to him. Then he moved forward and dropped to a knee. "Hold still," he told her.

She bit her lip, swallowing a gasp when he put his hand between her legs. His erection under denim told her he was as aroused as she was, and yet how he explored her, in such a functional way, confirming her smoothness, made her even wetter. He rose, drawing her to her feet with a hand under her elbow.

"Turn around, hold onto the back of the chair and spread your legs again."

When she did, he parted her buttocks and inspected her, again his fingers moving over the area. Her knees quivered. "I used an ointment, a cream to soothe the skin." She cleared her throat. "Yesterday. But I rinsed that area especially well."

"I'm glad you told me. It should be fine. Straighten and turn. Look at me."

When she did, he searched her face as thoroughly as he had the rest of her. "Are you okay, Les?"

"Yes, Sir. I want to please you. Serve you. Please let me."

"I will. You've already pleased the hell out of me. Put your arms around my neck."

When she eagerly did so, he carried her to the table, putting her on the mat. The table was long, nearly seven feet. He laid her on her back, and threaded her arms through the two tube-like things on either side of her torso. There were two for her ankles, holding her legs open at the end of the table.

"These are breakaways," he told her. "They'll hold up to a certain amount of tension, but if you jerk against them hard enough, they'll give way. If a fire got out of control and you needed to get off the table, drop and roll, you can do it. That's not supposed to happen, but I want you to know how to protect yourself, always. Do you understand?"

"Yes, Sir."

He trailed his hand down her front, circling her breast with fingertips, mouth tightening as she lifted into the touch. "I'm going to do a lot of things to you, Les. What's your safeword?"

"Jefferson." She saw no reason to change it.

He turned to the table, and she saw he was going to start with wands. He'd already dampened one in a cup. The alcohol smell reached her nose.

"How did Julie know how..."

"It's my own mix. These are my fireplay supplies as well. I brought them here yesterday while you were working at Dr. Spring's."

For the first time, she noticed the fire flogger was his, with the painted black handle and red crossed axes.

"Oh. Sneaky."

A half-smile touched his face, but when he circled her nipple with the damp wand, the humor left his gaze, and her desire to banter went with it.

Her gaze flicked upward, and she started. There were four mirrors.

One was suspended above her. It was at least as long as the table. She could see the wand moving over her.

"The mirror setup was suggested by one of the BDSM groups who partied here. You'll get to see everything I do to you, Les. If it becomes too much, let me know and I'll order you to close your eyes."

"I'd like to see." Her voice broke, though, revealing how much was happening inside her. He touched her face.

"I want you to see. If you need to safeword, it's okay. We can evaluate where we're at. It won't stop the play if you're not ready for that. But that said, be aware there will be times, as I go along, you'll feel moments of heat more intensely than others, especially in areas that might be more sensitive to it. You may think it's too hot, but anything you feel that startles you, see if you can hold your reaction to it a heartbeat or two. Then if it still worries you, safeword."

She nodded, understanding.

"Look at me, baby."

When she did, he gazed at her with lust, love, and hunger in his gaze. "I fucking adore you, Celeste Joy. All the things that happen in this theater, all the sexual energy, is absorbed into its walls, floors, ceilings, curtains, all of it. Your screams, your climax, your pleasure, and mine, are about to become part of it. When we come back for the Gallery, you'll remember that."

"We?" She wet her lips. "How do you know I wasn't going to ask Beulah to be my plus-one?"

He chuckled, a dangerous sound. "Go ahead and be a brat. See where that gets you." Then he became more serious. "Be quiet now, and just feel."

He lit the other wand. Now aware of what to expect from this part, she shivered as he passed it over the places he'd dampened. The fire lit and coursed over the alcohol, over her mound, her belly and around her nipples. He held both wands, kept passing the damp one over her, the flaming torch coming in right after it, lighting that track. Her skin warmed, just as he'd promised.

He moved the alcohol-damp wand over her thighs, on her mound just above her clit. She shuddered as the flame licked over all of it. Again, again. The heat building. Now the second wand caught fire, and he started to drum them against her flesh, her thighs, her mound.

He was right, that she was more sensitive around her nipples and her inner thighs. The fire bit into her there like teeth, but that reaction tangled with what she felt on less sensitive places. Like she was being petted, the wands and fire moving over her, his hand following.

Then he touched the flame to her clit, back over her belly, around her breasts, briefly over her nipples, making her arch, her hands tightening in the sleeves. She didn't want the restraints to let go, so she struggled to contain her movements, which just intensified her reaction.

When he bent to blow on the flames, making them ripple across her nipples, her mound and her thighs, the first throaty cry emerged from her lips. It was like a slow-building orgasm, but one that seemed to be reaching the intensity of a full orgasm, without pushing her over that edge. It held her there, not enough to push her over, but enough sensation to make her cry out like she was having one. Groans, whimpers, pleas.

He kept moving over her, his expression just as intense, absorbed. He ditched one of the wands and used the single one, passing his hand behind it, sealing in the heat. She shrieked when, right after he passed the flame over her mound, he spanked her cunt. One short, flat slap. That hot sense of combustion ricocheted sensation between her thighs, up through her belly to her breasts. Her toes were curled tight, knees bent up as far as the sleeves around her ankles would allow.

She was writhing, responding to his movements. He put his hand on her shoulder, stilling her, gripped her throat and came down to kiss her. She was so hungry for him, she tried to nip at his mouth, tangle with his tongue, clash with his teeth. He gave a dark chuckle and moved back, though he squeezed her throat, a warning.

When he set both wands aside, he freed her limbs and turned her over. He set the tubes aside, unlatching them from the table slots. Then he did something she didn't expect—not that any of this was predictable. He removed her necklace.

She'd noticed what looked like an empty banana hook on the table. He hung the necklace there, positioning a lit candle just beneath the dangling pendant. As he left that there to heat, he turned his attention to a metal bowl. When he ignited the liquid contents, it became a brazier.

"On your hands and knees, Les," he said. "Back level, head down."

When she obeyed, he placed the bowl in the center of her back.

She could feel the heat starting to conduct through the metal. Brick's gaze was on it as he circled around her, caressing her backside, offering a light pinch to her upper thigh. "I want to fire-cane you, Les. It will leave marks, not from the fire, but the cane itself. It will hurt, because it's a punishment."

"What part of the list is this?" The bowl was getting hotter.

"When you came to my place that night, you said you didn't come for me to be nice to you. You wanted me to punish you for the wrong reasons."

He paused, as if considering how far he wanted to take them down this road, if this moment was about that. But when she was deep in her head, belonging to him like this, all her emotions, laughter, tears, sadness, joy, they were all there, accessible and part of the moment. "This punishment is for that," he said after a moment. "How's that bowl feel?"

"Hot."

"Too hot?"

"Almost...but...not quite. I want it to mark me. That's where you touch me, when we go into a restaurant, or you help me out of the truck. I want it to be raw...want to know you know it, when you touch it."

"All right." He came to her front and traced her mouth with the pressure of his thumb. Let her take it between her lips, tease and bite it. His gaze flared at the provocation.

He kept doing that, letting her suckle and play with his thumb as he stroked her throat with his other fingers. The heat in the small of her back built. She could see it in the mirror in her peripheral vision. The bowl resting on her because her Dom wanted her to hold it balanced there while she sucked on his fingers and let him gaze upon her naked, trembling body.

A scant second before she would have had to safeword from the heat, he removed the bowl. He laid his hand over the area, making her flinch.

"That will be there a few days, Les. Will that make you happy?"

"Yes, Master."

The title felt right on her tongue. He seemed to agree. She sucked in a breath as he fished a small handful of ice out of a bucket, and placed it on that spot.

The fireplay had put her into a warm haze. This was a bright splash of sensation, and her skin was so warm the ice melted quickly, some of the water sliding outward, dripping down the side of her body.

"Oh..."

He picked up a damp towel, rolled it up and passed it over other areas of her skin while she shuddered from that more intense feeling. When he reached that area, removing the ice and blotting up the water, he went more lightly, gentle in that way he did so well, no matter his size and strength.

Then he removed the necklace from the hook. He fastened it around her neck, but he placed the pendants, the cross and fire badge, on her back, between her shoulder blades, instead of letting them dangle below. He put his fingers on them, side by side, holding them to her flesh.

"Oh..." He'd told her to give it a second if she thought she was going to be burned more than she could bear. This was definitely hotter, probably a safeword moment, but...

He was marking her. She quivered, held still, bit her lips so she wouldn't safeword. After a few seconds, he released the pendants and slid them back around, his knuckles brushing her jaw. The pendants bumped against her breastbone, a light tickle, before the necklace stilled, dangling from her throat. Or mostly stilled. She suspected it would keep shimmering from the compressed urgency within her.

"That won't be the first time I'll do that. I'll do it often enough they'll make a permanent mark over time. You'll know what that means, won't you?"

She nodded. "Yes. Thank you."

He helped her to her feet. Her knees were already shaking again, and the flesh between her legs ached for his touch. Enough that when he put his hand there, she cried out and shuddered against him. He held her fast, one hand gripping her hair, the braid, her nape, as he kept stroking her clit and labia with measured movements. "Don't you dare come."

The only thing that saved her from that was standing upright, her legs spread. It made the climax hover on the edge. But when she was so close she knew the air alone could make her orgasm, he guided her to the cross. He positioned her hands on it, aligning her feet on the bottom pieces. The cuffs he put in place were again breakaways, but he reminded her of it. He also readjusted the standing mirrors so she'd see her back as he caned her.

He rubbed her shoulders, touching the tender spots the pendants and bowl had left. "My beautiful sub," he said. "When this is done, I'm going to fuck you, Les. You're going to feel my marks, inside and out. Is that what you want?"

"Yes, Master. Always."

He went to the table and lifted the cane. He dropped two damp towels on the ground near her before he dampened the cane's Kevlar wrap with his fuel mix. The nervousness she felt combined with everything else he was making her feel, and how damn aroused she was. Her hands curled against the cuffs, chains clanking.

He lit the cane up.

The flash in the mirrors made it seem like a sword. He stood to one side and started batting it against her thighs, her ass, her back. When he touched that sore spot from the bowl, she twitched, but it was all right. He moved up, down, upper thighs, behind her knees, then back to her ass, her thighs.

Thwack. The sudden harder hit made her jump. It was like a hot oil splatter, that sharp zing of sensation that shocked all the nerve endings, but unlike the recoil from pain that oil would cause, they seemed to straighten back up and strain for more of the sensation right after. She gasped, swallowed the safe word and gave herself to whatever came next.

Another series of more gentle impacts, then another smack, another zing of sharp heat. On her ass. She could see the flame dancing, saw him douse a spot with his hand as it flitted across her sensitized skin. She trusted him. Had no fear.

But God, he meant it. Whenever he struck her harder, it hurt. *A punishment for wanting to be punished for the wrong reason.* That was because he cherished and protected her, and she was his submissive. As her heart and soul opened to that truth, it brought her another. He would always reserve his worst, true punishments for things she did that disrespected that.

Because he cherished and protected her—because he loved her— he expected her to care for his sub accordingly.

"Oh...God...Brick..." When he hit her this time, it felt like a raw wound had been opened. She could take it, she could, but on the third one like that, a shriek came from her lips.

He stopped. He doused the cane with a quick rub of the wet towel over it, like a warrior cleaning the blade, only he was cleaning it of fire. He set it on the table, then he was there, the wet towel on her back, so blissfully cool, his wonderful hands, the pressure of them, behind the terry cloth.

"Do I have any skin left?" she rasped.

He spoke tenderly in her ear. "Not even broken," he said. "But you'll see the marks, doc. And that redness like a sunburn. I'll tend to you with that vitamin E oil like I promised. I don't want my sub to feel the wrong kind of discomfort. But you're not done, are you?"

She wet her lips as he set the towel aside, freeing her leg and arm cuffs before he turned her around to face him. He gripped her wrists and lifted them above her head, arching her naked body up against his, her mound brushing his erection under his jeans. She made a needy sound and he pushed against her, a deliberate tease as he cuffed her arms above her head again. He left her legs free, so when he stepped back he could slide his hand between them. She moaned, a harsh sound.

"That's my girl. So wet and ready for your Master, aren't you? Answer me, Les."

"Yes, Sir. Yes. Please...oh..." She moaned again, head dropping back as he became more insistent, flicking and pinching her clit.

Thank God, he opened his jeans then. He shoved them and his underwear out of the way before he gripped her hips, lifting her so she could wrap her legs around him. She winced as the cross piece behind her scraped across sore places.

"Can you take the pain for your Master, Les? A reminder of your punishment, of what you owe him and yourself?"

"Yes, Sir. Please..." She was begging again.

"What do you want? This?" His cock, the broad head, was pushing against her cunt, but his arms were locked, holding them in place.

"Yes, please." She wailed it, her body shuddering. The mix of pain and pleasure were spiraling her right toward climax. She was going to come. She was going to go without him, and she would hate that, she wanted...

He slid into her, all the way to the hilt in one inexorable move that, despite her wetness, challenged her body to take all of his thick length in one go. She writhed, adjusting, needing to have all of him. He had her braid in his hand, his grip on her neck a clamp that held her to him, mentally and physically.

Her back felt like it was on fire, The mental image only pushed her closer to release. Her Master could put flame to her flesh. He could set her on fire in so many ways...

He'd gone still, lodged deep within her. "Now, Les. Come all over me while I hold you like this."

She convulsed in his arms. The scream that tore from her throat was strengthened by how he watched her, held control. He made her believe there was nothing he couldn't demand of her she wouldn't give. In his arms, the world would always make sense, even when it didn't outside of them.

In the grip of that crazed tumble of thoughts, he started to move. It was a rhythm as powerful as the hands that held her. His eyes never left her stretched and parted lips, her glazed gaze, the arch of her body toward him, taking him all with every new thrust.

When he came, it pushed her into a second orgasm. Her arms pulled against her bonds, the sense of helpless restraint adding to the overwhelming wave of reaction. When she finished, she was like a ring dancer in a circus, her mind spinning under the lights. He finished with his rough cheek against hers, his body shuddering with a climax that seemed as if it had been gratifyingly as strong as her own. He leaned against her, the cross holding them both up as their breaths lifted and fell.

Their hearts had charged up into the heavens together. Now they came back down with a steady, earth-bound rhythm, bodies reluctant to separate.

At length, though, he eased out of her body and freed her from her bonds. He held her with her arms and legs wrapped around him and brought her back to the table. He laid her face down on the mat, checked the marks he'd left on her, then kissed each one as she shuddered. He also kissed her fading bruises from their day in the river.

The aftermath of the fireplay really was similar to a sunburn, including that sleepy feeling that came with it. Like after a day on the beach, enjoying all the best things the vastness of the ocean, blue sky and sunshine could offer. She clutched his hand, and when he finally sat her up, she had to keep saying it, over and over, in a whisper like the tides.

"I love you. I love you."

She must be experiencing what they called subspace, if subspace was defined as becoming a little unhinged. But she guessed that was the way her Master wanted her. When she shared that, he smiled. It only made the hard planes of his face more attractive to her, the fire cop, the firefighter hero, the man who loved her.

"Let me show you something." He moved over to the other table, returning with a long-necked lighter and can of hair mousse.

As she watched, muzzy but curious, he clasped her hand with his free one. He sprayed a foam line on his own arm, starting at the biceps, moving down to their joined hands, over her wrist and forearm, up to her biceps. Setting the can down at the far end of the table, he picked up the lighter he'd left beside her and touched the flame to the mousse on his biceps.

She drew in a breath as blue flame followed the line of mousse like a living thing, going from his arm, over their clasped hands, to the top of her arm before vanishing. He touched the lighter to the mousse again, kept doing it, so she could watch the flow of the flame in her direction.

"Can I try?"

He handed her the lighter. "Just touch it to the edge of the mousse on your arm and let go of the trigger."

Enchanted, she watched the flame run back in his direction. She did it a couple more times, feeling the ripple of heat between them. It was a meditative exercise that centered and brought her back to earth, even as it had a dreamy quality that kept her pleasantly floating.

Leave it to her Master to come up with a unique form of aftercare. When he at last took the lighter back, he wiped the mousse off their arms with the towel. He had her drink some water and eat a Little Debbie oatmeal cookie, a reminder of childhood pleasures.

"Where's my juice box?" she asked. "Every kitten sub needs a juice box with her Little Debbie."

Brick was applying the vitamin E to her back with his strong, rough hands, but she heard the smile in his voice. "I'll ask Julie to consult with Mick on her future stock of aftercare treats."

He returned to her front. "Air and cool water are best, but you can

423

do more of the vitamin E if you think you need it until it stops being stingy. While I'd prefer to do it, have Beulah help you if I'm not there."

"Thanks, doctor." She looked at him, a crooked smile on her face. She was sitting naked before him. He'd re-fastened his jeans, but he hadn't found his shirt. She was good with that, even though...

"Come here." He bent and lifted her. Leaving the stage, he carried her down the hallway to the bedroom. As he laid her on the bed there, she voiced the desire. He'd said she could tell him what she needed, after all.

"Can you be naked, like me?"

"I can't be as pretty as you are that way, but yeah." When he took off the rest of his clothes and joined her, she nestled back into him, letting out a contented little sigh. She didn't mind the tenderness of her skin, though he didn't press as close to her as he normally would, treating the area with care. She only wanted him to do the vitamin E. She only wanted him, period.

"Are we staying here tonight?" She knew it wasn't a good idea, that she needed to do some things to get ready to go back to class and the hospital tomorrow. But how could any woman, feeling the way she did right now, in her lover's arms, think she should do otherwise?

"No. You need time to get settled and be ready to do doctoring."

He knew how to help her take care of herself. She liked that. Just as she liked hearing the same reluctance in his voice. "But we'll take a few moments. A short nap. You wore me out, doc."

She smiled. His cock was firm against her. She had a feeling after their cat nap, he'd want to be inside her one more time. A reminder of that marking and branding. He trailed his fingers over where he'd actually marked her, with the charm and cross, and pressed a light kiss next to it.

As they lay there, their dozing mixed with quiet murmurs, strokes and touches, her mind drifted to the past few days. It was astounding to think of how long a road she'd traveled in the short time since Llanzo's death. But as Brick and even her own mother had told her, the journey had reached much further into the past, and healed things she hadn't realized needed to be healed.

When she shared that, Brick kissed that same spot again, making the impression of the badge and cross tingle near his lips. "Physician, heal thyself. Before you go forth and heal the shit out of everyone else."

She laughed. "I'll make a plaque and put that on the wall of my first office."

"It will be my graduation gift to you. So you never forget."

"No. I'll buy that one for myself. You're already giving me a graduation gift."

He would bring her a ring. But in a surge of happiness, fragile and timeless at once, she knew he'd already long ago given her the gift that ring would represent.

His commitment and his heart. Her Master, who'd known just the right time to let her unwrap the gift she'd always wanted.

∼

WANT MORE? HOW ABOUT A FREE BOOK? While we're waiting for the next book in the Nature of Desire series, how about a **FREE** first-in-series from another of Joey's contemporary BDSM romance series?

He'll be there for her when she thinks no one will be... Savannah was groomed from birth to take the reins of her father's empire. Business rival Matt Kensington knows commanding her submission is the key to breaking through her emotional armor.

Calling on the unique sensual talents of his four-man management team, he engineers an aggressive erotic takeover, determined to rescue the woman he loves from the steel cage she's manufactured around her heart. Savannah will be theirs for this one night—and his forever.

CLICK HERE TO READ FOR FREE
BOARD RESOLUTION or go to
https://dl.bookfunnel.com/ns4cw7rwsr

Reading this book in print format?
Look for it at your favorite book vendor or use the BookFunnel link!
(Book not free at Nook)

Would you like to read the stories about the rest of the Wilder family?

Rough Canvas (Thomas and Marcus's story)

Worth the Wait (Julie and Des's story)

In His Arms (Rory and Daralyn's story)

See all the Nature of Desire books under the *Also by Joey W. Hill* section.

ABOUT THE AUTHOR

Having penned over fifty acclaimed BDSM contemporary and paranormal titles, which includes six award-winning series, *Joey W. Hill* has been awarded the RT Book Reviews Career Achievement Award for Erotic Romance. A submissive herself, Hill brings authenticity to her intensely emotional love stories.

She is grateful for the support of a wonderful and enthusiastic readership, which allows her to live on her beloved Carolina coast with her even more beloved husband and menagerie of animals.

- On the Web: https://storywitch.com
- Twitter: https://twitter.com/JoeyWHill
- Facebook: https://facebook.com/JoeyWHillAuthor
- Facebook Fan Forum: https://facebook.com/groups/ JWHMembersOnly
- MeWe: https://mewe.com/i/joeywhill
- GoodReads: https://www.goodreads.com/author/show/ 103359.Joey_W_Hill
- BookBub: https://bookbub.com/authors/joey-w-hill
- Amazon: https://amazon.com/Joey-W-Hill/e/B00IJSCIW0

ALSO BY JOEY W. HILL

Mirror of My Soul

Mistress of Redemption

Rough Canvas

Branded Sanctuary

Divine Solace

Worth The Wait

Truly Helpless

In His Arms

Ignition Sequence

Naughty Bits Series

Naughty Bits

Naughty Wishes

Vampire Queen Series

Vampire Queen's Servant

Mark of the Vampire Queen

Vampire's Claim

Beloved Vampire

Vampire Mistress *(VQS: Club Atlantis)*

Vampire Trinity *(VQS: Club Atlantis)*

Vampire Instinct

Bound by the Vampire Queen

Taken by a Vampire

The Scientific Method

Nightfall

Elusive Hero

Night's Templar

Vampire's Soul

Vampire's Embrace

Vampire Master *(VQS: Club Atlantis)*

Vampire Guardian *(VQS: Club Atlantis)*

Vampire's Choice